Faking
Grace

"*Faking Grace* is a witty, warm-hearted lesson in how *not* to be a Christian. Maizy Grace made me think about my own faith journey and how we all sometimes fake it until we make it. What a delightful book!"

LENORA WORTH, author of *Mountain Sanctuary*
and *Secret Agent Minister*

"I love this story of a *real* Christian struggling with *real* attacks of conscience and spiritual growth. As always, Tamara Leigh kept me entertained, laughing, and learning."

REBECA SEITZ, author of *Sisters, Ink* and
Coming Unglued

"Tamara Leigh does a fabulous job looking at the faults, the love, the hypocrisy, and the grace of Christians in a way that's entertaining and fun. Maizy Grace is a crazy character I couldn't help but like. I loved this book and highly recommend it!"

CAMY TANG, author of *Sushi for One?* and
Only Uni

"Clever. Insightful. *Faking Grace* is a joy to read, and Maizy Stewart is hilarious. I couldn't help but cheer for her along her bumpy journey to stop faking grace and start finding it."

MELANIE DOBSON, author of *Going for Broke* and
The Black Cloister

Faking
Grace

a novel

Tamara Leigh

MULTNOMAH
BOOKS

FAKING GRACE
PUBLISHED BY MULTNOMAH BOOKS
12265 Oracle Boulevard, Suite 200
Colorado Springs, Colorado 80921
A division of Random House Inc.

Scripture quotations are taken from the following versions: King James Version. The Holy Bible, New International Version®. NIV® Copyright © 1973, 1978, 1984 by International Bible Society. Used by permission of Zondervan Publishing House. All rights reserved. The Message by Eugene H. Peterson. Copyright © 1993, 1994, 1995, 1996, 2000, 2001, 2002. Used by permission of NavPress Publishing Group. All rights reserved. The Holy Bible, New Living Translation, copyright © 1996, 2004. Used by permission of Tyndale House Publishers Inc., Wheaton, Illinois 60189. All rights reserved.

ISBN 978-1-59052-929-4

Published in association with the literary agency of Alive Communications Inc., 7680 Goddard Street, Suite 200, Colorado Springs, CO 80920, www.alivecommunications.com.

Published in the United States by WaterBrook Multnomah, an imprint of The Doubleday Publishing Group, a division of Random House Inc., New York.

MULTNOMAH and its colophon are registered trademarks of Random House Inc.

Library of Congress Cataloging-in-Publication Data
Leigh, Tamara.
    Faking Grace : a novel / Tamara Leigh. — 1st ed.
        p. cm.
    ISBN 978-1-59052-929-4 (pbk.)
    1. Women journalists—Fiction 2. Nashville (Tenn.)—Fiction. 3. Chick lit.
I. Title.
    PS3612.E3575F35 2008
    813'.6—dc22

                            2008014982

Printed in the United States of America
2008—First Edition

10 9 8 7 6 5 4 3 2 1

This tale is for Maxen, my littlest love, who is hardly little anymore and who can make me laugh and smile like nobody's business (except when he's bugging his big brother…and vice versa). As you continue to grow toward the man you will become, it is my prayer that you will draw nearer to God and embrace the wonderful plan He has for you. I love you!

Acknowledgments

Here I go again, but it's true: The long trek from idea to manuscript to published book would not be possible without the dedication of the entire Multnomah team—especially my editor, Julee Schwarzburg, who brings order and insight to this wonderfully nutty thing called "writing." I would also like to thank publicity assistant, Elizabeth Johnson; line editor, Alice Crider; and literary agent, Beth Jusino, for their hard work and enthusiasm. And last, but never ever least, I am grateful to be so loved by the One who gave His life that I may have eternal life. Thank You, Lord Jesus.

Faking
Grace

ONE

~~MAIZY~~ GRACE STEWART'S 5-STEP PROGRAM TO AUTHENTIC CHRISTIAN FAITH

Name:
☑ Grace

Nice, upstanding Christian name—lucked out on that one. Must remember to answer to it.

Appearance:
☑ Monochromatic hair

I flip down my car's visor mirror and peer at the Marilyn Monroe hair that waves off my oval face. I *so* miss my stripes. But under my present circumstances, it's not as if I can afford to keep up the multiple-shade "do." Back to the list.

☑ Minimal makeup

Do I feel naked! Another peek in the mirror confirms the feeling. Since I had passed on foundation and blush, applying only a light powder to even out my tone, I look pale. The overall effect is that my hazel eyes practically jump off my face from beneath perfectly plucked eyebrows (the stragglers made me do it).

☑ Below-knee skirt

☑ Button-up collar

☑ One-inch heels

Almost wish I *were* naked.

☑ Cross necklace and earrings

☑ WWJD bracelet

I scrunch up my nose. *WWJD? Where would Jesus…? Why would Jesus…?* I tap the bracelet. *Ah! What would Jesus do?*

☑ "Love Waits" ring

Oh no, it doesn't. Still, it's a nice thought, especially considering the guy I left behind. But best not to go there.

Accessories:

☑ Bible

☑ Bible cover

And, I must say, it's a nice cover. I look to where it sits on the passenger seat with the "KJV" (whatever that means) Bible tucked inside—intensely spiritual with a tapestry print of a country church. And the faux tortoiseshell handles! Nice touch.

☑ Twist pen with seven different scriptures

One for every day of the week.

☑ "Footprints in the Sand" bookmark

Touching poem. And a surprise ending too!

❑ Fish emblem

"Oops!" I open the ashtray, dig out the emblem, and drop it in my lap. "Check!"

☑ "Jesus is my copilot" bumper sticker

☑ Crown-of-thorns air freshener

I glance at the scented disk that hangs from my rearview mirror. Stinks, but nicely visible—practically screams, "This is one serious Christian."

Christian Speak:
☑ "Jesus is my Savior."
☑ "Jesus died for my sins."

I close my eyes and run the lingo through my mind. "Got it!"
☑ "I'm praying for you."

I wonder how many Christians really do.
☑ "I need to pray about that."

Otherwise known as "No way, Jose!" Or, in these parts, as the "Nashville no."
☑ "Bless his/her heart."

Sympathetic aside tacked to a derogatory remark about someone to make it acceptable (possibly exclusive to the South, as I'd never heard it before moving to Nashville four months ago).
☑ "My brother/sister in Christ."
☑ "God's timing."
☑ "Have a blessed day."
☑ "Yours in Christ."

Must remember to use that last one for note cards and such.

Miscellaneous:
☑ Church

That one on West End should do—respectable looking and big enough to allow me to slip in and out undetected should I need to place myself in that setting. Of course, I hope the need does not arise.

Not that I'm not a believer. I am. Sort of. I mean, I *was* "saved" years ago. Even went through the dunking process—the whole-water-up-the-nose thing (should not have panicked). But the truth is, other than occasionally attending church with my grandmother before and after I was saved, my faith is relatively green. Hence the need for a checklist.

☑ Testimony

"Uh! Just had to leave that one for last, Maizy." Yes, *Maizy*, as in *Maizy Grace.* Courtesy of one Grandma Maizy, one Grandma Grace, and one mother with a penchant for wordplay. Amazing grace! And Mom isn't even a Christian. But Dad's mom is. According to Grace Stewart, the only thing my parents did right was to name me after her. I beg to differ. I mean…Maizy Grace? Though growing up I did my best to keep it under wraps, my mom blew it during a three-girl sleepover when she trilled upstairs, "Oh, Maizy Grace! How sweet the sound. Won't you girls come on down?" Fodder for girlhood enemies like Cynthia Sircy, who beat me out for student council representative by making an issue of my "goody two-shoes" name. And that's why I never use *Grace.* Of course, it could prove useful today.

I return to my checklist. "Testimony…" I glance at the dashboard clock, which reveals I've blown ten of my twenty minutes' leeway. Guess I'll have to think up a testimony on my way to the interview. Not that I don't have a story of how I came to know Jesus. It's just boring. Hmm. Maybe I could expand on my Christian summer-camp experience—throw in an encounter with a bear or some other woodland creature with big teeth. Speaking of which…

I check my teeth in the mirror. Pale pink lipstick is *so* boring. Glaringly chaste. Borderline antisexual. Of course, that *is* the effect I'm after. All good.

"All right, Maizy—er, *Grr-ace*—get in there and get that job." A job I badly need if I'm to survive starting over in Nashville. My part-time position as a lifestyle reporter at the paper has yet to translate into the full-time position I was led to believe it would after three months. Now, four months later, funds are getting low.

I fold my checklist and stick it in the book I picked up at Borders the day I surfed the classified ads and hit on "Christian company seeking editorial assistant." Hmm. Editorial assistant—a far cry from reporter. In fact, beneath me, but what's a girl to do?

Closing the book, I smile at the title: *The Dumb Blonde's Guide to Christianity*. Not that I'm blond—leastwise, not naturally. Another glance in the mirror confirms that although the $7.99 over-the-counter bottle of blond is no $75 salon experience, it lives up to its claim. Not brassy at all. Still, maybe I should have gone back to basic brown so I wouldn't have to worry about roots. But talk about boring.

I toss the book on the passenger seat, retrieve the fish emblem and my purse, and swing my legs out the open car door. After "hipping" the door closed, I hurry to the back. Unfortunately, unlike the bumper sticker, there seems no nonpermanent way to apply the emblem. Thus I have no choice but to pull off the backing and slap the fish on the trunk lid. Not sure what it symbolizes, but I can figure that out later—*if* I get the job.

I lower my gaze to the "Jesus is my copilot" bumper sticker. Nice statement, especially with the addition of the fish. Honestly, who wouldn't believe I'm a deeply committed Christian? And if someone should call me on it, I could be forgiven—it is April 1, as in April Fools' Day.

As I start to look away, the peeling lower edge of the bumper sticker catches my eye. Should've used more Scotch tape. I reach down.

"It's crooked."

The accented, matter-of-fact voice makes me freeze. I'm certain it was directed at me, but did he say, "*It's* crooked" or "*She's* crooked"? Surely the latter is merely a Freudian slip of my mind. And even if it isn't, I'm not crooked. Just desperate.

As the man behind me could be an employee of Steeple Side Christian Resources, I muster a smile and turn. His fashionably distressed jeans are the first thing I notice where he stands, six feet away. Meaning he can't be an employee. And he certainly isn't looking for a handout—even better (though I sympathize with the plight of the homeless, they make me *very* uncomfortable). So he's probably just passing through the parking lot. Perhaps heading for Steeple Side's retail store, which occupies a portion of the lower floor of their corporate offices.

The next item of note is his shirt—a nice cream linen button-up that allows a glimpse of tanned collarbone. I like it. What I don't like is his face—rather, expression. If not for his narrowed eyes and flat-lined mouth, he'd be halfway attractive with that sweep of dark blond hair, matching eyebrows, and well-defined cheekbones. Maybe even three-quarters, but that would be pushing it, as his two-day shadow can't hide a lightly scarred jaw. Teenage acne?

I gesture behind me. "My bumper sticker seems to be coming off."

He lowers his green eyes over me, and while I may simply be paranoid, I'm certain he gives my cross earrings and necklace, button-up collar, and below-knee skirt more attention than is warranted. He glances at the bumper sticker before returning his regard to me. "Yes, it is coming off."

British. I'm certain of it. Nowhere near the southern drawl one more often encounters in Nashville.

"Of course"—he crosses his arms over his chest—"that's because you're using tape."

That obvious? "Well, doesn't everyone?" Ugh! Can't believe I said that. Maybe there is something to the warning that you are what you read, as I could not have sounded more like the stereotypical dumb blonde if I tried.

He raises an eyebrow. "Everyone? Not if they want it to adhere permanently. You do, don't you?"

Guilt flushes me and is followed by panic even though I have no reason to fear that this stranger with the gorgeously clipped accent might expose me as a fake. "Of course, I do!"

Is that a smile? "Splendid. Then I'll let you in on a little secret."

Delicious accent or not, this doesn't sound good. It isn't, as evidenced by his advance. I step aside, and he drops to his haunches and peels away the tape. "You see…" Holding up the sticker, he looks over his shoulder and squints against the sunlight at my back. "Self-adhesive." He peels off the backing, positions the sticker, and presses it onto my bumper—my previously adhesive-free bumper.

He straightens. That *is* a smile, one that makes him look a bit like that new James Bond actor. What's his name?

"You'd be surprised at how much technology has advanced over the last few years," he says.

I nearly miss his sarcasm, genteelly embedded as it is in that accent. "Well, who would have thought?" *Be nice, Maizy—er, Grace.* My smile feels tight. In fact, my whole face feels as if it's been lathered with Lava soap. "I can't tell you how much I appreciate your taking the time to affix my bumper sticker properly."

He inclines his head. "If you'd like, I'll try to straighten your fish."

My...? *"It's crooked,"* he had said. Not the bumper sticker—my fish. Meaning he probably saw me stick it on. Were he more than a passerby, I'd be deeply embarrassed.

"No, thank you. I like my fish slightly crooked." I glance at the emblem, which appears to have its nose stuck in the air. "It makes him look as if he's fighting the current. You know, like a good Christian."

Very good, Ma—Grr-ace! Were he a Steeple Side employee, you would have won him over.

"So you're a Christian?"

So much for my self-congratulatory pat on the back. Of course, maybe his question is academic. I mean, it's obvious I'm a Christian. "Of course! A Christian. And proud of it." Good practice. Unfortunately, if his frown is anything to go by, I'm in need of more. "Er, Jesus is my Savior." *Knew* Christian speak would come in handy.

His frown deepens.

Or maybe not. I make a show of checking my watch and gasp. Nothing at all fake about that, as most of my leeway has been gobbled up. Thankfully, I was lucky to—

No, *blessed.* Must *think* as well as speak "Christian." Thankfully,

I was *blessed* to snag a parking space at the front of the building—the only one, as the dozen spaces marked Visitor were taken, and the remaining spaces on either side of mine apparently are reserved for upper management.

I fix a smile. "Thank you again for your help. If you'll excuse me, I have an appointment."

"Certainly."

I step forward and, as I pass within two feet of him, take a whiff. Some type of citrus-y cologne. Nice. Not sharp or cloying. Unlike Ben, whose cologne of choice made my nasal passages burn. And the Brit is nearly six feet tall to my five foot six. Not so tall I couldn't wear three-inch heels for fear of shooting up past him. Unlike Ben, who'd limited me to one-inch heels—

Go away! Another reason to leave Seattle. With his liberal application of cologne and compact height and build, Ben was nowhere near the man for me. Not that his scent and size were the worst of him. Far from it. And am I glad to be far from him.

As I step to the sidewalk, I'm tempted to glance behind at the nicely proportioned, bumper-sticker-happy Brit. Temptation wins out.

Thumbs hooked in his pockets, he stands alongside my passenger door. Watching me.

Feeling as if caught doing something wrong, I jerk a hand up and scroll through my Christian speak for something to reinforce my claim of being a Christian. "Yours in Christ!" I flash a smile that instantly falters.

At the rumpling of his brow, I jerk around and head for the smoked glass doors of Steeple Side Christian Resources. Can*not* believe I used a written salutation! Dumb blonde alert! Speaking of which…

The Dumb Blonde's Guide to Christianity is on the passenger seat. Fortunately, if the man is nosy enough to scope out the interior of my car, it's not as if I'll see him again. That scrumptious accent and citrus cologne were a one-time thing. Unless he *does* work at Steeple Side and I *do* get the job. Fat chance.

As I pull open one of several sets of glass doors, I glance behind. He's on the sidewalk now, head back as he peers up the twenty-some floors of the building. Definitely not an employee.

The lobby is bright and sparsely furnished, but what stops me is the backlit thirty-foot cross on the far wall. Fashioned out of what appears to be brushed aluminum, it's glaringly simple. And yet I can't imagine it having more presence.

Crossing to the information desk at the center of the lobby, I scope out several men and women who are entering and exiting the elevators. All nicely dressed. All conservative. I'll fit right in—

I zoom in on a woman stepping into the nearest elevator. Her skirt is above the knee by a couple inches. And that guy who just stepped out of another elevator? His hair brushes his shoulders.

I shift my gaze back to the towering cross. I'm at the right place, meaning those two are probably visitors. Same goes for the young woman who sweeps past and reaches the information desk ahead of me. Not only is she wearing ruched capris, but she has my hair. Rather, the hair I had. Ha! If she's after my job, I've got her beat.

She drops a jingly purse on the desk and points behind me. "Jack is *so* hot!"

"Really?" The chubby-faced receptionist bounds out of her chair, only to falter at the sight of me.

"Yes, hot!" The "ruched" young woman jabs the air again, looks around, and startles. "Er, not *hot* hot. *Hot,* as in under the collar... ticked off."

That's my cue to appear relieved that she didn't mean *hot* as in *carnal,* as she's obviously connected to this company—at least to the receptionist. I nod. "That's a relief."

She smiles, then puts her forearms on the desk and leans in to whisper in a not too whisper-y voice, "This time they stole his assigned-parking sign."

If someone stole mine, it would make me "hot" too. Doubtless, some visitor would snap up my space, and I'd have to park—

Oh no. The front parking space I snagged... The only unmarked space in the middle of dozens of marked spaces...

I peer out the bank of windows. The Brit whose parking space I took and who *does* work here is striding toward the doors. And he does look hot, though I can't be sure whether it's more in the carnal way or the angry way. Regardless, I am not getting this job.

"May I help you, miss?"

I focus on the receptionist, who has no idea how beyond help I am. Still, as the only alternative is to face the Brit on my way out, I step alongside the ruched young woman. "I have an interview with Mrs. Lucas."

The receptionist lowers her chin, and I hear a series of keystrokes.

Hurry up! I can handle being late to an interview for a job I'm not likely to get, but sharing an elevator with a man who in no way believes I was unaware that bumper stickers are adhesive backed? No.

"You're her one o'clock." The receptionist points to the elevators. "Fifth floor, take a left, a right, then another left. Human Resources is at the end of the hall."

"Thank you." *Fast feet!* Must get to an elevator ahead of the Brit.

"Hey, hold up!"

I falter as the ruched young woman draws alongside me. "I'm heading to Human Resources. I'll show you the way."

"Oh. Thanks."

"I'm Jem." She slips ahead of me into a vacant elevator. "Short for Jemima."

As she pushes the button for the fifth floor, I look at the very thin woman who can't be more than twenty-two to my twenty-six. She seems more like a Tiffany or Brittany. Of course *Jem* without the *ima* fits all right. As I turn alongside her, I'm snatched from my musings by the Brit heading across the lobby toward the elevators.

I jump forward, jab the Close Doors button, and hold my breath until the doors shut him out at ten feet and closing.

"Ah!" Jem bemoans. "Jack could have ridden up with us."

I look around. "Hot-under-the-collar Jack?"

Her pout flips right side up. "He doesn't stay that way for long. He's just miffed at the guys for pulling one over on him."

"The guys?"

"Yeah, Jack's the managing editor of Men's Publications."

Great. Might as well head back down and see if I can remove the fish and bumper sticker before the adhesive sets.

"Oh!" she exclaims. "Don't you think he looks like Daniel Craig?"

That's the name of the new James Bond actor that escaped me. "Um…some."

She exaggerates a scowl. "Obviously you need to take a closer look."

No thanks.

"Anyway, the guys are the editors and writers who work under Jack. They're always playing pranks on one another."

A melodic ping announces our arrival at the fifth floor.

Jem leads the way out and turns left. "Last week Todd was the target when the seat of his pants got super glued to his chair." She turns right, swerving to avoid a middle-aged man heading opposite. "Don't ask me how."

"So what happened?"

"The guys had a good laugh and started plotting their next prank—which, of course, likely manifested itself in the case of the missing parking sign."

"Are you telling me no one was written up? Or fired?"

She turns to me. "Fired? Are you kidding?"

No, merely confused. "Sorry, but I can't imagine someone getting away with that, especially at a Christian company."

She makes a face. "Because we're supposed to be uptight, keep our noses to the grindstone, and never crack a smile?"

I smile apologetically. "That is what I imagined."

"We're not like that."

Maybe working here won't be so bad after all. Maybe these people are normal. Just like me.

"Well…" Her smile falters. "We're not *all* like that."

Should have known there was a disclaimer. "It sounds like a nice place to work."

"Definitely." With a toss of her multiply shaded hair—how I miss mine!—Jem takes the lead down a long corridor. "Of course, Steeple Side does have its rules like every other place, but unlike every other place, there's a code of conduct you have to follow when you go home at night."

Whoa! They're going to tell me how to behave *outside* the workplace? Police my personal life?

"That's probably why they cut us some slack around here. You know, let us have a little fun. Of course, sometimes we go too far, like with the Super Glue—" Realizing I'm no longer next to her, she turns back. "Something wrong?"

I blink her into focus and, in a slightly cracked voice, say, "Could you elaborate on this code of conduct we're supposed to follow *after* hours?"

She stares at me, as if trying to reconcile the assembly instructions with the assembled product. "You have no idea what you're getting into, do you?"

Hate to admit it, but my tactless reaction—a far cry from how a serious reporter ought to conduct herself—makes my ignorance glaring. "I've never worked for a Christian company."

With a sigh, she waves me forward. "The code of conduct. You know, living the Christian life. You are a Christian, aren't you?"

I almost choke. "Absolutely!" Was that convincing? It should be, because I *am* a Christian. No reason to feel as if I'm here under false pretenses.

She pushes a hand through silky chunks of auburn, chocolate, gold, and bronze tresses. "Good, 'cause it's required to work here. So back to the code of conduct. As an employee, you're a reflection of the company and its Christian values, so you have to behave accordingly. I mean, can you imagine the harm it would do Steeple Side's reputation if its employees who are putting out materials on how to live the Christian life aren't living it? Doing drugs…stealing…cheating on spouses…"

True, but while I don't do any of the above, it still feels like a violation of my privacy.

"…lying."

Now *that* I do fall back on, though usually only little white lies, like when I told the Brit I did want the bumper sticker to adhere permanently, then said I appreciated him taking the time to affix it. But they're little lies, and very white, so they don't qualify as lying. Do they? And even if they do, it's not as if I don't pay a price, as I usually feel bad afterward. Though maybe only a little…

Jem lays a hand on my shoulder. "Don't sweat it. It's a great place to work." She draws me forward and halts alongside a door marked Human Resources. "Now go get that job."

I do need it. Even if "Big Brother" will be looking over my shoulder. "Thanks, Jem."

"You're welcome. It was nice meeting you…uh…" She wrinkles her button nose. "I don't think you told me your name."

"It's M…" I clear my throat. "Grace."

She frowns. "You don't look like a Grace."

"I don't?" Talk about shrill!

"Of course, I don't look like a Jemima, but that's why I go by Jem."

I stick out a hand. "Nice to meet you. God willing"—Ha! That one rolled right off my tongue—"we'll see each other around."

She clasps my hand. "You bet." Then she walks away.

I'm tempted to follow her and keep going until I'm miles clear of this place.

TWO

"What does *M* stand for?" Mrs. Lucas peers at me over her glasses.

Unfortunately, I couldn't avoid reference to my first name, as I had to provide my social security number, and surely the name has to match the number. However, I only gave the initial in case someone connects me with the Maizy Stewart who writes for the local paper—something my friend Tessie had warned me about. "You'll never get hired if they know you write for mainstream media," she said. "Too liberal for their taste."

I moisten my lips and mumble, "It stands for Maizy."

Mrs. Lucas frowns. "Did you say Mae?"

Close enough. "Yes"—hardly even a little white lie—"but I go by my middle name, Grace."

With a faint smile, she returns to my application. "Pretty name."

"And Christian. You know, 'Amazing Grace.'" Dumb blonde alert!

Her gaze flicks over me. "Yes. And you attend a Christian church?"

Uh-oh. And to make matters worse, I have yet to come up with an exciting testimony. My hands tingle where I clasp them in my lap, so I splay them on my thighs. "Since I recently moved here, I haven't yet found one I consider my…church home." Nice Christian speak! "But there is one off West End that I'm leaning toward."

"Wonderful. What denomination?"

No testimony, no denomination. "This is embarrassing, but I'm not sure. It just felt right." At least, driving by it…

Mrs. Lucas picks up my résumé. "It says that after you graduated with a degree in journalism, you postponed your plans to enter the work force for two years to travel the world."

It's true, though not to that extent. The summer after I graduated, I did travel the world. Well, Europe. But considering that the *Seattle Sound,* where I went to work three months later, is mainstream media and keeping in mind the circumstances under which I left, I couldn't put it down as work experience. Better to be considered "green" than incompetent. "Yes ma'am."

"So other than writing for the university paper and an internship at *Entertainment Seattle,* you don't have any real work experience?"

"No." Definitely a lie. Let's call that "Lie Number One." Easier to keep track of. Not that I intend to get in over my head, but if by some twist of fate I'm hired, I'm bound to have to crank out a few more doozies. "As I had to put myself through university, it took a couple of years longer to get my degree." The whole truth and nothing but the truth. "Of course, I did take out a student loan"—as evidenced by past due bills—"but it didn't come close to covering the cost, and I didn't want to be any further in debt by taking out another loan."

Mrs. Lucas's eyebrows rise. "Responsible of you." She leans forward. "Debt is a terrible thing."

Don't I know it. "It certainly is. A vicious cycle that…Jesus would not want us to get caught up in." Hey, I'm getting good at this!

She inclines her head. "You're not working anywhere at this time?"

"No." Lie Number Two.

"Well, as you know, the position is only part time at twenty-five hours a week."

"Perfect! That's all I'm looking for." Something to tide me over until I go full time at the paper.

Her brow rumples. "Most of the applicants view this position as a step toward full-time employment. You wouldn't be interested if the opportunity arose?"

Oh no. "Of course, I'd be interested." Lie Number Three. "I'm just saying that until then, I'm content to work part time. God's timing and all that."

Her brow clears. "When can you start?"

I blink. "Are you offering me the job?"

"I am."

"But what about a second interview?"

"Normally there would be an interview with Mrs. Stillwater, the senior editor who will be your supervisor. But she's out of town until Monday and has asked me to have someone up and running by the time she returns."

I've done it—and without a testimony. I'll be able to pay my bills, eat out from time to time, and feed my mutt something other than generic food. Maybe even re-stripe my hair! All good. "I can start tomorrow."

"Excellent." She pulls a piece of paper off a note block and begins to jot. "Your hours will be eight to one, Monday through Friday. You'll report to Fiala Cramer in Women's Publications on the eighth floor."

She hands me the paper. "I'll make sure she's prepared to get you started in the morning." She stands and reaches a hand to me. "It was lovely meeting you. I'm sure you'll be a blessing to our company."

I accept her handshake as I rise. So this is what flabbergasted feels like. Can*not* believe it was this easy, especially considering my encounter with the Brit… Ooh, I hope I don't run into him. Fortunately it's a fairly large company, so avoiding him may not be difficult.

I give her hand a final squeeze. "Thank you. I appreciate the opportunity."

"We'll see you tomorrow then."

"I look forward to it. Have a blessed day." At the door I glance back at her, then step through and pull the door closed. "Have a blessed day," I whisper as I start down the corridor. Icing on the cake. I *am* getting good at this.

Niggle, niggle.

And to think I only had to tell three lies.

Niggle, niggle.

I smile at a young man who sidesteps me, arms weighted with folders. Yes, only three. After all, half truths and omissions can't really be counted as lies.

Niggle, niggle.

Okay, so I'm a fake, a fraud, a phony. But what's a girl to do when facing another month of part-time employment and mounting bills? Play by the rules that nobody follows? Be honest to her detriment? A little embellishment never hurt anyone. And I *am* a Christian, so I didn't lie about that. Just the extent of my faith.

As I turn the corner and head for the elevator, that bad feeling I get when I'm not completely honest—*niggle, niggle*—once more flicks my hard-earned happy place.

"Stop it," I growl, only to force a smile when a woman passing by frowns at me. *Caught talking to myself. What's next?*

"Grace!"

With a shake of my head, I step into the elevator and jab the Lobby button.

"Grace!" A body leaps between the closing doors.

I stare wide eyed at Jem, who's wearing a frown so large it barely fits her pixieish face. *Better yet, caught* not *answering to your name, Grr-ace!* This is not going to be easy. Or comfortable, as I'm reminded of the last time I went by a fake name and the end result—humiliation and a seriously derailed career.

I draw a shaky breath. "Sorry, I must have been deep in thought."

"I'll say!" Her frown eases. "So have you been asked back for a second interview?"

Why does she look so hopeful? "No." As her face clouds with what appears to be genuine disappointment, I feel a grin coming on. "I got the job."

"No!"

"Yes—editorial assistant in Women's Publications."

She holds up a hand, and after an awkward moment, I high-five it. Beaming, she steps back from the elevator. "I'll see you soon, Grace."

"Bye, Jem."

The doors close, and I'm left alone to reflect on the turning of my luck, which begs the question of which bills to pay first.

"I can't believe they have books on how to do this stuff." Tessie—professionally known as Teresa Halston, columnist for the *Middle Tennessee Review*, as well as my friend, mentor, and landlord—runs a finger down the contents page of *The Dumb Blonde's Guide to Christianity*.

I shrug. "Neither could I, but when I told the clerk at Borders that I needed a straightforward book on Christianity, he led me to this one. Voilà! All the refresher course I need."

"And you weren't offended?" She makes a face. "I mean, *The* Dumb *Blonde's Guide*"?

Cradling a bowl of cereal—the strapped working girl's inexpensive, all-purpose meal—I sit back. "I *was* a little offended, but it's not as if I didn't act the part." At her scowl, I throw a hand up. "You know me. I can put words on paper, but getting them out of my mouth is a different matter, especially around cute guys. As for looking the part..." I tug a lock of my very blond hair. "Hello-o."

She winces. "I don't know why you wouldn't let me loan you the money to have your hair done."

And become even more indebted to her? I should be paying upwards of eight hundred dollars a month for this apartment over her garage in the uppity Green Hills area, but she rents it to me for six hundred. I refuse to take further advantage of her kindness.

She grimaces. "You are not a blonde."

"Yeah, but I don't want to be a boring brunette. And I certainly don't want to owe any more money. Besides, even though that Jem I told you about had my hair, I think straight blond better fits a

Christian woman than multiply highlighted hair, especially when said Christian woman has been away from her faith for so long."

Tessie shakes her head. "I'm still shocked to learn you're a Christian."

According to the book she holds, a statement like that is cause for taking a look at one's "walk," because one's speech and behavior should raise no question as to that person's relationship with Christ. See! I am getting this Christian thing down. Of course, it helps that when I got home after my interview at Steeple Side, I spent two hours skimming *The Dumb Blonde's Guide to Christianity.*

Feigning offense, I click my tongue. "Shocked that I'm a Christian? Hey!" I tug a cross earring and tap the matching necklace. "What do you call these?"

"Do you really want to know?"

"Probably not."

She crosses her arms over her chest. "So what have I missed that would have clued me in that you're a Christian?"

"I'm a good person."

Tessie drops to the couch beside me and peers at me from beneath a sweep of honey-colored hair. "As you know—or *should* know—being a Christian is much more than that."

"Who died and made you an expert?" I spoon up prematurely soggy frosted flakes. Boy, can't wait till the money starts rolling in so I can renew my acquaintance with Tony the Tiger. Not that I'm a brand loyalist. There are just some levels to which generics cannot ascend.

"Actually…" Tessie trails off.

Spooning the bite into my mouth, I look at her. "Hmm?"

She lowers her big blue eyes toward the book. "Though I don't advertise it, I once considered myself a Christian."

I stare at her. Tessie is—was—a Christian? The same Teresa Halston who student taught several of my journalism classes? Who was adamant that our writing be based on the known and observable? Who has it in for religion, as evidenced by some of the columns she writes for the *Middle Tennessee Review*? I'm shocked, just as she claims to have been shocked to learn that I'm a Christian. Not that she isn't a good person herself.

I swallow my soggy mouthful. "I'm surprised."

Her smile is tight—hardly a tooth in sight. "Me too." She blows a sigh up her face, which usually signals "discussion closed," then gives the book a tap. "A bit tongue in cheek. Listen to this." She bends her head, causing her hair to curtain her face. *"By all means, use Christian speak, a.k.a. Christian-ese, if you are comfortable doing so. However, keep in mind that it is best used sparingly. Too much, and you may be perceived as forcing it or, worse, faking it."*

Oops. Didn't read that part. Did I overdo it at Steeple Side?

"Also, be certain that your use is appropriate. For example, 'Yours in Christ' should only be used at the closing of a letter."

My stomach heaves.

Tessie snorts. "Have to say this for the book—it's appropriately titled." She snaps it closed. "Can you imagine anyone saying that to someone?"

I can do better than imagine. I can remember—a bumper-sticker-happy Brit folding his brow as I call out, "Yours in Christ!" I meet Tessie's gaze. "I can't imagine it."

Her all-seeing eyes narrow. "Maizy, tell me you didn't—"

"Grace! Would you mind calling me Grace so I can get used to it? Except at the paper, of course, where I'll remain Maizy."

She rolls her eyes. "I'll try to remember."

"Thanks. So, uh—"

"Yours in Christ?"

Thank goodness I skipped over my fish "fighting the current like a good Christian" faux pas. "All right, I said it. But it's that nosy Brit's fault. He got me all flustered."

"Brit?" The smile hovering about her mouth hovers no more.

"Yeah, the guy whose parking space I took. He's British and, according to Jem, the managing editor of Men's Publications. Jack something-or-other—looks kind of like that actor Daniel Craig."

Something curious glances across Tessie's eyes; then, in a thick monotone, she says, "Prentiss."

"You know him?"

"We've met."

Just met, or…? Aware that I'm treading on ground that could end in another "discussion closed" sigh, I ask, "In what capacity?"

"Work, of course."

No surprise, as work is her life, which may have something to do with her two failed marriages and her tendency to view life through a bitter lens.

She picks a piece of lint off her sleeve. "Shortly after I moved to Nashville, Steeple Side downsized—cut ten percent of its work force, from janitors to upper management." She gives a little sniff. "I smelled a story. Thinking there would never be a better time to expose the skeletons in Steeple Side's closet, I contacted those who were let go. Though most weren't interested in speaking to me—misplaced loyalty and all that—I rooted out half a dozen who were willing to talk. My ace in the hole was a middle-aged man who was passed over for the job of managing editor when it was awarded to Jack Prentiss."

Tessie laughs low. "Very upsetting. Unfortunately, before I could meet with him, I came down with the flu. When I tried to reschedule our interview a few days later, he told me he'd met with Jack Prentiss and that his differences with Steeple Side were resolved." She sneers. "Said he regretted his *un-Christianlike* behavior."

"Do you think Steeple Side got wind of your investigation and paid him off?"

She tilts her head to the side. "What do you think?"

"Possible, but also possible there never was a story."

Her eyes flash. "Maizy Stewart, there's *always* a story. Have you forgotten what got you into trouble in Seattle?"

I flush. "Of course not."

"Then repeat after me. There's *always* a story."

Feeling like an errant child up for discipline—and rightfully so, as my career can't afford another mistake like the last one I made—I draw a deep breath. "There's *always* a story." Eager to move on, I ask, "What happened to the other Steeple Side employees who agreed to speak with you?"

"I had conducted only two interviews before the flu struck, and while some of what I dug up was good, it wasn't enough to expose Steeple Side. Then one of the two I interviewed retracted his statement—told me he'd been angry and that, though the employees of Steeple Side weren't without their faults, they were good people."

Imagining Tessie's anger, which has one setting—frigid—I'm grateful I wasn't around when the walls of her story started crumbling. "Still, there were three others you hadn't interviewed."

"I'll give you one guess as to what happened to them."

"Backed out too?"

"Uh-huh."

"What did you do?"

"Called Jack Prentiss and arranged a meeting at a restaurant."

"Why?"

"A last-ditch effort to salvage the story. I thought I could charm him into letting his guard down." She shakes her head. "The man is charm-proof. So I attempted to bluff him into believing I had more on Steeple Side than I did. You know what he said?"

Offer to straighten her fish emblem? "What?"

"He said it would have been nice for us to meet under different circumstances, and then he got up from the table. So I gave him a piece of my mind, which is the only thing of interest my recorder captured—my raised voice and some choice words."

Meaning her anger has more than its one glaring, cold-shoulder setting? "Wow."

She frowns. "What?"

"I just can't imagine you losing it. You're always so in control."

She squares her shoulders. "It was a bad year—second divorce."

"Why didn't you say anything about this when I told you I was applying at Steeple Side?"

"Because I've put it behind me, something writers have to do when faced with a dead end." And there's that "discussion closed" sigh again, followed by the telltale breath that often precedes the announcement of "time to go."

"How about a bowl of cereal before you head home?"

"No offense, but that particular generic won't do it for me."

I understand completely, as does my Miniature Pinscher/Shih Tzu/something-or-other where he lies with his head on his paws ten feet from his untouched dinner. My poor, puffy boy. Unfortunately, with finances as tight as they are, we each have to do our part. Fortunately, there are advantages to being a mutt, as opposed to a purebred with a sensitive digestive system. Woofer may not like generic food, but when he gets hungry enough to eat, it stays down. Still, I feel guilty for not providing better for him, even though the change in diet has helped him shed a couple pounds.

"Your dog looks depressed."

"Yeah." I glance at my cereal bowl. While Woofer doesn't need the sugar, I set the bowl on the floor. "Here, Woof."

Floppy ears perking, bug eyes bugging, stub tail ticktocking, he scrabbles upright. Amazing how quickly he moves at the promise of something tasty. More amazing is that he's able to keep his balance on those peg legs. A moment later, his black and tan head is in the bowl.

"Do you have to do that in front of me?" Tessie gives a full-body shudder. "You know, I do accept your offer of a bite to eat from time to time, Maizy."

"Grace," I correct, then smile apologetically. "Sorry, but I assure you that the dishwasher sanitizes—"

"I know. It's just the thought. I don't care if we did come from apes, I refuse to eat after animals."

I almost laugh, but that niggling starts up again. No, I may not be the full-fledged Christian I seek to portray, but I believe in Him. "You don't really think we came from apes, do you?"

My usually direct teacher-turned-friend averts her gaze. "Who knows?"

"I do."

Her eyes snap back to me. "At best, Grace, you're a cultural Christian."

"A what?"

"Didn't get to that section?" She sets *The Dumb Blonde's Guide to Christianity* on the cushion between us. "It means identifying yourself as a Christian—often because it's merely part of your culture—but not being active in your faith. Chapter four."

Oh.

"You know, if you're going to pull this off, you'll have to dig deeper than this book. In fact, with your investigative skills, I'm surprised you didn't put more effort into what it means to be a Christian."

Great. Here's the one person who believes in my ability, and I've disappointed her. Sloppy, Maizy! "There wasn't much time to prepare. Too, not only was there no guarantee I'd get the job, but now that I have it, it's only temporary—"

"No excuses." She retrieves her purse. "Do your homework." At the door she turns and smiles big and bright. And, I declare, she looks just like Angelina Jolie, only honey blond and blue eyed, with softer cheekbones and lips that aren't quite as full. Oh, and she's almost six feet tall. But, really, she does look like that actress.

"Don't worry, *Grace*. You'll figure it out." She reaches for the doorknob. "And don't forget that you're covering the Mule Day event this Friday."

She had to remind me. Not that I'm ungrateful for the job she rooted out for me in the paper's Lifestyle department, but it's hardly serious journalism. "Mule Day. No problem."

But there is a problem, I acknowledge an hour later, following two readings of the fourth chapter and the removal of the cross earrings, necklace, and WWJD bracelet. Dropping my head back against the couch, I moan, "I don't want to be a cultural Christian."

In response, Woofer rises from beside the cereal bowl and attempts to leap onto the couch—hopelessly impossible, but more because of his girth than his height. I boost him up, and he settles beside me.

"I believe in God and Jesus." I stroke his head. "You believe me, don't you?"

He rolls over, wiggles his plump little rump, and offers up his belly for his evening scratch.

I grimace. "Don't ask, don't tell, hmm?"

THREE

I can't believe I have to sign this. Yes, Jem said employees are expected to conduct themselves in a manner consistent with Christianity, but she didn't say anything about agreeing to it in writing. Not that I steal, do drugs, or cheat on my spouse (that one's a freebie, since I've never been married), but I have cohabited outside of marriage (once, and I don't need anyone to tell me it was a mistake…and, uh, wrong). According to this statement, all are grounds for disciplinary action, if not termination.

Amid the ring of phones, the buzz of conversations, and the click of keyboards, I tap the signature line with my pen. Of course, as of this moment, any of my behavior that isn't consistent with Christianity is in the past. Providing I stay levelheaded and don't get tight with anyone, I might not have to lie again. Plus, I can always rely on evasiveness and quick topic changes. And, in the event I'm forced to tell a "black" lie, I can repent. God's forgiveness is the one that matters, right?

Cultural Christian.

I know. But I will "get right with God" (my current favorite Christian speak). I click the pen and lower the point to the signature line. Still, I hesitate.

Come on, Maizy, sign it.

Cultural Christian.

So you don't have depth. So you tend to make God into the God you want rather than the God who is. It's a start.

A start? Ten years you've considered yourself a Christian. At this rate, you'll be lucky if you make it through the first chapter of the Bible by the time you're old and shriveled.

No kidding. With all those thees and thous and thys—

"Is something wrong?"

I swivel my head to see a twenty-five-ish woman who has come around the wall of the cubicle. "Not at all." I sign my name, gather the paperwork she set before me a half hour earlier, and hand it to her. "All set."

Compressing perfectly painted lips (note: *red* lipstick), Fiala Cramer scans each page. Though until now she's been brusque—so much that it's been a struggle to keep my defenses in check—she appears to be in no hurry to get me started on my new job.

At last she levels gray eyes on me. "Everything looks in order." She tucks my paperwork in a folder. "If you'll follow me, I'll show you around the department."

Like the inexperienced underling I'm expected to portray, I jump up and follow her from the cubicle.

On svelte legs (*black* hose) and jacked-up heels (*three* inch), she trots me along the left side of the office. "I should tell you that you now hold the position I held until six months ago, when I was promoted to junior staff writer."

A position that, if not for mounting bills, would still be beneath me. "Oh?"

She indicates a group of low-walled cubicles to the right. "Associate editors."

Guess she didn't hear the question in my "oh." I draw alongside her. "So the editorial assistant—your replacement—was promoted as well?"

Fiala snorts. "Hardly." She gestures to glass-fronted offices on the left side of the department. "These are the staff writers' offices." A moment later, she halts before one that bears a plaque: Fiala Cramer, Jr. Staff Writer. "My office, should you need me." With a toss of her chin, she strides past. "My replacement quit two weeks ago without notice. Very unreliable. Bless her heart."

Hey! Christian speak—a sympathetic aside tacked to a derogatory remark to make it acceptable.

"Thus, once again I have the responsibility of training an editorial assistant."

Which doesn't sit well with her. Just as it doesn't sit well with me that I have to answer to a woman who is likely younger than I, less experienced, and on the unpleasant side. Must keep in mind: student loan, MasterCard, utilities, rent, and a little left over to do something about my hair.

Fiala halts and dips her chin at a large glass-fronted office ahead, the other side of which boasts a view of Nashville's west side. "That's the office of the managing editor of Women's Publications—not that you should have much contact with her."

Not as an editorial assistant, but were I one of her writers…

You're not, Grr-ace!

Fiala points to the right. "Linda Stillwater's office—one of two senior editors and your direct supervisor. Which means that's yours."

She nods at a cubicle-less desk that's visible to anyone who cares to check on me. "When Linda returns on Monday, she'll be keeping the same hours as you."

"She works part time?"

Something flickers across Fiala's face. "Until recently she was full time, but she has decided she needs to spend more time with her family." She nods at a desk ten feet from mine where a young Asian woman sits (showing a bit of *cleavage*). "Pamela Vanderpool, editorial assistant to our other senior editor."

Pamela smiles. "Welcome to Steeple Side."

I step forward and offer my hand. "Grace Stewart."

"Nice to meet you."

I open my mouth to say something in kind, but Fiala interrupts. "We'll come back." She heads down the opposite side of the office with its floor-to-ceiling windows that would offer a decent view of the Nashville cityscape if not for the building across the street. "Editors there." She walks me past three large cubicles, making no attempt to introduce me to the women within. "Eventually you'll meet everyone, but for now you need only concern yourself with the layout."

Fiala sweeps a hand toward two high-walled cubicles, from the depths of which comes the clacking of keyboards. "Copyeditors there." A moment later she halts before the glass doors I entered at 8:00 a.m. sharp. "And across the hall is the editorial department for Men's Publications, headed by Jack Prentiss."

Not on a different floor then.

"Their layout is pretty much the same as for Women's Publications, so if Linda sends you over, you shouldn't have any problem finding your way around."

If she sends me over? "Then there's interaction between the two departments?"

"Of course, not only with regard to advertisers but also magazine content. We want our men and women subscribers on the same page, you know. Oh, there." She nods at a thick-necked thirtyish man exiting the double doors across the hall. "That's Todd Wynde, lead writer of Men's Publications."

Todd of glued-to-the-seat fame?

"He often works on joint projects with our women writers." Fiala leans near and, in a low voice, says, "Very smart and knowledgeable, but best to steer clear of him."

"Why?"

She lifts an eyebrow. "Incontinence of the mouth, bless his heart."

There it is again—the blessing of the heart.

"If he corners you, you can kiss productivity good-bye." Fiala does a U-turn and crooks a finger for me to follow. "Let's get you settled at your desk."

"Grace!"

Though I don't immediately recognize the woman's voice behind me, I recognize the name called out. *Grace. Must remember Grace.* Fixing a smile, I turn back to the glass doors, through which steps the young woman who clued me in on the "seedier side" of Steeple Side yesterday. This time she's wearing three—maybe four—layered tops of varying colors over leggings. "Hi, Jem."

"Hey!" She looks to the woman over my shoulder. "Hi, Fiala."

"Jem." Making no attempt to disguise her irritation, Fiala is no poster child for Christian joy. Hopefully she's just having a bad day. "You two know each other?"

Jem nods. "Met yesterday, before and after Grace's interview. Hit if off, didn't we?"

Did we? "Uh, yes. Do you work in this department?"

"No. Children's Sunday school materials, two floors below. Just thought I'd drop in and see how you're liking your first day at Steeple Side."

"It's hardly even begun," Fiala says dryly.

"Am I interrupting?"

"Yes."

Jem looks back at me. "So what do you think of your job so far?"

Is she really that thick? I glance at Fiala, whose pale cheeks have bloomed with color. "So far, so good," I venture.

"We were just heading back to Grace's desk."

Jem points a finger at Fiala, closes an eye, and makes a clicking sound. "Gotcha." She turns away only to whip back around. "Wanna have lunch, Grace?"

Another glance at Fiala, whose cheeks are brighter yet. "I'm only part time, so…"

"You have a half-hour break," Fiala says. "Eleven to eleven thirty."

I'm surprised. "That's great."

"Meet me in the cafeteria." Jem scoots toward the doors, the charms suspended from her purple belt *clink clinking.* "Second floor."

Though the unexpected break would provide an opportunity for me to check out Steeple Side's retail store on the first floor, how does one turn down an invitation like that? "All right, I'll see you then."

As the doors close behind Jem, Fiala heaves a sigh. "I apologize. Jem thinks she's *every*one's friend. Has a bit of a problem with boundaries."

"Bless her heart," I murmur, only to catch my breath at the realization that I spoke aloud what was merely an anticipation of Fiala's use of the expression.

To my dismay, she looks at me as if seeing me for the first time, then smiles. "Yes, bless her heart."

Ugh. Feels as if we're in agreement. It's true that Jem is a little too friendly for comfort, but I kind of like her. And it's not as if I couldn't use a few friends—

Wrong! You shouldn't be at Steeple Side long, and considering the exaggeration required to nail the job, it's best that you not befriend anyone.

"If you'd like"—Fiala pats her chignon—"I'll talk to her for you."

"No!"

Her hand freezes at her temple.

"I mean, I can handle it. But thank you."

She shrugs. "Follow me."

Shortly, I'm seated at my desk, staring between a pile of folders (to be filed), a pile of mail (to be opened), and a pile of paperwork (to be copied).

Face it, the once hot-and-upcoming investigative reporter, turned leprous-and-unemployed reporter, turned part-time lifestyle reporter, has sunk to a new level.

Still, there are worse things. Like being unable to pay one's bills.

Two hours later, all that's holding me together are those bills. Half hoping Jem doesn't keep our lunch date, as I'd like to huddle down in a corner and recharge, I make my way to the second floor cafeteria, which is teeming with empty tables. Eleven *is* a bit early for lunch. Good thing I was too nervous this morning to scarf down a bowl of cereal. Now if it hadn't been generic...

A poke on the shoulder precedes a voice in my ear. "Did Fiala behave herself?"

I spin around, and there's Jem smiling so brightly I could almost forgive her for keeping our lunch date. "Behave?"

She tickles back a lock of striped hair. "She can't help it. She's just been testy since…"

So Fiala does have an excuse for being unpleasant.

Jem shrugs. "I can't say. Gossip, you know. A weakness of mine, which my supervisor has asked me to work on."

Grounds for termination. Still, though I know I should lay off the curiosity (a natural inclination for any great reporter) and respect Jem's compliance with her supervisor's request, I can't help but test her resolve. "I imagine Fiala must have gone through a difficult time." Catching a flicker of sympathy in Jem's eyes, I draw a deep breath. "Something to which I can certainly relate, but I'm sure our circumstances are different."

Her eyes widen. "I'm sorry, Grace. Are you okay now?"

While conscious of my tactics, the tightening of my chest and pang in the vicinity of my heart are real. That's no lie. Which is good, as I'd prefer to avoid Lie Number Four. Or delay it for as long as possible. I nod. "Getting better every day."

She's thinking about letting me in on Fiala's troubles. I can tell from her shifting jaw and lowering gaze. But she sighs. "I'm glad to hear it."

Although I know that if I open up about my own troubles, she might open up about Fiala's—a little old-fashioned give and take—I can't go there.

Jem steps past me. "Let's get something to eat."

Five minutes later we settle at a table with a carton of milk and a turkey croissant in front of me, a bottled water and peanut-butter cheese crackers in front of Jem.

"Aren't you hungry?"

In the process of removing the cellophane from her paltry lunch selection, she stills and colors slightly. "Not really."

When she returns her attention to her crackers, I peer more closely at her. She's tiny. In fact, stick-model thin despite all those lay-ered tops. Might she be anorexic? Or is she simply petite? I hear there are still some naturally skinny women around. Too, eleven o'clock is early for lunch, especially if she's accustomed to late lunches. Mustn't jump to conclusions.

Jem carries much of our conversation as I wolf down my sandwich and she nibbles at her crackers. As most of the other tables remain empty, she chats up everything from Steeple Side's position in the Christian publishing market (midsize, but held in high regard) to a day in the life of a graphic artist (pulls back her layered sleeves to reveal a bulge-eyed turkey she sketched on her forearm while stuck in morning traffic) to last week's boyfriend who lasted all of forty-eight hours. All interesting, especially compared to what I have to plod through after my lunch break.

I glance at my watch. "I have to be back at my desk in five minutes."

A few moments later we toss our waste in the trash bins, and Jem looks at me. "I just realized that I did most of the talking. Next time we'll talk about you."

"Me?" My voice comes out unnaturally high.

"Sure. If we're going to be friends, you have to share too. You know, what you like about your job…"

I don't.

"…where you've been…"

Not a pretty sight.

"…where you're going…"

God only knows.

"…who you're going with…"

Nobody, as evidenced by my breakup with Ben.

Jem grins. "Same time, same place tomorrow?"

As a seasoned reporter—well, not exactly seasoned, though I was on my way to becoming so before the mistake that cost me every-thing—I ought to have a ready excuse to decline her invitation. But I'm as dry as a dust bowl. "Sure."

I walk with her toward the cafeteria doors as the thick-necked man, identified by Fiala as lead writer of Men's Publications and of glued-to-the-seat fame, enters.

"Hi, Jem."

"Hi, Todd."

He turns his smile on me, only to frown. "Hey, aren't you the gal who took Jack's parking space yesterday?"

He knows? How?

Jem gasps. "You're the one? Oh, my goodness." Her eyes sparkle like a child's on Christmas Day.

"I'm afraid that *was* me. Of course, I didn't realize I was taking anyone's space. There wasn't a sign."

He chuckles. "That's because we snatched it."

So he participated in the prank, though that doesn't explain how he found out I played a role.

He thrusts out a hand. "Todd Wynde, writer for Men's Publications."

I accept his handshake. "Grace Stewart, the new…editorial assistant to Linda Stillwater." The title, if it can be called that, sticks in my throat. Here I am, a writer in my own right, and I have to make like I'm some just-out-of-school lackey.

Todd releases my hand. "Nice to meet you, Grace."

"Um…" I glance at Jem, who looks about to burst, then back at Todd. "How did you know I was the one who took Jack's parking space?"

Looking pleased, he rolls back on his heels. "We were watching from the office." He nods at the ceiling.

So that's why Jack was peering up at the building. Must have known he was the channel of choice.

"It was a bonus that you were there when Jack returned from lunch." Todd glances over his shoulder as if to confirm no one has entered behind him, then leans in. "What did he say? And what was he doing at the back of your car?"

While the first question is uncomfortable, the second is cause to break out in hives. No way am I going to admit that the Brit was permanently applying my bumper sticker. *You know, this might be a good place to use that lie you've been saving for an emergency.*

As Jem's curiosity shudders between us, Todd's brow beetles.

No, this isn't an emergency. But there is a way out—evasion. I smile brightly. "Jack was just being helpful. So, Todd, what do you do here at Steeple Side?"

I deserve the look he gives me. And Jem's snort of disbelief. Not to mention a trophy for proving there is evidence for the existence of dumb blondes. I have *got* to change the color of my hair; it's having a very bad influence on me.

Todd's smile is weak. "I'm a writer in…uh…Men's Publications."

"Right. You mentioned that." I smack myself upside the head. "Sorry. First day and all, you know."

He nods. "Well, nice meeting you, Grace."

"Nice meeting you, Todd." Surely there's some redemption in remembering his name?

As he steps past, Jem grabs my arm and pulls me around to face her. "I can't believe you're the one who took Jack's parking space! How cool is that?"

Cool? "It was only a chance meeting."

"Yeah, but why didn't you say something yesterday? Here I was giving you the lowdown on Jack Prentiss, and you didn't say a word about meeting him."

"Maybe she had good reason not to say anything," says a decidedly British, decidedly amused-at-my-expense voice.

By the way, that was an anvil that just dropped through me, and I wouldn't be surprised if those within a fifty-foot radius felt its impact.

"Jack!" Jem emits sheer delight as she turns to face the dark blond man who is on a fast track to becoming my nemesis.

"Hello, Jem." Head tilted where he stands inside the cafeteria doors, he looks me over. And I look him over, noting that yesterday's shadow has been shaved clean, making the lightly blemished skin of his jaw more pronounced and setting off those nice cheekbones.

As for the rest of him…I suppose he's decent enough—no jowls, no slouch, no paunch. In fact, he looks fit, though not in a he-man way. He's probably a jogger.

He shoves a hand at me. "I suppose we ought to formally introduce ourselves. Jack Prentiss, Men's Publications."

I slide my hand into his, and there's that citrus-y scent again. "Grace Stewart, Linda Stillwater's new editorial assistant."

He squeezes my hand. "Right across the hall."

"Yes." Right…across…the hall.

As he releases my hand, Jem steps near him. "So what's this about Grace having good reason for not telling me the two of you met in the parking lot?"

"You mean after you gave her 'the lowdown on Jack Prentiss'?"

She giggles. The tip of my nose warms. And Jack's eyes return to me—smug, as if he knows my secret. Which he doesn't. I think. I hope. Should I pray?

Oh, God. And I really am talking to You. Though it's true I'm being a little deceptive, I'd appreciate it if You'd get me out of this. In fact, if You do, I'll crack open that new Bible tonight.

"Maybe Grace is shy," Jack offers to my dismay. "Or perhaps she was too embarrassed to mention our encounter in the car park."

"Embarrassed?" Jem glances at me. "About what?"

"Look at the time!" I gasp. And it *is* past time that I was back at my desk. "I've got to—"

"When I pointed out that her 'Jesus is my copilot' bumper sticker was coming off, I think she may have feared it reflected poorly on her Christian beliefs that she hadn't taken more care with its application."

Dirty dog!

"So that's what you were doing."

He blinks. "Sorry?"

Jem hitches a finger over her shoulder. "Todd asked Grace what you were doing at the back of her car. All she would say is that you were being helpful."

"Ah. I repositioned her bumper sticker."

It's Jem's turn to blink. "But you can't reposition a bumper sticker. Once they're on, it's for life."

Please don't tell her about the tape!

He looks back at me. "This one was an exception. The adhesive was rather…tenuous."

Hold up! Was that a double entendre? Am *I* the bumper sticker? *My* Christianity the tenuous adhesive? And is that a smirk?

The smirk broadens into a smile that reveals slightly crowded teeth. "In fact, I wouldn't be surprised if, come a spot of bad weather, it drops off altogether."

Man! That *was* a double entendre. I am toast—blackened, crumb-smoking toast. Probably won't even be allowed to finish out the day. Good-bye, Steeple Side. Hello, repo man.

Jack looks past me and juts his chin at someone. "Though I'd like to chat, I was supposed to meet Todd for coffee five minutes ago… Late as usual." He pins me with his gaze. "Seems I'm always fighting the current. You know, *like a good Christian.*"

Ah!

Jack steps forward, but as he draws alongside, he winks and says, "Yours in Christ."

And I feel like such a fake. Of course, to a degree, I am. Meaning I probably shouldn't bother returning to my desk. Late or not, it's over.

"Yours in Christ?" We walk into the corridor outside the cafeteria, and Jem shakes her head. "Nobody says that. Especially Jack."

Rub it in, why don't you?

She halts before the elevator and pushes the button. "He was acting strange, don't you think? Well, you wouldn't know, but that was *not* the Jack I know."

Grabbing the opportunity to move the topic away from me, I chirp, "Sounds like you know him well."

"I wouldn't say that, but he was definitely distracted and—like I said—a little strange."

Why this feeling that the topic is once more moving toward me?

Thankfully, the elevator doors open, and two men step out, both of whom Jem greets. They reciprocate, sweep me with curious smiles, and walk past.

Jem punches the buttons for our floors and settles back to contemplate the ceiling. Her wheels are turning. I can almost see them. Any moment—

"I've got it!" As another anvil threatens my toes, she moves closer. "I'll bet he's disengaged."

Disengaged? Christian speak for... "What?"

"Disengaged—as opposed to engaged."

"You mean...?"

"Not engaged anymore. Again."

I feel like a dog chasing a too-short tail. "What do you mean 'again'?"

"The on-again, off-again with him and his fiancée, Bette."

Now I'm curious. The, uh, reporter side of me. "So he and this Bette…"

"That means he's available!"

If his peculiar behavior were attributable to another broken engagement, but I know better. It's all about me and our…encounter.

Jem sighs. "That will certainly make some women around here happy."

As if! I mean, the man is hardly pleasant. Of course, that may have more to do with what he thinks of me. But what woman in her right mind would want a man whose every word is smug and judgmental? Of course, smug and judgmental isn't half bad when delivered in a tasty accent. But what about his jaw? Pockmarked. Still, it is firm, and he does make up for any shortcomings with impressive cheekbones.

"Oh ho!" Jem punches my arm. "You too, hmm?"

I frown with all my might. "What?"

"Don't tell me you didn't notice what a catch Jack is—nice build, roughly attractive, good personality. Then there's that accent." She sniggers. "He's too old for me, but it makes my toes curl every time he opens his mouth."

Ping!

"My floor!" Jem steps forward as the doors whoosh open. "I'll see you tomorrow."

No need to enlighten her as to the slim chance of my holding a job at Steeple Side tomorrow.

As she turns left, she rubs her hands with glee. "I can't wait to tell the gals about Jack's disengagement."

Though she wouldn't budge on cluing me in about Fiala Cramer's troubles, she obviously doesn't think the same right to privacy applies to Jack. Because he's a guy? Because his series of "disengagements" is common knowledge? Perhaps a running joke he takes lightly? But what if he doesn't take it lightly? And what if she's wrong and he isn't disengaged?

You are not her mother. Let it go. But I can't. As the doors close, I lunge forward.

Jem looks around. "Wrong floor, Grace."

"I know. Listen, I'm thinking that you might not want to spread it around about Jack and his fiancée. You don't know for certain he's…disengaged." As disappointment shuts down her joy, I smile apologetically. "You don't want to take any heat for passing along news that might not be founded." Which I'm pretty certain isn't.

She mewls with regret. "I guess you're right."

Good. Unfortunately, now I'm going to be even later getting back to my desk, which brings me that much closer to a pink slip. "I'd better get back to work."

"Grace?"

I look over my shoulder.

She wrinkles her cute little nose. "I have to ask—'Jesus is my co-pilot'?" She holds up a hand. "No offense, but it threw me."

Ugh. "How's that?"

"I didn't take you for a 'Jesus junk' Christian."

Is that what I am? Great. "I guess I have a soft spot for Jesus junk." Was that a lie? Nah. Surely that was what drew me to that particular bumper sticker—a soft spot. Now that I think about it, I *was* touched by the wording.

"To each his own." Jem waves and hurries down the hall.

I grit my teeth. That sticker is history. I will scrape every trace of it from my bumper—soft spot or not!

When I return to my desk, Fiala is reclining against it. "Nine minutes late." She taps her watch. "Not a good way to kick off your future with Steeple Side."

The only consolation, if it can be called that, is that I won't be here much longer if Jack Prentiss has his way.

FOUR

"Face it. Jack's the cat to your mouse." Tessie shifts on the corner of my newsroom desk, dips my last french fry in the ketchup pooled on my hamburger wrapper, then pops it in her mouth.

Glad I made it through my ninety-nine-cent burger before she showed up and raided the vegetable portion of my dinner. I roll my chair closer to the desk and poke a finger in the ketchup. Trying to imagine a salty fry beneath the tangy sauce, I lick the red from my fingertip.

"Did you hear me, *Grace*?"

I tilt my head back and give her a look. "Here at the paper, the name's Maizy."

"Sorry. I keep getting you two mixed up." She grins. "You look so much alike."

I sigh. "Yeah, we're definitely playing cat and mouse."

She scoots farther back, paying no mind to the items scattered across my desk, among them Mule Day clippings, brochures, and notes. My life is *so* pitiful.

"Well..." She shrugs. "At least it makes the job interesting."

"Interesting!" I gag, causing heads to turn. I lean toward Tessie. "You try spending five hours a day filing, photocopying, answering phones, and gofering, and in the midst of all that boredom, avoiding a man who's out to get you."

"I see your point, but what about this new friend…Jem?"

Some of my tension drains. "She's sweet."

"And knows everyone's business, from the sound of it." Tessie considers the ceiling. "Jack Prentiss disengaged… I like that."

Likes what? The odd use of *disengaged* to refer to his on-again, off-again relationship? Or the possibility that he's having trouble with his fiancée? Though Tessie says she put the failed Steeple Side story behind her, I wonder.

"So you think Jem may be anorexic?"

I toss my hamburger wrapper in the wastebasket. "As I said, it crossed my mind, but she's probably naturally bone thin and just wasn't hungry."

"Regardless, I assure you that Steeple Side has plenty of skeletons in its closet. Holier-than-thou though they pretend to be, they're human like the rest of us—full of troubles of their own." Her mouth curves. "And gossip."

"Yeah, but at Steeple Side, gossip can get you fired." Which is why I had to warn Jem after lunch. "Speaking of which, I still can't believe I wasn't handed a pink slip today."

Tessie slips off my desk. "Well, Christians are all about forgiveness. In fact, if you play your cards right, you might end up writing for Steeple Side."

Another gag. "Are you kidding?"

She picks up the Mule Day brochure. "Then you like writing about good ol' boys getting together to swap mule stories?"

Aargh! "You know this is only until Ray puts me on full time and"—I lean toward her—"transfers me out of this department."

She doesn't look so certain. "That's what I'm hoping for—that he'll give you a chance to prove you're capable of solid investigative reporting."

"But?"

"But it looks like it's going to take longer than expected."

As much as I don't want to ask, I have to. "Do you think you could talk to him? Find out where I stand?"

"If the opportunity presents itself."

Hope flutters through me. "I appreciate it."

She smoothes her hands down her pencil skirt. "I'd better get back to my desk. Deadline, you know."

I do, though none of my current deadlines are as urgent as hers. Mule Day! "See you later."

Tessie does an about-face only to turn back. "You do know that I have only your best interests at heart?"

"Of course. Why?"

A determined glint enters her eyes. "I believe you have what it takes to do something big with your writing, but you need to toughen up. What happened in Seattle can't happen here. Understand?"

Gulp. "Yes."

"If it does, your career is over. For good."

My heart skips a beat. "I know."

"You've moved beyond *The Dumb Blonde's Guide,* haven't you?"

Maintain eye contact. Do not avert. "I've done a bit of online research and picked up a couple more books at the library." No need to tell her that I still prefer the simplicity of the first book, even if the tone is tongue in cheek. *So* much easier to grasp a concept written with humor than one written for the serious theology student.

"Good." She straightens. "I'll let you get back to…" She glances at the items on my desk. "Mule Day."

"Gee, thanks."

She chuckles. "Cheer up, Maizy. Who knows, maybe this meeting of mules will solve world hunger or some other important social issue."

That stings, but also serves as a reminder to never again allow my feelings to interfere with my career.

As she walks away, I finger the Mule Day brochure—my present and possibly my future. Yeehaw!

"Maizy Grace!"

I shove *The Dumb Blonde's Guide* beneath a sofa cushion. Of course, Grandma Grace is only a voice in my ear—but one capable of conjuring an image of her standing over me, finger wagging.

I sit up straight. "Hi, Grandma."

"Why haven't you called in over a week? You know how lonely I get."

I guess Dad didn't make it by to see her, or Mom (no surprise there), and certainly not my kid sister, who avoids her for fear she'll be dragged off to Sunday school—or worse, a Christian camp like the one where I was saved. "Sorry, Grandma. It's been a busy week."

Her gasp is one of delight. "The paper put you on full time?"

"Not yet, but soon, I hope."

She harrumphs. "Hope! Best be praying, else you'll end up out on the streets."

I do *not* want to have this conversation. "So how have you been keeping yourself busy?"

"Same old, same old. Sitting by the door twiddling my thumbs—"

Cross-stitching.

"—waiting for my son to drop by and acknowledge his mother is still alive and kickin'—"

Literally.

"—idling away the hours in hopes that you'll call—"

Groan.

"—and feeling as if no one loves me."

"I love you, Grandma. In fact, if I were still in Seattle, you know I'd have already visited you at least once this week."

"But you aren't in Seattle, are you?"

And all because I messed up. "You need to get out more often. Volunteer at the hospital or library, spend time at the senior citizen center—"

"So I can meet some old man who'll want me to spend my last good years taking care of him? No, thank you. Bert was all the husband I needed, rest his soul. From here on out, Grace Stewart is a single-seater, single-engine plane."

"But you're lonely."

"Which is your father's fault, your mother's, your sister's, and to a lesser degree—considering the pickle you got yourself in—yours."

Desperate to turn the conversation, I scan the living room and light on Woofer, who's propped against the door with his peg legs in the air, floppy ears spread on either side of his disproportionate head, wheezy snores quivering his nose. "What about a dog? I know you're not an animal person, but—"

"Maizy Grace! You know I can't stand animals! They poop, pee, vomit, leave fur and dander everywhere, and nickel-and-dime you with trips to the doggy doctor."

At least I'll never have to worry about her moving in with me. I *really* love Woofer. As if I had spoken aloud, the little mutt turns his head slowly to keep from losing his balance against the door.

I smile at him and mouth, "Cootchie-coo."

His stub tail ticks once…twice…then he closes his eyes and returns to his snoring.

"—fly out to visit you."

Grandma's words jolt me. "What did you say?"

"You heard me. In a little over three weeks, I'm flying out to Nashville to visit you."

Three weeks. Grandma. Here. "But you said you'd never get on another plane."

"Desperate times call for desperate measures. And I'm desperately lonely."

"But what if you panic like you did last time, when we had to blindfold you to get you on board?"

"We'll just have to pray it's a smooth ride so I won't have trouble making the return flight to Seattle. Otherwise, once they pry me out of my seat, I might have to stay in Nashville."

I did *not* hear that! "You're kidding, right?" I'm hopeful. And desperate. *Oh, please, Lord, don't let it be a bumpy ride. I love her, but I haven't missed her griping and groaning.*

"I am not kidding. In fact, the more I think about it, the more certain I am that change is in order. Wouldn't hurt to shake up my life a bit."

I don't mean to be dramatic, but I lower my head between my knees and breathe deeply.

"You there, Maizy Grace?"

I stare at the carpet between my feet. "I'm concerned about you giving it all up—your church, and what about your friends? You don't want to leave them behind."

"If they want to follow, they're welcome, but it's not as if there are many left. If it's not one funeral, it's another. Depressing, I tell you, watching them drop like flies."

I sit up. "Grandma!"

"It's true! We buried Lottie three weeks ago, Joseph Pulliman this past Monday, and Edith…" She draws a shuddering breath, and I feel her ache over the pending loss of her best friend. "They've called in hospice. A matter of weeks, they say."

"I'm sorry. Are you sure you ought to be traveling at this time?"

Grandma makes a choked sound. "It's too hard watching her fade away. Why, yesterday she didn't even recognize me—thought I was her little sister who passed away when Edith was ten." After a long silence, she clears her throat. "Write this down."

A few moments later, I jot out her flight information.

"So, three weeks from Friday." Lowering the pen, I eye the necklace, earrings, and WWJD bracelet where I laid them yesterday after reading all about cultural Christians. "And you're going to stay… where?"

"With you, of course."

I lift the simple silver cross on its chain and rub the horizontal bar. "You do remember that I share my home with Woofer? And that you don't like animals?"

"I remember, but it's only for two weeks."

Only two weeks.

"You just keep him out of my way, and we'll get along fine. However, should it prove a problem, you can always put him up in a doggy hotel."

Though I make no sound, Woofer throws his weight to the side, bobbles to his paws, and stares bug-eyed at me as if to plead, *"Say it isn't so."*

I nod sympathetically.

Like an inflatable bouncing cage losing its air, Woofer drops, sprawls, then practically melts into the floor—*practically,* because there's no deflating his gut.

Grandma sighs. "I look forward to spending time with you. Fortunately, from the sound of it, we won't be wanting for plenty of opportunities, unless of course, the paper puts you on full time between now and my visit."

It seems as good a time as any to tell her about my job at Steeple Side. But it isn't. One—it's possible that before three weeks are out, Ray will give me my chance. Two—if I tell her about Steeple Side, she might get ideas about me giving up my newspaper dream to work full time at a Christian company—something that is *not* going to happen. Whatever it takes, I *will* atone for the mistake I made in a moment of weakness, *will* prove I'm worthy of Tessie's faith in me.

I drop the cross necklace beside the notepad. "I'll let you know if anything happens at the paper."

"Good girl. Now don't forget to call me this weekend."

"I'll call. Love you." I slip the phone into its stand, pull the sofa pillow forward, and retrieve *The Dumb Blonde's Guide*. As I flip through it, a section I'd read while putting together my "5-Step Program to Authentic Christian Faith" catches my eye:

Show and Tell:
The "Living-Out-Loud" Christian Woman

They're out there—proclaiming their faith by means of a kindergarten favorite: Show and Tell. Let's begin with the lighter side of "show." "Living-out-loud" Christians—or those attempting to appear to "live out loud"—are most easily identified by clothing, personal accessories, and car accessories. Although young Christian women may push the envelope with their choice of clothing, modesty is still in order—the less flesh, the better. Older Christian women, regardless of whether they fall into the category of "living out loud" or "living by example," tend to prefer longer skirts, looser tops, and lower heels.

Tend is the key word, which I didn't pick up on during my first read.

As evidenced by quite a few of my female Steeple Side co-workers, a gray area exists between "pushing the envelope" and "longer, looser, and lower." For which I'm grateful, as it means I'm not stuck wearing one-inch heels, below-knee skirts, and boring pink lipstick.

Of course, there are some living-out-louders whose modesty is questionable. However, what they lack in this area, they often make up for with personal accessories. These accessories often take the form of symbolic jewelry, such as the cross—

I glance at the necklace and earrings I wore to the interview.

—angels, doves, nails, etc. Then there are WWJD bracelets, though this fad is fading.

I zero in on my WWJD bracelet beneath the necklace and earrings.

Fading or not, I thought it was a nice touch.

Popular car accessories include fish emblems, bumper stickers, license-plate frames, antenna balls, and rearview-mirror air fresheners.

Got that down.

Now for the heavier side of "show." A living-out-louder shows by words and acts that her faith is her mainstay. She honors God by keeping His commands and allowing herself to be used by Him to show His love for others.

Okay, so I'm not a living-out-louder. Probably not even a candidate, but I do agree that's how it should be.

The final piece of Show and Tell is, of course, the "tell." A living-out-loud Christian isn't afraid to let others know her story, or "testimony" (see appendix C). With believers and nonbelievers alike, she shares it with sincerity, enthusiasm, and lack of embarrassment.

Will never happen—*if* I can even scrape together a testimony.

Another way Christians "tell" their faith is by a willingness to speak about how God is working in their lives and by sharing Scripture.

Won't happen either—certainly not with all of those *thees* and *thous*.

> Another device is the judicious use of "Christian speak" (see appendix D for a list of commonly used words and phrases).

Which I did. Unfortunately, I didn't use them "judiciously."

> Keep in mind that Christian speak is something of a code and should be used exclusively with fellow Christians.

Understandably so.

> A final word: If being a living-out-loud Christian comes naturally, then live out loud; however, be aware that your outward display of faith carries the risk of being perceived as pretentious. Or faking it.

No kidding.

> If it doesn't come naturally, then living by example may be for you.

Sounds just as hard. Maybe harder. Though I consider reading the next section, I'm too tired. Too, I have to believe that my days at Steeple Side are numbered—that I'll soon be reporting newsworthy, life-changing stories rather than shuffling paperwork.

I squeeze my eyes closed. *Come through, Tessie. Please come through.*

FIVE

"Coming through!"

I jump back against my desk, which I was coming around when the perpetrator appeared carrying a large box labeled Gourmet on the Go.

"Sorry about that!" calls the young man, who doesn't alter his rush toward the managing editor's office, which is the setting for a working lunch.

I blow a tendril of blond hair off my brow. Friday couldn't have come soon enough, though not because of my Mule Day assignment. It has everything to do with the monotonous tasks Fiala throws at me. Then there's Jack, who was hard to avoid not only on my second day on the job, but also now, my third day. If the man's not in our department coordinating the upcoming men's issue with the women's, I'm in his department in the capacity of gofer. Not that I've had direct contact with him since our run-in at the cafeteria, but I'd bet a hundred bucks—which is saying a lot considering my present circumstances—he's keeping an eye on me. Fortunately, my first week at Steeple Side is almost over.

I glance at my watch. Ten minutes and counting…

Warmth spreads against my backside. With a gurgle of disbelief, I thrust off the edge of my desk and whip around. Yep, that would be my coffee, which is slowly chugging out the plastic lid's drink hole to pool across my desk.

As I right the cup, which must have tipped over when I collided with my desk, the *D* word peels off my lips as easily as a peel slips off a banana.

"Good thing most of your colleagues are out to lunch." Jack's voice runs like ice down my back. "Otherwise you might have offended someone."

Keeping my back to him, I stare at the brown spill on my desk that, mercifully, hasn't spread to the paperwork. And as I stand there, I yield to the temptation of Lie Number Four. "You really think someone would be offended by 'darn'?" I pull a handful of tissues from a box on my desk and mop at the spill.

"Darn? That's not what I heard." He leans in, and his warm breath tickles my ear. "Either you're a liar, Grace Stewart, or my hearing is terribly off."

A shiver goes through me, but knowing that the longer I avoid his gaze, the guiltier I'll appear, I force myself around.

His intensely green eyes, less than a foot from mine, sweep my face. "If it's the latter"—he smiles wryly—"I apologize."

His proximity disturbs me inside and out, which is usually evidence of attraction. But I can't possibly be attracted to this smug Brit. I'm nervous. Nothing at all to do with curiosity over his curved mouth or citrus-y scent. Using the excuse of my sopping handful to distance myself, I step around the desk, toss the tissues in the wastebasket, and reach for more. Unfortunately, Jack doesn't move, and when I wipe up the last of the coffee, he's still there.

I look to his face only to find his attention somewhere in the vicinity of the base of my throat. "What?"

His eyes flick to mine. "Sorry. Not sexual harassment. I was just wondering what happened to that pretty cross necklace you were wearing the day we met." He points to my right ear, then the left. "And the earrings."

Annoyance clenches my jaw, the side benefit of which is that it keeps me from rolling out a lie about an unfortunate incident with the necklace and earrings. I clear my throat. "I have a question for you, Mr. Prentiss."

Up go his eyebrows. "Jack."

"All right—*Jack*. Even if I said what you think I did, are you telling me that no one at Steeple Side ever uses offensive language?"

He shakes his head. "That would be a lie. Christians are fallible. Whether employed by Steeple Side or elsewhere, we all say and do things we regret. It's how we handle our mistakes that attests to our faith."

So there, cultural Christian! Putting a face on the guilt flushing me, I reach for the unopened mail. "At least we can agree on that." Hoping my cheeks aren't as bright as they are warm, I lower my face. "I have work to do before I leave today."

"Have a nice weekend." He turns away but then turns back. "Don't forget about your bumper. If you don't get it off now, it won't come off at all."

The bumper sticker again—he's holding it over my head, threatening to expose my use of tape.

He grins. "I am, of course, referring to the coffee stain."

I clap a hand to my damp backside. I did forget about my "bumper."

"Thank you."

With a nod, he enters the managing editor's office.

I decide my stained skirt is a legitimate excuse for leaving early and grab my purse. However, as I step around my desk, a half dozen editors and writers from Jack's department appear. I acknowledge them with a smile, hanging back until they disappear inside the managing editor's office, then it's off to the ladies' room. Fifteen minutes later, I grudgingly accept that I may have to write off the skirt. Wishing I hadn't been tempted by the flattering above-knee skirt and had stuck with the conservative black skirt I originally pulled from the closet, I head home.

"What's with the bumper sticker I saw on the back of your car?" asks Porter Mitchell, the paper's photographer assigned to capture the visual charm of Mule Day.

Eyes irritated by the dust kicked up by a team of mules that passed by earlier—sporting bonnets, no less—I grind my teeth. Why haven't I removed that sticker?

"Did you get cinched in by the 'Buckle of the Bible Belt'?"

I nearly smile at the label by which the Nashville area is known, due in part to being home to the headquarters of many denominations, and I peer up at the middle-aged man. "What do you mean, did I get cinched in? I *am* a Christian."

"I didn't know."

There it is again.

He smiles sheepishly. "Sorry. The bumper sticker wasn't there last week when I helped you change your flat."

Which made him late for bowling. Still, he hadn't seemed to mind, though he'd changed into his bowling shirt and shoes to save time before leaving the office.

Porter shrugs. "That's why I thought religion might be a new thing for you."

"I was saved ten years ago."

Shifting as if suddenly uncomfortable, he takes a noisy whiff. "Don't you love the smell? Reminds me of my granddaddy's farm."

I'm glad it holds fond memories for him. "I'm sure it's an acquired smell."

He chuckles. "Columbia's a long way from Seattle, ain't it?"

Columbia, forty-five minutes southwest of Nashville. Wondering how an event like this can attract upwards of a quarter of a million people from across the country each year, I scan those who throng the park, many of whom sport coveralls and high-crowned tractor hats. "A very long way."

"I suppose that means you haven't given any more thought to joining our bowling league?"

I narrow my lids at him, but the twinkle in his eyes tells me he isn't any more serious about me joining now than when he issued the invitation months ago. "Nope."

With a bounce of his eyebrows, he looks past me. "Mmm." His face is canvassed with bliss. "Smell them funnel cakes?"

"You mean that greasy smell above the scent of animals and waste?" The latter of which I've almost stepped in despite valiant attempts by workers to remove the piles.

Porter smiles. "That would be it. Let's get one."

"No thanks. The sooner I get the story, the sooner I can leave."

"Your loss. Anything in particular you want me to shoot?"

I pull my notebook from my backpack. "I plan on covering the arts-and-crafts show, knife-and-coin show, gaited-mule show, liars contest, and"—I snort—"clogging event."

"Gotcha." He pats the camera around his neck, then turns his baseball cap front to back and strides away, leaving me to contemplate the meaning of life as it relates to Mule Day in Columbia, Tennessee.

Two hours later, as darkness settles like a fluffy blanket, I'm surprised to have six pages of material after elbowing through the enthusiastic masses. Much of it was supplied by an old-timer at the gaited-mule show. Everything I never wanted to know about mules I now know. And it's actually interesting. Though I knew a mule was a cross between a donkey and a horse, I didn't know they are unable to reproduce themselves. Duh. This of course creates a constant mule market, which had the old-timer—a sought-after breeder—gleefully rubbing his hands.

Sidestepping a pack of laughing children trailed by tired-looking parents, I dance opposite and the toe of my right sneaker sinks into what can only be a pie. "Ugh." I step off the pavement beneath a park light to scrub my shoe in the grass. *So* glad I didn't wear my suede ankle boots. When in Rome—er, Columbia—do as the Columbians do, I'd counseled. And I'm glad I did, as the dirt, smell, and dung of Mule Day can easily be removed from my sneakers, jeans, and close-fitting top by a spin in the washing machine.

Leaning against the light post, I consult my notebook. I've covered all but two of the events. A glance at my watch reveals it's fifteen minutes till the liars contest begins. I consider the booths across the way that waft all manner of aromas, not the least of which is funnel cake. But somewhere in between the greasy tendrils is the smell of roasted corn.

Five minutes later, I'm munching happily on a cob as I join those making their way to the high school that adjoins the park. Surprised by contentment, I smile as I snap up the last mouthful of sweet, juicy corn.

See, this isn't so bad. It's all about attitude. All about making the best of your circumstances, even if it means stepping around, and occasionally in, mule pies. Not bad at all.

"Grace!"

Though my forward motion doesn't fail me, I get a kink in my stride, which I correct. It must be a different Grace the guy is calling.

"Grace Stewart!" a second male voice calls, and oh-so-British.

As much as I long to pretend I didn't hear, my fear of raising *his* suspicions further by not answering to my Steeple Side name makes me halt fifty feet from the auditorium. I turn.

"I thought that was you," exclaims Todd Wynde, the owner of the first voice. As for the second, that would be Jack, whose arm is loosely held by a tall woman with fashionably short black hair that flips up on the ends (the possibly disengaged fiancée?).

"Todd! Jack!" *Ooh, that didn't sound genuine.* "What are you doing here?"

They halt before me. "Enjoying the festivities." Todd grins. "You?"

"The same." With a wave of my picked-clean cob, I punctuate the statement that surely can't be counted a lie, considering I have started enjoying myself—a bit.

"By yourself?"

Jack is watching me. I can feel it, and it's then that I become aware of my appearance—soiled sneakers, jeans that follow my every curve, and a snug knit top that makes the most of my small bosom and, when I raise my arms, reveals an inch or so of bare midriff. Hardly Steeple Side–approved apparel. Of course, this isn't Steeple Side, and Todd and Jack, in their jeans and T-shirts, fit in with Mule Day as well as I do. As for the woman, she's overdressed in embellished jeans and a white ruffled top—poor choice in the midst of so much dust and dirt.

"Hey, Grace." Todd waves a hand before my eyes.

I blink. "Yes?"

"I asked if you're by yourself."

I am, aren't I? "Yes." Not a lie, as Porter doesn't count. Though we're here as employees of the paper, we came in separate cars and may not even meet up again. All good.

"I'm surprised," Jack says. "I didn't take you for someone who would enjoy an event like this."

Thinks he knows me, does he? Well, in this instance he's right, but this instance only. "Obviously there's a lot you don't know about me, Jack."

"Not yet."

Silence expands between us, and I glance at the woman regarding me with a deepening frown. I flounder, look to Todd, whose eyes dart between Jack and me, and spit out, "But what about you, Jack? This hardly seems your cup of tea." Oh, cute! Brit…cup of tea. "Who dragged you along?"

"That would be me." Releasing Jack's arm, the woman with a soft southern twang steps forward. "And since neither Jack nor Todd sees fit to introduce us"—she extends a hand—"Bette Bruin. I'm a close friend of Jack's."

Not fiancée? Meaning Jem's right? As I accept her handshake, I look to her left hand. No ring. Disengaged then. "Grace Stewart. I just started at Steeple Side as an editorial assistant."

She releases my hand. "Enjoying the job?"

Oh dear. If I tell one more lie I'll have to start writing them down to keep track of them. Evasion! I wrinkle my nose. "It's interesting." No need to clarify that "interesting" only kicks in over lunch with Jem, whose struggle against gossip is weakening. But then, once upon a time I *was* an investigative reporter and wheedling information out of people was my job. *One you failed at.*

Bette's head lists right. "I assume you're working in Women's Publications."

"Yes."

"And aspire to become a writer? editor?"

"Writer." I clear my throat. "I like writing." But enough about me. "So you dragged Jack to Mule Day."

She glances at him. "As you say, it's hardly Jack's cup of tea, but he always comes through when I need him." She looks back at me. "And I certainly didn't want to do this gig all by my lonesome."

"Gig?"

She pushes a hand through her flipped locks. "My band is performing on the main stage this evening."

The outfit makes sense now. "You're a musician?"

She smiles. "Small-time, but yes. If you have the time, drop by the main stage. We're on from eight till nine."

Though I had hoped to be heading back to Nashville by then, curiosity makes me nod. "Sounds like fun."

Jack steps forward. "If you want a decent seat, Bette"—he inclines his head toward the auditorium, where a line is forming—"we ought to queue up."

"Right." She raises her eyebrows at me. "Join us?"

Oh dear. I do *not* want to spend any more time beneath Jack's watchful gaze, especially as Porter might be getting shots of the event. If he sees me, he could blow my cover—

Cover! As if I'm attending Mule Day in an investigative capacity.

"It's not a life-or-death decision." Jack's amusement deepens his accent. "And, correct me if I'm wrong, but you were heading into the liars contest."

Grateful for the dim light that camouflages my flush, I nod. "Yes."

"And you are alone." Todd joins forces with Jack and Bette.

Think! Maybe you could come down with an allergic reaction to mule dander. A lie. *A queasy stomach?* It does feel a bit off...

"Well?" Once more Bette loops an arm through Jack's.

I bite into a smile. "All right." At least until I can come up with something believable and just this side of a lie.

As Jack and Bette step past, Todd draws alongside me. "This should be fun."

Trailing the other two, I say, "Did you get dragged along too?"

"Hardly, though I wouldn't have attended if Jack hadn't asked me along."

Further proof that Jack and Bette are disengaged? That he's here only in the capacity of a friend?

"I love events like this," Todd continues. "A step back in time to a simpler life—the smell of farm animals, being jostled by real people, dodging their squealing kids. It feels good, you know?"

I do. As much as I groan over covering such events, they do impart a sense of belonging...community...harmony. Not that log-loading competitions, mule seminars, clogging, or mule parades have anything to do with real life, but it's a nice respite. "Yeah."

"That sounded heartfelt."

Oh boy. If I'm not careful, I'll give into my baser instincts and go all sentimental, which is not a desirable quality for an investigative reporter. In short, I'll never get out of this rut, warm and fuzzy though it feels at the moment.

I toss my emaciated corn cob in a trash can and nod at the two ahead. "I'm assuming Jack and Bette are significant others."

Todd snorts so loudly I wouldn't be surprised if something came out of his nose. "Significant others! Whatever happened to boyfriend, girlfriend? Husband, wife?"

I couldn't ask for a better opening to probe Jack and Bette's relationship. "Or fiancé, fiancée."

"Fiancé, fiancée." He grunts. "That's like Ms., Miss...begging the question of is she or isn't she married?"

So much for the perfect opening.

"Of course, that's the bachelor in me talking. I guess the single life is starting to get old—coming home to a silent apartment, dining on microwaved food, watching the news, playing video games, hoping that when the phone rings it'll be someone other than my mother."

This must be the incontinence of the mouth Fiala spoke about. "Yeah."

"Then you're tired of the single life too?"

Uh-oh. He seems like a nice guy, but I don't like where this conversation could be heading. "Not yet, but I do have my moments."

We halt behind Jack and Bette, who are next in line to purchase tickets. I swing my backpack from my shoulder and pull out my wallet. A moment later, I hit on the perfect excuse to bypass the liars contest. "Oh, da—shucks!" Nice save. "Looks like I've spent my last dollar." I open my empty wallet wide for Todd's inspection. True, I have a twenty tucked behind a credit card, but that's for emergencies. And watching a liars contest hardly qualifies, even if I did plan on including it in my article. Oh well.

"I'll cover you." Todd pulls some bills from his wallet.

"No! I wouldn't impose."

"You're not."

"But—"

"If it makes you feel better, you can pay me back on Monday."

I start to protest further, but Jack turns to me. "Careful, Grace, or you'll leave us with the impression that you don't want to spend time with your Steeple Side colleagues."

Should have known he was listening. "That's not it!" Well, not exactly, as my main concern is the possibility of an awkward run-in with Porter. "I just…"

Bette leans near me. "Let Todd spring for you. It will make his evening."

What's the use? I give Todd a smile. "If you insist."

Okay, Big Guy, here's the deal. You keep Porter away from me and I'll crack open my new Bible. Promise.

"Spectator or teller?" drawls the teenage girl who's collecting for the tickets.

Todd frowns. "Teller?"

She bobs her head. "If you'd like to compete in the contest, you register with the clerk."

"What does it involve?"

"When the master of ceremonies calls your name, you have five minutes to tell your biggest whopper. If you win, there's prize money."

Todd looks around. "What do you think, Jack?"

"Only five minutes? I can't imagine you telling any story—whopper or otherwise—in under half an hour."

Todd feigns offense. "Ow."

"But as for Grace…" Jack eyes me. "I have a feeling she could do it."

And I have a vision of grabbing him by an ear, hauling him to a Porta Potti, and locking him inside. I open my eyes wide. "Embarrassing as it is to admit, I'm not very good at expressing myself verbally." But give me a pen and paper and I'm pretty good at leveling the playing field. And how I'd like to level his!

"Stop giving Grace a hard time." Bette punches Jack's shoulder. "She'll start thinking you don't like her."

I believe we're *way* past "start."

"So?" The teenage girl comes to my rescue. "Spectator or teller?"

Todd hands her the bills. "We'll have to content ourselves with being mere spectators."

Shortly, we step into the auditorium that, though far from capacity, is filling fast. Jack snags four seats a half dozen rows from the
front, and I find myself sandwiched between him and Todd with
Bette on Jack's right.

Trying not to appear too obvious, I scope out the room and cringe
at the sight of Porter standing to the right of the stage. Hands shrug-
ging up his pants pockets, he rocks toe to heel. Hopefully, he'll stay
pointed in that direction. He doesn't.

As his head comes around, I slip down in my seat.

Todd leans over to me. "You all right, Grace?"

Ignoring Jack's probing gaze, I nod. "Just relaxing a little. It's been
a full day."

"But you can't see over the guy in front of you."

True, but neither can Porter see over him to me. "I'll sit up when
the contest starts."

Todd shrugs and looks forward again.

Great! Why don't I just stamp "something to hide" on my
forehead?

Once the contest starts, I straighten, though only enough to see
the stage in the gap between the man and woman in front of me. Surprisingly, the contest is entertaining, and I find myself laughing with
the audience. And wishing I could pull out my notebook and jot
down impressions of it for the article I'll be writing this evening. Jack
Prentiss is *really* cramping my style!

When Porter finally withdraws—likely to get pictures of the clogging event—I can barely contain my relief. Summoning the energy to
sit upright, I slide up in my seat to enjoy the show. And I do enjoy it,

especially the performance of a thirteen-year-old boy sporting a cap of brown hair and a smile that contorts time and again as he tells his tale of "the mule that got away."

"That was funny!" Bette says as the four of us step into the crisp night air.

I nod. "That thirteen-year-old boy…" Remembering his parting shot, I laugh. Laughter, which trails off into a giggle, which trails off into a…

I press my lips. Too late, according to the eyes that spotlight me.

Bette tilts her head to the side. "Did you just…purr?"

Haven't done that in a long time. Of course, I haven't had much to laugh about. "I've been told it sounds like that—what comes out at the end of my laugh when I'm excited…er, happy." And which I try to keep under control as much as possible, especially as it was another "laughing point" for my girlhood nemesis, Cynthia Sircy.

Todd nods. "Definitely a purr. Have you ever heard anything like it, Jack, outside of a cat?"

"Can't say I have. Grace is a very interesting person."

Though I'm growling on the inside, I'm smiling on the outside. "Why, thank you. And thank you for inviting me to join all of you. I'd better get going."

"Oh," Bette groans, "I thought you might catch some of my show."

And dodge Porter again should he decide to stop by the main stage? And subject myself to more of Jack's derisive comments and scrutiny? "I appreciate the invite. Unfortunately I have a date." With a deadline, so not a lie. Exactly.

Jack narrows his eyes. "Unfortunately?"

Cannot believe I said that. "You know how dates are—some good, some bad. We'll just have to see how this one goes." I'm hoping that, with a pot of black coffee at my side, it will be productive.

"Wow, unless your date is in Columbia, that's going to be some late date." Todd consults his watch. "It's going on eight."

Bette gasps. "I've got to get to the stage!"

I couldn't be more grateful for the diversion, as otherwise I might have had to pull a "night-shift" boyfriend out of my hat—a.k.a. a lie.

Bette gives Jack's cheek a peck, Todd's shoulder a squeeze, and me a smile. "Nice meeting you, Grace. See you at the show, guys." She hurries across the park, leaving me with Jack and Todd.

I shift my backpack. "I guess I'll see you at work on Monday." I step past them, holding my breath, fiercely hoping they don't call me back. They don't.

Thank You, God. And thank You for keeping Porter away. I'll definitely crack open my new Bible. If not tonight, then tomorrow night, or the next. Regardless, You can count on me.

It is done. And, if I say so myself, I did the article justice. Of course, it helps that, with the exception of spending nearly an hour in the company of Jack Prentiss, I actually enjoyed myself. As dull as lifestyle writing is compared to investigative reporting, I really am good at this.

With Woofer tucked under an arm, nostrils flaring as he attempts to inhale the peanut-butter sandwich I'm carrying in the opposite hand, I cross the living room and plop down on the sofa.

Woofer whimpers. Woofer wiggles. Woofer waddles out from beneath my arm and onto my lap to stick his nose inches from my sandwich. As usual, I share—a bite for me, a pinch for him—until all that's left are crumbs.

As he settles alongside my thigh, I retrieve my Bible from the lamp table. "And now for some light reading." *See, God, I'm keeping my promise—even though I'm really tired.*

I spread the tortoiseshell handles of the tapestry cover, unzip, and am pleased to immediately translate the KJV initials stamped on the cover into "King James Version." Despite the tongue-in-cheek title, *The Dumb Blonde's Guide to Christianity*—or *DBGC* as I've begun to think of it—is a wealth of information.

I start to open the Bible, only to feel the tug of *DBGC*. Surely it will tell me the best place to embark on my journey. I grab it. And—lookie there!—a chapter titled "So You Want to Attempt to Read the Bible: Sixty-Six Books in Sixty-Six Minutes or Less." Attempt? That doesn't sound promising.

I turn to the chapter that explains the structure of the Bible. Two divisions—Old Testament and New Testament.

I know that.

Thirty-nine books in the Old Testament, twenty-seven books in the New Testament, for a total of sixty-six.

Simple addition, but what's with the number sixty-six?

A list of the Old Testament books, from Genesis to Malachi, with all kinds of strange names like Leviticus and Ecclesiastes.

Sure hope I won't be expected to know their pronunciation. I stifle a yawn.

A list of the New Testament books, from Matthew to Revelation.

More strange names, though sprinkled with some nice, solid "100 Most Popular Baby Names" like Matthew, John, James, and Peter.

Three types of books in the Old Testament: historical, poetical, and prophetical, each book placed under one of the three headings. "Oo...kay."

Shortly, I give myself a pat on the back when the author explains how to find something in the Bible using its standard reference system—the book of the Bible, a chapter in that book, followed by a colon, followed by the verse. Easy, especially since I figured it out years ago when I was saved at the Christian summer camp. What won't be easy is memorizing the order of the books to avoid fumbling through nearly fifteen hundred pages *should* that become necessary.

The thought of memorizing all sixty-six names makes me yawn again. *Don't worry, Tessie will come through.* And if she doesn't? Fortunately, throughout the *DBGC* are sidebars titled Very Blonde Tips for the extra-challenged (or, in my case, busy).

VERY BLONDE TIP #16

Navigating the Bible Without Wearing Out the Contents Page

You're either very blonde, very busy, very lazy, or memory impaired. Regardless, the alternative to memorization of the sixty-six books of the Bible is the use of color-coded self-adhesive tabs printed with the name of each book (see appendix for a detailed explanation of how to apply these handy-dandy tabs). Sets are available at your local Christian bookstore for around five dollars.

Another yawn prompts me to "rest" my eyes for a second...

"Mmm." With every intention of cracking open my Bible, I shift sideways, then a little more. Oh, why not? I stretch out across the sofa cushions (just need to recharge my batteries), causing Woofer to reposition himself alongside my tummy.

As for my Bible...I eye it where it lies beside Woofer.

You promised.

But I didn't say tonight—or is it morning now? Regardless—

Stop being so cultural!

I poke a finger between the covers of the Bible and crank it open to Psalm 25:4–5. "Shew me thy..."

"Shew? Thy?" Now I remember why the Bible I received at summer camp ended up in a garage sale. "Shew me thy ways, O LORD; teach me thy paths. Lead me in thy truth, and teach me: for thou art the God of my salvation; on thee do I wait all the day."

I drop the cover. There. Not only did I take the time to research how to begin my journey through the Bible, but I cracked it open and read a verse. All good.

SIX

I'm beaming. Not because Linda Stillwater, senior editor and my immediate supervisor, is back from a two-week absence (though she seems nice enough). Not because I've nearly made it through my workday without running into Jack. And not because I splurged on Tony the Tiger cereal and gourmet dog food yesterday. I'm beaming because I overheard two junior staff writers talking about my Mule Day article that ran on Sunday. One said she loved the witty tone and style; the other added that Maizy Stewart never disappoints. And if my beam wasn't bright enough, it cranked up when Fiala added, "Nice that they finally hired someone with talent."

"Me!" I wanted to shout. Not bad for someone who'd rather make a difference with her writing by tackling the dregs of life—the good stuff, like embezzlement, drugs, and illegal political contributions.

My beam falters in direct proportion to the bitterness that oozes through the cracks in my memories, and I'm forced to admit that "good stuff" isn't an apt description, especially if the reporter is "faint of heart." Which, according to my last editor, I am.

She's wrong. I was just green. And gullible. But that has changed, and once Ray gives me a chance, I'll prove it. Maizy Stewart is going to expose the gritty underside of Nashville…is going to bring justice to the downtrodden…is going to make a name for herself and prove her detractors wrong.

I wince at that last statement, which is obviously self-serving, but there has to be some gratification to keep a good reporter going. Right? Right. In fact, I can see it now: "And this year's recipient of the award for best investigative reporting…"

I fantasize, yet not for much longer, I hope. Er, pray. *Please, God.* Now back to this pile of unopened mail.

"Grace."

That's my name, and I haven't forgotten it once today. I look over my shoulder at the middle-aged Linda Stillwater as she pokes her head around her office door. "Yes ma'am?"

"Can you come in? I have an assignment for you."

Assignment. How sweet the word! Too bad it's not being used in its purest form. Expecting to be given a task along the lines of labeling folders, I push back from my desk and step into her office.

"Having been out these past weeks, I've fallen behind." She lowers to her chair. "I don't know how I'm going to write this article for the upcoming issue and at the same time keep my writers on track."

"I'd love to help however I can." *Which is far more than you realize.*

She gazes at me through the same red-rimmed eyes she sported this morning when I introduced myself. If she hadn't just returned from vacation, I'd say she's been crying. Probably allergies.

"I'm assuming you know how to research."

Do I ever! "Of course. Just tell me what you want."

She gives what seems a halfhearted smile. "I like your enthusiasm. It'll get you far in this company."

Not in my plans, but if it makes her feel better. "Thank you."

She pushes a folder toward me. "Teenage drug use. I need current statistics among Christians and non-Christians."

Serious research. And interesting. This should make the day go by faster.

As I open the folder, she continues, "Frequency, duration, drug of choice, who with, where, why—" Her voice breaks, and when I look up, her eyes have reddened further and the tip of her nose is flushed.

Maybe not allergies. Might she be going through a rough time?

"Also, I'd like to know how our churches are dealing with teen drug use. Big and small congregations. Make a few calls, talk to a few youth pastors."

"Should I stick with local churches?"

"Sure. In fact, start with your church."

Gulp.

"By the way, which church do you attend?"

Why am I not surprised? Which begs the question: why am I not prepared? I had every intention of scoping out a church yesterday, maybe even peeking inside a couple. *But no, just had to sleep in. Had to indulge in a long shower. Had to take Woofer for a walk at Percy Warner Park.*

I clear my throat. "Unfortunately, I'm still fairly new to the area, so I haven't yet found a church I'd call my church home. But I'm getting close." Close to making the drive down West End. Today. After work. No excuses.

"Which church are you leaning toward? Maybe I can offer some insight."

"Uh, this one on West End…big, brick, nice landscaping." On West End, they *all* have nice landscaping. At her frown, I scrunch up my nose. "Embarrassing as it is to admit, the name escapes me."

Her frown eases. "Is it—?"

"The right or the left side of the road as you head west?"

It's *him*. My own personal plague rolled up in a British accent, always appearing at the most inopportune time. That pharaoh guy who thought he had it bad when Moses descended on Egypt? He had nothing on me. Not that I've been reading my Bible, though I had every intention of doing so this weekend. It's just that one of Grandma Grace's favorite Bible stories is the one about Moses and the plagues visited on that stubborn pharaoh.

Drawing a breath to avoid appearing rattled, I turn to where Jack stands in the doorway, arms crossed over his chest. "It's on the right side of the street."

"Big…brick…" His brow furrows as if he's truly deep in thought, but I know better. He's trying to catch me. "Brown brick?"

Was it brown? "I believe it's some shade of brown and not far off the interstate."

His eyebrows rise. "You don't mean the one with the Star of David out front?"

Uh-oh. *Does* it have a Star of David? I don't remember seeing one. And even I know what that signifies. Wrong religion. "Of course not. It's past the synagogue. Actually, probably farther from the park than I'm thinking. Maybe a mile? Really big"—the better to get lost in—"with a tall steeple." *Very* Christian.

"Sovereign Church?" Linda says.

Posting a bright smile, I turn. "That's it. In fact, I'm certain it's going to be my new church home. The pastor's sermons are wonderful." I'm sure they are. "As are the people." Okay, as tempted as I am to call those little white lies, there's no denying that each of these statements is a lie. But they can be lumped together as one, so Lie Number Five.

Linda nods. "Though I attend elsewhere, I've heard it's a wonderful church and has a strong singles' program."

Hmm. I'm nowhere near manhunt mode, but it wouldn't hurt to dip a toe in the water.

Suddenly Linda's eyes light. "Isn't Sovereign your church, Jack?"

Oh, God. Yes, You. You're laughing with Jack, aren't You? Well, I hope You're happy, because I really regret that lie. And, uh, the others. Of course, that's the point, isn't it?

I peer over my shoulder. "Is that right? I haven't seen you there." The truth.

"And I haven't seen you." He smiles. "Strange, hmm?"

"Yeah. Maybe next Sunday."

"Splendid. I'll watch for you."

Of course he will. I look back at Linda and tap the folder. "I'll get right on this."

She glances at her watch. "About to go to lunch?"

"Yes."

"Don't worry about starting on it today. Tomorrow is soon enough." She shifts her attention to Jack. "I've asked Grace to do some research for the article on teen drug use."

As I turn toward the door, Jack drawls, "Research. Really?"

Yes, *really!* Must do something about this blond hair that's giving him the impression there's nothing under it. Clasping the folder to my chest, I force my gaze to meet his so I won't appear shifty eyed.

"In fact," Linda continues, "since Grace is new to your church, perhaps you can put her in contact with your youth pastor."

His mouth curves lazily. "My pleasure."

Well, it's not mine. Curiously aware of my slightly above-knee skirt, the flattering cut of my blouse, and the embrace of two-inch heels, I start toward him.

To my relief, he steps aside. To my chagrin, he says, "Stop by my office on your way back from lunch, and I'll give you *our* youth pastor's name and number."

"Thank you." I clear the doorway. A moment later the door closes behind me, and I hear the muffled sound of his voice. Is he telling her about my crooked fish? my taped bumper sticker? the "yours in Christ" faux pas? the *D* word slip of the lip?

With a sigh, I set the folder on my desk and envision a pink slip there when I return from lunch. And just when the job's starting to get interesting.

"So he *is* disengaged!" Jem collapses back in the chair she had sat tensely in throughout the selective retelling of my Mule Day encounter with Jack. "I knew it."

"That's how it appears, but just because Bette wasn't wearing an engagement ring doesn't mean they're no longer engaged."

She snorts. "You're not engaged to a man like Jack without proclaiming it to every female within sniffing distance."

"What about her hanging on his arm?"

She waves dismissively, scattering cracker crumbs. "They're just friends again."

I take a nibble of my pickle. "What kind of relationship is it where two people bounce back and forth between wanting to marry and not? Either you do or you don't."

"Cold feet."

"But Jack doesn't strike me as someone who gets cold feet."

"I didn't say the cold feet were his. From what I've heard, Bette's the one who's in need of a pair of thick wool socks."

"And he keeps taking her back?"

"Must be love."

I almost feel sorry for Jack.

Jem sighs. "So how do you like Linda?"

"She seems nice."

"How does she look?"

Strange question. "Um, fine."

Jem's mouth forms an O. "No one's told you?"

That there's something more to Linda's red-rimmed eyes than allergies? "No."

She leans forward to impart the gossip she's supposed to be gaining control over. But far be it from me to stop her—at least, in this case. She opens her mouth, only to narrow her lids. "I am not gossiping again, as Linda was very open about the trouble her teenage son got into." She frowns. "Fiala or Pamela should have told you."

Fiala, whose exchanges with me are limited to instruction on how to perform my job. Pamela, who's so busy running everywhere for the other senior editor that we're lucky to exchange a dozen words throughout the day.

"What kind of trouble did Linda's son get into?" Oh, wait—

"Drugs."

Duh. And *ow.*

"That's why she was gone—getting her son into rehab—and why she's now working part time. Though her daughter's also a teen and in school most of the day, this whole mess made Linda reevaluate her situation and decide she needs to be more available to her husband and children."

I feel the tug of empathy that sometimes gets me in trouble—*big* trouble. "And Steeple Side doesn't have a problem with that?"

Jem stops fiddling with her charm bracelet. "Of course not. They're behind her all the way."

That didn't sound like a stupid question to *me.* Christian company or not, the work still has to be done. "Who's going to pick up the slack?"

"I've heard they may open up another senior editor position, possibly full time since the magazine is growing. In the meantime, now that Linda's back, expect to be doing more than filing."

I look at my watch. "Speaking of which, I'm supposed to be meeting with Jack in three minutes." I sweep up my lunch remains and move toward the trash bin.

A few moments later, Jem taps my shoulder as we head out of the cafeteria. "What do you mean you're meeting with Jack?"

I know what the glint in her eyes means. "He's helping me with some research that Linda asked me to do."

"That's how it always starts."

I halt before the elevator and punch the button. "Not with me."

"Well, just remember there are others ahead of you and you're not going to make any friends by cutting in line."

I roll my eyes. "I have no interest in Jack."

The doors of the elevator part, and as we step inside, she says, "We'll see."

I blow a breath up my face. "I'm ignoring you." And I do, until she gets off at her floor.

Jem glances over her shoulder as the doors begin to close. "If anything of consequence happens, I want to be the first to know."

I wave. "See you later."

Shortly, Jack motions me into his office. "Close the door behind you."

"You think that's a good idea?"

He looks to the large windows left and right. "Nothing happens in here that can't be seen by all."

Right. I close the door with reluctance.

"Sit down." He nods at the chair in front of his desk.

"Oh, I don't want to take you from your work. All I need is a name and number."

"Of *our* youth pastor?" With a pen, he points to the chair. "Sit down, Grace. Please."

He doesn't mean that. Still, I cross his office and lower to the edge of the chair.

"Comfortable?"

"Hardly."

"Well, then, let's get this over with." He rises, comes around, and leans back against the edge of his desk—three feet from me.

I tip my chin up. "Is this supposed to make me more comfortable? Because it doesn't."

"Why? Because I'm near enough to see that you aren't who you pretend to be?"

There's definitely a pink slip waiting for me on my desk. Why did I splurge on Tony the Tiger? Why?

"No more games, no more lies." He crosses his arms over his chest. "Why are you at Steeple Side?"

My stomach clenches as I mentally skitter backward and forward in search of a way out. In short, the perfect lie. But it's elusive. And besides, I'm tired of lying. "I needed a job."

One eyebrow raises, as if the truth is unexpected. "Badly, hmm?"

"Don't we all?"

"True. So what's real and what isn't?"

I *hate* heart to hearts. "If you're asking if I'm a Christian, I am. If you're asking if I'm deeply committed, we both know the answer to that." Here comes the pink slip, and I'm kind of grateful.

"Yes. However, if you're truly interested in pursuing your faith, I may be of help."

"Excuse me?"

His grim mouth starts to turn up. "Your job is not in jeopardy."

A thrill goes through me, only to spill into indignation. After all, hasn't he been messing with me since that day in the parking lot? Backing me into corners? Playing cat to my mouse?

"If you're willing"—he lowers his arms to curl his hands over the edge of his desk—"I believe I can point you in the right direction."

As if he's even qualified! "What makes you think I need you to point me in the right direction?"

He stills, the only movement about him the lowering of his mouth and a tightening jaw. "Let's see...a little fish fighting the current like a good Christian, a *taped* bumper sticker, a curse word followed by the denial of it being spoken." He tilts his head. "Overall, a feeling that Grace Stewart is lost."

Ooh! "I am not lost. I'm saved, just like you."

His green eyes widen slightly. "I doubt 'just like me.'"

I push to my feet. *Whoa! Pull hard on those reins! Don't—* "You think you're more of a Christian than I am?"

His jaw tightens. "I wouldn't say that. But I will say that I believe I'm more certain of my faith and that the path I'm on is pointing me in the right direction."

Pull, do you hear?! "Whereas the path *I'm* on is not?"

He stares at me. "You, Grace Stewart, need to get your story straight. Or, to put it more bluntly, get your lies under control."

I take a step toward him. "You—"

"Careful." He glances past me. "As I said, nothing happens in here that can't be seen by all."

Wondering if the twinge between my shoulders has anything to do with his co-workers on the other side of the glass, I step back. "Well..." I draw a breath that quivers all the way down. "I'm glad we got that over with. Now, can I have the contact for Sovereign's youth pastor?"

The anger drains from Jack's face and is replaced by what appears to be disappointment. Ha! As if he really cares about my "walk" (flavor-of-the-day Christian speak).

He straightens from his desk. "Then you're not accepting my offer of help?"

"I'm a big girl. I can find God on my own, thank you."

"All right, but if you change your mind—"

"I won't." I hold out my hand. "Name and number, please."

His jaw tenses again, and I believe I see a spark of anger. However, before I can confirm it, he walks around his desk and lowers to his chair. A few keystrokes later, he jots down names and numbers. "So how was your date?"

I frown. "Date?"

"The unfortunate one." His delicious accent wrapped around *unfortunate* momentarily distracts me from my search for a point of reference. "Was it good or bad?"

My date with writing the Mule Day article that I led him to believe was a man. "Good. Very good, in fact."

He nods, then pushes a paper that lists five contacts across his desk. "Different churches, from Nashville to Goodlettsville. I suggest you ring up all of them."

"I'll do that. Thank you."

"I'll see you at church on Sunday."

No surprise that he's holding me to it. I start to turn away only to come back around. "It sounds as if I won't be seeing you between now and then." Can*not* help sounding hopeful.

He leans back. "I'm leaving tomorrow for a conference in Memphis."

Thank You, God! Obviously I'm not as lost as Jack thinks. Were I, surely You wouldn't give me this reprieve. Five days without the insufferable man!

"I'll miss you too, Grace."

His derisive tone makes me intensely aware that my lips are stretched so near to the snapping point that they may be permanently distorted. I drop the smile, pivot, and toss over my shoulder, "Have a nice trip."

"He wants to point you in the right direction?" Tessie's upper lip curls. "How arrogant!"

I consider her as she once more perches on my desk in the Lifestyle department, this time filching Tater Tots. "I was a little offended myself, but in retrospect he seemed sincere and didn't tattle on me."

"It's still early in the game."

"True, but at least he's good for contacts. I did tell you he gave me names and numbers for the research Linda asked me to do?"

"You did." She snags another Tater Tot. "Funny, isn't it?"

I grab the last one. "What?"

"Your boss, who brought up her son 'right' with church, Sunday school, vacation Bible school, and God knows what else, has a drug addict on her hands."

I twinge. Though I wouldn't call it funny, it does make one question the impact of faith, especially on children being dragged along in the wake of their parents' search for meaning.

Tessie points a manicured finger at me. "What do you want to bet she's written and edited articles that tell others how to keep their children drug free?"

"She might have."

"Why don't you look into it?"

"Why?"

"Because…" She glances at her watch. "Oh, we're going to be late for our meeting with Ray."

I gape at her, then jump to my feet. "We're meeting with Ray?"

She slips off my desk. "In two minutes."

Does this mean what I think it does? Wiping my mouth, shirt, and blouse to remove any crumbs, I catch up with Tessie as she exits the Lifestyle department. "Please tell me he's going to put me on full time."

"Maybe. I ran an idea past him that could get you back into full-time investigative reporting."

"Really?"

"It's up to him." She narrows her lids at me. "And you."

I feel so bouncy! "Well, the answer is yes. A hundred times yes!"

She halts before Ray's office and thrusts out a hand. "Then welcome back."

I clasp her hand with both of mine. "I owe you big time."

"First let's see what Ray has to say."

We enter the outer sanctum, where Ray's secretary gestures at the door that leads to the inner sanctum. "Go in." A few moments later, Ray gruffly tells us to park ourselves in the chairs before his desk.

With his faintly green lenses perched atop a large-pored nose and salt-and-pepper hair pulled into a ponytail, Ray regards me with the same calculating expression with which he seems to regard everyone. As always, it's hard not to smile. Though his sense of style differs from the stereotypical news chief, his behavior and mannerisms are right on.

He leans back in his chair. "So, Maizy, you think you're ready to get back on the horse that threw you?"

Horse that threw me? He doesn't look like a cowboy—and isn't, as evidenced by his New England accent. "Yes sir."

"Then you've matured…toughened up?"

"I have, sir."

"And you think you can set aside your personal feelings and get the stories our readers want?"

"I do, sir."

He shoots another glance at Tessie. "Then you're on."

I jerk. "Full time?"

His thin lips curve. "That's right."

Dare I ask? "In-investigative reporting?"

"Investigative reporting."

I should be more dignified, but every muscle in my body goes limp with relief. No more scraping together rent, no more soggy generics, no more excuses to keep the bill collectors at bay, and no more Steeple Side.

Thank You, God. And You know what I'll do to show You how grateful I am for this second chance? I'm going to church this Sunday. Not Sovereign Church, but some nice little church. And maybe I won't scrape off that bumper sticker after all. Might even let the fish stay. But the stinky air freshener has to go. As for the Bible, I'll make more of an effort to read it. Perhaps I'll even pick up one of those One Year Bibles. Not KJV, though. Some other translation that won't give me permanent frown wrinkles.

With a glance at Tessie, who lifts her lashes to meet my gaze, I sit up. "When do I start?"

He chuckles. "First thing tomorrow."

Once he decides to move on something, he really moves. I like that—at least until I'm twinged by what it means to Steeple Side. It's hardly professional, let alone considerate, to leave without notice, especially now that Linda has entrusted me with the research she needs to keep her head above water. "Um…"

Ray raises an eyebrow.

"I don't know if Tess—er, Teresa—told you that I took another part-time job—"

"She told me." Suddenly there's more to his mouth than a curve. I think it's a smile. "Don't worry, Steeple Side will get all the notice they deserve."

Then he'll allow me to give proper notice *and* work full time at the paper? Hard on me, as it will require putting in late hours, but considerate of him. Maybe he's not the hardhearted, bull-nosed boss he portrays.

I smile. "I can't tell you how much I appreciate your working with me." And I can't begin to thank Tessie for going out on a limb. I turn to her, but she's too intent on examining her fingernails to look up.

I return my attention to Ray. "What's the story you're after?"

He slides a folder across the desk. "Steeple Side Christian Resources."

My hand shoots out to retrieve the folder only to freeze. "Steeple Side?" I glance at Tessie, but her fingernails continue to hold her attention. Back to Ray. "This is a joke, right?"

He defers to Tessie with a sweep of the hand. "Teresa?"

She retrieves the folder. "Not a joke, Maizy." The folder lands in my lap. "You wanted to redeem yourself. Here's your chance."

The folder tab is labeled "SSCR: An Inside Investigation."

"What's it really like working for a Christian company?" Tessie says. "Do those who are telling the rest of us how to live practice what they preach? What skeletons lurk in Steeple Side's closets? That's the story the *Middle Tennessee Review* wants, and who better to expose the hypocrisy than someone on the inside?"

I feel sick, though I shouldn't. After all, I said that I'm capable of setting aside personal feelings…that I've matured…toughened up. And yet I'm balking at investigating my current employer. But this is different. While I've been at Steeple Side for only a week, I *know* those people—at least some of them. And I like them, Jack Prentiss excepted. Now Ray and Tessie want me to spy on them…

"You know"—Tessie lays a hand on my arm—"if you're not ready for this, we can give it to someone else."

Meaning Steeple Side will be investigated regardless of my involvement? "Who?" Hopefully not Lance, whose motto is Take No Prisoners.

Tessie looks at Ray. "Lance would be a good choice, don't you think?"

He inclines his head. "Or Arlene. She's anxious to move up the ladder."

Panic sets in at the realization that the job is being pulled out from under me. No, I'm not so naive that I don't realize I'm being manipulated, or that the idea of this investigation came out of Jack's thwarting of Tessie's investigation, but it's true that another writer could get the scoop. Not as easily as someone who is already on the inside, but I'm hardly irreplaceable—certainly not at this point in my pathetic little career. A career that's going nowhere unless I grab the opportunity to prove I have what it takes.

"No." Tessie shakes her head. "I think Lance is the better pick. If we can get him on the inside—"

"I'll get you the story."

I hate the glint in Ray's eyes. Isn't there something in the Bible about plucking out an eye if it offends you?

His smile ripens. "You do that, Maizy, and your future is assured."

Redemption. If only it didn't feel so foul…

Gripping the folder, I stand. "I won't let you down."

"Better not, or it's the Dumpster for you." He chuckles, as if I should find the threat funny. "My secretary will let Payroll know about your new full-time status and increase in salary." He reaches for the phone. "Now get out of here."

I exit ahead of Tessie, but the moment we're in the corridor outside the outer sanctum, I turn on her. "Why didn't you tell me?"

She regards me with studied patience. "I knew if you had too much time to consider what you were being asked to do, the soft-hearted Maizy who blew her chance in Seattle would blow her chance in Nashville." She crosses her arms over her chest. "You asked me to help, but if you don't have the stomach for investigative reporting, you might as well resign your career to Mule Day reporting."

Her face is drawn up in hard lines, but there's hurt in her eyes over what she perceives to be ingratitude.

Caught between begging her forgiveness and recoiling, I stare at my white-knuckled hand on the folder.

Tessie touches my shoulder. "I won't pretend that what I've done isn't self-serving. You know that, I know that, and Ray knows that. But I also care about you."

My throat tightens, while my hand on the folder eases sufficiently to allow color to return to my knuckles.

Tessie steps nearer. "You're my friend, and I don't want to see you writing dreary articles about mules when you possess the talent for so much more."

I do, don't I? Even if writing those "dreary" articles is never as bad as anticipated. Eyes moist, nose tingling, I meet her gaze.

She smiles tightly. "Think about your future, because there isn't a single *Christian* at Steeple Side who cares about it as much as I do."

She does care. She's the only one who stuck her neck out for me following the Seattle disaster. "I know, but—"

She drops her hand from me. "What good did it do you to care about that politician, huh?"

State senator Leona Nettles. I don't want to go there, as I've expended far too much emotion and energy on reliving the eight weeks I worked undercover in her campaign headquarters. But Tessie's words place me firmly back in that setting.

Armed with the anonymous tip that led to my first assignment as an investigative reporter and a tweaked name—Mary Stewart—I had been thrilled to turn my skills from spotlighting events about town to exposing those who shamelessly take advantage of others. Slowly, the evidence of illegal campaign contributions mounted, as did suspicions that the phone conversations of Leona's opponent were being taped. Close but no cigar, so I got closer. And was undone when Leona took a personal interest in me.

On the surface, it was ideal to serve as her assistant, but doubts about her culpability arose from beneath. She was kind, considerate, and full of praise and motherly advice. But what made me take two big steps back from the evidence against her was the vulnerability she let slip when a story broke that her husband had cheated on her years earlier. Not that she was unaware of the affair, but the public airing of it reduced her to a hiccupping mass of sobs. I offered a shoulder, not expecting her to accept, but she did and I hurt with her. Though it was another week before my world fell apart, that was the point of no return.

"You got scooped, Maizy," a voice pulls me forward in time, but as I focus on Tessie, her words pull me back.

Ben. My television reporter boyfriend had been on me for weeks, probing and pushing and warning that I was getting too close to Leona when I expressed doubts about her guilt and frustration toward my boss, who was pressuring me to deliver the story. Then one night Ben lost it—got in my face and said that if I didn't expose Leona, someone else would and I could kiss my career good-bye. I told him I would rather that than ruin an innocent woman's life. The next day he scooped me with the aid of my investigative notes and pictures.

"You were fired, Maizy."

Tessie again, and I go back once more—this time to the long walk past my co-workers at the *Seattle Sound,* their eyes and whispers following me as I answered the summons to my boss's office. I knew what was waiting for me, having turned on the television that morning to find Ben's face staring out at me from headlines that heralded the end of Leona's political career. My boss left the door open for all to hear what a pathetic excuse of a reporter I was and that I wouldn't work in Seattle again—or anywhere if he had any say in it. Then the never-ending walk past my *ex*-co-workers…

"And you didn't get so much as a thank-you for being gullible enough to give that woman a running start at getting away with the goods." Tessie drops in the last piece of my shame.

Leona was guilty—of everything—and somehow made it out of the country.

And here I am, gullible again, and all because I've grown attached to my co-workers at Steeple Side. Co-workers who would surely turn their backs on me if they knew the true depth of my faith.

"Do you hear what I'm saying?"

I nod Tessie into focus. "I hear."

"And you're going to take this opportunity?"

"I am, but…" Dare I say it? "What if there isn't a story? Nothing newsworthy?"

Her teeth snap. "Then you won't have done your job."

And that pink slip that has yet to land on your desk at Steeple Side? It won't have any qualms setting up camp on your newsroom desk.

"Repeat after me, Maizy: there's *always* a story."

I clear my tight throat. "There's always a story."

"Good. Now go get it." She strides past me, then looks over her shoulder. "And don't forget that, between the two jobs, you're going to be paid very well to tell that story." Her mouth turns up. "If that's not incentive enough, I don't know what is."

Paid by the *Middle Tennessee Review* to investigate Steeple Side. Paid by Steeple Side to be investigated. How I wish I hadn't eaten those greasy Tater Tots.

Tessie walks away, and when she disappears around the corner, I suppress the longing to sink against the wall.

I am not gullible.

I press my shoulders back.

I am not weak.

I lift my chin.

I am not sentimental.

I put one foot in front of the other.

I can do this.

I don't *know* those people at Steeple Side. They're just acquaintances. And if Steeple Side isn't all it seeks to portray, then people have a right to know. Yes. They most certainly do.

SEVEN

Steeple Side Lies

#1. No real work experience (Mrs. Lucas)

#2. Currently not working anywhere else (Mrs. Lucas)

#3. Interested in full-time work at Steeple Side (Mrs. Lucas)

#4. Didn't say the *D* word (Jack Prentiss)

#5. Attend Sovereign Church and like the congregation (2 lies in 1—Jack and Linda)

#6. Do freelance editing (Jem)

I had to do it, even though the lies seem worse in print. Unfortunately, because of my pursuit of the truth behind Steeple Side, there are bound to be more lies, and the more there are, the more likely one will turn on me. Hence, the need to track them.

Snapping the small notebook closed, I sigh at the irony. In pursuit of the *truth*, it's necessary to *lie*. Makes me feel a bit like James Bond, but rather than holding a license to kill, I hold a license to fib. Of course, those first five lies were before the license… As for the sixth lie, that was necessary on Friday when Jem asked what I do when I leave Steeple Side at one o'clock. I'd nearly shrugged off her question with, "Oh, this and that," but it occurred to me that she might have designs on my "leisure" time. Leisure time spent at my desk at the paper. Thus, I told her I do freelance editing.

And it isn't a very big lie, as I am editing other Lifestyle writers since Ray decided to keep me in that department for the duration of the Steeple Side investigation. Having expected to be given a new desk among different co-workers, I was a bit put out, but the message was there for the reading: botch the Steeple Side story and this is the best you can expect. But I *will* get this story, even if it means entering the immense church across the parking lot.

Hoping Jack's return to Nashville is delayed, I toss my notebook on the passenger seat, grab my purse and Bible, and step out into a cloudless spring day looking to all the world like I fit in—thanks to the *DBGC:*

Dressing the Part

So, it's your first time at church, and the all-consuming question is, what to wear? Yes, shallow, but when you're learning to swim, you're less likely to drown if you start out at the three-foot end of the pool. Here are your options for determining what is suitable attire:

a) The Sunday before, slip into the parking lot and observe the clothes worn by women your age (use binoculars if necessary, but be discreet).

b) Check out the church's Web site, where

pictures of members are often posted. (This also serves as a gauge of the age range and, if you're single, a peek at the possibilities.)

c) Dress in layers and remove articles of clothing as necessary. (This does add pounds to your figure, so you may want to rethink.)

d) Bring a variety of outfits into which you can change in the backseat of your car (park away from others to avoid an embarrassing situation).

I opted for *b,* and sure enough, there were plenty of pictures showing the congregation at worship, in Sunday school, and at church functions. As for a peek at the possibilities, they were there, as evidenced by the ringless left hands of several good-looking men. The really good news was that Jack was absent from the pictures, so it's possible Sovereign Church is as much a front for him as it is for me and maybe I won't run into him.

I tug the waist of my collared white blouse with its flared cuffs, smooth my black slacks, and wiggle my toes inside two-inch closed-toe shoes. I should fit right in.

The sun warms the back of my neck, and I cross the parking lot to join the stragglers who, like me, will walk into the service a few minutes late.

"By yourself?" asks the elderly man who greets me outside the sanctuary.

"Yes." I accept the bulletin he hands me. "Is there still room? If not, I can sit in the balcony."

"For a single—certainly. I'll show you to your seat."

How sweet. And gentlemanly.

Unfortunately, when we enter the sanctuary, it becomes obvious there are few seats in the back that don't require clambering over those who are on their feet singing the words projected on a screen at the front of the sanctuary.

I touch the man's arm. "I don't see any seats down here. Maybe the balcony would be better."

He shakes his head, causing the loose, weathered skin of his neck to swing alarmingly. "There are plenty of single seats near the front, miss."

The front? "Oh, I don't want to trouble you—"

"No trouble." He keeps going, straight down the aisle, and grudgingly I allow him to escort me to a seat two rows from the front. Not good.

He pats my shoulder. "May you be blessed by the service."

"Thank you." As he turns away, I glance to my right where a family of—

Oh my. Surely those five kids, ranging from toddler to teen, don't all belong to that smiling couple? No. You don't have that many kids and look that perky. They must be keeping someone else's brood.

As if feeling my eyes on her, the woman looks around and smiles. Her husband peers past her and does the same, as does the four-year-old girl on his hip.

I smile back, then find my place in an unfamiliar song of praise. For the next fifteen minutes, the rhythm of that one amazing summer of belief and my sporadic attendance at my grandmother's church comes back to me—the ups and downs (as in "Please stand," "Please sit," "Please stand"), the greeting of one another, whereby I learn that the group beside me is the Rooter family and not only are the five children theirs but they have six-month-old twins in the nursery.

Finally the pastor steps to the podium and I settle into my seat. So here I am at Sovereign, turning Lie Number Five into the truth…

Hmm. Might I remove that one from the list? Surely future attendance counts for something. As for the second part of the lie about liking the congregation, the Rooters seem nice enough. Overpopulated, but nice.

During the next half hour, the pastor expounds on the book of Habakkuk, which, though unfamiliar, tempts my tongue to curl around the name. Surprisingly I find myself caught up in the sermon about a prophet who is bewildered by God's seeming inattentiveness to His people and, later, his realization that God works everything—including the bad—into something good.

Meaning He'll turn my Steeple Side deception into something good? No sooner does the thought occur than I sweep it back to its dark corner.

At the end of the service, I pop up, raise a hand to the Rooters, who turn their shining faces to me, and join the throng exiting the sanctuary. The lobby is packed with those waiting to enter for the second service, so it's with slow, halting steps that I make my way to the doors.

A hand curls around my arm—a hand I'd know anywhere, even though I've only felt it once in a brief handshake. Of course, the citrus-y scent attached to it probably has something to do with the familiarity.

"Leaving so soon?"

I turn and look into Jack's green eyes. "Hello, Jack."

"Grace."

I glance at his hand on me. "Did you enjoy the sermon?"

Releasing me, he inclines his head. "And you?"

"Oh, yes. Habakkuk"—did I say that right?—"is a fascinating book."

"Then the Rooter children didn't distract you."

He knows I sat with the Rooters… Meaning he was watching me?

"I was in the balcony. That's how I saw you."

A bird's-eye view. I push my sleeve back to consult my watch. "Well, I should—"

"Can we talk?" He nods at the doors that lead outside. "Where it isn't crowded."

Do I have a choice? "Okay."

I follow him outside, and he halts at the corner of the building and out of the flow of churchgoers heading for their cars. "I'd like to apologize."

Suspicion leaps through me. "For?"

"Offering to assist in your pursuit of faith."

What game is he playing? "Really?"

"I thought you could use some help." He shrugs. "Presumptuous of me. And arrogant."

I search his eyes for a glint, his mouth for a twitch, but either he's good at disguising his feelings or he's sincere. Caught between wanting him to remain the arrogant, bumper-sticker-happy Brit and liking what appears to be a new and improved Jack Prentiss, I shift my weight. "I appreciate that."

"And there's the matter of how I've behaved since we met. We both know you're forcing your faith, but it was wrong of me to bait you." He turns his palms up. "I have no defense, but judging others is a failing to which I sometimes succumb." He offers a hand. "Truce?"

While he seems genuine, I know how gullible I can be. I look to his hand, the back of which is lightly tanned, the fine hairs on which are golden, the thought of which makes my pulse leap.

Just shake it! I clasp his hand. "Truce."

"Brilliant." He releases me. "Which Sunday school class do you plan to attend?"

I avert my gaze. I wasn't planning on attending one. "Probably the singles' class." Probably, so not Lie Number Seven.

"Then I recommend Avery's." With a broadening of his shoulders beneath his navy jacket, he walks forward. "He's good."

I fall into step with him. "Do you attend a singles' class?"

He nods, causing a dark blond lock of hair to brush his brow. "I am, after all, *disengaged.*" That last said with a grin.

Meaning he's aware of the gossip about Bette. "Yes, but from what I understand, tomorrow you could be re-en…gaged." That last said on a breath of disgust. *Why didn't you think that through?*

Jack looks sidelong at me. "Might you be interested in my personal life?"

I falter and have to quicken my pace to draw even with him again. "Of course not. You're an object of gossip, that's all."

His eyebrows rise. "You are aware that Steeple Side frowns on gossip?"

More black marks against me. "And you are aware that it's human nature to talk about others?"

"Even so, that doesn't mean we shouldn't try to rise above it."

Aha! "Just as we should try to rise above judging others."

As we halt to allow a family of four to pass on their way into church, Jack turns to me and smiles broadly, and for some reason those slightly crooked teeth enhance, rather than detract from, his mouth. "You're right." He resumes his stride, which I match. "As for becoming reengaged, I'll let you in on a secret."

Me? Maizy Stewart pretending to be Grace Stewart pretending to be a deeply committed Christian? I tilt my head. "What?"

"It's not going to happen, Bette and me."

Is the cat really confiding in the mouse? I snap my teeth shut to keep from asking what I shouldn't, but that doesn't stop my tongue. "What's so different about this latest disengagement?"

Two more strides and he turns to me. "This time *I* broke it off."

As opposed to the rumor that Bette's the one who keeps disengaging. "Why?"

He considers me, as if weighing the wisdom of allowing further insight into his personal life. "A couple of months ago, I finally conceded that Bette and I were little more than a habit. We talked and she agreed." He inclines his head. "And now I have told far more than I should to someone I hardly know beyond a crooked fish and a taped bumper sticker."

Though he says it lightly, I wince. And all because of the guilt that spreads through me like a weed. The fish and bumper sticker were originally a means to secure a job, but their continued presence represents a means to expose Steeple Side and further my career. And what of those whose lives are laid open?

Stop it! You have what it takes to write life-changing stories, and if you don't, you'll get it. Must get it or you can kiss your career good-bye. And don't think that a soul at Steeple Side cares what happens to you. Remember all those "friends" you had at the Seattle paper? How many sympathized with you? In the end, it was Tessie who pulled you out of the muck, and you are not going to fail her.

A hand touches my shoulder, the warmth causing me to jerk my chin up.

"I'm teasing." Jack's eyes delve into mine. "Truce. Remember?"

"Yeah. Truce."

He drops his hand, and I almost go limp at the realization that I can put Sovereign Church behind me and head home to Woofer.

"So this is it." Jack juts his chin at a door over his shoulder. A door to a building separate from the church.

How did I get here? One moment we were right outside the church, and now the church is…

I look back at the immense structure behind us. Guessing I must have followed Jack and wondering where I laid my brain between there and here, I ask, "This is what?"

"Avery's singles' class."

Did I tell him I planned on attending Sunday school? No. I said "probably," which doesn't mean "yes."

"I'll introduce you around." Before I can wiggle out an excuse that will return me to Woofer's orbit, Jack opens the door and gestures for me to precede him.

My hesitation earns me raised eyebrows, and I step forward. Ten minutes later, following introductions to at least two dozen singles who welcome me with varying degrees of enthusiasm—from ardent (mostly males) to guarded (those who view me as competition)—Jack leads me to Avery, a sparkly eyed, goateed thirtyish guy.

He clasps my hand. "First-time visitor?"

"Uh…just to your class." *Not* a new lie, as it's covered under Lie Number Five, when I told Jack that I attend Sovereign Church.

He releases my hand. "We're glad you're here." He looks to Jack, and a moment later the two are engaged in guy talk that provides me the opportunity to slink to the back of the class. To my dismay, and the dismay of several women who frown at me, Jack settles into the chair beside mine a few minutes later.

"You're staying?"

He looks to his left hand. "I *am* single."

And not soon to be reengaged, if he's to be believed.

As Avery calls the class to order, I lean toward Jack. "Does Bette attend Sovereign?"

"Occasionally. She shies away from organized religion."

That surprises me. Considering his position at Steeple Side and the face his employer surely expects him to present, I would have thought that his future wife would be an unswerving churchgoer.

"Today I want us to look at desire," Avery says, to which I startle and several college-age guys snicker.

Avery chuckles. "Not carnal desire, but desire for the things dear to God's heart—the exaltation of His name and enlarging His kingdom."

Amid a murmur of good-natured disappointment, Jack bends toward me and rasps, "He had you worried for a moment?"

There's that citrus-y scent again, and it makes my mouth go moist. Ignoring him, I unzip the tapestry cover and open my KJV Bible. Unfortunately, the spine is so stiff that the cover closes on me twice before I resort to force to bend it back.

"New?"

I lean toward him. "Are you judging me again?"

To my surprise, he seems repentant—until he grins. "Just wondering aloud."

"Are you with us, Jack?"

I look to the front of the class and catch the teasing smirk Avery directs at Jack. Great. Caught in the middle of their guy ribbing.

"With you, Avery."

"Then why don't you read Matthew 6:9–10."

Jack opens his Bible and quickly locates the passage—without the benefit of index tabs like those I meant to purchase for my Bible. Fortunately, more than half of my battle to find the book of Matthew is won by elimination when I notice that Jack bypassed the first three quarters or so.

"This, then," he reads, "is how you should pray: 'Our Father in heaven, hallowed be your name, your kingdom come, your will be done on earth as it is in heaven.'"

A thrill goes through me at the familiarity of the words. They're part of the Lord's Prayer, which Grandma Grace has posted in every room of her home.

"Thank you, Jack." Avery glances around the room. "So let's talk about God's will and its fit with our fleshly desires."

"I see you found Matthew all right." Jack leans toward me again to ensure that his words don't travel.

I bristle even though his baiting seems more of the teasing than entrapment variety. "Of course I did."

"Then you know your Bible pretty well."

That was a statement, right? Meaning it's not a question I have to answer. Meaning I'm free of the temptation to claim a thorough knowledge of the Bible. Meaning no Lie Number Seven.

"Jack!"

Caught. Again.

"Do I have to separate you two?" Avery grins.

The men chuckle, as do a few of the women, but it's the muttered comment from a red-headed guy that swamps my cheeks with warmth. "Guess Jack has moved on."

Moved on. To me? While the curve of Jack's lips doesn't falter, he has definitely stiffened.

Over the next half hour, a lively discussion follows of how, by spending time with God and seeking to understand His heart, Christians learn to delight in the things that please Him—to desire those things for themselves.

Will I ever be able to do that? Put God and His desires first? It sounds hard.

"So," Avery says, "when you pray, pray for God to be exalted and His kingdom increased. Then pray for your own desires to fall in line with His."

Very hard.

"In closing, let's turn to Psalm 37:4–6."

Out of the corner of my eye, I see Jack turn to the center of his Bible. Doing the same, I land on Psalm 36, with Psalm 37 a mere flip away.

"Who'd like to read?"

I don't know what comes over me, though it probably has something to do with proving to Jack that I'm not completely ignorant of the Bible, but my hand shoots up.

Avery smiles. "All right, Grace."

Feeling Jack's eyes on me, I dip my chin, causing my hair to curtain my face. "'Delight thyself also in the LORD, and he shall give thee the desires of thine heart. Commit thy way unto the LORD; trust also in him; and he shall bring it to pass. And he shall bring forth thy righteousness as the light, and thy judgment as the noonday.'"

"Thank you, Grace. So how does that passage speak to you?"

Avery's gaze continues to hold mine, meaning...? Meaning he's asking *me* how I was affected by the words? But I did all the reading, and everyone knows it's hard to comprehend what you're reading when you do it aloud.

As expectant eyes fall on me, I return my attention to the passage and quickly reread it. But now I'm all nerves, and the words refuse to attach meaning to themselves, especially cluttered as they are with thees and thys. I swallow. "Uh..."

A young brunette raises her hand. "I can tell you what it means to me."

Please do!

Avery nods, and she launches into her interpretation of how, as our relationship with God deepens, we set aside our selfishness and make His priorities our own.

As the others hang on her words, I scan the passage and mutter, "So many thees and thous."

"Perhaps another translation would help."

Should have smelled that coming—the citrus-y scent, that is. "Don't talk to me, Jack. You'll get us in trouble again."

Five minutes later, those of us eager to get on with our Sunday head for the door. Unfortunately, my nemesis is at my side as I join the line.

"Jack, I didn't get the chance to talk to you earlier." A young woman lays a hand on his arm—the same one who saved me from the embarrassment of trying to interpret Scripture.

"Dinah." Jack smiles down at the petite woman. "Have you met Grace Stewart? She recently started at Steeple Side in Women's Publications."

"We haven't met." She lifts her hand from his arm and reaches to me. "Dinah McDonald." We shake. "I work in Payroll."

I almost startle at the realization that Jem had pointed her out the other day when the woman exited the elevator as we approached. As I barely caught a glimpse of her before she turned away, I can be forgiven for not recognizing her. However, I do remember her name and reputation as a shameless flirt who, Jem says, has caused tiffs between her and her co-workers. Thus, I added another page to the notebook I've started keeping—Christian women who flirt, much to the annoyance and jealousy of other Christian women.

"It's nice to meet you, Dinah." I release her hand.

"And you."

As we inch toward the door, an awkward silence falls, during which Dinah looks between Jack and me with curiosity in her eyes.

"Well…," She flashes Jack a smile, then waves her ringless left hand. "Just wanted to say hi."

Jack and I emerge into sunshine, and I wince at the sight of those streaming out of the church following the second service. Wishing Avery hadn't taken so many prayer requests at the end, I quicken my pace.

"I'm guessing you won't be back," Jack says as I veer toward my car ahead of the wave of churchgoers.

He guessed right. I glance across my shoulder. "Why do you say that?"

"You couldn't wait to leave."

And I thought I was being discreet checking my watch every few minutes. But I am not going to lie again. "It was a little uncomfortable."

"New things often are."

I'm tempted to deny that Sunday school is a new thing for me, but I zip my lip. "Well, my car's over there." I jut my chin toward the far end of the parking lot.

"I'll walk you."

I am struck by the way the sunlight glints off his hair. Though it's usually on the dark end of the blond spectrum, out here it looks almost golden. "I don't want to put you out."

"You won't. I parked two spaces down from you, which is how I knew to look for you."

Why didn't I park a block away? "Then you arrived later than me."

"Always running late. A shortcoming I've already confessed to."

I remember—the cafeteria…saying he was late as usual…looking me in the eye…giving back the "I'm always fighting the current like a good Christian" excuse I gave when I refused his offer to straighten my fish emblem.

I don't say anything further on the matter, and neither does he. At least until we reach my car.

"No more bumper sticker problems?" He eyes the one in question.

I cease trying to dig my keys out of my purse. "No more problems. It's...not going anywhere." Not without a razor blade and some elbow grease.

"The good thing is, neither is Jesus. You know that, don't you?"

Though "of course!" is on my tongue, my heart skips a beat. It should be a comfort to know that Jesus isn't going anywhere, but considering my situation, it's far from comforting. *Will* He stick with me even though I've been assigned to root out the hypocrisy in a company that seeks to educate others about Him? I'd like to think so, as surely He doesn't want someone doing things in His name if they aren't sincere, but...

"I spoke with Linda."

I'm so relieved that Jack's given up on awaiting my response that I'm only vaguely aware of the growing number of cars filing past. "You did?"

He slides his hands into his pockets. "She said your research was thorough and well organized, and if she didn't know better, she'd say you had practical experience."

Did he hear that gulp? I declare, it felt as if my Adam's apple *were* the size of an apple. I resume my hunt for the keys. "I've always been good at research and, of course, had plenty of practice while pursuing my degree." Not another lie—ha!

"Linda thinks you could go far at Steeple Side."

I whip out my keys. "I appreciate you passing that along. I really enjoyed—"

A piece of paper flutters to the ground between us, but before I can catch sight of what came out of my purse with the keys, Jack retrieves it.

"Your paycheck." He hands it to me.

"Oh. Thank you." A nervous tremble goes through me as I pinch my first paycheck from Steeple Side and return it to my purse. Hardly where it belongs, but unlike the masses who flocked to their banks this past Friday to deposit life-sustaining funds, I hesitated. Not that I had any qualms about depositing the *Middle Tennessee Review*'s paycheck. But the one from Steeple Side… Considering that the paper is now paying me to work at Steeple Side and the assignment I've been given, it gave me pause. But I will deposit it. And I will remove that silly bumper sticker.

"Didn't make it to the bank on Friday?"

"You know how Fridays are. So, as I was saying, I really enjoyed the research Linda assigned me. It was interesting and eye opening."

It takes him a moment to switch gears. "Found out that the problem of teenage drugs and alcohol isn't limited to those outside the faith, did you?"

As further evidenced by Linda's son. I suddenly feel morose, just as I felt while compiling the statistics and opinions of the church leaders who were generous with their time. "I knew it wasn't. I'm not that naive." Well, not always. "It's just sad."

"Sad that Christianity isn't an impenetrable shield? that even after we've accepted Jesus as our Savior, we keep messing up? doing things we know we shouldn't? things He has to wash away again and again?"

How depressing…

Jack laughs, and only then do I realize the gloomy state of my face. "Sorry, Grace. I didn't mean to ruin your day. And what I said shouldn't ruin it, because there's joy in knowing He loves each of us so much that He never stops washing no matter how big or dirty the piles of laundry."

I'm swept with gratitude for words that evoke an image of Jesus amid mile-high piles of laundry, using an old-fashioned washboard to clean every single garment. Then comes confusion. "I don't get it. Why are you being so nice to me?"

Remorse shadows his face. "My grandmother told me to play nice."

"Your grandmother?"

"Yes, she—"

A car honks as it passes, and Jack waves before returning his attention to me. "I visited with her while in Memphis, and somehow you came up in the conversation."

Somehow—how?

"If I weren't so much bigger than she, I think she would have dragged me to the loo and washed out my mouth with soap."

I laugh, and though there isn't anything special about the sound (except that it doesn't end on a purr, thank goodness), Jack lowers his gaze to my mouth. "I'm glad you came today, Grace."

Strangely, so am I. More strange, I feel "convicted"—an over-whelming urge to right a wrong, according to my all-knowing *DBGC.* When I first read the explanation, I wondered at the word *convicted,* as I've only ever thought of it in terms of crime and impris-onment, but maybe there's something more to it. Perhaps if I admit to the wrongs of this "convict," who now has to keep track of her lies, I'll work off some of my sentence and free myself of guilt.

Giving it no more thought, I say in a rush, "This is my first time at Sovereign."

Jack doesn't look surprised. "Yes."

"And that day when my coffee spilled, I did say, you know, the *D* word."

"Yes."

Just 'yes'? Well, I feel better. Sort of. There are still those other four lies, but I'm no saint. Actually, according to the *DBGC,* followers of Jesus *are* saints. But the author must be mistaken, and when I get the time I'm going to look up the scriptures referenced.

Another car honks, and Jack waves again. This car, however, stands out, as it appears to be in no hurry to sweep past us. Because it can't.

I groan at the line of cars attempting to exit the parking lot. "I knew I should have gotten out of here pronto."

"Give it ten minutes and most of the traffic will be resolved."

Startled at the realization I spoke aloud, I look to Jack.

He smiles. "Would you like to have lunch with me?"

"Uh…" I want to. I really do. And if not for fear of once more being convicted, I would. But confessing two lies is enough for one day. "I can't."

"Then I'll see you at work on Monday."

"Yeah." I press the Unlock button on my keychain. "Have a nice day."

In three strides, he's at his car—the sporty silver sedan with the rounded fenders that I'd noticed in the parking space I stole from him that first day.

I nearly jump when, across the roof of the car between us, he looks at me. "You might try *The Message.*"

"What?"

"A different version of the Bible, without the thees and thous."

I do remember seeing it in the store the day I picked up my KJV but from the title concluded it was shelved in the wrong section. "Maybe I will give it a try." As I step to my door, I'm struck by something. "Hey!"

Jack straightens. "Changed your mind about lunch?"

"No, just wondering if you're trying to assist in the pursuit of my faith again."

His mouth quirks. "Do me a favor. Don't tell my grandmother."

With a smile, I slide into my car. Only when I turn the ignition do I realize that I've engaged in banter with Jack. If I'm not careful, I may get to like him, which could prove detrimental to my investigation.

Must remain neutral, get the story, and get out.

I draw a deep breath only to grimace. More important—at least for the time being—*must* get rid of that crown of thorns air freshener! I glance left, right, and behind, then snap the string of the cutout that dangles from my rearview mirror and stuff my least favorite piece of Jesus junk in a discarded fast-food bag. As for the others, I'll worry about them later.

Steeple Side Lies

#1. No real work experience (Mrs. Lucas)

#2. Currently not working anywhere else (Mrs. Lucas)

#3. Interested in full-time work at Steeple Side (Mrs. Lucas)

#4. Didn't say the *D* word (Jack Prentiss)

#5. Attend Sovereign Church and like the congregation (2 lies in 1—Jack and Linda)

#6. Do freelance editing (Jem)

Two lies made right, four to go.

My smile falters. Four to go. Not anytime soon though, especially those first two. If I am to keep from blowing my cover, they'll have to wait until the end of my investigation. Of course, then I won't need to tell anyone they were lies.

"Whatcha doin'?"

I nearly come up off my chair. *Please don't allow Jem to have seen my list,* I pray as I snap my notebook closed. But it's merely a knee-jerk prayer, as I'm hourly besieged by doubts that God has anything to do with this.

"Sorry, Grace. I didn't mean to scare you."

I shove the notebook in my purse and wonder at my disregard for discretion. Until today, the only time I've pulled out the notebook at Steeple Side is while in a bathroom stall. Only a genuine dumb blonde would do what I just did—go for a piece of gum and end up happily black lining lies as if none of my co-workers could return from lunch at any moment. I have *got* to get out of blond!

Jem comes around my desk. "What's the big secret?"

Once again I wonder if I may no longer be cut out for investigative reporting. Though the sly and secretive part was always a challenge, I was on my way to having it down when I got "tight" with Leona. Leona who is still somewhere out there enjoying her ill-gotten gain.

"Boo!"

I yelp at the thrust of Jem's face near mine.

She pulls back. "What's up? You seem out of it."

I drop my purse to the floor. "I didn't get enough sleep last night." Which is true. And it's all the fault of *The Message,* which I picked up at Borders after leaving Sovereign yesterday. As Jack said, it's the Bible without the thees and thous. Not that I understand half of the big chunk of Genesis I read, but it kept me turning pages.

Jem leans back against the edge of my desk. "Let me guess… You had a hot date."

I blink. "No." Of course, if I'd taken Jack up on his lunch offer… *Absolutely not!* "I was up late reading."

"A romance?" She gives a little bounce. "I love romances."

Jem *would* admit to that. "No. So what are you doing here?" We did, after all, have lunch together not long ago.

"At lunch you said you were tired of being blond and that as soon as you save enough money you'll go back to brunette."

Which, hopefully, won't be much longer now that I'm full time at the paper. I push a lock of blond hair behind an ear. "I'm counting the days."

She beams. "Well, count no more. I'll do it for you."

"What?"

"I know I didn't finish beauty school"—she had mentioned that—"but I know enough about hair coloring to get you back to brunette and then some. You know, nice highlights. All it will cost you is a few boxes of color."

Hmm. *This is Jem who's offering.* It will hardly cost me a thing. *Jem who admits to being easily distracted.* This time tomorrow, I could be blond-free. *She doesn't do her own hair.* The first step in putting my dumb blonde days behind me. *Do you really want to trust your hair to her?*

"So what do you say, Grace?"

"Uh…"

"Tonight?"

"Okay."

She pushes off my desk, grabs one of my Steeple Side business cards, and jots her address on the back. "Five thirty."

I nod. "See you then."

That niggling starts up as I watch her flounce away, but I'm being silly. After all, it's not as if we're going from brunette to blond—a radical change I managed all by myself. How hard can it be to go from blond to brunette? "Jem?"

"Yep?"

"How about I bring pizza?"

A stricken look crosses her face. "I don't eat dinner until real late."

And when she does, does she eat anything other than those peanut-butter crackers she crumbles her way through when we meet for lunch?

The smile that suddenly brightens her face seems forced. "But if you want to bring a personal pizza for yourself, go for it."

"Maybe I'll do that."

Then she's gone, and I'm tempted to pull out my notebook to jot down my ever-increasing suspicion that she has an eating disorder.

"I don't know what went wrong." Jem wrings her hands. "Guess we should have done a strand test."

Mirror, mirror, on the wall, who's the darkest of them all? Ten minutes ago my stomach was carrying on with hunger; now it's eerily silent as I stare into the hand mirror.

Why didn't I go to a salon and fork over a credit card? By the time the bill arrived, I could've afforded it. But I had to be cheap, and all because I put Tony the Tiger and gourmet dog food ahead of my looks.

"Sorry."

I drag my gaze from my Elvira-Mistress-of-the-Dark reflection to Jem's worried face. "What do you think went wrong?"

She tugs a tress (if those damp, black-as-tar strands can be called that). "Your colorings must have been too closely spaced, hair too porous." She sighs. "I don't know why I didn't think of that."

I thought of it, but figuring she knew better, I went into her kitchen chair like a…dumb blonde. Visions of what it'll cost me to correct my hair disaster dancing in my head, I draw a breath. "Jem, how much beauty schooling did you have?"

She looks down. "A few months."

Calm. "Just a few months, and then you…quit?"

"Actually…" She's back to wringing her hands and I'm tempted to wring her—

No. Mustn't entertain such visions, no matter how sinister I appear with this mess of black surrounding my face and mascara smeared from the overspray of rinsing out the color in the kitchen sink. "Are you saying you didn't quit?"

"Sort of."

"You were kicked out?"

She glances at me, only to look away. "That about sums it up."

Calm. It was an accident. Which could have been prevented! As evenly as possible, I say, "I wish you had said something."

"I thought I could do it." She drags a deep breath, causing her narrow shoulders to broaden slightly. "It seemed so easy, and last year I did it for a friend who went from ash blond to chocolate brown"—*ash* blond, not Marilyn Monroe blond—"without any problem. She looked great. Very natural. Not…"

Scary?

"Of course, maybe once we add highlights—"

"No highlights! We're already in over our heads."

She bites her bottom lip. "You're probably right."

Calm. "Let's just figure out how to fix it."

"Right." She slaps her thigh. "First, a shower. Lots of hot water to tone it down. And the sooner the better."

"Are you sure?"

"Hot water is notorious for fading colored hair, and the spray will help versus simply sticking your head under the spout."

I follow her into the bathroom, where she sweeps the shower curtain aside and turns on the taps. "While you're in there, I'll call the number on the box and see what they suggest."

Maybe *I* should call. However, the clock is ticking. Five minutes later, standing beneath borderline scalding spray, I monitor the water that swooshes down the drain. A little gray, I think. "Please be gray," I whisper. "Please be gray…gray…"

It seems I'm in the shower a long time before Jem taps on the door. Flushed, I inch back the curtain. "What did you find out?"

Despite the steam obscuring her features, I catch her smile. "Though the hot water should tone down the black, the solution I'm mixing will help more."

"Solution?"

"Yeah. Shampoo, peroxide, and water."

"That's what the hair company suggested?"

"Actually, their toll-free hot line is closed for the evening."

If I had a weaker constitution, the combination of heat and bad news would make me swoon. "So where did you come up with this solution?"

"My stylist. She said this kind of thing happens all the time, and women ought to leave something as important as hair color to a specialist."

I clench my teeth.

"She said there's usually a forty-eight- to seventy-two-hour window before the color locks in, and until she can get you in tomorrow afternoon, the solution is the best way to go."

This is going to cost me. "What do I need to do?"

"Get dressed and meet me in the kitchen."

A half hour later, with the solution applied and my hair wrapped in plastic, Jem is aiming two hair-dryers at my head. And that's when my stomach revs up again. I check my watch. Seven forty.

"How much longer, Jem?"

She switches off the dryers. "I've been applying heat for a half hour, so that should do it."

"Good, 'cause I'm starved. How about you?"

She looks down. "Not yet."

"But it's late."

"Yeah, but with all the excitement over your hair, I don't feel like eating."

I frown, and before I can think of something tactful, I say, "Do you *ever* feel like eating?"

With a little gasp, whatever muscles weren't tense become tense, and then she goes still. Or nearly so. I observe a quivering of her nostrils, downcast eyes, and a slight convulsion of her mouth. As color begins to creep up her face, the emotion coming off her hits me in waves.

I don't know what to do, but I can't just sit here—not when my blundering question caused her distress. So I rise and step forward. "I'm sorry, Jem. I shouldn't have pried."

Her lids flutter, and when I touch her shoulder she lifts them. Pain-inflected eyes meet mine, and she shifts her jaw side to side as if to loosen it, then in a small voice says, "You care, don't you... about me?"

If my eyebrows weren't attached to my brow, they would have bounded right off. "Of course I do!"

She searches my face, then draws a deep breath. "I have anorexia, Grace." Moisture rims her eyes. "And bulimia. You know, when I sometimes give in and binge."

Though struck by a need to embrace her, I'm afraid to overstep the bounds. "I'm sorry." Is that my voice that just crackled between us? "Is there...anything I can do?"

Her eyes get bigger in her reddening face, and then a sob pops free. A moment later she's in my arms, and I can't say if I stepped forward or she did or if we met in the middle. Alternately patting her back, smoothing her hair, and murmuring, "It's okay," I hold her as her shoulders convulse with nearly soundless sobs. She allows me to comfort her until I attempt to move her out of the kitchen and into the living room.

"I'm okay." She pulls back and presses the heels of her palms into her eyes to rub the moisture away. "Just having a bad day."

That's an understatement. "Jem, are you getting any help?"

She squares her shoulders. "I beat it before on my own. I can beat it again."

Then this is nothing new. Amazed at how much I can hurt for another person's hurting, I return a hand to her shoulder. "Other than the couple of times I purged as a teenager after eating too much and wanting to look good in shorts"—*not* worth it—"I don't know much about eating disorders, but maybe you should get professional help."

"I can do it on my own." She steps out from beneath my hand. "Besides, this time I'm a Christian and have what I didn't have the last time: salvation and prayer."

Meaning Christianity is all the cure she needs? Not that I discount its power and the possibility her faith may indeed be enough, but for her to turn her back on the help that's out there… "That's great, Jem, but—"

"Just pray for me. That'll help more than anything."

But if God isn't answering her prayers, what makes her think He'll answer mine? Still, I nod. "Okay." Not a lie. I *will* pray for her.

"C'mon." She heads out of the kitchen. "Let's wash that goop out of your hair and see what the damage is."

I think we already know that, and if not for the turn the night has taken, I'd feel bad. And though it might cost a bundle to fix my hair, it's cosmetic. Jem's problem is not.

Lord, I'm praying for Jem as she asked me to. Though I know You can do anything, I understand You do some of your best work through others. So please give Jem a nudge to seek help to overcome her eating disorder. And please help me help her any way I can.

"Oh my—!"

No, Tessie doesn't stop there. She has no qualms about throwing around the Lord's name, and I've done it myself, but it's started to bother me. Because it wouldn't be tolerated at Steeple Side? Because

I redoubled my efforts not to use it for fear of being caught as I was by Jack when I said the *D* word? Because when I say it now, it's more often in an appropriate context—actually referring to God? Because I'm talking to Him more than usual?

From where she stands on the other side of the door, Tessie shakes her head. "This can't have been intentional."

I finger my dark "do"—only dark because the hot water and solution toned it down to the point it can pass for very dark brown. "Not intentional, but I'm seeing Jem's stylist tomorrow to see what it'll take to make it presentable."

"Jem's?"

Shouldn't have said that. I step back to hold the door wide and motion Tessie in, but she doesn't move.

"She did it, didn't she? Messed up your hair?"

"She was trying to help me save money."

"Ha!" Tessie moves inside. "Wait till you see what this is going to cost you."

With a sinking feeling, I slowly close the door to give Woofer adequate backup time, then follow her to the sofa. "It's a good thing I'll soon have the money to pay for it." *Must* deposit the Steeple Side check.

"If you come through."

Halfway lowering to the sofa, I pause. "You don't think I will?"

She crosses one leg over the other. "I worry that you're getting too close to these Steeple Side people."

Defenses rising, I drop to the sofa. Though I know it will bother Tessie—at times I can be so petty—I scoop up Woofer and plop him on the cushion between us.

Sensing my friend's vibes, he teeters on his peg legs amid the fluff of the cushion, as if in preparation for flight should she pull out a can of flea spray.

I pat my thigh. "Here, Woof."

With a wary glance at Tessie, he bounds into my lap, scrambles across, and seeks cover alongside my opposite thigh. Smart dog.

"So…" I scratch him between the ears. "What makes you think I'm getting too close to the people at Steeple Side?"

"Well, let's see. You attended—"

Woofer groans and flops over to offer up his belly.

As I comply with his request, Tessie draws a deep breath. "You attended Jack's church yesterday."

I start to shrug it off, but then I catch sight of *The Message* on the chair to Tessie's right. I do *not* want her to give me a hard time about buying another Bible version. Fortunately it doesn't look like a Bible, so maybe she won't notice.

I look back at her just as she starts to follow my gaze to the evidence of my attempt to understand the Bible. "Jack's church. Well, yes, I told you how that came about. Damage control, pure and simple." *So* glad I didn't tell her I confessed to Jack the lie of having previously attended Sovereign.

"All right. What about leaving the paper early today so you could play beauty shop with this Jem girl?"

I'm starting to feel incompetent—and wet. Protesting the cessation of his belly scratching, Woofer is licking my hand. I resume my duty to him. "You make it sound as if I was derelict in my work. I assure you, I got it done before leaving this afternoon."

"But your work now includes this investigation. Tell me how allowing Jem to make a mess of your hair has anything to do with that."

"As you know, she's given me more insight into the goings-on at Steeple Side than anyone."

Her eyebrows rise. "Insight is good, but it does not a story make—nor does getting too close to someone you're supposed to be investigating."

As I know well, and the memory of that career-altering naiveté gives me a hard shake. Maybe Tessie's right. Maybe I am getting too close. Liking Jem more than I should. Praying for her, for goodness' sake. Then there's Jack, whose lunch invitation I wanted to accept. Whose accent I wanted to savor. Whose laughter I wanted to hear.

I'm definitely heading down the wrong path again, and when I get to the end of it, neither Jem, nor Jack, nor any of the other Steeple Side employees will be there for me. I'll be alone again, and likely worse off, as Tessie will have every reason to turn her back on me after all she's done to help me get my act together.

I frown as the word *act* reverberates through me. That's not all I'm about, is it? That's not all this is? No, this is real. Even if I do find myself acting out a bigger Christian life than I've known, it's for a worthy cause.

"Are you with me, Maizy?"

Once more abandoning Woofer, I clasp my hands in my lap. "I am. In fact, I found out something tonight when I was with Jem."

Her face brightens. "Why didn't you say so?"

Because I *wasn't* going to say so, and now my conscience is going to town on me, just as it did before I flubbed the Seattle story. But I am *not* going to flub this one. "It's not much…just another piece of the puzzle."

She relaxes into the pillows. "Pieces add up to pictures, and once we fit all the pieces we can get our hands on and fill in the holes with educated guesses"—she sniffs—"a story is born."

But what if those educated guesses are wrong? I start to ask, but it doesn't require every piece of a puzzle to see the big picture.

"So what piece did our little Jem provide?"

"Remember my feeling that she's anorexic? She is." Ignoring my groaning conscience, I continue. "When I probed to find out if she was getting help, she told me she wasn't ready but asked that I pray for her."

Tessie's eyes roll. "Christians are so cliché."

I'm not surprised by her reaction or by my own—indignation—which is in direct opposition to my renewed determination to get the story. Indignation that is going to get me in trouble if I don't control it. And at the moment, it seems the only way to control it is to eliminate the one causing it.

I check my watch. "No wonder I'm so tired. It's after ten—and on a Monday night."

Tessie unfolds from the sofa. "I'll let you get to bed." She steps forward, halts at the sight of *The Message,* and peers over her shoulder. "I'm not going to ask."

"What's to ask?"

She considers me. "You're not going to find the story you're after in that silly Bible, so don't waste your time. Or mine."

A moment later, she's gone, and I'm left with an unsettled feeling that leaves me tossing and turning the whole night and causes Woofer to migrate farther and farther down the bed until I hear a thump. With a low growl, he pads over the carpet and out of the room.

"Fair-weather mutt," I mutter and drag the pillow over my head.

NINE

Of all people…

I catch Jack's widening eyes as I slam to a halt on my approach to the sidewalk. Great! Not that I didn't know I'd have to face him, but I hoped it would be later rather than sooner.

Gripping my purse hard to keep from fingering the dark hair I subdued with a headband, I give a wooden smile. "Good morning, Jack."

He halts in front of me. His eyes move left to right and right to left before settling on my face which, according to my mirror, is as pale as my hair is dark. He shakes his head. "I was fairly certain you weren't a blonde, but I'm positive you're not a brunette—leastwise not on the darkest end of that spectrum."

Act as if it's perfectly normal to go from one extreme color to another and everyone will forget about it. I smile. "Are you saying you don't like my new 'do'?"

Jack's eyebrows peak. "Are you saying this was planned?"

Not even his British accent can soften the blow. Though I know I shouldn't care what he thinks, I hate that he's seeing me like this. Thus, the pressure to save face makes me consider Lie Number Seven: *of course it was intentional!* Or might that be Lie Number Five?

After all, as I confessed to Four and Five, Number Six could move into Number Four's slot, and Number Seven into Number Five's slot...

Too complicated. And all the more reason not to tell another lie. "Not intentional. Amazing how much trouble one can get into with a box of hair color."

Jack crosses his arms over his chest. "I wouldn't know."

Envisioning Jem twittering about his head with a coloring bottle, I chuckle. "No, you wouldn't."

"Do you mean to go back to blond?"

"Actually, at this point I'd be thrilled to return to middle-of-the-road brunette—my natural color."

He smiles. "I thought so. It goes with your eyes and coloring."

He noticed? As I struggle with the implications, Todd Wynde appears and slaps Jack on the back. "This looks promising."

Is he implying that Jack and I...?

He grins. "Didn't recognize you at first, Grace."

I shrug. "It's a different look for me."

"I'll say! Decided a change of scenery was in order, huh?"

I glance at Jack, whose lower jaw is slightly thrust forward. "Something like that."

"Well, I don't know what Jack thinks of it, but I prefer your blond days."

One would think I'd asked for his opinion. "Thank you. I'll take that into account the next time I color my hair." I consult my watch. "I'm going to be late." Avoiding Jack's gaze, I step past him. "Have a nice day."

The consensus is that blond is better, and a medium brunette would be best. But what do they know? It's all about adjustment. If Jem's stylist can't do a thing about my hair, that's what my opinionated co-workers will have to do—adjust. Hope I can.

Perched on the edge of the toilet seat in a stall at the far end of the ladies' room, I balance the notebook on my knee to complete my notes about Gwen's husband. While I didn't mean to eavesdrop on her and her friend, both of whom work in advertising, I had no choice. After all, there I was, alone in the cafeteria, Jem having pulled a no-show, and there they were two tables away, making no attempt to prevent others from straining to listen in on their conversation.

I was saddened to learn that Gwen's husband, who converted to Christianity shortly before they married, is on the brink of a change of heart. As for her friend, though she was eager to console, twice she reminded Gwen that she had warned her that something like this could happen. In the midst of nose blowing, Gwen nodded, and I bristled.

It's true that I'm new at Christian etiquette, but I can't believe an "I told you so" attitude is what Gwen needs. However, in defense of Gwen's friend, the woman's sympathy did seem sincere, and I was touched when she asked if she could pray for Gwen. To my surprise, she did just that—right there.

So here I am, on the edge of a toilet seat, compiling notes that will allow others a glimpse of the faces behind the mask Steeple Side wears—a good thing, especially as I intend to be fair by presenting the positives alongside the negatives. No hidden agenda. No misleading slant. Just the truth.

I scan my newly inked notes, then flip to the notes on Jem. I'd glimpsed her earlier on my return from the Graphic Arts department. She was heading the other way and didn't see me—at least, didn't appear to. Then, for the first time since I started at Steeple Side, she didn't join me for lunch. Because she feels bad about my hair? Because of her anorexia? Coincidence? I'll have to call her.

I snap the notebook closed, but as I start to stand, someone enters the ladies' room.

"Thanks for having lunch with me," Fiala says. "It means a lot to have someone to talk it over with."

Talk what over with? The reason behind Fiala's chill behavior, which Jem has yet to spill on?

"Certainly." This from my boss, Linda.

I glance at my stall door, which is several inches ajar, just as the other unoccupied stalls were when I entered. I usually latch it, but this time I forgot. So it appears as if there's no one else in the ladies' room. As I waver between alerting Fiala and Linda to my presence and adding to my investigation, I hear a door close farther down the line of stalls, then the one immediately to my right.

The bad news—I lose my grip on the notebook. The good news—the notebook tumbles to the left and hits the floor in concert with the sharp latching of the door beside mine. More bad news—my feet are showing. I lift my knees and swing my feet to the side.

"It's so hard not to be angry at God." Fiala's voice sounds from two feet away.

A stall talker. I've never been comfortable carrying on a conversation across restroom stalls, but some women think it's the most natural thing in the world. Now if Linda is one of them...

"I've been there too, Fiala."

We have dialogue. Unfortunately, my abdominal and thigh muscles are starting to cramp, evidence that it's not only Woofer who needs more exercise.

Fiala sighs. "I just can't believe God would allow this. It's as if He doesn't care."

"You know He cares."

"Do I?" A note of bitterness, to which Linda doesn't respond and which leaves me hanging—rather, teetering—on a hard piece of plastic.

My thighs! And stomach! I lean back and wrap my arms around my knees. It helps, but not much. Perspiration forming on my brow, I'm relieved by a distant flush and nearly go limp when Fiala flushes. *Thank you, thank you!*

"He cares," Linda says as she and Fiala approach the sinks. "But as I've learned with my son, the problem doesn't always go away with prayer alone. Until your husband wants to change enough to get help for his—"

The taps come on, garbling the rest of it, but I believe I heard the word *gambling*. If so, it's no wonder Fiala is less than amiable.

The taps go off. Footsteps retreat. The towel dispenser clunks.

"I'm going to talk to our pastor again," Fiala says as she and Linda go out the door. "Maybe he can convince Will to come in and speak with him."

The door closes.

I drop my feet to the floor and clap a hand to my abdomen. An instant later, my groan turns into a yelp when the automatic toilet I'm perched on assumes I've done my business and flushes. At the realization that it could have done so anytime during my covert operation, I feel dizzy. *Way* too close. Another sign that I'm not cut out for this kind of work?

Mustn't think like that. It could as easily be a sign that God approves of my mission. That He's watching out for me.

"Yeah." I reach for my notebook. "Watching out for me."

But when I return to my desk and Fiala approaches with an armful of folders, an impassive face, and eyes that at first glance appear shot through with annoyance but at second glance lean more toward sorrow, I feel guilty.

"I'll be there, Grandma."

"Seven seventeen sharp. Don't forget."

I wouldn't dare. "Seven seventeen sharp." A week and a half from now, yet she makes it sound as if she's flying in tonight.

"And call to make sure the plane isn't ahead of schedule. I don't want to be waiting around at night in a strange city. I'm too old for that."

Peering at the fingernails on my left hand, I nod. "I'll call ahead."

"About that dog, what are you going to do with him while I'm visiting?"

I search out "that dog," but he's nowhere to be seen. Probably has his head under a rug in anticipation of Grandma's visit. "Woofer and I had a little heart to heart, and he's agreed to keep a low profile."

"Well, so long as he stays out of my way, we'll get along fine."

No doubt Woofer will be happy to accommodate. "I don't think that will be a problem, Grandma."

"Good. Now about my visit. I've drawn up a list of the places I want to get all tourist-y over. Top of the list is the Grand Ole Opry."

I bite my tongue.

"I also want to see the Ryman Auditorium, Cheekwood Gardens, and the Parthenon, which I understand is worth a trip to Nashville all by itself."

Obviously she needs to know that the paper put me on full time. But not about Steeple Side. That would be awkward.

"Then there's the Belmont Mansion, The Hermitage, the… Sche…Scher…"

"The Schermerhorn Symphony Center. Grandma, I'm sure we can fit in some of those, but now that I'm working full time—"

Gasp. "Full time?" Her pitch has shades of relief as well as disappointment. "When did the paper put you on full time?"

"Fairly recently, and of course I'm thrilled to be able to pay my bills, but it means I can't take you to all those places."

"Of course not, but that doesn't mean I can't enjoy the sights. I'll just hook up with a tourist company. You'll look into that for me, won't you?"

Relieved that she's taking it well, I nod into the mouthpiece. "I'll be happy to." And now to check in on her friend. "How's Edith?"

A sharp breath whistles across the phone line. "She's hanging in there. Though they're still telling us it's only a matter of weeks, Edith is having nothing to do with their doom and gloom. In fact, at times I think she might beat this, but then she has a bad day."

"Maybe there's hope yet."

"There's always hope with God, Maizy Grace."

She says stuff like that—upping the ante with God when I don't include Him. "Of course."

"But I do think the doctors are right, that the Lord is calling Edith home. I just…" Her voice thickens. "I hope He comes for her while I'm visiting you. I can't take much more of this. It's hard on my poor heart."

Dare I ask? "Grandma, has Dad—?"

"He hasn't. Busy, busy, busy. And that wife of his too."

"That would be my mom." Although I often let her backhanded slaps pass, something impels me to speak up. Maybe it's this dark hair of mine, which Jem's stylist said would benefit more from a series of deep conditionings than another bottle of color.

"Yes, your mother. She and that husband of hers—"

My *dad*. Her *son*.

"—never have the time to visit. As for that daughter of theirs—"

My *sister*.

"—she doesn't even pretend to be busy."

"I'm sorry, Grandma, but the good news is that you'll be here with me in a couple of weeks, and as much as possible, I'm going to show you a good time."

"That is good news, isn't it?" She sighs. "Well, it's late there. I'll let you go."

"I look forward to your visit."

"Remember, 7:17 sharp."

I finger a tress of hair. "You may not recognize me."

"How's that?"

"I'm a solid brunette. And very dark."

"Like your mother?"

"Sort of."

"Why on earth would you go and do that? Not that I much liked your skunky look, but dark brunette?"

"I needed a change."

"Now, Maizy Grace, you know"—her teeth clack—"I certainly understand the need for change."

Thank You, God.

"All right, I'll let you get to bed. Good night."

"'Night, Grandma."

I push the handset's Off button and glance at my watch. Has Jem picked up the message I left on her answering machine? I gave her the scoop on her hairstylist's recommendation, told her I missed her at lunch, and said I hoped we could get together tomorrow. Did she try to return my call? At times like this, I wish I had call waiting.

I set the handset down and groan as I unfold from the sofa. My thighs! And abs! Can*not* believe my balancing act in the bathroom stall would make my muscles so sore. I need to start working out.

I glance at the *DBGC,* then at *The Message.* Though I'm too tired to do any serious delving, surely I can squeeze in ten minutes before bed. In fact, it might be just what I need to put me to sleep.

TEN

What's a Hypocrite to Do?

So you're starting to feel that Christianity might be the thing for you. Starting to feel you're part of something big and life chang-ing. Maybe even starting to look like one of the "in crowd" (that is, Jesus's crowd). Hold it! Before you get all goopy eyed and mushy kneed, let's talk about...hypocrisy.

An ugly word. But if you're in this for the long haul (a.k.a. eternity), you'll have to get up close and personal with the hypocrisy that piles into pews on Sundays. Imagine a man whose hand is always raised high in praise but was raised for an entirely different rea-son when he was cut off in traffic. How about a young woman who dresses conservatively for service but abandons modesty for a day at the mall? Then there's a stiffly starched mother who disciplines her children for impolite behavior only to snap at her own mother. Not to be overlooked—the guy at the end of the pew who proclaims, "Amen," when the minister preaches on treating the poor fairly. He owns a pawn shop that does a thriving business.

Ah! A deacon's wife. Sunday after Sunday, she presents a spotless example of Christianity, but last Sunday she ripped into a library volunteer who wasn't shelving books in the prescribed manner. Then there's *you*. Hate to break it to you, but to some degree or another, you have been, are, and will be a hypocrite no matter how much effort you put into being like Jesus. You're not alone. Not only "seekers" (those searching but not yet committed to the faith) but also mature Christians put on their best faces when they walk into church, struggle to hold them in place, and sometimes let them slip. But that's no excuse not to reach for something beyond your grasp—to get as close as possible to overcoming hypocrisy. So what's a hypocrite to do?

a) Pray that Jesus will reveal the hypocrisy in your life. (No denial, now!)

b) Read the Word (a.k.a. the Bible).

c) Strive to be your Sunday best all week

long (at home, at church, and among the masses).

d) Refrain from judging others, and be as quick to forgive as you want to be forgiven (time and again).

Doesn't sound easy, does it? It isn't, which is the reason prayer is listed first. Now get to it! That is, if you're in it for the long haul.

I want to be, but the author's right. It's not easy, especially when you're me. But once my work at Steeple Side is complete, things will be better. Easier. More attainable.

Cultural Christian.

I toss the *DBGC* on the chair beside my purse and check my watch: 7:17. I glance at the security checkpoint that Grandma should be coming past in the next ten minutes. Should I have sought clearance to meet her at the gate with a wheelchair? Not that she can't get around on her own, but she may be expecting to see me when she disembarks. Not the way to kick off our visit, especially if it was a rough flight. But it's too late now, as the plane is arriving on schedule.

I groan in anticipation of her displeasure. It's been a bad enough week without adding to it. Not only does Jem continue to avoid me (haven't lunched with her in a week and a half), but Fiala's on my case for everything from missing files to missed phone calls. Then there's all the gofering between Women's and Men's Publications. The icing on my sorry week was the discovery that my paycheck from the paper didn't stretch far. *Must* cash the Steeple Side checks.

Deep breath.

There's more. Yesterday Ray charged Tessie with monitoring my progress on the investigation, meaning I'm to update her regularly. Meaning they don't trust me to bring in the story. As for Jack, I must be crazy, but though he and I haven't exchanged a word since he caught me in the parking lot with my new hair color, every time I see him in passing...every time he acknowledges me with a raised hand...every time our eyes meet and his mouth turns up...I go carnal. Not *carnal* carnal, but "Wonder how he kisses?" carnal. "Wonder how he links fingers when holding hands?" carnal. "Wonder if his palm against mine will produce delicious shivers?" carnal. All bad.

"Grace! Is that you?"

It's me, but *that's* not Grandma. Jolted by the appearance of a thirtyish man whose goatee and sparkling eyes strike a chord of familiarity, I jump up. "Uh...?"

"Avery." He releases the handle of his wheeled bag and thrusts out a hand. "We met two Sundays ago in the singles' class at Sovereign."

"Oh, right." Certain I'm about to be badgered for not attending this past Sunday, I slide my hand into his and steel myself, just as I've done each time I see Jack. Strangely, he has yet to ask about my absence. Meaning he was absent himself?

"You've changed your hair color." Avery releases my hand.

Angling my body to block his view of the book, which may or may not be faceup on the chair, I push fingers up through my hair and draw them out to the ends. "I'm surprised you recognized me."

"I'm good at faces. Especially pretty ones."

Is he flirting with me? "Thank you."

"So what are you doing at the airport—picking up someone?"

"My grandmother. What about you?"

He switches his laptop bag from his right to his left shoulder. "I just flew in from Seattle."

Not Seattle. "Really?" *Please, God, don't let it be that he sat next to Grandma. You name the version—King James, Queen James, Prince James, whatever!—and I promise to carve out time tonight.*

"I was there on business."

I hazard a glance past him, hoping Grandma is taking her sweet time walking from the gate.

"I'm a sales rep for industrial pipe fittings. I was in Seattle setting up a new account."

"Sounds exciting."

"Not really, but I like my job. How about you? Do you enjoy working at Steeple Side?"

I do not have time for this. Any moment now—

There she is, all five feet, one hundred pounds, and elegantly coifed silver hair. And she appears...not happy, but not unhappy either. I look back at Avery. "Uh, yes, Steeple Side is a very nice work environment."

"That's hard to come by."

I steal another glance at Grandma. Fortunately she hasn't seen me. Because of my dark hair? Because Avery is partially blocking her line of sight?

I smile big. "Yes, hard to come by." Back to Grandma.

Avery follows my gaze. "Is that your grandmother?"

Oh no. And it goes from bad to worse when she catches sight of me and raises a hand. "That's her."

"We came in on the same flight."

Tell me they didn't sit together, that she didn't go on about her Maizy Grace, who's the only one who cares a whit about her.

I press my shoulders back. "Small world. Well, it was nice chatting—"

"Looks like she's recovered all right."

"Recovered?"

"Yeah, though she was several rows ahead of me, it was obvious she was anxious about flying."

How obvious? "I'd better go see to her." I flash a smile and grab my purse.

"Nice talking to you, Grace."

I wave over my shoulder. "And you."

"Hey!" His voice causes me to break my stride. "Is this yours?"

I turn as he advances, *The Dumb Blonde's Guide to Christianity* in hand.

Heart thwacking, I put on my best never-seen-it-before face. "Was that sitting there? Hmm. I'm sure whoever left it will come back for it." Hey, that was pretty good. Not *exactly* a lie. Unfortunately I should probably track it, so Lie Number Seven it is.

"Maizy Grace!" Grandma exclaims a moment before her arms come around me.

Oh dear. Did Avery hear the *Maizy* part? Since it's her habit to emphasize *Grace,* maybe he didn't catch it. "Grandma!" As I return her hug, I dip my head and put my mouth to her ear. "Call me Grace. Okay?"

She pulls back. "What?"

"Grace," I hiss. "Don't call me Maizy. I'll explain later."

Before she can confirm that she understands, Avery is beside us, fingers wrapped around the spine of that stupid book, his other hand outthrust as I draw back from Grandma. "I'm Avery Kenwood. I understand you're Grace's grandmother."

Her gaze flicks to me as she accepts the handshake. "That I am. Grace Stewart."

His smile broadens as he releases her hand. "Then Grace here is your namesake."

Another flick of her gaze at where I stand awkwardly alongside her. "Yes, her father and"—she clears her throat—"mother named her after me."

"For good reason, I'm sure."

Her lips edge upward. "I'd like to think so." She clasps her hands at her waist and gives him the twice over. "Are you my granddaughter's boyfriend?"

Avery startles, and I don't know whether or not to take offense. "I believe someone else has claimed that honor."

I'd be flattered except that he's surely referring to Jack—and Grandma is giving me the evil eye, as in, "Why didn't you tell me you had a boyfriend?"

"I'm just her Sunday school teacher."

Her penciled eyebrows jump. "You're Grace's"—gray eyes dart to my face and back to Avery—"Sunday school teacher?"

"Yes, we just ran into each other here. In fact, you and I were on the same flight from Seattle. I was a few rows back. I couldn't help but notice how nervous you were." Sympathy curves his mouth. "You're all right now?"

Grandma nods. "My feet are on the ground again."

"Good." Avery twists the wrist of the hand holding *my* book and checks his watch. "I should get going. It was nice meeting you."

Grandma inclines her head. "And you, young man."

What about my book? Surely he's not going to walk off with it?

"Interesting title, hmm?"

I startle at the realization he's caught me staring at the *DBGC*. "Yeah. Imagine that: a Christianity guide for dumb blondes."

Grandma frowns. "Surely that's not your book, Avery?"

"No." He nods over his shoulder. "Someone left it on the chair near where Grace was sitting."

Grandma's eyes land on me with an almost audible *thunk*. "Wonder what fool paid good money for something like that when the Bible is all a person needs?"

Itching to snatch the book from Avery, I shrug. "It must have some value if it was published. And, um…" I tilt my head to the side to peer at the cover. "It does say 'National Bestseller.'" *So there!*

"Amazing what sells nowadays," Grandma mutters.

With a noncommittal nod, Avery zeros in on me. "I'll see you Sunday?"

Sunday? Just because I attended two Sundays ago doesn't mean I'll attend this Sunday. "Maybe. You know how it is when you have out-of-town guests."

"You're welcome to bring your grandmother."

"Oh, she will," Grandma says.

I silently implore her to look *deep* into my eyes. "But, Grandma, what about all those places you want to see?"

She smiles. "You know the importance I place on church, *Grace.*

Besides, I'm here for two weeks. If that's not enough time to be a tourist, I'll alter my plans."

Can this day get any worse?

"I look forward to seeing you both." Avery shifts his laptop bag. "Now I'm off to drop this book at the Lost and Found and head on home."

I raise a hand. "Bye."

"Good-bye, Avery." Grandma wiggles her fingers and, when his back is to us, pins me with those sharp gray eyes. "You've got a lot of explaining to do, young lady."

"I know, but first let's get your luggage and drop by the Lost and Found."

Steeple Side Lies

#1. No real work experience (Mrs. Lucas)

#2. Currently not working anywhere else (Mrs. Lucas)

#3. Interested in full-time work at Steeple Side (Mrs. Lucas)

#4. ~~Didn't say the D word (Jack Prentiss)~~

#5. ~~Attend Sovereign Church and like the congregation (2 lies in 1—Jack & Linda)~~

#6. Do freelance editing (Jem)

#7. *DBGC* not mine (Avery)

Grandma sighs into her teacup, causing the steam rising from it to cloud her face. "Some pickle you've got yourself into, Grace."

Amazing how receptive she is to dropping my first name. Of course, she never much liked my mom's mom. And in defense of Grandma Grace, her counterpart was not easy to like. I stare at the tea leaves at the bottom of my own cup. Generic tea bags just don't hold up as well as the leading brands.

"Did you hear me, Grace?"

"I've gotten myself into a pickle. Unfortunately, I don't have much choice."

"You can say no."

I look up. "Is that what you think I should do? Tell the paper no? Risk my career again? Resign myself to writing mindless articles about county fairs and the newest eatery in town? Barely scrape by? Maybe not even scrape by?"

She sets her cup in its saucer. "You are not an orphan. You have safety nets."

I've heard this before—*many* times. "Grandma, how old am I?"

She waves dismissingly. "I know. 'I'm twenty-six, a grown woman, and I can do it on my own.'" She harrumphs. "That's pride speaking, and pride will lead you into sin, Grace."

Grace, Grace, Grace! I slump back into the pillows. "You know, Grandma, around here you can call me Maizy."

"Why?"

"Because it's my name."

"Not at Steeple Side or Sovereign."

"Neither of which we're at."

"But we will be. So if I'm to stay in character—"

In *character*?

"I need to practice." She raises the cup to her lips.

I glower. "Why do I have this feeling that's just an excuse, that you prefer *Grace* over *Maizy*?"

"Because I do. I can't tell you how often I argued with your mother before you were born that you should be named Grace Maizy."

At least once a week, according to Mom.

"But she preferred to honor *her* mother over your father's mother." She wags a finger. "And you know how she convinced my son? With that silly wordplay of hers. As if she cares about an old hymn."

Lord, I know Grandma loves and believes in You, but why doesn't it show at times like this? Even I know You don't want to see this from her—bitterness over what she perceives to be wrongs done her. Regardless of whether or not she's right, why can't she try harder to get along with Mom? Maybe then Dad and Mom would visit more often. Isn't there something I can say? Something that will make her see that she's only hurting herself? Some verse—

As if I'd even know where to begin looking for a verse to cover something like this. After all, the Bible is little more than a prop for me despite my good intentions to read it.

Cultural Christian.

I set my cup and saucer on the end table, lean forward, and lay a hand on Grandma's bony little knee beneath polyester slacks. "This day has given me more than my share of headaches. If we're going to talk into the wee hours of morning, let's talk about something pleasant."

She shrugs. "Honestly, Grace, what is there pleasant to talk about? The flight was so nerve racking I had to take hits of oxygen. When I finally made it off the plane, there you were looking like a shorter version of your mother with all that dark hair. One moment I'm thrilled to learn that you not only have yourself a boyfriend but a church home; the next, I find out it's a farce. Then there's this business about Steeple Side, whose publications I've enjoyed for years. And now…" She rubs her nose. "Now my nose is itching from all that dander and hair your little dog deposits."

She's right. There isn't anything pleasant to talk about—not even the good news that Edith took a turn for the better yesterday, as Grandma is certain everyone's getting their hopes up for nothing.

I push up off the sofa. "How about we start all over again tomorrow after we've had some good sleep?"

A shadow of regret crosses her face. "You're right. I am tired."

Twenty minutes later, she's tucked in my bed, I'm stretched out on the sofa with Woofer at my side, and *The Message* is open on my lap to Matthew, the first book of the New Testament. Yes, I'm reading the Bible. While I long to pull the covers over my head and sleep away the remainder of Friday, I made a promise I intend to keep.

Though much of what I read over the next half hour merely skims the surface of my gray matter, time and again I return to the sixth chapter of Matthew that we touched on in Avery's Sunday school class. Especially the part that precedes the Lord's Prayer and which *The Message* puts into language I'm better able to understand: "Find a quiet, secluded place so you won't be tempted to role-play before God. Just be there as simply and honestly as you can manage. The focus will shift from you to God, and you will begin to sense his grace."

I try it out, and burrowed beneath the warm covers, I sense something. Is it all in my head? Perhaps, but it's comforting, especially when I turn my self-centered prayers to others: Jem, Linda's son, Fiala, Gwen and her husband, Grandma, and Edith.

Prayer. Who would have thought that something so simple could feel so good?

ELEVEN

"So this is your young man?"

I could just die. I look from Jack's startled expression to Grandma, who's beaming as if he's the answer to her prayers. Unfortunately, as she was set on attending church, it had been necessary to alert her to the situation with Jack and the reason behind Avery's assumption that we're seeing each other. Why didn't I stay in bed? In light of all the sight hopping we did yesterday—Opryland Hotel, Opryland Mall, and the Country Music Hall of Fame—surely we could have skipped church?

"Grandma, Jack and I are just…" I nearly roll my eyes to find him staring at me with raised eyebrows, no doubt enjoying the thought that I've been talking him up. "We work together and attend the same church. That's all."

She gives me a scowl and Jack another smile. "Is that really all, Jack?"

His eyebrows resettle, and for a moment it seems possible that he's going to let me off the hook, but his eyes turn luminous. "If Grace says so."

Embarrassment vying with dread over what Grandma will read into his response, I search for something to turn the conversation, but she gets there first.

"Don't mind what Grace says." She pats Jack's arm. "Truth be known, she likes to be chased."

"Grandma!"

"Well, you do. How many times did Ben have to ask you out before you accepted?"

Did I just crack a tooth? *Two days down, twelve to go before she returns to Seattle.*

Grandma sighs. "Of course, he turned out to be a horse's patootie."

An understatement, but I refuse to talk about him in front of Jack. I curl a hand around Grandma's forearm. "Let's find a seat."

She looks back at Jack and winks. "Lovely meeting you. Oh, and delicious accent, Jack. I'm sure it drives the women wild."

A groan escapes me, then another when I see the heads of other singles turn our direction. *Two days down, twelve to go.*

As I hustle Grandma toward the back of the class, I put my mouth to her ear. "What are you doing?"

"Endearing myself."

I falter. "What?"

"Endearing myself and giving you and Jack plenty of stories to tell my great-grandbabies one day."

I declare, I'm having heart palpitations. I turn down the back row. As she settles into the chair beside mine, I hiss, "You know the situation with me and Steeple Side. There is no way that Jack and I will be walking down the aisle together."

"You're probably right, but I can fantasize."

"Fantasize?" That word does *not* belong in the vocabulary of a senior citizen!

She flutters a hand to her throat. "Imagine having a grandson-in-law with a British accent. The ladies in my 'experienced' Sunday school class would be envious."

I glower. "Correct me if I'm wrong, but Christians aren't supposed to be envious."

She rolls her eyes. "This is silver hair, not a halo."

My grandmother, the "experienced" Christian. Not that I'm any better—far from it—but at times like these I better understand my mother's reluctance to explore her mother-in-law's faith.

As I send up a prayer that the remainder of our Sunday school experience will be uneventful, Grandma brightens. "You know how much Edith loves those BBC productions of the Brontë sisters' and Jane Austen's books! If I had a Brit in the family, it might be enough to get her out of bed."

I give up. Sitting back, I scan the room, which is filling with those who exited the first service behind Grandma and me. I'm not looking for Jack, so when I pick him out where he stands alongside Avery at the front of the class, it's accidental. Head bent toward a petite woman— Dinah from Steeple Side's Payroll department—he nods.

"Oh dear," Grandma says. "There's a pretty little brunette talking to your Jack."

Two days down, twelve to go. "He is not *my* Jack."

She shifts her gaze to my hair. "Not with you looking like that. Honestly, you need to do something about that color."

Avery saves me from saying something I'll regret. "Okay, people, let's get started."

And just like that, Grandma forgets about my hair. "Lovely." She gives her sweater a tug. "I've always wondered what goes on in the young singles' class."

Worn out by her antics, distracted time and again by Jack and Dinah sitting side by side at the front, I tune out much of the discussion. Thus, when a clipboard comes around near the end of the class and Grandma writes down our names, I assume it's an attendance sheet.

"There." She passes the clipboard to the woman across the aisle. "That ought to provide an up-close look at the plight of the less fortunate."

"What are you talking about?"

She nods at the clipboard as it grows distant. "The sign up for working at the soup kitchen next week in lieu of attending Sunday school. Weren't you listening?"

Suppressing the impulse to lurch after the clipboard and scribble out our names, I pitch my voice low so it won't distract the others from their prayer requests. "Unfortunately, no."

She arches one heavily penciled eyebrow. "You have other plans?"

"Maybe."

"Now there's no 'maybe' about it. Next Sunday you and I are going to roll up our sleeves and dish up meals for those who have nothing."

"Since when have you been interested in feeding the homeless?"

She cants her head toward the front of the class. "Since I saw your Jack sign up to serve." She pats my hand. "Trust me, it will make a good impression."

I start to sputter, but when heads turn in our direction, I switch to seething.

Five minutes later, I hurry Grandma through the parking lot.

Twenty feet from my car, she puts on the brakes. "Spill it, Maizy Grace."

I turn to her. "I do not require your services as a matchmaker. Delicious accent or not, Jack and I are incompatible. As for serving soup to the homeless, you know that is not my thing. Or yours. Yes, I sympathize with their plight, but I am not comfortable spending time among them—or faking being something I'm not." Oops.

She unpurses her lips. "I would think you've become quite comfortable with faking, Grace. *Humph!* 'Jesus is my copilot'!"

Not for much longer. That sticker is coming off today. And that little fish too. "I'm only doing what I have to."

As she stares at me, her stern features ease. "Are you, Maizy Grace?"

"I don't want to talk about it. Let's get lunch."

"Now we're getting somewhere." Tessie peers across my kitchen table at me. "I told you that if you kept digging, you'd discover your boss has written articles about how Christians can keep their children drug free." She chuckles and returns her attention to my laptop's screen.

I shouldn't feel violated that she's monitoring my investigation, but I do. And it's no one's fault but mine. Though I tell myself that my co-workers at Steeple Side are merely subject matter, I'm lying. They're people, several of whom I like, all of whom could be hurt by my investigation. Maybe I'm not cut out for—

"You've got what it takes."

I blink Tessie back into focus. "You think?"

"I do. However, you need to dig up more on Steeple Side's actual employees. This stuff on Fiala and Gwen's husbands is good, but it doesn't show *them* to be hypocrites. What's going to blow the lid...er, steeple"—she grins—"are things like Jem's eating disorder and the brainwashing that God is all she needs to overcome it."

Alarmed, I shake my head. "You're reading more into my notes than there is. I never said anything about brainwashing. Even if someone has convinced Jem that she can overcome her problem without professional help, that doesn't necessarily have anything to do with Steeple Side."

Tessie lowers her lids to half staff, then continues as if the speed bump I poured in the middle of her road never was. "While Linda's inability to parent is pretty good stuff, you need to be on the lookout for infidelity, embezzlement, pornography—the juicy stuff."

If it's so juicy, why does it make my stomach heave?

Grandma lowers the Sunday paper behind which she ducked shortly after Tessie walked in. "Did you tell Tessie about working the soup kitchen next Sunday?"

Inwardly groaning—not only over my dilemma of how to wriggle out of the commitment, but what Tessie might read into it—I give Grandma "the look" as she sits in the armchair beside the sofa.

"Soup kitchen, Maizy?"

I look back at Tessie. "We signed up at church."

"You went to church again?"

An accusation in sheep's clothing. "That's right." Though tempted to explain that Grandma insisted, something in me protests the disapproval that sloughs off Tessie like dander off Woofer.

She sets my laptop aside. "It's good that you take your research so seriously, but don't forget that it's the end product that pays the bills."

Is she letting me off the hook, or does she really think that's all this is—research? Of course, for now that *is* all it is. And obligation. After all, it was Grandma's idea to go to church. And I'm not the one who signed us up for the soup kitchen.

"Did I mention that nice young man from Steeple Side, Jack, will be working the soup kitchen with us?"

Oh no.

Tessie brightens. "Really? Maybe your priorities are straight, Maizy."

"Well, you just give my granddaughter time, and she'll dish up plenty of dirt for that article of *yours.*"

Tessie whips her head around. "It's not my article, Mrs. Stewart. It's Maizy's. I'm simply overseeing it."

"Hmm." Grandma gives the newspaper a shake and raises it before her face. "I must have misunderstood."

Tessie looks to me, then pushes back her chair. "I'm sure you and your grandmother have plans for the rest of the day, so I'll be going."

I want to be sorry to see her go, but I'm not. I want to protest, but I don't. And I feel guilty. Tessie may be a die-hard skeptic, but she's my friend. If not for her, Nashville would be lonely, especially now that Jem's avoiding me. Er, not that Jem is friend material. Under the circumstances, that would be a very bad idea.

I rise and, despite what feels like a strained friendship, say, "Grandma and I are going to Cheekwood to see the gardens. Do you want to join us?"

Tessie glances at Grandma, who shows no signs of coming out from behind the paper. "I'll pass. But you two have fun."

Grandma raises a hand above the paper. "Nice to meet you, Tessie."

"And you, Mrs. Stewart." Tessie crosses to the door, and I follow.

"Thanks for dropping by and reviewing my notes," I offer as she pulls the door open. "It's good to know I'm on the right track."

Her smile is forced and disappears altogether when the cross-stitch picture on the wall beside the door catches her eye. "The Lord's Prayer?" She frowns over her shoulder at me.

"Grandma made it for me." And hung it. Right where Tessie couldn't miss it.

She glides her lips from side to side. "Nice needlework." Moments later she descends the steps and crosses to her house, which sits fifty feet from the detached garage.

"I never liked that woman." The newspaper *thumps* as Grandma tosses it aside.

I close the door. "Never liked her? You just met her."

She makes a face. "Yes, in person. But it's not as if I don't know her. After all, you talked about her when she was your instructor at the university, and now that you work with her"—Grandma's nose twitches—"or should I say 'now that you work *for* her'?"

I don't protest, as she's not far off. Still, I have to defend Tessie. "She was there for me when I needed someone—got me the job at the paper, rented this place to me at below market value, and has provided companionship. I owe her."

"I'm not saying you shouldn't be grateful. I'm saying that she doesn't sit well with me and that if you're not careful how you spread around your gratitude, she'll take advantage of it. That woman has an agenda."

The agenda being the story that Jack nipped in the bud years ago? The agenda being her mission to shake up beliefs she once embraced?

I cross to Grandma and kiss her cheek. "I'll be careful."

She captures my hand and squeezes it, and in her eyes I glimpse the love she often shutters. "Promise, Maizy Grace?"

"Promise."

She releases my hand and pushes up out of the chair. "Let's go see what Cheekwood is all about."

I feel like a thief—carefully picking my way through the dark, flashlight in one pocket, razor blade in the other, gaze shifting between the car, the house, and my apartment. Not that I'm trying to be sneaky. It just seemed a good time to remove that bumper sticker. Of course, there was the added incentive provided by a group of teenagers earlier when I experienced some difficulty with parallel parking at Cheekwood.

As I jimmied the car back and forth, a skinny kid with jeans slung low had commented to another, "So much for Jesus being her copilot."

"Yeah," his hefty pal said. "Either He bailed on her, or He has no idea what He's doing."

Just banter, I told myself. Nothing to get uptight about. But I had, because I took their comments personally. As in, what if Jesus *has* bailed on me? What if He *doesn't* know what He's doing where I'm concerned? Worse, what if He doesn't *want* to know?

To top it off, Grandma stuck her head out the window and raised an aged fist. "If Jesus were *your* copilot, you'd be more careful about showing your hiney in public!"

At which point, I slammed the brakes, closed Grandma's window, and locked the doors.

Peripherally aware of the teenagers staring at us, I'd met Grandma's glowering gaze. "You can't talk to people like that." I gave a discreet nod toward the teenagers who, thankfully, resumed their course.

"Did I lie?" She grunted. "No self-respecting senior citizen ought to be subjected to a view like the one I just got an eyeful of. My diaper days are long past and are going to stay that way."

I gritted my teeth and took my time getting the car situated, the window shade positioned, and Grandma out of the car. All to put distance between us and the teens. Fortunately the remainder of our outing was uneventful. But to be certain something like that never happens again...

Now I'm hunkering before the bumper, shining the flashlight on the sticker that Jack was so kind to *permanently* apply, and positioning the razor blade at the lower right corner. "Here goes nothing."

Sliding the blade beneath the edge, my eyes are drawn to the word *Jesus.*

As in Savior.

I return my attention to the task and ease the blade up...up...

Then there's the deceptively insignificant word *is.*

As in "being." Right here...right now...

"Stop it!" I mutter. "It's coming off." I wiggle the blade until the corner releases from the bumper. I smile, but in doing so, my eyes land on *my*.

As in "mine." Belonging to me…

"But not my bumper." I set the razor blade on the asphalt and grip the corner of the sticker between thumb and forefinger. Though I know there's not much chance of it coming off in one piece, I slowly pull and it begins to release.

And there's the word *copilot*.

As in "counselor." Guiding me…

"Cliché," I grumble.

With a jerk, a large portion of the sticker releases, causing a tear that cuts across the *t* in *copilot*, which is drawn as a crucifix.

Gulp. I'm not superstitious, but this is not good. In fact, it's bad. Borderline sacrilegious. Not that I meant for it to happen. Well, I *was* prepared to take off the sticker piece by piece. But now…

"It's just a bumper sticker. A piece of paper with goo on the back and words on the front. Jesus junk." I nod. "Yeah, just like the fish." I shine the light on the latter and feel the tug of a smile. It is kind of cute, especially angled as it is. Fighting the current…

A few minutes later, I trudge up the steps to my apartment, while below the fish still has its nose in the air and the torn bumper sticker is pressed back into place. I'll take them off later when this whole thing with Steeple Side is over.

TWELVE

I'm eavesdropping again. And feeling bad, though I keep telling myself this is why I'm still at Steeple Side—to get the story. And there's *always* a story, especially if I'm reading this one right.

Four tables away, a guy about my age is sitting with an older man who, I believe, works in the department that produces adult Sunday school materials. The younger man has his head down, and the older man has a hand on his shoulder. They speak in hushed tones, but not so hushed that I can't catch sound bites. Thus, I can now add "pornography" to the list of struggles faced by Steeple Side employees.

So where's the thrill of unearthing the truth? of bringing it out into the open? of making the world a better place by exposing those who seek to deceive others? Where's the satisfaction in knowing that my investigation has the potential to make a splash among the readers of the *Middle Tennessee Review*? in it finding its way into other papers across the country? in its ability to redeem my career? At the very least, there ought to be a frisson of excitement.

But my conscience isn't having any of it. Is this why there aren't more Christians working in secular media? Because it's too hard to live with oneself?

I blow a breath up my face. Regardless of what my conscience has to say, I will add this to my research, which ought to make Tessie happy.

Catching the word *Internet,* I once more turn my ear toward the young man and his gray-haired mentor and my unseeing gaze to the paper on the table before me. Mustn't be too obvious.

"Anything good?"

Jack's voice not only makes me jump my seat back several inches, but causes my dry palms to start perspiring.

Calm down! But my heart is doing double time, my face is hot, and the eyes I lift to him are painfully wide. "What?"

"Are you all right?"

"You surprised me." Of course, he does that a lot. Intentionally? Perhaps he's still set on proving I'm a fraud.

"I apologize." His smile is thin. "Must be an interesting article." He angles his head to read the paper's caption. "Gardening."

Nice one. Couldn't open to something more headline worthy? Who is going to believe you have an interest in gardening? Remember Cheek-wood? Pretty, but if not for Grandma, you'd have been out of there in fifteen minutes flat.

I smooth a hand over the article. "Very interesting. If you're a gardening enthusiast."

"I am. Any good tips?"

If only I knew how to speed-read! "The same old stuff—sunlight, water, good soil." I catch a glint in his eyes. Suspicion? "So what are you doing in the cafeteria at this hour? Taking an early lunch?"

Whatever that glint was, it fades. "I dropped by to see if I might catch you here."

Though my first thought is that I've done something wrong—perhaps been found out—the next is quite the opposite. In fact, it's warm and fuzzy. Which it shouldn't be. I have no business liking Jack.

I fold the paper and push it to the side, where my half-eaten lunch clutters a tray. "Is there something we need to talk about?"

He reaches for the chair beside mine, only to still as the word *porn* drifts toward us. "I believe our neighbors require more privacy."

"Certainly." I gather my tray and newspaper. "Let me dump these."

"Not the gardening article." Jack relieves me of that section. "I don't usually read the *Middle Tennessee Review,* but this is of interest."

Meaning the rest isn't? A bubble of offense rises, and I nod. "It's yours."

I cross to the table he's chosen in the far corner, where none of the men's conversation can reach, and lower to the chair opposite him.

Jack clasps his hands on the table. "First, I want to say that I was pleased to see you in Sunday school yesterday. When you didn't show last Sunday, I was afraid I had run you off."

He had—or partly so, due to my forbidden attraction to him. The other reason for my absence was due to my present circumstances. As an investigative reporter attempting to root out hypocrisy among Christians, it didn't seem right to sit in a pew or Sunday school chair and soak up God.

"Also, I want to tell you that I enjoyed meeting your grandmother." Jack smiles, which causes my stomach to engage in activities unrelated to the production of acid. "She's quite a character."

My lips begin to tug. "Should I pass that on?"

He chuckles. "Not in so few words, perhaps."

How do the British do that—turn something as unsensual as a chuckle into something spine tingling? "You'd like me to embellish?"

"Please."

Oh boy. I really am attracted to this man who would be the first to string me up if he knew what I'm doing at Steeple Side. And that grounds me. "Thank you for sharing." I start to rise, but he lays a hand on my forearm.

"There's more."

I look to his hand on me, and there's that thrill I was bemoaning the lack of earlier. Though not your ordinary unearthing-the-truth thrill. This one is better. And dangerous. I lower to my chair again. "Oh?"

He removes his hand. "I was pleased to see that you and your grandmother signed up to serve in the soup kitchen next Sunday."

While I already know the answer, I ask, "Did you sign up as well?"

"I did."

"Then we'll be working together."

"Yes, and that's the primary reason I wanted to talk to you. Would you be interested in writing a piece about your experience helping to feed the homeless?"

He's asking *me* to write a piece? The part-time editorial assistant? The *Middle Tennessee Review* mole?

"I'll be writing one for the men's June issue, and I think it would be beneficial to do the same for the women's issue—to run jointly."

"You're serious? You want *me* to write it?"

His brow creases. "I wouldn't ask if I wasn't serious. Now the question is: are you serious about moving up at Steeple Side? If so, this could be the first step to realizing your dream of writing for publication."

Not the first step. I'm many steps from being fresh out of college. And there's my party-pooping conscience again. My former nemesis is trying to help me, completely unaware that it's the last thing he should be doing.

"Are you all right, Grace?"

Only then do I realize my eyes are puddling.

"I hope those are happy tears."

A better excuse than the truth. "Of course." I wipe my eyes.

He considers me with that glint in his eyes again, and I hold my breath until it passes. "Then the next step is for me to get Linda's approval and input."

"You didn't run this by her first?"

"I wanted to be sure you were receptive so you wouldn't feel pressured to do something you're not ready for."

I'm *not* ready for this, but only because the emotions churning through me are reminiscent of what got me into trouble in Seattle. Jack's belief in my ability will only make it harder to sleep at night.

"You are ready, aren't you?"

If a smile could light up a room, mine would—regardless of how fake it feels. "You bet!"

He reaches across the table and once more lays a hand on my forearm. "I know you won't disappoint us."

Jack Prentiss is a fool.

"You did what?"

Grandma sighs. "I invited Jem for dinner."

Cupping a hand over the mouthpiece of my cell phone, I dart my gaze around the Lifestyle department, then swivel around to give my back to those who don't appear the least interested in the events unfolding at my desk. "Grandma, Tessie is my landlord. I can't risk having my life at Steeple Side overlap my life at the paper."

"But you've been worrying yourself over this Jem, and when she called and said she wanted to speak with you, what could I do?"

"Say I'd call her back?"

"Well, it's too late now as I've given her your address, so pack it up and head home."

"I can't just walk out. I'm in the middle of editing—"

"Jem and I will visit until you get here."

"I'll be there as soon as I can." Even if it means doing a second-rate job on editing this article for tomorrow's edition.

"So are you in the mood for spaghetti or baked chicken?"

Meaning she must have gone grocery shopping. "Neither."

"Then spaghetti it is. Drive safely."

"Grandma!"

"Yes?"

"Do me a favor. From now on, let the answering machine take my calls."

She sighs gruffly. "But what if your father or mother calls?"

I didn't think she cared. "Then if you're moved to do so, pick up."

"All right. I'll see you in a little while."

I flip the cell phone closed and look to the ceiling. "You're not going to make this easy, are You?"

"Talking to God now, are you?"

I swivel around, and there stands Tessie, arms crossed over her chest. "I do that sometimes."

"And I suppose He talks back?"

Curling my fingers into my palms, I'm struck with regret at the rift opening between me and this woman I want to continue looking up to. I don't want to feel resentful or question our friendship. "What's up?"

"I just wanted to tell you 'good work' on the porn guy."

Porn guy? Is that all he is to her? She didn't see his sorrow, his struggle...

"Of course, we'll want to develop this angle further, so keep an eye out for other opportunities to sit in on his lunchtime confessionals."

Bitterness rolls through me. "I'll do that." Maybe.

She turns on her heel.

Should I warn her that Jem's coming to dinner? Wouldn't want her dropping by, as she's fairly visible in the Nashville area with her picture appearing alongside her columns. I teeter before deciding against it. Tessie will probably be here several more hours, and if she does get home early, I can't imagine there's anything that would bring her to my door.

Despite my attempt to wrap up the editing assignment, it's nearly an hour before I head home to what I hope isn't a disaster.

"There's my girl!" Grandma rises from the kitchen table, crosses the living room, and embraces me. "I've been discreet," she rasps into my ear.

How I wish our definitions of *discreet* matched. Returning her embrace, I smile at Jem, where she looks up from a plate of spaghetti. "Hi, Jem."

With an apologetic smile, she adjusts the lacy, long-sleeved top she wears over a burgundy scoop neck. "Hi, Grace."

Grandma leads me forward. "I believe Jem and I have pretty much had our fill, but we'll sit with you. Maybe have a cup of tea. Would you like that, Jem?"

"Yes, thank you."

I take a seat across from Jem, and we stare at each other until I look away from eyes that evidence the strain of tears. "Grandma, where's Woofer?"

She holds the teapot under the tap. "I stuck him in the bathroom. All that dander was making my nose crawl."

At that moment, Woofer gives a pitiful *woo-oof* from the other side of the bathroom door.

"How long has he been in there?"

"Since I got back from my tour of downtown Nashville."

Meaning several hours. And since she probably didn't let him out before locking him away, I start to rise.

"Don't worry, I took the mutt out to do his business—nasty business, that—before putting him away."

Putting him away? Like an old pair of shoes? Poor Woofer. Considering how mopey he's been since Grandma's arrival, it may take a while for him to recover from her visit. I hope he doesn't require therapy.

I spread my napkin on my lap, then spoon spaghetti from the bowl at the center of the table. "Looks good, Grandma."

"It is. Ask Jem."

I glance at her plate, which appears to have been picked at. "Did you like it?"

She nods. "Your grandmother's a good cook."

"Thank you." Grandma sets the teapot on the stove.

I add a breadstick and a scoop of salad—neither of which was in my refrigerator this morning—to my meal.

Grandma comes up behind me and lays a hand on my shoulder. "Don't forget to say grace."

Lord, get me through this evening and I'll…well, I'd appreciate it. Also, while You're at it, would You help Jem with her anorexia? Amen.

Grandma lowers to the chair between Jem and me. "Before you got home, we were talking about anorexia."

What was it she said about being discreet? *Lord, tell me she didn't come right out and say something like, "So, Grace tells me you're anorexic."*

"You do know she's anorexic, don't you?" Feigned surprise jumps off Grandma's face. "Of course, you know. Jem told me she talked to you about it."

I dig my fork into the spaghetti and look to Jem. "How are you doing?"

"Okay." She grimaces. "I'm sorry I cut you off. It was just awkward—not only the anorexia part but the mess up with your hair." She takes a deep breath. "I was embarrassed and sure you regretted our friendship. And you're so nice that I figured you'd feel obligated to keep it up."

I set my fork down. "You were letting me off the hook?"

"That's what I thought, but"—she laughs nervously—"you keep calling. And when I saw you today, I thought you were going to chase me down."

"I considered it but had visions of being arrested for stalking."

This time her laugh is smooth. "I appreciate your friendship. You're a good person, Grace."

I open my mouth to give back the compliment, but the sound of Tessie's car in the driveway reminds me of the reason for my continuing relationship with Jem. Me, a good person? At the moment the best I can say is that I'm a good investigative reporter. And that pinches. I lower my untouched fork.

I glance at Grandma, whose wrinkle-framed eyes speak volumes, then look back at Jem. "I appreciate that."

"You're welcome." She picks up her fork and spools a bite of sauce-drenched spaghetti. "So your grandmother and I were talking about my…eating disorder." She inserts the fork in her mouth, removes it, then chews, and I'm thrilled at the demonstration of her willingness to eat. But it's not that easy. Nothing's that easy.

"We prayed," Grandma says.

They did? My grandmother and a stranger? She's never prayed with me. Sure, when I was young and spent the night with her, she made sure I said a prayer before bed. And of course there's always grace before meals, but she's never prayed *with* me.

Jem smiles sheepishly. "I asked your grandmother to pray with me."

That might be why. "That's great." I wait for her to elaborate on what they talked about regarding her eating disorder, but she returns her attention to her plate. Though the reporter in me itches, I take command of my own fork, and this time the spaghetti makes it to my mouth. The sauce isn't canned, as evidenced by fresh oregano and garlic that send my taste buds into sigh city. "This is good, Grandma. Thank you."

"No trouble." Her smile slips. "Actually, it was some trouble. I had to walk to the grocery store, and my word! The traffic, the humidity, and the cost! I know those health-food grocery stores are pricey, but this was ridiculous."

"I would have been happy to drive, and I'll certainly repay you."

"I'm not complaining, Maizy Grace—"

She catches her breath, I catch mine, and we look to Jem. However, she doesn't appear to have caught Grandma's use of my first name, as her attention is fixed on drawing the tines of her fork through her noodles.

Grandma clears her throat. "The good of it is that you now have a full refrigerator and pantry."

Full? But she walked—

"The better of it is that I didn't have to catch a cab back and throw more good money after bad."

"Then…"

"A nice gentleman offered me a ride. Loaded up the groceries and, when we got here, helped me carry them up the stairs."

I set my fork down with a clatter. "A stranger?"

"We met over melons. He has this interesting way of determining which ones are at their peak. He uses the knuckle of his middle finger. Like this." She knocks on air.

"Grandma! Cantaloupes or not, you don't take rides from strangers."

"Not normally, but I had a good vibe about this William. He's only three years older than me, widowed, and a transplant to the Nashville area. Like me."

I feel lightheaded. "You're not a transplant. You're visiting. For two weeks."

"One never knows." The teapot begins to whistle, and she jumps up. "Anyway, seeing as you're working two jobs now and hardly around—"

I glance at Jem, whose placid face gives me hope that the nugget Grandma just dropped didn't make it through the sieve.

"—William will give me something to do." She pours boiling water into two cups.

That made it through *my* sieve. "You made plans with this William?"

"He promised to show me the sights. No telling how much money I'll save on the tours I was going to take all by my lonesome."

"That's so nice of him," Jem croons.

I sit straighter. "Am I the only sane one here?"

"If so"—Grandma sets her cups on the table—"we're in trouble."

I swallow my *humph* as Jem pushes her plate aside and pulls her tea close. That's all she's going to eat? Of course, I don't know how much she started with, so maybe she ate more than an infant's portion. Deciding to put aside my concern over the Casanova who swept Grandma off her feet, I ask, "Are you sure you ate enough?"

"Oh yes." Jem nods as she lifts her cup. "If I don't ease back into eating, I'll be sick."

I guess that makes sense. "I've been praying for you."

"Thank you." She glances at Grandma, who glances at me. "The more prayers, the better."

"I agree, but…" Here goes. "I've been reading up on eating disorders."

She rakes her teeth over her bottom lip. "I'm handling it. Really."

Stomach protesting as I push away my spaghetti, I assure it that I haven't gone over to the other side and that occasions like this are what microwaves are for. "Jem, I know some people are able to face down a problem like yours without intervention and that prayer can be powerful, but this isn't the first time you've gone through it. Maybe you should give counseling a try."

"I can't."

"Why?"

She puts the cup to her lips and sips through a struggle, which I sense is between hotfooting it out of here and dumping her messy burden at my feet.

A look at Grandma yields raised eyebrows and a staying hand discreetly lifted alongside her cup.

Finally Jem sits back. "Counseling is out. Number one, I can do this without help. Number two, I can't afford it. Although I'm making it on my own, there isn't a lot left over at the end of the week."

I can certainly sympathize. "But you have insurance."

"Yeah, and deductibles and noncovered portions. I simply don't have it." She raises her eyebrows. "And number three, I need my job. If Steeple Side found out…"

A chill goes through me. Then Tessie was right? Steeple Side *has* brainwashed her? Expects prayer alone to get her through? "You think they'd fire you over this?"

"Look, I cause them enough trouble without adding another reason for them to throw their hands up."

"I don't understand."

"Gossiping. Remember I told you my boss asked me to work on it? What I didn't tell you is that she's asked me a half-dozen times and wrote me up the last two times."

"But this is different."

Grandma nods. "Grace is right."

"Maybe, but then there's the matter of my work."

I lean forward. "What about it?"

"I'm slow, can't keep up with my assignments. I try, but…" She shrugs her thin shoulders. "It's the perfectionist in me. And when my fiancé broke up with me last year, it was even worse."

"You were engaged?"

Her eyes moisten. "For a month. I really loved him and he said he loved me, but when his mother refused to accept me, he wouldn't go against her."

"Well!" Grandma puffs up. "Obviously he doesn't have a backbone, so good riddance. Imagine being tied down to a mama's boy. A man is what you want. A man who, though he respects his mother, doesn't allow her to set the tone for his marriage."

I cannot believe I'm hearing this. Cannot believe Jem's *not* hearing this. However, it does hit her, as evidenced by her startled expression. I long to say, *"Listen to her, Jem. She raised such a man who didn't allow his mother to run roughshod over him and the woman he loved,"* but I can't.

"Did your boss write you up for being unable to keep up with your assignments?" I ask.

"No, she's nice about it, but I can tell she's frustrated."

"So you're afraid that if you asked for help—"

"The final straw."

Would Steeple Side decide she's more trouble than she's worth? While I know how Tessie would answer that, I don't believe it, but maybe I'm just naive. Again.

"I think you're wrong. Those are good Christian people." Grandma flicks her gaze to me so I'll know she's not just talking to Jem. "Not perfect, but good. After all, if they didn't care about you, do you think you would have received so many warnings? They're trying to shape you. Trying to bring out your full potential."

Jem's eyes widen. "You think so?"

"I do. As for your eating problem, you're not the only one at Steeple Side who has burdens and"—she regards me again—"secrets."

If she thinks reminding me of my deception is going to shut me up about her diatribe on mama's boys, then she…may be right.

Grandma picks up Jem's left hand and cradles it between her aged palms. "When you're ready to ask for help—whether just for prayer or for counseling—I'm sure Steeple Side will be there for you."

Jem sighs. "Thank you, Mrs. Stewart. And thank you, Grace. I don't know what I'm going to do, but I feel better." She chuckles. "If that makes sense."

Five minutes later she drives down the street. As I turn away, I catch the shifting of Tessie's curtains. I close the door, hoping she won't come knocking.

"Two minutes ought to do it." Grandma sets the microwave to warm my spaghetti, then turns. "That went well."

"Thank you, Grandma. You were very kind to Jem."

She pats her hair. "She's a nice girl. A bit lost and strangely dressed with those tops and that pleated skirt and those striped tights, but nice."

"Yes, she is. I hope she heard what you said and will get some help."

Grandma parks herself in her chair. "If that's what she needs." She picks up her cup. "You know, sometimes prayer *is* all it takes."

"That's what I hear." I sink into the chair beside her, momentarily wrestle with bringing up the matter of the strain between her and Mom and Dad, and lose. Of course, there is another matter that needs to be addressed. "About this William…"

She pats my hand. "Maizy Grace, how old am I?"

"You're…" I frown. "I don't exactly know." Of course, she did say William is three years older.

"Let's keep it that way." She clears her throat. "My point is that I'm old enough to take care of myself. And go on a date if I choose."

"A date? I thought he was just going to show you around Nashville."

"That too."

I am *so* confused. "But you don't date. In fact, you told me you didn't want to waste your last years taking care of some old man… said Grandpa Bert was all the husband you ever needed. And something about being a single-seater plane."

She shakes her head. "That was before I met William. He's very fit, you know."

"I don't know."

"Well, he is. Quite muscled and spry for someone his age."

"And what, exactly, is his age?"

"Eighty-two."

"Aha!" I point a finger at her. "You're seventy-nine."

Her eyes widen, her jaw unhinges, and the microwave dings. With a pursed smile, she says, "That would be your dinner."

For which I no longer have an appetite. Still, I rise and turn toward the microwave. Only to turn back. "In the words of a very concerned grandmother to her granddaughter two years ago, 'no hanky-panky.' Got it?"

For a moment she appears offended, but then a smile that doesn't portend well appears. "Don't you worry about me. This grandmother can hold out far better than her granddaughter did."

I knew it didn't portend well. When Ben and I started dating, Grandma had extracted a promise from me that I would set boundaries. More than any man I had dated, he worried her. Not only was he seven years my senior, but he ranked among Seattle's most eligible bachelors and was known for his high rate of girlfriend turnover.

I had kept my promise. That is, until Ben's proposal—rather, "pre-proposal." With my left hand in his, he stroked my bare ring finger and...asked me to move in with him.

Just move in?

To determine if we were compatible as life partners, he said, then raised my hand and kissed my ring finger.

Though the faint pealing I heard sounded like warning bells, I told myself they were wedding bells. I should have heeded my suspicions.

I nod. "Okay, so I made a mistake—"

"A big mistake."

"A big mistake." I throw my hands wide, as if to size up an exceptional catch. "But that doesn't mean I can't see that you're playing with fire."

"Fire?" She caws like a crow. "As you so lovingly pointed out, I am seventy— Well, I am *somewhat* past my prime. And if that's not enough, my Christian values will keep me in line. And William… He's a Christian too."

I'm still worried. However I am too tired to reason further with her. "It's been a long day, Grandma. Can we talk about this later?"

She snorts and rolls her eyes. "I'm going to bed. I've got a big day ahead of me tomorrow."

Oh, Lord.

THIRTEEN

If I get fired, it's Grandma's fault.

Regardless of what I said, she had insisted on allowing William to show her around Nashville. Thus, I did what any concerned granddaughter would do: called in late. Fiala was not pleased, but it allowed me to meet William before he and Grandma embarked on their tour. He seemed harmless enough and appeared only a little offended when I had him write out his plans for the day so I'd know where Grandma was at all times. As for Grandma, she was definitely offended and, as she allowed William to help her into his baby Hummer, gave me a look that would have melted a teenage me.

When I step from the elevator at Steeple Side, a glance at my watch confirms I'm an hour late. Everyone has settled into their day, and all is quiet—at least until the door of Men's Publications whooshes inward and a young man flies out. Right into my path and into me. I stumble back with a squawk, unable to balance on two-inch heels.

We go down—me on the bottom, Flyboy on top.

"Sorry, sorry, sorry." He scrambles off me, but before he can right himself, he's lifted by Todd Wynde.

"Look what you did." Todd sets the young man on his feet. "You okay, Grace?"

I am flat on my back, one shoe has gone south, my at-knee skirt is no longer at-knee, and my tucked-in blouse is untucked. *So* embarrassing. And soon to be the talk of Steeple Side if those streaming out of the two departments are any indication of how thirsty these people are for something to gab about.

"Grace?"

I catch a glimpse of Fiala's wide-eyed face before accepting the hand that Jack thrusts out to me. "Thanks." Though I could blame the sensation that zips through me on frazzled nerves, I know some of it is from Jack. More than some of it.

He pulls me to standing. "All right?"

Unsteady on my feet, largely due to one side of me aspiring to rise two inches above the other, I smile. "I'll be fine."

He releases me, and none too soon, as the onlookers have begun to murmur.

I smooth my skirt with one hand and work my blouse into my waistband with the other.

"Clear out, people," Jack says. "It was fun while it lasted, but it's over."

Fun? For whom?

As I accept the shoe retrieved by my fellow editorial assistant, the onlookers siphon back into their respective departments.

Jack turns to Todd. "What happened here?"

"Sir"—Flyboy raises a hand—"it was my fault. I was having a little fun with the guys, and it got out of hand."

"He crawled under my desk and tied my shoelaces together," Todd grumps.

Then how did he…? I glance down. Sure enough, he left his shoes behind in his pursuit of the rascal.

"I did it." Flyboy looks momentarily sheepish. "But I'm telling you, it wasn't me who glued your pants to your chair."

As I step into my shoe, Todd crosses his arms over his chest. "Well, I'm the one who coated the inside of your baseball cap with axle grease."

Flyboy lights up again. "That was *you*?"

Jack grunts. "Enough! I want to see both of you in my office."

As Flyboy starts to turn away, Jack says, "I believe you owe Miss Stewart an apology."

"Sorry, Miss Stewart."

I nod. "It was an accident."

He and Todd stalk back into their department.

Now where did my purse land? Unfortunately Jack spots it against the far wall before I do. Unfortunate because some of its contents have spilled out, among them the book that contains the notes I often jot down while perched on a toilet seat.

And it's wide open.

I hurry forward, but my two-inch heels have nothing on Jack's loafers. Of course, the first thing he picks up is my notebook. And to think Tessie believes I have what it takes to be an investigative reporter…

Play it cool. But I don't. The moment I'm within reach, I snatch the notebook from him. "That's personal."

He looks up. "Jem's anorexia is personal?"

"Uh…" I drop down beside him and shove the notebook into my purse, then heap the remaining contents on top. "It was told to me in confidence, so it is personal."

"And you're keeping notes?"

Lie Number Eight is nipping at my heels. Short of blowing my cover, there's no way out. Mind working, I attempt to regulate my breath as I rise.

Jack also straightens, and I feel his gaze attempting to bore through my brain.

I lodge my purse between my arm and side and raise my eyes to his. "Since you expressed an interest in my writing a piece on the soup kitchen experience, I thought I might also write one on eating disorders."

His brow smoothes—a little.

"I know it wasn't solicited, but when Jem told me she's struggling with anorexia, it occurred to me that it might be an issue that impacts nearly as many young people as drugs."

That sounded convincing, and from the further smoothing of his brow, it was to some degree. Though I ought to feel relieved, my conscience kicks in—in spike-heeled boots.

Jack nods slowly. "Is Jem aware that you're taking notes?"

I have to look away. "No. I don't want her to think my concern is based on self-interest. Because it's not."

Look up…into his eyes…hold.

"I really do want to help her." Not a lie. *Please let him see that in my eyes.*

Finally he says, "I'm sorry to hear about Jem. Is she getting help?"

"No. Not only does she think she can handle this on her own but she's also worried about her job."

His face grows troubled. "She's afraid of being sacked?"

"Yes. She's already been written up twice for gossiping and apparently is having trouble turning in her assignments."

He shoves his hands in his pockets. "That has nothing to do with this."

With Lie Number Eight only a vague—albeit unpleasant—memory, I step toward him. "That's what I told her, but she's adamant that she doesn't want or need counseling. I don't know what to do."

"I don't either, but—" He glances left then right. "I think we'd better part ways before we provide more fodder for gossip."

Those in the two departments aren't overly obvious about their interest in our exchange, but they're definitely keeping an eye on us. I step back. "Absolutely."

A corner of his mouth crimps. "Not that I don't like the smell of your perfume."

If my attraction for him were measured by a carnival machine, it would have hit the bell with that comment. Only problem is… "I'm not wearing perfume."

His left eyebrow arches. "Must be your shampoo."

Yep, I was standing *way* too close. I push a lock of semi-Goth hair behind an ear and do an about-face.

Jack heads the opposite direction, but I pause as I put a hand to the door of Women's Publications. "Jack?"

He looks over his shoulder.

"I don't think Jem would want me to share about her…you know…so I'd appreciate it if you don't mention it to her."

"Of course." He pushes through the door of Men's Publications.

I set my shoulders. "Here I come, Fiala." But Linda is the one standing alongside my desk.

Feeling a jolt of "uh-oh" when her unsmiling eyes meet mine, I halt before her. "I'm sorry I called in late."

"Is everything all right?" Automatic response, of course, as she can't possibly have the time or desire to listen to my grandmother woes.

"Yes." Oh, I hope everything's all right. What if William doesn't bring Grandma home? What if he turns out to be a serial killer? What if—?

"Are you sure?" Though Linda's eyes still aren't smiling, they're bearing down on mine with something like concern.

"Er…" I shrug apologetically. "It's my grandmother. She's visiting and…" *Do you know how ridiculous this is going to sound?*

Linda touches my arm. "Is she all right?"

Her concern seems genuine, and in that moment I want her to care for me beyond the paperwork I shuffle and phone calls I field. I want a bit of the shoulder she offered to Fiala in the ladies' room. Still, I'm surprised when out of my mouth comes, "I suppose that depends on how you define 'all right.'"

She nods over her shoulder. "Let's talk in my office."

I'm rushed with gratitude until reality breaks its stride. More than likely, we're back to the reason she was at my desk. Oh no. Have I done something wrong?

Suppressing a groan, I step into her office. Quickly I claim the edge of a chair before her desk, and she surprises me by sitting on its twin two feet away.

"So what's happening with your grandmother?"

Whew. I think. "You really want to know?"

She cracks a smile. "Only if you're comfortable talking about her."

I shouldn't be, but strangely I am. "It's her judgment. She's almost eighty, and she just met this older gentleman in a grocery store and accepted his offer to show her around Nashville. That's why I called in late—to check him out before I let her go off with him."

"And what did you think of him?"

"He seemed nice enough, and he's certainly old enough—in his early eighties. Not one of those younger men who pays an elderly woman attention in order to get his hands on her life savings." I frown. "Of course, maybe that's his M.O. You know, pull them in with an arthritic gait and age-spotted hands and a gravelly, worn-out voice—"

A laugh sounds from Linda, but she claps a hand over it. "Sorry, I don't mean to make light of your concern. It's just the way you said it and the picture that popped to mind."

I can imagine what picture that was, and it is humorous. I make a face. "I'm being ridiculous, aren't I?"

"No. That's part of loving someone—worrying about him and trying to prevent him from making bad decisions." In the next instant, her son is there between us, as evidenced by her moistening eyes.

Don't do it. Don't reach out to her. Not your place. Nuh-uh. She's your boss. Among other things... "I'm sorry about your son." I startle at the words that slip under the radar while I struggle to keep from squeezing her hand. "I've been praying for you...and him." *Enough already!*

She searches my face and I nearly squirm. Not because I haven't prayed for them—I have—but because I admitted to it. It makes me sound like a...well...a committed Christian, which would be good

if not for the circumstances under which I now work at Steeple Side.
It's only a matter of moments before I start squirming like a worm on
a hook. Time to move on. "You, um, were at my desk. Is there something you need to talk to me about?"

She blinks and, a moment later, rises and steps around her desk
to lower into her high-backed chair. "On Jack's recommendation, I'm
giving you the go-ahead on the soup kitchen article."

My heart surges. "Really?"

"Yes, and I'd also like you to start fielding reader feedback—handling the correspondence and making suggestions on letters and
e-mails to be included in the next issue."

Not as exciting as writing a piece, but better than filing and wield-
ing a letter opener. "Thank you. I won't let you down."

"Of course you won't." She reaches for her phone. "You're going to
go far at Steeple Side, Grace. I look forward to watching God's plans
unfold for you."

Ooh. Reality check.

"Do you know what time it is?"

Grandma ignores my question until she waves William out of
the driveway. "It is a quarter to seven."

"That's right. Way past time for grandmothers to be safely home.
What were you thinking? What was he thinking?"

She sashays past me, then creaks down onto the sofa. "I had a
wonderful time. We went here, there, everywhere. Did you know that
the Ryman Auditorium was originally called the Union Gospel Taber-
nacle and that Patsy Cline and Hank Williams performed there?"

I close the door and go to stand over her with arms crossed over my chest. "I didn't know, but did you know that William doesn't answer his cell phone? I called him three times in the last two hours and not one answer."

"That's because he lost his phone at the bar with the bull you can ride."

I gasp. "He took you to a bar?"

"Just to see the bull." She frowns. "Didn't look like a bull. Just this leather-covered thing that bounces up and down and spins around. Honestly, I was expecting something more realistic." She settles back among the cushions. "But it was fun watching those young folks try to hang on."

I flop down beside her. "Do you really think a seventy-nine-year-old woman ought to be visiting bars? And with a stranger?"

"Stop tossing my age in my face, young lady."

I groan. "Tell me you're not going out with him again tomorrow."

"I am. He's going to show me around his retirement community."

I think I liked the bar and bull better.

"It's on a golf course." A smile emerges. "If it's not too hot, we may even play half a round. You know, a dozen holes."

"Grandma, you don't play golf. And half a round is not a dozen holes. It's nine."

She huffs and puffs. "Well, Miss Snooty, since you're not going to be supportive of my attempt to enjoy the little life I have left, I'm not going to speak to you about William."

"Fine." Well, not really, but if she's set on gallivanting around town with a stranger, what can I do short of tying her up while she sleeps? Hmm…

"So how was your day?"

Outside of nearly being exposed as a fraud? "All right."

"How is Jem doing?"

"Good. In fact, she joined me for lunch and ate half a chef salad."
Without dressing, but she did get through some of the meat, egg, and
cheese. I only hope she kept it down.

"Wonderful. Maybe she'll beat this thing on her own."

"Too early to tell."

She sinks into a short-lived silence. "And how is that nice young
man Jack?"

"He's fine."

"For now. Of course, when that article of Tessie's—er, *yours*—
appears in the paper, that will be a different matter."

As if I need reminding.

"Now about this soup kitchen thing we signed up for on Sunday…"

We? I narrow my lids at the sheepish look on her face. "What
about the soup kitchen thing *you* signed *us* up for?"

"There's a special event that William's church is holding on Sunday."

"And?"

"I told William I would go with him. Wasn't that nice of him to
invite me?"

Steeple Side Lies

#1. No real work experience (Mrs. Lucas)

#2. Currently not working anywhere else (Mrs.
Lucas)

#3. Interested in full-time work at Steeple Side (Mrs. Lucas)

#4. Didn't say the *D* word (Jack Prentiss)

#5. Attend Sovereign Church and like the congregation (2 lies in 1—Jack & Linda)

#6. Do freelance editing (Jem)

#7. *DBGC* not mine (Avery)

#8. Notes on Jem's anorexia—article proposal for Steeple Side (Jack)

I switch on the light, fish my notebook out from under the sofa, and flip to the list of lies. Eight strong now—or six if I subtract the two made right. Is it possible to make any others right? Maybe the last one, as I *could* start researching an article on anorexia. Not that I'm likely to write the thing, as my time at Steeple Side is running down; however, just going through the motions is bound to make me feel better about myself. Or will it?

Cultural Christian.

I shove the notebook back under the sofa, and my fingers brush the spine of one of two books I now keep under there. I pull out *The Message* and am struck by a longing to read it. Instead I return the book to its hiding place and switch off the light.

"Oh God, I want to know You better, but now isn't a good time."

FOURTEEN

Hands on hips, I stare at the back end of the Hummer as it pulls away and merges into traffic—and lament my "ploy gone bad." I had tried to get out of working the soup kitchen, even though it meant appearing unreliable.

Awakening before Grandma, I crept to my car and let the air out of a front tire. Of course, I didn't "discover" my car trouble until I was running late for the morning worship service. I groaned at having to pass on the experience of helping the homeless.

To my surprise, Grandma sympathized and didn't appear the least suspicious. Thus, I was up to my neck in self-congratulatory pats on the back when William's arrival forty-five minutes later ushered in an unwelcome solution.

Standing in the doorway, arm looped through that of the elderly gentleman I took a grudging liking to during our official introduction this past Tuesday, sly Grandma gasped. Next thing I knew, William agreed that it would be no trouble to drop me at the soup kitchen on their way to church. And—talk about convenient—about the time I'm finished with my Christian act of service, they will be heading back and can pick me up.

So here I am in the heart of downtown, standing before a massive brick church that was built in the late eighteen hundreds and trying not to fantasize about the café across the street, where it would be so easy to while away a couple of hours.

Determinedly, I focus on the church's carved door, which, doubtless, leads to the sanctuary. The paper taped to it reads: "Soup kitchen volunteers, please use south entrance. Guests, please use north entrance."

I look to the right end of the building, where a line that was two dozen strong when William and Grandma dropped me off has grown by another dozen. And it's a half hour before the mission begins serving.

The homeless men and women come in all shapes and sizes, but even at this distance, there's one thing they appear to have in common: a shabby sense of fashion. Of course, it's not really a sense, as that would mean they made a conscious choice to wear dirty, worn clothes, the scent of which is carried on the breeze—dirt, sweat, decay, and other things less pleasant.

My mouth goes chalky at the realization of what I'm about to do, and I work my tongue around my gums. I really could use something to drink. And I bet that café has just what I need.

You committed to this.

That was Grandma.

You accepted the Steeple Side writing assignment.

But my days there are numbered, so I don't have to impress anyone.

What about Jack?

Yeah, I'm attracted to him, but the only future for us is adversarial. Once that article hits the streets, he's not going to want anything to do with me outside of organizing a lynch mob.

My conscience heaves a sigh. Meaning I've won—

Oh yeah? What about Jem? She said she might join you. If she has the guts to look involuntary hunger in the face, what does that say about you, you big chicken?

I waver.

Lord, You know this isn't my thing. Couldn't I just write a check? I do have two Steeple Side paychecks I haven't deposited...

Unfortunately, the dilemma over Jem, coupled with the realization that I'll have to make up another lie to cover my absence, decides for me. I cross to the south entrance, and my tentative tap is answered by a middle-aged man with a bald head as round as the belly beneath his tightly stretched apron.

"You're here to help in the soup kitchen?"

"That's right." I cross the threshold.

He closes the door, then catches my hand and gives it a shake. "Thank you for agreeing to help the less fortunate."

But I didn't agree. I was manipulated. I follow him across the room to where an elderly woman stands with a clipboard in hand.

"Welcome." She smiles. "Your name?"

"Grace Stewart."

She scans the list. "With Sovereign." *Scritch scratch.* "The others are in the basement cafeteria suiting up to serve, so take the stairs"— she sweeps a hand to indicate the corridor beyond the doorway— "and we'll put you to work."

Aren't people supposed to rest on Sunday? *Deep breath. It's only for a couple of hours. It will soon be over, and you'll have done a good deed.*

"Is this your first time, Miss Stewart?"

I blink at the bald man. "Yes, I've never done anything like this."

He pats my shoulder. "Believe me, it will bless you."

Bless *me*? Maybe the homeless, but not me. All it's going to do is make me a nervous wreck.

"Would you like me to show you the way?" He nods at the stairs.

"I think I can find it on my own."

And I do—down fourteen steps, where I catch the scent of broccoli, down a short corridor rife with the scent of pinto beans, down a long corridor through which the scent of warm rolls wafts, and into an enormous kitchen bustling with activity.

A young woman wearing a hair net and a white apron is at my side in seconds. Pulling her gaze from my ominously dark hair, she says, "I'll bet you're Grace."

I squelch the impulse to tuck my hair behind my ears. "That's me."

"Jack asked me to keep an eye out for you and direct you to the serving line."

I look at the counters where volunteers are preparing food, then to stove tops with huge pots that are tended by yet more volunteers. "The serving line…as in out front?"

"Yes. You'll be serving our guests. But first let's put your purse away and get you a hair net and apron."

As she starts past me, I lay a hand on her arm. "Don't you need help back here?"

"We've got it under control." She smiles. "Besides, Jack says you're writing an article, so you'll want a close look at what the soup kitchen is all about—the hungry."

The ones I'm supposed to write about in such a way that others will be touched by their plight and all the more receptive to reaching out to them. But considering how uncomfortable I am, can I really do the article justice? Will it be as well received as the magazine's other articles are according to the reader feedback I'm now handling?

Recalling an e-mail from a woman whose child was recently diagnosed with autism and who found comfort in an article that celebrated the blessings that children born with mental handicaps pour out on others, my nose tingles. Honestly, some of the letters and e-mails are so moving that I've had to accessorize my desk with a box of tissues. I never would have guessed that issues addressed from a Christian perspective could make such a difference in people's lives.

"Ready?" prompts the young woman in the hair net.

Realizing I've been staring through her, I jerk my chin. "Yes. Uh, lead on."

Though everyone is outfitted in hair nets and aprons, I feel self-conscious when I step from the kitchen and am greeted by Avery and half a dozen others from the singles' Sunday school class. And more so when I catch sight of Jack as he leans back against the counter from which the meal will be served.

He's a guy whose looks greatly benefit from hair. Not that he's unattractive beneath the hair net. He just doesn't rank as high.

He motions me forward. "I saved you a place."

He shouldn't have. I cross to his side and stare at a pan of carrots. Though I like them raw, I can't stand them cooked. Would it be rude to ask if they provide surgical masks for those who are sensitive to odors?

"I was beginning to think you had changed your mind about volunteering…and the article."

Did I ever. "Car trouble." *Not* a lie. Regardless of who let the air out of my tire, it's still car trouble.

"Nothing serious, I hope?"

"Nope." In fact, I'm pretty sure my bicycle pump will get me out of my jam. I peer into Jack's pan. And envy him. "So you get to serve mashed potatoes."

"And gravy." He nods at a smaller pan. "Unless you'd like to trade places?"

I would, but that would mean acknowledging his ability to read me. "I'm good with carrots."

"Sure?"

"Sure."

"You seem uptight."

I give the carrots a stir. "Just a day that didn't start off well."

"Missing church can do that to you."

Was that judgmental? "So will car trouble." Our gazes lock.

"Will you need a ride home?"

For a stupid moment I feel a thrill, but accepting a ride from him would be a bad idea. "No, thank you. Have you seen Jem?"

"No. You're expecting her?"

"I told her about the soup kitchen, and she said she might drop by and help."

He consults his watch. "We serve for two hours, so there's plenty of time for her to show."

Somehow I don't think she will. I look past Jack to the volunteers near the beginning of the food line, then to those near the end. "I thought we would be serving soup, and I don't even see soup."

He chuckles. "Today the entrée is some type of goulash; that's

Avery's baby." He nods at the man to his far right. "Sometimes it is just soup, but when donations are up, the church passes on the blessing." He smiles crookedly. "Hardly gourmet to us, but it's a feast to the men and women who'll come through those doors any minute."

Turns out "any minute" happens to be *this* minute. I don't mean to stare, but when the homeless and hungry stream in, that's all I can do.

"Get ready," Jack says in my ear.

I whip my head around and there he is, almost close enough to kiss. Not that I'm thinking of anything like *that* at a time like *this*.

I avert my eyes, only to avert them again to avoid looking at the masses of homeless people descending upon us, which is the reason their scent—far stronger than what the outside breeze carried—reaches me before their faces.

Oh my.

Once more, Jack's breath warms my ear. "They're looking to you to represent Jesus to them."

Me? What if *I'm* more in need than they?

Get ahold of yourself!

Okay. I can do this—an up-close-and-personal look at the plight of the less fortunate, according to Grandma, who is conspicuously absent. Bless her heart.

I glance down the line to where the homeless are converging upon us. *People just like you. Sort of.* Soon I have my first customer, a greasy old man who, at second glance, isn't that old. Just tired and scruffy. When he passes on Jack's mashed potatoes, Jack pushes his tray across the counter to me.

"Carrots?"

He wrinkles his nose, but as I start to pass his tray to the woman beside me, he says, "Yeah. Good for the eyesight."

Eager to send him on his way—not that the painfully thin, dark-skinned man coming behind him is less daunting—I scoop up a portion of carrots.

He points to his eyes. "Some punk busted my glasses."

"I'm sorry." I deposit the carrots and push the plate on.

The dark-skinned man passes on the carrots but accepts a scoop of corn on a plate so full it ought to hang a No Vacancy sign. He must be really hungry. Of course, this may be the first meal he's had in days. Or longer.

"Jack?"

"Hmm?" He ladles gravy over mashed potatoes.

"What about second helpings? Can they come back if they're still hungry?"

He passes the plate to me. "If there's enough food."

I look to the squat woman whose weight contrasts sharply with the man who came before her. "Carrots?"

She wipes the back of a hand across her dripping nose, leans forward to peer into my pan, and begins to cough. Fortunately, there's an acrylic barrier between her and the food. Unfortunately, if her germs decide to go out and greet the world, I could be their next target.

She waves a hand, and as she trudges to the next offering, I release my breath.

"You all right?"

I nod in Jack's direction. "Um-hmm." Not really, but I *will* get through this.

"It gets easier. Before you know it, you'll be smiling and greeting them."

Is that what he's doing? Have I been so caught up in my adventure in discomfort that I missed what was going on beside me?

Sure enough, he greets the next one in line, a man who wears what appears to have been a very nice business suit. Years ago. Or, on the streets, perhaps months ago.

"I'm good," the man says, "especially now that I've got this fine meal to look forward to. Thanks." He smiles with teeth that seem intact and only moderately yellowed. "I'll take some carrots, miss."

"Certainly." My smile feels only partly fake as I scoop and pass on his plate.

Next in line is a man whose wild tangle of hair sticks out all over, gnarly beard evidences his last meal, and scent threatens my gag reflex. As Jack greets him, I lean down and draw a deep whiff of the steam rising off the carrots. A glorious, if tinny, aroma that offends me no more. So much in life is relative.

And so they come. Some are exactly what one expects a homeless person to be—ragtag, dirty, drunk, high, and emitting odors for which it's best not to ponder the source. Others are less stereotypical. In fact, at first glance, some simply appear to be availing themselves of a free meal. On second glance, I notice frayed hemlines, dirty wrists above hands that have been washed, teeth in need of brushing, and eyes that reflect loss, desperation, and emptiness. Stereotypical or not, nearly all of them clutch their plates like treasures as they make their way to tables set throughout the enormous cafeteria.

"The name's Iris," says a middle-aged woman with a southern drawl.

Ridiculous as it is, I'm jolted at being given a name to go with a face. Of course, they all have names, just like me, but this makes it more personal. And moving.

My throat tightens. "It's nice to meet you, Iris. My name's Grace."

Her eyes sparkle. "A fitting name. Um-hmm. Just right."

No, it isn't, but in that moment I wish it were. "Would you like some carrots, Iris?"

"Oh yes. They look delicious, all nice and orange and piping hot." She sniffs the air. "And do they smell good!"

I draw a breath myself. Yes, they do smell pretty good. I scoop a portion onto her plate.

"Bless you, dear."

I smile. "Why, thank you. And, uh, bless you back."

She looks to the ceiling and shakes her head in wonder. "That God does. Over and over."

But she's homeless.

"Gives me a new day every mornin'. Keeps me safe on them mean streets. Provides rest when I'm tired. Keeps me company. And when I'm hungry and can't handle one more day of garbage can scraps, He goes and puts you here to feed me." She grins. "That's blessed."

I'm feeding her? Strange, but I have a feeling that *she's* feeding *me*.

As she moves on, I notice she does so with a limp. Her bulky sweater, which ought to be too hot for early May, has large holes in it. And her hand, the one with which she taps the glass to indicate she'd also like a serving of corn, is an angry red. A burn? Some kind of rash? Regardless, it looks painful. And yet she smiles at each server and lets them know how blessed she is for their kindness.

How does she do that? How does she thank God for her desperate situation, a situation that makes my problems seem nonexistent?

"Pretty powerful, hmm?" Jack's eyes shine with compassion. Can it be found in my own?

He returns to his mashed potatoes. "It certainly puts things in their proper perspective."

My next customer is a young man who looks perfectly normal until I tune in to the conversation he's having with himself. Actually, an argument. *He* wants carrots, but *he* does not.

"Maybe just a small scoop?" I suggest.

He smiles, then sneers and lunges forward in line.

"Okay." I suppress the longing to rub goose bumps from my flesh.

"Quite a few people with mental disorders on the streets," Jack murmurs.

So grateful for this barrier between us.

Strangely, time whips by, and I'm surprised when the line starts to thin out and my third pan of carrots is nearly empty. Still, the tables remain filled despite the majority of the homeless having finished their meals. My guess is we served at least 250 men and women, many of whom returned for seconds.

I start to relax and reflect on Iris, who blessed me—not only with her words but with an attitude that made God seem much closer. It's as if He really is here. Not just hovering, but in this very place and moving among the destitute.

Vaguely aware of Jack removing his tray of decimated mashed potatoes, I look across the cafeteria and feel loss to discover that Iris is no longer seated at the center table. Nor is she at the beverage station or making her way toward the stairs as some are. Gone. Just like that.

"All gone!"

The growl, which expels a stench of alcohol so strong it makes my eyes burn, comes from a man who stands half as broad as he is tall. He's been through the line twice, but despite my previous exposure to him, he's no less intimidating. Actually, more, when I find Jack conspicuously absent, along with his tray.

I peer up the man's six-and-a-half-foot figure. "It does look like the mashed potatoes are gone. Carrots?"

"Ain't talkin' 'bout 'tatoes." He folds back his lips to reveal his very few teeth. "Talkin' 'bout sugar." He points a grimy finger that comes within inches of my nose, then redirects it over his shoulder. "Them little packets is all gone."

I glance at the young woman who serves the corn. Correction: *was* serving. She has now retreated several steps.

The counter is between you, and it's not as if you're alone with him. In fact, here comes Avery. Still, my heart is pounding so hard that if I don't channel more oxygen to it, I might go down for the count. I fill my lungs. "I'm sorry, sir."

That finger comes across the barrier again. "I need sugar!" Then he's cursing. And though I command my legs to retreat, all I can do is stumble back.

Hands grip my arms and steady me.

"We'll handle it, Grace." Jack eases me aside as he and Avery step forward.

I need air. On trembling legs I pass through the kitchen, acknowledging the others with a forced smile. Then it's down the corridors I passed through earlier, up the stairs, and out a door marked Exit.

It's an exit all right, but not the one I had in mind. Nor the air I had in mind. Faced with a shadow-entrenched alley and Dumpsters on either side, overpowered by the brutal scent of refuse that once more threatens my gag reflex, I reach behind to the door—as it clicks closed. And locks.

FIFTEEN

I lift a hand and rap once…twice…three times.

Nothing.

I rap louder.

Still nothing.

Calm down. It's an alley. There's a way out. Therefore, a way in. Meaning I may not be alone. I peer at the overflowing Dumpsters. Outside of possibly carrying the seeds of plague, they appear harmless. Of course, what lies beyond…

I step forward and crane my neck to see on either side of the huge trash bins. More alley stretches toward light at both ends, more Dumpsters, but no movement other than birds that would have to be starving to look for a meal in this place.

As the alley to the left appears shorter, I turn in that direction but halt when I hear a sound from the far side of the nearest bin. I do an about-face, dive for the door, and begin pounding.

The door opens. I jump back to avoid having my teeth knocked out, then lurch forward into a solid chest.

"What happened, Grace?"

"I got locked out," I mumble into Jack's shoulder. "There's someone out there."

He lifts an arm from me and pushes the door open. "I see a dog."

Gripping his shirt, I look over my shoulder. It is a dog. Something knee high, fluffy, and apparently well fed and a little put out if his turn-tail-and-saunter attitude is anything to go by.

Jack draws me back inside and the door closes. I know I should let go of him, but I don't. Won't. Can't. And he doesn't make me.

"I'm guessing you needed some fresh air." His breath is warm against my scalp.

"That was the idea." Continuing to hold his shirt, I close my eyes and breathe in his citrus-y scent.

"Let's get you some."

"Where?"

"There's a café across the street from the church."

A good choice, as Grandma said she and William would pick me up in front of the church. From there I'll be able to keep an eye out for them. "Okay."

He drops his arms from me, but I wish he wouldn't. "If you want to get your purse, we can leave."

I let go of him. "All right."

"I'll see you at the side entrance." He nods at the doorway to the room I came through this morning.

A few minutes later, hair net and apron shed, I cross the street alongside Jack. As it's well past the lunch hour, the tables outside are vacant, and Jack chooses one near a large window that provides a view into the establishment. Three employees are gabbing behind a glass case that offers a selection of breads, pastries, salads, and sandwiches. But I'm not hungry, even though it's been hours since I ate breakfast.

Jack pulls out a chair and gestures for me to sit. "Just something to drink?"

"How did you know?"

"It's not unusual for one's appetite to diminish after serving in a soup kitchen." He places his palms on the table and leans in. "Some say it's a result of being inundated by the smell of food, others that it's the sight and smell of destitution. But I hold with those who believe it's more a subconscious awakening of what real hunger is." He straightens. "So what can I get you?"

"Iced tea, please."

He returns with two iced teas, sets one in front of me, and settles in the chair beside mine. While I should be dismayed that he chose to sit beside me rather than across the table, I silently welcome his proximity, which makes me feel safe.

We sip in silence, watching the flux of traffic less than fifteen feet away, until he pushes his tea aside.

"I'm sorry your experience took an untoward turn." Jack's British accent seems more pronounced than usual. Or perhaps it's more his choice of words. "He frightened you."

"The man has a rather aggressive sweet tooth."

"It's more of an addiction. If you watch, you'll see that some of those who come for a meal are also looking for a temporary high to hold them over until their next fix. That's where the sugar comes in. I've seen them dump twenty or more packets in their coffee, while others eat it straight up."

I grimace. "Well, at least now I know why he was so upset...nothing personal."

With his straw, Jack attempts to maneuver a wedge of lemon up through his iced tea. "You might want to incorporate the incident into your piece for the magazine."

"I hadn't thought of that." In fact, I'd forgotten about the piece. Not the mark of a good reporter. Maybe my boss at the Seattle paper was right. Maybe I don't have what it takes. Maybe I'm strictly a fluff writer who, according to Tessie, covers "none of the news fit to print." But what about her encouragement all these years? If *she* believes in me, there must be something to it.

Jack clears his throat, and I look up to find him smiling. With yellow teeth.

I do a double take, but the lemon rind remains firmly wedged between his lips. And I have to laugh at this juvenile version of Jack Prentiss. A laugh that ends on a purr. Eyebrows arching, Jack stares at me.

Lest the kitty cat put in another appearance, I press my lips inward and look down. However when I return my gaze to Jack and his yellow smile, my mouth twitches anew, and the hum in my chest starts up again. I clear my throat. "What are you doing?"

He pops out the lemon and runs his tongue over his front teeth. "Making you purr."

Cheeks threatening to go up in flames, I struggle for composure. But in the end, I laugh again—this time sans purr. Thank goodness.

Jack laughs with me, and I find myself fascinated by the curve of his mouth, the show of his teeth, the roll of his tongue...

He draws a deep breath. "Better?"

"What do you mean?"

"You were in dire need of comic relief."

I eye the lemon wedge. "You know, you British aren't supposed to do stuff like that. You're supposed to be sophisticated, uptight, and snooty...*not* turning lemon wedges into dentures."

He makes a face. "Stereotyper." Then he takes a bite of the lemon, rind and all.

"Ew!" I shudder at the imagined bitterness. "And you eat them too?"

"I do."

"And here I thought it was cologne that made you smell so citrus-y."

His face stills, only to be splashed with a broad smile. "Why, Grace, have you been smelling me?"

Warmth suffuses me, and I grip my glass of iced tea and will the chill beneath my palm to reverse the effects of this man. "Of course, I wasn't smelling you. At least not intentionally. You know, we *have* been in close proximity a time or two."

His expression turns almost serious. "Which is how I know that you prefer the scent of vanilla."

My shampoo, as he guessed last Tuesday when he helped me up after Flyboy knocked me down. And I thought I was warm before.

He leans near. "In case there's any question as to what's happening here, I'm chatting you up."

I blink. "Doing what?"

He grins. "Flirting."

Tongue stuck to the roof of my mouth, I look into his eyes. Nice eyes, especially with those flecks of gold amid green. Nice lashes, short but thick and dark. And the skin of his jaw isn't as rough as I first thought. In fact, the light scarring lends an air of mystery that tempts my fingers from around my glass—

I sit back and, at the risk of shattering the glass, lock my fingers in place.

Jack sighs. "For a moment there, I thought I had you."

"What?"

"I thought you might be as honest with me as I was with you."

Honesty is hardly your strong suit, Maizy Grace Stewart. Not under my present circumstances. Nor my future, meaning it would be a very bad idea to accept an invitation to play in Jack Prentiss's sandbox. "I'm flattered, but I'm not in the market for a relationship."

His face washes clean of emotion. "In the market?"

That *did* sound cold. "What I mean is that the last relationship I was in ended badly. So I'm...cooling my heels."

Emotion creeps around the edges of his face, opening a way for understanding. "How badly did he burn you?"

Out of one frying pan and into another. "A minimum of second-degree burns." And if I don't kick this attraction for Jack, I might be looking at third degree. "Well, if you need to get going, don't let me keep you. My grandmother and her...gentleman friend ought to be here at any moment." Actually, fifteen minutes ago. Where are they?

"I'm in no hurry."

Great. But we're certainly not going to talk about me. "I hoped Jem would show."

Jack's brow ripples, but he settles into the change of topic and sits back. "You thought it might make her appreciate true hunger—of the involuntary sort. Make her grateful for the food opportunities she's passing on."

"Something like that. But the good news is, she does appear to be eating more. At least, when we lunch together."

He nods. "I checked with Human Resources to see what help is available."

"You did?"

At my widening eyes he holds up a hand. "I didn't name names. Just a casual inquiry."

"What did you find out?"

"If Jem is willing, her insurance covers a program for eating disorders, and Steeple Side will help her with any deductibles or uncovered portions she can't meet."

More good news. Maybe. "You don't think she'll lose her job?"

"Steeple Side isn't like that. If she gets sacked, it won't be over this. In fact, by being open about her problem, any shortcomings with regards to her work will likely be overlooked. After all, a starving person can hardly be expected to work at optimum level."

Some of the weight on my shoulders eases, and I realize how much I've come to care for Jem. Foreboding creeps through me. It may be the Christian thing to do, but such feelings have no place in the career of an investigative reporter. Tessie's right. I'm getting too close. Again.

I consider my glass and note that the ice cubes are half the size they were a short while ago, which is the reason the tea has turned so pale. I can relate, as my dream of being something more than a lifestyle writer is beginning to feel diluted by the bonds I have no business forming at Steeple Side.

When I look at Jack, he's watching me. "Thanks for checking with Human Resources. I don't know what I'll do with the information, but it's good to know."

He inclines his head and reaches toward my glass. "Refill?"

"That would be nice."

As he rises with both glasses, I add, "No ice for me."

"Then you'd like a hot tea."

"No, an iced—" Of course iced tea needs ice, especially when it's freshly brewed and strong. "Never mind." I wave a hand. "I'm just distracted."

He grins. "My fault then." Before I can correct his assumption, he pulls open the café door and disappears inside. When he reappears, his exit coincides with the entrance of a man built like a quarterback. Jack holds the door for him, but as the other man starts past, Jack says, "Ron?"

The man halts. "Jack Prentiss?"

"That's right."

Ron gives Jack's shoulder a whack. "I haven't seen you in years."

"It has been years."

"Your girlfriend...uh...Beth?"

Jack's smile slips slightly, and though he doesn't look at me, I have the feeling he's very much aware of my presence. "Bette."

"Right." Ron pushes his hands into his pockets. "I was sorry to hear that the two of you broke up and you moved out."

I'm surprised. Not judgmental, just surprised. I moved in with Ben despite pangs of conscience, but I would never have guessed Jack had done the same, especially considering his position at Steeple Side. Of course, Ron said it's been years since he last saw Jack.

Ron snaps his fingers. "You were engaged, weren't you?"

"We were." Jack still doesn't look at me. "In fact, we've been engaged a couple of times since."

"Can't get enough of each other, hmm?" A suggestive smile is in his voice. "So what's it now? On or off?"

"I believe my colleagues call it *disengaged*." Jack looks at me. "In fact, this is one of them."

Ron whips around, and his expression falters.

No doubt, he was expecting a *male* co-worker. I lift a hand. "Hi."

He turns back to Jack. Though I know I'm not meant to hear his words, the lull in traffic lets them slip through. "Hope I didn't mess up anything for you, Jack."

"As I said, Grace is a colleague. Let me introduce you."

The two men stride to the table, and a moment later my hand is swallowed by Ron's beefy one. "Nice to meet you." He gives me a sizing-up look. I'd be offended if Jack hadn't told him I'm just a "colleague." No fault of Ron's that it wasn't mentioned I'm also a recipient of his flirtations.

"Nice to meet you." I pull my hand free.

Ron nods his buzz-cut head in Jack's direction. "We go back a ways. We were neighbors when he and…"

"Bette." Jack's eyes seek and find mine as he sets the iced teas on the table.

"Right. When they lived in the complex on Hillsboro. Years ago."

I smile.

"I'll let you get back to your co-worker chat." Ron heads for the door. "Got to pick up a loaf of bread to take to my folks for Sunday dinner."

"Nice seeing you again, Ron." Jack takes his seat. "I should explain—"

"Hey, Jack!" Ron turns back around. "Can I talk to you?"

With a sigh, Jack rises. "Sure."

A minute later a business card lands in front of me. "I told Ron I had it straight from you that you aren't interested in a relationship, but he insisted that I pass that on." Jack takes his seat. "He said he felt an instant connection and thought you did too."

I have no reason to be embarrassed, but I am. I pick up the card. "Jeffers and Sons Engineering, Ronald Jeffers III, Senior Engineer."

"Single and successful. A good combination."

My knee-jerk response is to assure him that I have no intention of calling Mr. Jeffers the third, but Jack might think it's because I'm interested in *him.* I drop the card in my purse and lift my glass. Refreshingly cold tea slips down my throat, and I have to concede the importance of ice cubes—just as Steeple Side is important to my career. Not the bonds with its employees that I need to break, but the story I'm being paid for.

"I should explain about Bette and me."

And I should be thrilled, as Tessie will be when she learns of this latest development. Jack Prentiss, head of Men's Publications and the one she believes is responsible for pulling the story of Steeple Side's hypocrisy out from under her, has exposed his back. And she's not above shooting him—and Steeple Side—between the shoulder blades.

But are you? Because you're the one providing the ammo. More, that article you're being paid to write places your *finger firmly on the trigger.*

"I met Bette in Memphis shortly after I came to the States." Jack sticks his voice in the middle of my muddle.

"No!" I throw a hand up. "You don't have to explain." And I mean it. After all, Ron's just a guy Jack knew years ago. Hardly reliable. And he only alluded to something that I may have interpreted wrong. Hardly verifiable.

Except for that business card, Miss Investigative Reporter. As for that other voice that's questioning what you have no reason to question, you've heard it all before. Remember Seattle?

Jack leans in. "If I don't explain, there will be questions and wrong answers running around your head, so I prefer to set them straight now rather than later."

I shake my head. "What's between you and Bette is none of my business."

He raises his eyebrows. "If you're forming an opinion of me based on what Ron said, it is something of your business. After all, you signed a code of conduct just as I did in order to represent Steeple Side and its beliefs. And those beliefs don't include an unmarried couple living together."

You heard him. But he wouldn't be telling me this if he knew what I'm doing at Steeple Side. *Exactly. So what about "investigative reporting" don't you understand? Of course, if you can't hack it, there's always lifestyle reporting. If they'll still have you after you trash this assignment. And they won't, not even part time. No one will.*

I feel like one of those toy poppers turned inside out—on the edge of popping sky high, after which the only place to go is down.

"Grace?" Jack's fingers lightly graze the hand that grips my glass. "Are you all right?"

Far from it, especially with him touching me. "I guess I'm still a bit shaken by my soup kitchen experience."

"That's all it is?"

Am I that transparent? "I—"

"Hey!" Ron exits the café carrying a handled paper bag. "Keep in touch!"

"You too, Ron."

The man grins at me, then raises an imaginary phone and mouths, "Call me."

As Ron strides down the sidewalk, Jack takes a drink of his tea, then clasps his hands in front of the glass. "I met Bette when I moved to Memphis eight years ago to accept my first management position in publishing. As my grandmother lives there—my mother's an American—I had a place to stay until I found something more permanent. Bette lived with her parents next door to my grandmother, and as shallow as you're going to think I am, it was something like love at first meeting. Bette was different from most of the British women I dated. Very…well, American. And then there was that drawl of hers." He smiles. "Soft and lingering and musical and more feminine than any woman's voice I had ever heard."

I wish mine could be described in such glowing terms. Unfortunately the best I can hope for is that if I remain in the South, some of the "southern belle" drawl will rub off on my lips.

"Of course, she's also gorgeous," he continues.

Remembering how Bette looked at the Mule Day event, I nod. I may be attractive in my own right (pre-Elvira, of course), but no matter how long I remain in the South, no one is ever going to describe me as gorgeous.

"And when I learned that she also attended my grandmother's church, I was done in. Bette wasn't eager to rush into marriage, or we probably would have wed that first year. Instead we dated two years before she agreed to marry me. A month after our engagement, I was handed the opportunity to work at Steeple Side. It meant less money, something of a demotion, but room for advancement in a Christian publishing company."

He cups his perspiring glass. "Bette wasn't happy when I told her it would be best if she remained in Memphis and worked on the wedding arrangements while I settled into the new job. You see, Nashville was always her dream, but her pursuit of a singing career meant she couldn't afford a place of her own. And I certainly couldn't afford two places." His gaze lowers to my glass. "Your ice cubes are staging a coup."

I sip the paling tea.

"Two months later she came to stay. I tried to send her home, but she was determined to take her singing career to the next level. So I allowed myself to be convinced that, as we had every intention of marrying, there was no reason we should pay for two places we couldn't afford." He smiles wryly. "My good intentions to keep our relationship platonic lasted a week."

Emotion streaks through me, pausing only long enough to flash its jealous face. I clear my throat. "What about Steeple Side?"

"They didn't know. Though I told Bette we should marry without the elaborate ceremony, she insisted we wait. So for several months we lived together as husband and wife, and I drifted further from my beliefs. Until the day I walked out."

"*You* walked out?"

This smile is less tight than the other. "You've heard about our series of disengagements."

"I have."

"I didn't break it off with Bette. I just told her that we needed to be apart until the rings were in place. She didn't agree and ended our first engagement."

"Then Steeple Side never found out that the two of you lived together?"

"No, I told them."

"Why?"

"I'm ashamed to admit it, but the offer of the managing editor position six months later prompted me to make a clean breast of my break with the code of conduct. I had my sights set on the job, but I couldn't accept it without alerting the company to the baggage I brought with me, which would reflect poorly on Steeple Side if it became public knowledge."

Which is what Tessie is aiming for. I nibble my lower lip. "And yet they still awarded you the job."

"After withdrawing the offer and months of reconsideration." He shakes his head. "They should have fired me, but I was shown grace."

Would they show me as much? No. Jack made a mistake, but he recognized it and did something about it. Me? If it's true that the public has a right to know about the shortcomings of a company that presumes to tell them how to live the Christian life—and why wouldn't they?—then what I'm doing isn't a mistake. Even if it feels like one.

"That's great. And you and Bette haven't…?"

"No. Despite our on-again, off-again, we've maintained separate residences since."

"At least until you take the plunge."

Jack frowns. "I told you, this disengagement is final."

"People change their minds."

"No. Bette and I aren't as compatible as I thought. The lifestyle she seeks is different from what I'm after. As for her faith, it's more at her convenience than God's."

"Are you saying she's a cultural Christian?" Wow. That rolled right off my tongue. As if I know what I'm talking about. Of course, maybe I do.

"Believing merely because it's expected? I don't think so. Living a Christian life is just hard for her. Not that it's easy for any of us."

Maizy Grace Stewart, case in point.

"Believe me, there have been times when I've questioned God." His eyes begin to lose their focus, as if a memory has taken the place of my face. "Times when I wanted to turn away and get on with my life."

When he doesn't elaborate, I whisper, "Like when?"

"When my father died. All those years as I was growing up in England, he rejected my mother's faith; however, once I became an adult, our discussions often turned to God. Just when it looked as if he was beginning to believe, he passed away. I nearly had a falling out with God over that."

Is this the reason Jack's taken an interest in my faith? "I'm sorry."

His eyes refocus on me. "I don't know why I'm telling you all this."

"Maybe because I asked?"

He settles back in his chair. "Well, now that I've bared a bit of my soul, tell me something about yourself."

What I want to know is: where is Grandma? "Like what?"

"Your parents. Are they living?"

"Yes."

"In the Nashville area?"

"No."

He raises his eyebrows. "Where?"

"Seattle." Maybe I shouldn't have volunteered that.

"And that's where you lived before Nashville?"

"Yes."

A corner of his mouth hitches. "This feels more like an interrogation than a conversation."

"Sorry." I glance at my watch. Where *is* she?

"What brought you to Nashville?"

A job. No, better not.

"Were you running from your second-degree-burn boyfriend?"

There was that too. "I needed a change of scenery."

"Where did you work before Steeple Side?"

Lie Number Nine alert! And it even comes with a blaring horn.

"I suppose that's your ride."

"What?" I follow Jack's gaze across the street to the Hummer drawing up in front of the church. William is waving at us, and so is Grandma as she leans over him.

I jump up so fast my thighs hit the table edge, nearly causing the glasses to upend. "That's my Grandma and her gentleman friend."

To my chagrin, Jack joins me at the curb. When the traffic clears, he walks me across the street.

"Sorry we're late," Grandma says as Jack opens the door for me. "The program lasted longer than expected; then we got stuck in traffic." She peers into the backseat as I slide in. "But we're here now." She cranes her neck further and smiles at Jack. "Thank you for keeping my granddaughter company."

"A pleasure, Mrs. Stewart." I feel his eyes on me. "We used the time to become better acquainted."

Grandma "oohs," and I could just pinch her. "Isn't that nice?" She winks at William. "Don't you think that's nice, William?"

He nods. "If I had a single granddaughter, I'd be pleased."

I could pinch them both. I look at Jack. "I guess I'll see you at work tomorrow."

Jack starts to close the door but sticks his head back in. "If you're not too wrung out, you may want to get a start on that article."

"The one on Steeple Side?" Grandma asks innocently. At least, it appears that way.

Clenching my teeth, I push a smile past lips that feel as if they might fall off my face. "No, Grandma. The article *for* Steeple Side. You remember…about the soup kitchen? The reason you dropped me here earlier."

Her lids fly wide, and the alarm in her eyes seems genuine. "That's right. The soup kitchen. Silly me." At least the smile she turns toward Jack seems more real than mine feels. "Don't worry about Grace. She won't let you down."

Won't I?

"Good. I'll see you tomorrow."

I don't have the nerve to look as he closes the door. And twice on the way home, I nearly ask William to pull over so I can be sick. Unfortunately, it gets worse when I discover what's waiting for us when we walk through the door.

SIXTEEN

"Ha! Told you so." Grandma turns her back on the answering machine, which in addition to delivering a message from Jem, who apologized for not making it to the soup kitchen, unloaded a frantic message from Dad. "They don't love me. Which is why I'm leaving everything to you when I pass through those pearly gates."

I step in front of her. "You didn't tell Dad and Mom you were flying out to visit me?"

"No." She crosses her arms over her chest. "And look how long it took them to notice I was gone. Nine days. Why, I could have gasped my last breath and the only thing to bring it to their notice would be the stench."

"Now, Grandma—"

"It's true!" Her eyes sparkle with tears.

Letting go of my frustration, I put an arm around her. "I love you." It's all I can say; I know she doesn't want to hear that her son loves her. Not that he doesn't. Dad has not-so-simply chosen his wife over his mother, refusing to be a mama's boy. As for defending Mom's feelings for her mother-in-law, that would involve lying.

Grandma snuffles into my shoulder. "I ought to just stay in Nashville."

What?

"Nothing left in Seattle now that you're gone and Edith is going. Yes, maybe I will stay. Perhaps move in with you."

Over her shoulder, I catch sight of Woofer peering around the sofa, and—I declare!—he looks like I feel. Grandma's visit has been hard on him. When she's here and I'm not, he's locked away. Once I get home, he stays as far from her as possible, which often means watching me from a distance. Short walks to relieve himself and curling up against me at night is about as good as it gets for him.

Grandma pulls back. "I suppose I should phone your father before he files a missing persons report."

"Good idea." A whine from the front door reminds me of Woofer's need to get personal with a bush. I start toward him. Though normally his floppy ears perk and his stub tail ticktocks, he stares at me with as close to a frown as a dog can come. My poor puffy boy—

Well, not anymore. Despite his earlier enthusiasm for a higher grade of dog food, he's lost a couple of pounds, which is significant for a small dog.

Remembering my incapacitated car, I hold up a finger. "Just a minute, Woof."

As I rummage through the coat closet in search of my bicycle pump, Grandma punches in my parents' number. "Oh. Lily."

I wince at the disappointment in her voice.

"Is Sam there? He's not? Yes, I'm fine. Here in Nashville with Maizy Grace. For nine days now."

Poor Mom. Although she doesn't care for Grandma any more than Grandma cares for her, she tries. To a point.

"Why?" Grandma sniffs. "Because I'm a lonely old woman, that's why."

Where is that pump? I dig deeper and wrap my fingers around a thick tube.

"Yes, I fly home this Friday."

Then her talk of moving in with me was a bunch of hot air. Whew! Clutching my trusty old bicycle pump, I cross to Woofer.

"Unless I decide to stay awhile longer. And I might. Perhaps indefinitely."

Hoping she's just pushing Mom's buttons—not that I condone it—I wave a hand to catch her eye.

"One moment, Lily." Grandma raises her eyebrows at me.

"Tell Mom I'll call her tonight."

"Maizy Grace will call you tonight."

I open the door, and Woofer darts out in front of me.

"Why would I want to move to Nashville?" Grandma harrumphs. "Well, that's pretty obvious considering my absence has only now been noted."

Wishing my dad were home so he could deal with her, I close the door.

Five minutes later, with Woofer sniffing out a bush worthy of his attention, I place my feet on the pegs of the pump and start pumping. But when the first bead of sweat breaks loose on my brow, I have yet to see any change in the slumped tire. So I pump harder, causing my dark hair to swing and my chest to send up an SOS for a bra better suited to vigorous bouncing.

Yes! The tire is inflating. Slowly, but definitely inflating.

Woofer trots over to investigate the recipient of my efforts, then lifts his leg.

"No!"

He looks up but continues, which is odd, as he's usually quick to respond to correction.

"Stop it, Woof! Can't you see I'm working here?"

I do believe he's staring me down. Has some rebellious hormone kicked in? Not that he doesn't have a right to be upset over the situation, but I can't handle any more drama right now.

All tires—er, peg legs—once more on the ground, he moves away.

"That's disgusting."

At the back of the car, he turns to me. For a moment I sense he's tempted to give the rear tire the same treatment, but he drops and spreads.

I glare at him. "All out?" I resume my pumping. Ten minutes later, the tire's still a long way from full inflation, and I investigate the pump. Which doesn't say much for my investigative ability, especially when I discover that the hose is cracked.

Clothes clinging, moist hair hanging down around my face, I seat myself on the driveway and stare at the tire. No one's fault but my own. Still, it would be nice to have someone to commiserate with. I view Woofer, but he doesn't even lift his head. Fortunately the tire should be inflated enough to limp me to the nearest gas station.

I push to my feet and cross to the garbage can outside Tessie's back door. In goes the pump. Out comes Tessie.

Lugging an engorged garbage bag, she pauses outside her doorway and looks me up and down. "Rough day?"

"That obvious?"

She steps forward, and I hold the lid as she tosses her bag in. "Guess you won't be working another soup kitchen anytime soon, hmm?"

That definitely contributed to my rough day, but I don't want to bore her with the other contributors—my self-inflicted flat tire, Grandma running away from home, and Woofer's bad attitude.

"It was an eyeopener." The first memories to rise are those of the angry man who was looking for a sugar fix and my time in the alley, but they're overwritten by the worn-out woman with the drawl and unwavering faith despite her circumstances.

"There were so many people. Dirty and sad and lonely and scared and hungry. Who knows where their next meal will come from?"

Tessie folds her arms over her chest. "True, though I'm sure some are more concerned about their next fix."

I can't argue that. Still, I'm shot through with a need to defend them. "There was this homeless woman named Iris who had the most incredible attitude. You'd never know it to look at her, but she's blessed."

Tessie scowls.

"Her sweater was barely holding together, and she had what looks like a bad rash on one hand, yet she went on and on about how God is good to her and how He keeps her safe. It really puts things in their proper perspective." Jack's words, not mine.

Tessie's hand slices the space between us. "I'm happy for her. But tell me: how's your investigation shaping up?"

I stare at her, missing the Tessie I knew before Steeple Side. Why is *my* story so important when she has plenty to occupy her? It goes beyond being thwarted when she attempted to throw the curtain wide on Steeple Side years earlier. It must have something to do with her loss of faith.

She steps nearer. "Have you got anything new? It's been almost a week since you updated me."

There have been several additions to my findings since, not the least of which is the revelation about Jack and Bette. The day gets rougher yet.

"What is it?" She smiles. "Something juicy?"

Me and my face. "Not really. Just gossip here and there."

"Like?"

"Some intern was let go when it came out that she had paid some-one to write her college papers."

Tessie's enthusiasm falters. "Intern? What else?"

"The marketing director was detained for a week in a third-world country for smuggling Bibles while vacationing."

Disgust bounds from her throat. "We're not looking for things that martyr Steeple Side's employees. We're looking to discredit them. What about the porn guy? Have you listened in on any more of his conversations?"

"No." She doesn't need to know that the last time I was in the cafeteria at the same time as the two men, I had the beginnings of a headache and opted for a table as far from them as possible.

"And the woman whose husband has a gambling addiction?"

Fiala. "She's still trying to convince him to get help."

"No talk of divorce?"

"Not that I've heard."

Tessie blows out a breath. "Anything on Jack Prentiss?"

In danger of blanching, I turn to the only distraction I can think of. "Over here, Woof!"

He doesn't have the decency to acknowledge me—just lays there.

"Jack Prentiss." I look back at Tessie. "What can I say?" How about nothing?

How about your job? You know, the one with the paycheck you cashed to make good on your bills? The one that will continue to pay those bills if you prove yourself? Well, Miss Investigative Reporter, this is it. This is what they're looking for. In fact, it might be enough to wrap up the assignment. Enough to write your piece and get out of Steeple Side for good.

"Are you not telling me something?" Tessie's drawl is tainted with suspicion.

Must buy time. "It's just that I've yet to run across a person who has anything bad to say about Jack. He's well liked." Not a lie.

"So you have nothing for me?"

For *her.* "I'm working on it."

"And being paid for it, don't forget. Or that I stuck out my neck to give you this chance, and if the ax falls, it's likely to take off my head as well."

Doesn't the Bible frown on indebtedness? This must be one of the reasons. "I won't forget."

"Good. Now I've got a piece to finish writing." She pivots and then disappears inside her house.

"Come on, Woof." I pat my thigh.

He pries himself from the ground, follows me up the stairs, and refuses to go farther. So I scoop him up and close the door behind me before depositing him on the living room carpet.

"How did it go?" I look to Grandma, who sits with her hands folded in her lap and her bottom lip tucked over the top one. "You didn't get into it with Mom, did you?"

That lower lip remains locked in place, even as a tear falls.

"Oh no." I drop down beside her, pull her in, and squeeze.

A shudder goes through her. "She said I needlessly worried your father, conveniently forgetting that it took him nine days to discover there was anything worth worrying about." She heaves a deep breath. "That woman will be the death of me. And my son. No matter how hard I pray, she refuses to let go of my boy."

The hand I pat her shoulder with freezes. I can't believe she said that.

Eyes glittering, Grandma pulls out of my arms and throws her hands up. "For someone who doesn't believe in God, she certainly believes in the sanctity of marriage."

Clearly she's been praying for divorce all these years, and that hurts. "Grandma—"

"I prayed for a godly woman for my son, and what did he end up with? Someone who stole his faith and denied his daughters a proper upbringing in our faith."

I'm trembling. Part anger. Part ache. "We're her daughters too, Grandma. We wouldn't exist without her. Is that what you'd prefer?"

She jerks. "That's not what I meant."

"That's how it sounds. I know you don't like my mother, but she's my mom. A good mom. And I love her. As for a proper upbringing in your faith, what would that be?" *Don't do it.* "One that makes a person wish bad on those she's supposed to love? That sets an example that causes those outside the faith to turn away?"

She blinks as if a blinding light has been shined on her.

You've said more than enough. I know, but the spring in me that's been compressed for so long has popped. "Mom may not be the daughter-in-law you envisioned, but when it came to choosing her, Dad proved he had a backbone. Which is what you told Jem she needed—a man with a backbone, who wouldn't allow his mother to run his life."

She seems to be adjusting to the light, as evidenced by a decrease in the fluttering of her lids.

This would be a good place to stop. "Did you ever consider that maybe the reason Mom never investigated Dad's faith and didn't encourage him to continue growing in it was because of how you represented it to her?"

She gasps, and what may have been the beginning of remorse does an about-face. Firming her trembling mouth, she narrows her gaze. "Maizy Grace Stewart, you wound me." She pokes her chest. "Your grandmother, a woman who has only ever wanted what's best for her son and granddaughters."

You're already in up to your neck. What's a little more? "Mom is what's best for us."

"Not if she stands between you and salvation."

Practically over your head. I push up off the sofa. "Have you ever thought that Mom might not be the problem?"

"Are you saying I am?"

That's water coming up your nose, in case you're wondering. "I'm saying that your behavior toward Mom has made your faith seem shallow and uninviting. You say you believe in Jesus's teachings, but she sees little evidence of it. Yes, you go to church. Yes, you read your

Bible. Yes, you pray every night. But there has to be more to it." I shake my head. "Even *I* know that."

In a trice she's on her feet. "And how do you know that? From attending one Christian summer camp as a teen and saying—*saying!*—Jesus is your Savior?"

Her dart lands to the right of the center of my conscience.

"Or maybe you learned it from that *Dumb Blonde's Guide to Christianity* that you sneak around."

This dart lands slightly left.

"Perhaps you learned it from those nice folks at Steeple Side. The ones who are in for quite a surprise when they find out you've been spying on them."

Right on the line.

"Of course, you have started attending church...for appearances' sake."

Bull's-eye.

Well, that about seals it for this being among my roughest days. As much as I'd like to defend myself, Grandma's aim is too good. At best, I'm a cultural Christian. I nod. "You're right. It's wrong of me to question your faith."

Her color comes down a bit.

"I'm sorry, Grandma." Intensely aware of being a fake, I start to turn away. But there's something I have to say for her sake and my parents'. "It's true my faith may be little more than a prop, but it doesn't require a mature faith to know that this thing between you and Mom is wrong and it's hurting everyone."

Her expression wavers.

"We're all we've got. Yes, you have your dear friend Edith, but—"

She gulps air and releases it on a sob. "Oh, Maizy Grace." Then she cannons into my arms. "Edith's…Edith's…"

The reason for the phone call. The reason Grandma let loose on Mom. And me.

With a pitying groan that empties all of my resentment, I pull her close. "I'm sorry. I know what a good friend she was."

"Better than I d-deserved. I'm going to m-miss her so much."

"I know. Let's sit down."

For a half hour, she wears herself out, crying and relating little things about Edith that make her cry harder. She refuses food and drink and, exhausted, asks me to help her to bed.

I tuck her in and kiss her cheek. "What about the funeral?"

She draws a strident breath. "Tuesday."

Three days before she's scheduled to return to Seattle. "Will you go?"

"I don't know. It's hard enough as it is without seeing her like that."

I squeeze her shoulder. "We'll talk about it later. Get some rest."

Closing the door softly, I notice Woofer laid out by the front door. In need of a bit of cuddling, I pat my thigh.

He lifts his head, then drops his chin back to his paws.

I cross the room and halt before him. "I know this hasn't been easy on you, but it hasn't been easy on me either. So let's not forget that we're supposed to be here for each other."

He rolls his eyes up to meet my gaze.

I drop to my haunches. "Come on. I know you can sense how conflicted I am."

His stubby whiskers twitch.

"I'm all jumbled up." I pat my chest and lay my hand to his back. "Feel that?"

He flops onto his side, and for a moment it looks as if he's going to offer up his belly, but he gives me his back.

"Fine." I straighten. "Be like that."

I carry the phone into the kitchen and settle at the small table. Mom greets me cheerily, but there's no mistaking the strain in her voice. "Mom, I'm sorry about Grandma."

"Yes, lots of needless worry. That last patch of hair holding out on your father's head? Gone. He's completely bald."

It had pretty much abandoned him before I left Seattle, but I give it to her. "I should have been keeping in touch with you. Had I, you and Dad would have known that Grandma was with me."

"True. It does seem that most times when you call it's to remind us to visit her."

And a lot of good that does. "Sorry."

"Well, it's not as if you aren't busy with that new job. And, I hope, some nice young man."

Hope on.

"I guess the worst thing about this whole fiasco is that your grandmother should have been here during Edith's final hours. That woman was a good friend to her."

I draw my feet onto the edge of the chair and wrap an arm around my knees. "I think that's why she left. It's been hard for her to watch Edith slip away this last year, and when Edith didn't recognize her anymore... I just don't think she could stand to take the last leg of the journey with her, especially after it was so painful with Grandpa."

Mom releases a breath I wouldn't have expected her to be holding. "That was difficult. For all of us."

Although Mom spent little time with Grandpa, as it meant spending time with his disapproving wife, she cared for him. "She's been very lonely since, and it worsened when Edith fell ill, so please don't be too upset with her."

A long silence ensues, but she finally blows it off. "I'll try. Now, your grandmother wouldn't say whether or not she'll be coming home for the funeral. Did she tell you?"

"She wouldn't commit, said it would be hard to see Edith like that."

"Well, she needs to decide soon. The funeral is in two days."

"I know." Meaning she ought to fly out tomorrow.

"Keep after her, Maizy, and let us know what she decides."

"I will."

"So how's everything with you, outside of your grandmother's visit?"

A little jab, but still a jab. "It's been a nice visit. Grandma's taken Nashville by the horns and is seeing everything there is to see."

"And you get to be her personal tour guide. Wearing you out, I'll bet."

"Actually, I'm working full time at the paper now, so I haven't been able to take her around much."

I hear a gasp of delight, and I can almost see the long braid that trails down her back, bouncing as it does when she animates. "Full time! That's wonderful."

I wish I felt the same. "It pays the bills."

"That's all that matters."

Is it?

"So your grandmother hooked up with a tour company?"

I smile. "More like a man."

"*What?*"

"A nice elderly gentleman offered to show her the sights, and she accepted. In fact, today she attended church with him."

"That doesn't sound like your grandmother."

"It's the truth."

"Strange. Might be Alzheimer's…"

"Mom!"

She chuckles. "Back to you. Any nice young man I ought to know about?"

Jack pops to mind, but though it turns out he's on the nice side and fairly young, there's no reason to mention him. "No one."

"Your grandmother said you're attending church."

I tense. What else did she tell her about? Steeple Side? "Uh, a couple of times now."

"No harm in that. Just don't get too caught up in it."

"Why?"

"One Bible card-carrying member in the family is more than enough. Oh, I know you started calling yourself a Christian after that camp, but at least you had the smarts to leave it at that."

I have no reason to be upset with her for an impression that's my own doing, but it hurts. "So you don't think I'm a Christian?"

There's a long pause. "Do you want to be a Christian?"

"Yes, and I believe in Jesus even if I haven't done much with Him all these years."

"Meaning you want to do something with Him now?"

I consider the Bible I have yet to take seriously, the cross necklace and earrings, and lastly Steeple Side. No, not now. But soon. "I'm tired of just saying I'm a Christian. I want something more."

"Well, tell me when you find it, and we'll talk about it."

That surprises me, as I was wincing in anticipation of her giving the leaky faucet a hard crank. "I'll do that."

"Your father just walked in. Would you like to talk to him?"

"Yes. I love you, Mom."

It takes five minutes to assure Dad that his mother is fine, but when it comes to the matter of Grandma attending the funeral, Dad's decided. "I've made all the arrangements to fly out first thing in the morning to bring her home."

"You have?" I imagine Mom in the background, mouth opening and closing.

"Yes. If not for Edith's passing, I still wouldn't know Grandma had disappeared. That's not right. God knows she's a handful—"

He said "God," but does he really mean *God*?

"—but I've neglected her for too long."

Though I long to ask him how he's going to handle this with Mom, now isn't the time. "I'm glad to hear that."

"I knew you would be." I hear a smile in his voice and hope it won't be dislodged easily when he gets off the phone. "Have your grandmother packed and at the airport at two tomorrow afternoon, and we'll catch the next flight back. I'll e-mail you the flight information."

"Thanks, Dad."

I set down the phone and throw my arms wide in thanksgiving.

It wasn't supposed to happen this way...should have been harder... more conflict ridden...

My arms falter at the reminder that Grandma has no idea of Dad's plans. Meaning there's still room for conflict.

I hesitate, as all cultural Christians probably do, then sweep up the cross necklace from the table and drop to my knees. "God...Jesus... whichever One's listening...maybe both...please give Grandma a nudge. And Mom..." I sigh. "Help her to accept Dad's decision.

"I'm praying for Jem too, and Linda and her son, and Fiala and her husband, and Iris who spoke so highly of You. Even that angry man who wanted sugar. In fact, all of those homeless people. Please help them to recognize Your blessings. And me too."

SEVENTEEN

My sleep is disjointed. So is Grandma's, as evidenced by the rustling that sounds from the bedroom throughout the night. Clearly the only one getting any good sleep is Woofer. He remains camped out by the front door, having refused my invitation to curl up on the sofa despite my assurance that things would soon return to normal.

As the first morning light creeps past the parted curtains, the bedroom door opens and Grandma's slippers whisper into the room. "You awake, Grace?"

I reach for the pull chain on the table lamp. A moment later we blink at each other as we adjust to the glare.

"Want to sit down?" I swing my feet to the floor.

She eases down beside me. "I don't know what to do. I should go back for Edith's funeral, but I don't want to. It would be too lonely."

"What if Dad went with you?"

With a puff of disgust, she shakes her head. "You know he won't."

I touch her veined hands in her lap. "I talked to him last night, and he's flying in to bring you home for the funeral."

There's the conflict—pride bashing against joy—visible in the smile struggling against a frown to come out on top. Neither does. Mouth flatlining, she peers at me. "Is he doing it because you asked him to?"

"No, he's doing it because you shook him up when you left without a word. And he loves you."

Hope flits in and out of her eyes. "Are you being honest?"

"Yes."

"What about Lily? She can't be happy about this."

I squeeze her hands. "Dad loves her too, but this is about you. About getting you back and being there for you when you tell Edith good-bye."

Her eyes brighten and her hands quiver, but a determination rises in her eyes. "It's rather presumptuous of your father to think I'll just up and rearrange my vacation plans."

I groan. "Do you want Dad to come or not? If you don't, I'll call him and save him the trip."

Another struggle with pride, and then she slumps. "It won't change anything. He may take me to the funeral, but then he'll drop me at home and that will be that."

"Not if you and Mom declare a truce."

She shakes her head. "I would, but there's too much water under the bridge."

"What water?"

"I...it started when your father and mother were dating." She pulls her hands from beneath mine. "I was just being honest when I told her she wasn't right for my son."

I sit back. "You actually said that to her?"

Her back straightens. "I certainly did. Marched right up to her parents' house and told her on the front porch. And what did she do? Went and told my Samuel and got him so upset that he didn't talk to me for weeks. Next thing I knew, they were married." Her mouth pinches. "Do you know how I found out? Edith showed up at my door with the announcement from the paper. Not even Bert could console me." She glowers. "Of course, for some reason your grandfather liked Lily, so I can't say he tried all that hard."

"Did you ever apologize to Mom?"

"Humph! Did she ever apologize to *me*?"

There's only one thing I can think to say and only because I read it fairly recently. "You're the Christian, Grandma. I know that won't make it less difficult, and there's no guarantee she'll accept your apology, but at least you'll have done what you're supposed to do."

Grandma's eyes flash. "Is that what your *Dumb Blonde's Guide* told you?"

Caught. "Um...something like that."

She wiggles her fingers. "Hand it over."

"Well, it's—"

"Under the sofa."

How does she know where I keep it? Feeling as if caught reading an unsavory magazine, I fish out the book I claimed from the airport's Lost and Found where Avery so kindly turned it in.

She frowns at the wide-eyed cartoon blonde on the cover, turns the book over, skims the blurb, then hands it back. "Read me the part about forgiveness."

"But you know what the Bible says."

"Yes, but I want to know what that book says."

If I hadn't decided to call in sick so I could spend the morning with Grandma before taking her to the airport, I'd beg off. "All right." I turn to the page and begin to read.

Crazy Little Thing Called Forgiveness

You said. She said. You meant. She meant. You're offended. She's offended. Then—*woohee!*—toss a few friends into the mix, give it a good stir to make sure they know *your* side of the story (as she's doing on her end, right?), and you have a recipe for unforgiveness. Get the picture? Not a nice one. In fact, as you've probably already discovered, unresolved conflict can be u-u-u-u-gly. So ugly that you'll lose sleep over it, perhaps even friends or family—

I peek over the top of the book and look at Grandma. "Don't stop now."

—maybe even years of your life. No, it won't necessarily kill you (directly), but it will eat at you. However, you as a Christian, regardless of whether or not she's one, can turn it around.

Eyes downcast, Grandma waves a hand for me to continue.

No buts! You may be the one who was wronged (or, at least, who received the first blow), but it's time to suck up your pride and get right. How? Though offenses come in all shapes and sizes, forgiveness comes in one: Jesus. He set the example. And what an example! *Psst*—it might be a good time to open your Bible and take a look at Matthew 6:12; Mark 11:25; Ephesians 4:32; and Hebrews 8:12. You know what you have to do now, don't you? If possible, seek out the other person and ask her to forgive you.

Grandma winces.

Yes, it's gonna hurt, especially if she won't accept your apology or ask for forgiveness in return. But God has you covered. He forgives you, and being right with Him matters above all else. Slate wiped clean (until the next time—and there will be a next time).

In conclusion, this crazy little thing called forgiveness is actually big. Huge. Ginormous even. But you must master it, as it will not only aid in your healing and the other person's but will also help you to grow toward a more Christlike life. What are you waiting for?

Grandma sighs. "Not bad, though a bit cheesy."

"Would you like me to look up the Scripture? Uh, Matthew 6:12?"

"The Lord's Prayer." She juts her chin at her cross-stitched hand-iwork beside the door. "'Forgive us our debts, as we also have forgiven our debtors.' Believe me, I know that one by heart."

I'm struck by those last two words, the literal meaning of which not only escapes me more often than I care to admit, but probably escapes her—at least where Mom is concerned. I decide to draw her attention to them in a roundabout way. "I wish I knew it by heart."

"*Tch!* All you have to do is read it over and over until it sticks." She taps her temple, then stills. "Actually"—she lowers her hand—"there's more to it than that."

As I'm also learning.

The silence stretches. In her aged face I can almost see the gears of forgiveness engage.

And then, as if someone plugged her in, she slaps a thigh. "I'd better get packed."

Woofer scrambles to his feet. Grandma probably thinks it's in response to her thigh slapping, but I know better. That little mutt senses a turning of the tide.

I nod at him as I rise.

Perk goes his ears, ticktock goes his stub tail.

"It's the right decision, Grandma." I kiss her cheek.

"Yes, that it is."

I want to ask about Mom, as I long to hear that things will be different between them, but I don't want to push. "I'll grab a shower; then we'll go out for breakfast."

"What about work?"

"I'll call in…" No, I'm not sick. "I'll call my boss. I'm sure she won't mind if I take the day off to spend with you before you leave."

"Wonderful."

"Then Pancake Pantry it is."

"Ooh, William was going to take me there. He said it's scrumptious."

"I've heard that too, but speaking of William…"

She nods. "He'll be disappointed by my early departure, but he'll understand."

As she bustles toward the bedroom, hope burgeons that God may take something bad—Edith's death—and heal the rift between Grandma and my mother and thereby my father. Feeling light on my feet, I start for the bathroom, only to pull up short when my computer catches my eye.

A few moments later, I sign on to my e-mail account. Besides Dad's e-mail with the flight information and instructions on how to obtain a pass that will allow me to accompany my elderly grandmother to the departure gate, there's a message from Tessie. I open it. It's a reminder of what we discussed at the garbage can (appropriate) with emphasis on discovering Jack's Achilles heel. Which I've already done and have no intention of divulging, even if it means disappointing Ray.

As I move my cursor to delete the message, I read the line beneath Tessie's name: "PS—Don't forget your rent is due in three days."

Reality check. I need my job at the paper.

As Dad approaches behind the others disembarking ahead of him, wariness is entrenched in his face. And with good reason, as Grandma is glowering beside me with her arms crossed over her chest.

I lean down. "Remember how far he's come. He's here because he loves you."

Her lids flicker.

"What shape and size does forgiveness come in? Come on."

She grunts. "I'll try, Grace."

As she starts toward Dad, I lay a hand on her arm. "We should probably go back to plain Maizy. Or Maizy Grace. We don't need to burden Dad with the pickle I got myself into."

"Is that all it is—a pickle?"

Understatement of the year. "No, but I'll work it out. You'll see. One day we'll laugh about it."

She lays a hand over mine. "That seems a stretch, but I suppose it depends on how you handle the situation."

How *am* I going to handle it? "Of course."

"Mom?"

We look up, and there's Dad.

After a long moment, Grandma steps forward and puts her thin arms around her thick son. "I'm so glad you came, Samuel."

Over the top of his mother's head, a surprised Dad meets my gaze.

I smile and join in the embrace.

An hour is all we have, but we make the most of it, sitting at the departure gate with Dad between me and Grandma. As the safest topic is Grandma's exploration of Nashville with William, that's where we stay until the boarding call.

Dad's hug and kiss on the cheek make my eyes mist, and I realize how much I've missed him and Mom. Grandma's hug is more of the same, and a tear spills over as I watch them walk away.

"Maizy Grace."

I flick away the tear and raise my eyebrows at Grandma where she's stepped out of line.

"That guide of yours—you know the one."

I glance at Dad, who's frowning across his shoulder. "Yes?"

"Why don't you see what it has to say about integrity?"

My grandmother. Always looking out for my best interests. But does she really know what those best interests are? Lately I'm not sure myself.

"And while you're at it, see what that newfangled Bible of yours has to say."

"I'll do that. Have a nice trip."

Dad takes Grandma's elbow. "What was that all about?"

"Just an article your daughter's working on for the paper."

"Ah. And the new Bible?"

"She's rediscovering her faith. Isn't that wonderful?"

I sense Dad's hesitation, but he nods and says something that is swallowed by the bend in the walkway.

So back to normal. Back to the way things were before Grandma. And that's a good thing. I think. Though Woofer will be thrilled by a return to two, I might just miss three.

Or maybe not.

"I'm sorry about your grandmother's friend."

Jem's concern sounds genuine, and I'm touched that she called to discover if my absence from work was a result of illness. "Thanks, Jem."

Phone between ear and shoulder, I sink deeper into the stiff bubbles that only a $1.99 bottle of dishwashing liquid can produce. No, I won't smell like sun-drenched gardenias when I climb out, but these bubbles aren't going anywhere anytime soon. In fact, I'll probably have to squeegee them off.

"How was your weekend?" I ask.

"It was...all right."

I'm so tired that her hesitation almost slips past. "Are you eating?" Ooh, that was direct.

And her further hesitation confirms it. However, just as I'm about to apologize, she sighs. "It's hard. I thought I was doing good easing back into it, and I even had a decent-sized dinner on Friday night..."

I push back to sitting, and the bubbles stick to me like peanut butter on bread, preserving my modesty even though Woofer's the only one to see me. "But?"

"I totally bloated. I could hardly button my pants, and when I looked in the mirror, my back flab was puffing up over my waistband."

I draw a hand up through the suds and rub my temple. "Jem, did you...?" I leave the word *vomit* unspoken.

"I had to one last time."

"*One* last time?" I know I should temper the judgment in my voice, but a throb has set up shop between my ears.

"Look, I can do this. I need to take it slower, that's all."

"No, you need help. Jack checked with Human Resources, and—"

"You told Jack?"

I did not think that through. "It was unintentional. It just came out. I'm sorry."

"Well, thanks. I trust you and what do you do? Blab my troubles to everyone."

"Not everyone. Just Jack. And I didn't mean to—"

"I have to go." *Click.*

Wishing I hadn't answered the phone, I push the Off button, drop the handset to the rug, and sink into the tub. Guess I'll get to see how long these bubbles last, 'cause I'm not getting out anytime soon.

EIGHTEEN

It's all for the best, I tell myself as the week wears on into Friday and Jem pulls a U-turn on every potential encounter. Yes, for the best, as I'm not here to make friends. I'm here to rebuild my career by exposing the truth. Case in point: the strawberry blond Steeple Side store employee who just knocked over a display of books and said a very bad word.

Turning down the greeting card aisle, I locate the "Thinking of You" cards. Surprisingly, the selection is expansive, meaning I've just saved myself a trip to a card store. Now to find the perfect card to let Grandma know I'm thinking of her. And one for my parents, who have gone above and beyond to support her by letting her stay with them during this difficult time.

I grimace in remembrance of the strain in my mother's voice last night when she mentioned that she and Grandma had argued over the length of my sister's skirt. Mom backed down, but she won't do that indefinitely. Which is why I encouraged Dad to transition Grandma back to independent living. He agreed. Wholeheartedly.

Fifteen minutes into my lunch break, I start toward the front of the store only to draw up short when the "I'm Sorry" cards to my left bring Jem to mind.

Just leave it. Remember? All for the best.

I ease a bright blue card out of its slot. Above a cartoon rendering of a plucked, repentant-looking chicken are the words "My Bad." That surprises me. It's so hip. Guessing a scripture like those referenced in the "Thinking of You" cards is tucked inside, I open the cover. No scripture, just: "Your grace. Puh-leeease forgive me." Cute. While I need to back off my relationship with Jem, that doesn't mean I shouldn't try to mend the fence. It certainly would be the Christian thing to do.

Three cards it is.

The checkout line is four deep. As I move into position, I glance at my watch. I should be able to make it back to my desk with a few minutes to spare. But then in walks Jack, whom I've caught little more than glimpses of over the past four days.

Though I have no reason to hide, I duck my chin.

Moments later, canvas shoes appear to my left. "I see you've discovered our convenient retail store."

Oh, that accent. Which has no business shimmying down my spine. One order of surprise, over easy. "Jack!"

His eyes dance and lips tilt.

So much for faking it. "What are you doing here?"

"Picking up an audio book for my grandmother. Her birthday is next week." He looks around, then back at me. "Is Jem out ill today?"

I blink. "I don't think so."

"I thought the two of you were steady lunch buddies."

Lie Number—no. And no reason for evasion either. I hold up the chicken card. "We had a falling out."

His eyes slide to the woman ahead of me, who has turned her ear toward us. "Want to talk about it while I browse the audio books?"

I do. Of course, it may mean inciting the wrath of Fiala. I hesitate, but decide that Jack should probably be told of his part in the falling out. "Sure."

I fill him in on Monday's events, which begin with a sketch of Grandma's early departure from Nashville and conclude with the ill-fated call from Jem.

Leaning an elbow against a shelf, he nods. "Sounds like she needs help."

"I know, but I handled it wrong, then alienated her further by letting it drop that I confided in you."

"Did you tell her about the article on eating disorders you're writing?"

"I...under the circumstances, I didn't think it was a good idea to mention it."

"You prefer that she believes you're a gossip?"

"I guess I didn't think it through."

He pushes off the shelf. "I could speak with her. We've known each other for a while, so she might be receptive."

"Or resentful."

He inclines his head. "Let me think about it."

"I'd better get back. Thanks for listening."

"Any time."

I start to turn away, but he says, "You could return the favor by giving me two minutes of your time."

I'm late already. What's two more minutes? "Sure."

He scans the spines of the audio books and picks out two. "I was here yesterday and couldn't decide between these." He holds up a CD case with a glowing cross center stage. "A daily devotional with emphasis on the New Testament." The second CD case shows a dirt path through a misty wooded area. Very peaceful. And familiar. "Or this one that sets Psalms and Proverbs to music."

I tap the latter. "That picture looks as if it was taken at Percy Warner Park."

He turns it toward himself. "It certainly does."

"I love that park."

His eyebrows rise. "You go there often?"

"As much as possible. My dog loves long walks." I make a face. "Providing I lug him most of the way. He's a bit lazy."

"I hope he's a little dog."

"He has his moments." Or did. With Grandma's departure came a return of appetite, and it's been hard to ignore his begging, especially as I'm not completely back in his good graces.

"I haven't seen you at the park," Jack says.

"Do you go there often?"

"Regularly. It's a great place to jog."

Remembering the conclusion I drew on my first day at Steeple Side, I gasp. "I knew you were a jogger!"

The surprise that flashes across his face nearly makes me groan. "How's that?"

Catching his citrus-y scent, I take a step back. "You look like one."

"And how does a jogger look?"

"Fit, I suppose, in a..." This is embarrassing. "...lean way."

He smiles and I'm reminded of when he made it perfectly clear that he was flirting with me this past Sunday. "Thank you."

That *was* a compliment, wasn't it? And now he probably thinks *I'm* flirting with *him*. I clear my throat. "So you jog regularly at the park?"

The smile I hoped to send packing takes on an impish slant. "A few days a week around 7 a.m."

"I usually only make it on the weekends, and it's always after eight."

"Which explains why we haven't run into each other."

And if we did—outside of Steeple Side, outside of church, outside of mission work? Oh boy. Mustn't forget the reason I'm here, or before much longer my name will be tantamount to a curse.

I consider the audio books in his nicely shaped hands, square my shoulders, and give the one with the glowing cross a nod. "I think she'll like the daily devotionals. And now I have to get back to my desk."

"Thank you for your input. And don't worry about Jem. Steeple Side won't let her down."

Unlike the real world, where giving someone the benefit of a doubt for fear of ruining their life will get you canned. Unfortunately, that's the world I live in, and though every day that passes makes Steeple Side more appealing, there's no future here for me.

Right. You made your bed; now you have to sleep in it.

Wait. That doesn't make sense. I don't have to sleep in it. After all, it's made. Maybe on the sloppy side, but made. Meaning I can walk away from it.

And where would you go? The unemployment line? You'd be ruined. This time for good. An utter failure, proving your detractors right—

Maizy Stewart doesn't have what it takes to shine light on the injustices of the world and make it a better place.

"Is something wrong?"

Not if I complete the assignment I've been given. Bringing Jack into focus, I shake my head. "Just thinking about all I need to get done today."

He consults his watch. "You'd better get to it then. Your day's almost over."

Not even close.

"Out-of-wedlock pregnancy." Ray's chest puffs up in concert with his smile. "Perfect. More stuff like this and we'll have an article that will blow the steeple off Steeple Side."

I know I'm supposed to be amused, but I'm not, especially as the out-of-wedlock pregnancy is barely a notch above a lie—a snippet of conversation overheard in the parking lot between two women who may or may not be Steeple Side employees. But I had been desperate. Ray's finger was in my face as he ranted about the poor quality of my leads and how long the investigation is taking, while beside me Tessie's eyes were rolling. So it was the out-of-wedlock pregnancy or the revelation about Jack.

Ray flops back in his chair and laces his fingers over his chest in a rare show of contentment. It doesn't last. He thrusts his chin forward. "We'll need more, of course."

"Of course," I murmur.

He consults his calendar. "I'm being generous here, but I'll give you two more weeks to get me this story."

I startle. "Two weeks?"

"Ms. Halston led me to believe you could handle this. She vouched for you. Are you telling me you can't?"

Tessie's foot ceases its tapping.

I dig my nails into my palms. I don't have to sleep in this bed. I can walk away.

And throw Tessie's friendship back in her face? Leave her holding the bag?

But Ray wouldn't fire her. She's too valuable. Even so, there would be mud on her. And for what? As Tessie and Ray pointed out the last time I was in this office, there are plenty of others who'd like to advance their career on the back of Steeple Side, leaving me bringing up the rear of the unemployment line. I've felt torn before but never to this degree. In fact, if conscience and reason had physical form, they would be bloodied.

"Well," Ray snaps, "can you get me the story?"

I don't have a choice. Walk away and not only is my career trashed but Tessie gets the backlash. Stay the course and my career is reinstated, and Tessie's belief in me is rewarded. "I'll get the story. Two weeks."

"That's my girl."

Girl?! Were I a die-hard feminist, I'd…I'd…

You'd grit your teeth and keep your job. And hate myself for it. Of course, it's not as if I'm overly fond of myself at the moment. In fact, I can't say I like myself much at all.

As I turn toward the door, the parting words Grandma spoke at the airport pop into my head: *"Why don't you see what that guide of yours has to say about integrity?"*

NINETEEN

"Just you and me, Woof." Eyes closed against the steadily rising sun, I reach for him. Guided by his heavy panting—one would think *he's* the one who carried *me* the last half mile—I locate him sprawled in the grass near my thigh. "Told you we'd get back to normal." I scratch his neck.

He rumbles low in his chest.

I yank my hand back. He growled at me! And after we agreed to put the past behind us. I lift my head from the grass. Half expecting him to be showing a bit of teeth (of course, that's all he has), I'm surprised to find he's not even looking at me. The silent treatment. He must be really mad. Of course, I did forget to bring water.

He scrambles to all fours, whips around, and looses a bark that sounds something like a cross between a toy squeaker and a hairball-coughing cat.

Then he wasn't growling at me? Shielding my eyes, I look up. Nope. The one who set him off is the last person I want to see after the ultimatum Ray delivered yesterday—Jack in jogging shorts, a T-shirt, a sheen of perspiration, and a smile.

I'm not really surprised, as it crossed my mind that this might happen, especially since he has been flirting with me.

"Just the person I'm looking for," he says as he nears.

Then he's not going to pretend this is a chance meeting. Of course, it would be rather obvious since he told me he jogs at seven and it's well past eight.

He halts near my feet. "So this is the little dog."

Another growl. Another squeaky cough.

"Woofer."

Jack chuckles. "He looks fierce."

His gaze returns to me, and I realize how I must look laid out in the grass. Hoping I didn't pick up any ticks, I sit up. "You said you were looking for me?"

He drops down beside me—near enough for me to silently bemoan the absence of his usual scent, but not so near as to suffer the smell of his physical exertion. Woofer, on the other hand, busily sniffs the change in the air while he holds his ground on my opposite side.

Jack tosses his water bottle to the grass, slides fingers back through his damp hair, then loosely wraps his arms around his knees. "I want to talk to you about Jem. I would have rung you last night, but I didn't have your number and you aren't listed."

Not under *Grace* Stewart. "I'm fairly new to the area, so I probably missed the last printing of the phone book."

"Directory assistance couldn't pull up a listing either."

Imagine that. "Maybe I went unlisted. I'll have to look into it." Honestly I don't remember, so not a lie. "What did you want to tell me about Jem?"

"I shared a lift with her yesterday when we were leaving work and asked her to join me for coffee. She agreed, though somewhat reluctantly."

I'm surprised she agreed at all. "I assume you spoke with her about her eating disorder."

He grins. "I'm not sure if it was my charm or the three cups of coffee that got her to open up, but she came around."

"And?"

"I gave her my word that Steeple Side will stand beside her. She agreed to think about it."

"You think she will?"

"I believe she was sincere."

"And if she decides against help?"

He sighs. "I don't know if she can beat this on her own. In fact, I'm doubtful, but she has her faith, and I've learned never to underestimate the power of prayer."

I underestimate it, which is why I didn't give in last night, though I felt pulled to my knees to ask God to help me out of the mess I'm in. Would He really listen to a cultural Christian who has to keep track of her lies? And if He answered my prayers, what price would He exact? There has to be a price, and I know I'd be the worse for it. Unemployed. Ostracized. Friendless.

"You look like you just swallowed a nasty pill."

Plummeting back to earth, I mentally land beside Jack with a gasp. "Sorry?"

"Are you all right?"

"Yeah. Just worried about Jem." Which is true. "Anyway, I appreciate that you adjusted your jogging schedule to let me know you met with her." Of course, he could have told me tomorrow at church. Er, providing I showed, as it's a strong possibility I would have found an excuse not to attend again. It just feels wrong. And yet right. Might this be the onset of schizophrenia? Or merely a deeply disturbed con-science?

"You swallowed another one."

I land beside Jack again. "Sorry, my mind's all over the place today. So much going on… Overload, you know."

"Then I suppose now would not be a good time to ask how the article's coming?"

How did he find out? I teeter. I totter. I ground myself. *He's talking about the article* for *not* on *Steeple Side*. "I'm, uh, working on it."

Though the space between Jack's eyebrows remains pinched, he nods. "So long as you have it to Linda in two weeks."

Not even in my current state of frazzle do I miss the irony. Two weeks to prove that Steeple Side is a den of hypocrisy. Two weeks to write a piece about the soup kitchen that reflects the Christian's commitment to showing by example how to live the Christian life. I don't feel so good.

"Are you sure you're all right?" Jack leans toward me. Still no citrus, but a not-too-unpleasant masculine scent tempts me nearer. And makes Woofer rumble.

Poor guy. If it's not Grandma, it's some strange man. I pat his back, but he bristles and trots to the end of his leash.

"I'm all right. Just a bit overwhelmed."

"Is it the editing?"

I freeze. "Uh…?"

"Jem mentioned that you do freelance editing."

Knew that would come back to haunt me. "I do." Not a new lie, just a new recipient. And it's not even a big lie as it's only the adjective *freelance* that qualifies it as a lie since I *am* editing lifestyle articles. "Oh, just the odd piece here and there, but it helps to pay the bills." But enough about me. "So do you have anything special planned for this weekend?"

He reaches for his water bottle. "Just kicking back. You?"

Other than organizing the notes on my Steeple Side investigation? "Same."

Jack tips the bottle to his lips, which not only makes me salivate but Woofer as well.

Jack chuckles, pours a splash in his hand, and extends it. "Want a drink, pooch?"

It appears that Woofer might take him up on the offer, but he drops back to sitting and gives another growl. Meaning the water is up for grabs. But even if I were crawling across the Sahara, dehydrated and near death, it would be a bad idea to drink from Jack's hand.

I startle when he reaches the bottle to me. "You look thirsty too. Have a drink, providing you're not afraid of a few germs."

I look to his face, which has a grin so appealing that the voice telling me to tread carefully goes mute. "What?" I smile and, as if from a distance, hear myself chuckle. "Was I drooling?"

"Nearly." He winks.

Oomph! *All systems alert! Maizy Grace Stewart is* not *treading carefully.*

I snatch the bottle and tip the spout to my lips. When I lower it, I become aware of a strangely disturbing sound—like lapping. What is Jack doing?

Not Jack, but Woofer. Drinking out of Jack's hand.

Jack shrugs in response to my wide eyes. "He was feeling left out."

I refuse to relate.

Lifting his head, Woofer gives a single tock of his tail and moseys back to my feet.

I hand Jack his water bottle. "Thank you."

"You're welcome. So how about breakfast?"

Tempting, but therein lies the problem—temptation. "I should get home."

He leans in. "Still not in the *market* for a relationship?"

Is that what he's offering?

His gaze settles on my mouth with a deliberateness that makes me drop my eyes like two hot potatoes. *Now would be a good time to grab your little dog and get out of Oz.*

Jack's shadow shifts, and now I'm really afraid to look up. Afraid of what I'll see because of this thing between us...afraid of what a difference two weeks will make.

"Grace."

Lifting my chin, I'm struck by the proximity of our mouths. So close. And getting closer. Contact.

"Grace," he whispers against my lips.

As his fingers slide along my jaw and curl around the back of my neck, I lean into the kiss. And feel like ice on a hot tin roof...a Popsicle on a midsummer day...butter on a sizzling griddle. All my nerves may be standing at attention, but I'm me-e-e-elting. Thus, when Jack pulls back—first his mouth, then his hand—I'm in danger of dribbling down into the earth. I open my eyes to find his face still near.

He smiles. "How was that?"

Yummy. And served with a side of British accent, better than yummy. Totally, positively—

Dangerous.

He runs the backs of his fingers down my cheek. "It seems that Grace Stewart—"

Grace.

"—may not be as averse to a relationship as she thought."

Neither is Maizy. I sit back to add more inches to the space between us. "I admit that was nice, but *you* have to admit that it's not a good idea to allow this to go further. We are co-workers."

"I've considered that, and you're right. It isn't a good idea. Office romance can get sticky, which is why Steeple Side cautions against it."

"Then why are you here?"

"It's true that I wanted to tell you about my meeting with Jem, but…" His smile takes a crooked turn. "…more true that there are some things worth throwing caution to the wind for."

Is he saying *I'm* one of those things?

He nods as if I spoke aloud. "I didn't want to be attracted to you, but I am."

The feeling is mutual. "This is probably a case of rebound."

"No. I'm the one who broke it off with Bette. And that was over six months ago."

"Six months?" I pull back further. "But no one at Steeple Side knew about it."

"I hope I don't sound egotistical, but my job is easier when the Closed sign is hung as opposed to the Open sign."

Jem did mention that if Jack and Bette broke off their engagement again, a line would form to catch his eye. And speaking of catching his eye, I follow his gaze to a ribbon of stomach peeking from beneath the hem of my top. "Uh…" *Tug, tug, tug.* "It might still be rebound. You know, me being the first woman to turn your head and all."

"You aren't the first. I've had several dates since the breakup with Bette. The women were all nice but not what I'm looking for."

That begs a question I shouldn't ask. "What *are* you looking for?"

He leans back on his elbows. "This may sound wishy-washy, but I'm not sure." Squinting against the brightening day, he looks across the lawn. "All I'm sure of is that, despite a strange first meeting, followed by several peculiar encounters and a shocking change of hair color, I fancy you."

My heart leaps only to land with a *splat* when he turns his face to me and adds, "Grace."

I long to correct him, to tell him the name is Maizy, but that would require too much explanation. And the truth.

"You're attractive."

Even with this dark hair?

"You have a nice smile."

Just nice?

"You're different."

Is that a good thing?

"Amusing."

At my own expense.

"Caring."

Must be talking about Jem.

"Interested in knowing more about your faith."

Of course, that's on hold.

"Mysterious."

With reason.

He shrugs. "Though you pretend to be someone you're not—"

It's all I can do not to clap a hand to my chest.

"—I believe I've seen enough of the real you to warrant a closer look."

The need for CPR is fast becoming a reality.

"So what do you say to a closer look?"

Mouth-to-mouth resuscitation is imminent. *Are you insane? Like it or not, once is enough.*

I shake my head. "You'll thank me for this, but I have to pass."

"Pass?"

Time to go. I rise so suddenly that Woofer jumps several inches and scoots to the end of his leash.

Jack is on his feet seconds later, his brow furrowed. "I'm a bit at sixes and sevens here."

I frown. "Sixes and sevens?"

"Confused. Will you humor me a moment?"

I bite my lip. "Okay."

"Is this about the boyfriend your grandmother spoke of? The one who gave you second-degree burns?"

Ben. Self-absorbed, controlling Ben who was wrong for me from the start. Whose betrayal brought every doubt I'd had about us into the chill light of reality.

He's in the past. Leave him there.

I shove the memory of that day back into its closet. However, no sooner do I step away from it than the door bursts open and the confrontation is before me again in Technicolor and surround sound.

"You stole my story."

Standing in the doorway, toothsome smile absent, contact-enhanced blue eyes dull, Ben slides his hands into his pants pockets. "No, Maizy, I salvaged it from the garbage. 'One man's trash is another man's treasure' and all that."

Springing from the chair I had sunk into hours earlier to await his return, I advance on him. "There wasn't enough proof."

"Tell that to the judge and jury. Speaking of which—new development. Looks like your pal Leona has skipped the country."

Anger sinks through the cracks in my life, and I halt. And feel a deeper pang at his slow smile that has endeared him to Seattle viewers—and once endeared me.

"You got too close, Maizy."

I lower my chin. As his too-musky cologne causes my nostrils to pinch, I stare at the two feet between us that seems like miles. Yes, I messed up—and may regret it the rest of my life—but he had no right to do what he did to me. His fiancée!

"Look at it as a learning experience." Ben straightens his sapphire blue tie. "The next time—"

"Next time?" I step closer, bringing us eye to eye and shattering the illusion that he's as tall as he appears on television. "You scooped me, remember? End result—I was fired. F-i-r-e-d."

Regret flashes in his eyes, and he reaches forward and cups my shoulder. "I did warn you what could happen if you didn't deliver the story."

I jerk from beneath his hand. "Well, that makes me feel a whole lot better!"

With a grunt of frustration, he drops his chin but then pops it back up. "Look, let's talk about this later when you're thinking more clearly."

"There is no 'later.' This is it."

He frowns. "What?"

As intelligent as he is, sometimes he can be incredibly dense. "Good-bye, Ben. That's what it is—g-o-o-d-b-y-e." As petty as it sounds, it feels good to spell it out for him.

"Ah, come on, Maizy." He whips a hand up through the air. "You'll get over it."

"Yes, I will, but not with you."

He stares at me, and I neither flinch nor flutter as he searches my face. Finally, with a muttered deprecation, Ben steps past me. Strangely, though, in the next instant I feel his hand on me again.

"Bad memory," he says with a distinctly British accent.

I blink. I didn't know he could—no, that last wasn't Ben. It was Jack.

I catch my breath and look down at his fingers on my forearm. Much nicer fingers than Ben's...

I shake my head. "Sorry. I didn't mean to go there."

"My fault. So is it safe to conclude that this guy is the reason you're *passing* on me?"

Actually it would be safer—for me—if *Jack* were the reason I'm passing on him. But not another lie. Feeling as if the "up" muscles of my mouth are on the verge of conceding defeat to the "down" muscles, I try to smile. "It's not you. And though it does have something to do with Ben, it's really about me. I'm not at a good place in my life to get involved." How's that for honesty?

After a long moment, he says, "All right. I respect that."

That was surprisingly easy, especially if I don't allow myself to dwell on the fact that, under different circumstances, what just happened between us would have me head over heels. "Thank you."

He snags his water bottle from the grass. "Let me know when you are at a good place in your life. Providing I am as well, I'd like to see how we match up."

Sadly, if and when I arrive at that good place, I will have attained the rank of pariah where those at Steeple Side are concerned. "I'll do that." I take a step away. "Thank you for filling me in on Jem."

"You're welcome. I hope to see you at church tomorrow…and bowling afterward."

Did he say the *b* word? I whip around. "Bowling?"

His eyebrows arch. "Avery said you signed up."

Me? The thought of hefting a weight-challenged ball is no more appealing than it was the day Porter teasingly invited me to join his bowling league. Grandma! Must have been at the same time she signed me up to work the soup kitchen.

"You didn't sign up?"

If I told him it wasn't me, might that raise suspicions about my participation with the soup kitchen? I clap a hand over my face. "Like I said…overload. So what time tomorrow?" Me. Bowling. This can't be happening. "And where?"

"Two o'clock. Brentwood. I can count on you, can't I?"

I drop my hand from my face. "Why would you want to do that?"

"Being the matchmaker he is, Avery assigned you to my team."

Lord, are You trying to tell me something? "Well, you might actually be better off without me as I'm lucky to score ninety *with* the aid of bumpers."

He crosses his arms over his chest, and I can't help but admire the way it further defines his biceps. "Ninety, hmm?"

"Sorry. Holey balls that weigh more than my purse on a bad day don't do much for me."

"Then we'll have to focus on the fun of it."

That's his solution? "You still want me on your team?"

"Sure."

I toss my hands in the air. "They're your toes."

"I'll watch out for them. See you tomorrow."

As I head across the lawn with Woofer in tow, I feel Jack's eyes on me but squash the temptation to turn around. After all, Jack and temptation are a bad combination, especially with the remembrance of his kiss on my lips.

"I'm just happy to be back in my own bed."

Despite the sturdy pitch of Grandma's voice, I don't believe her. "It was nice of Mom and Dad to ask you to stay with them."

A long pause. "Your mother's little habits and outlook on life were starting to rub my nerves raw, yet it distracted me from my grief." She harrumphs. "Did you know she refuses to allow red meat in the house?"

So she's on that kick again. I roll from my back to my stomach and lever onto my elbows to pick at the lint peppering my bedspread.

"Though my son is no longer a growing boy, he needs meat…of the red variety."

I shrug. "So long as Dad's fine with it, I wouldn't worry."

"Fine with it? Do you know what he ordered when he took me to dinner last night when it was just the two of us?"

"A steak?"

"Medium rare. I tell you, it's not right that a grown man has to sneak around to get his red meat. You should have seen your mother's face when he told her that he'd taken me to a steakhouse."

That changes things a bit. "Then he's not sneaking around?"

"Your father's a good man. He may have abandoned his faith, but he's no liar. God's commandments are still in there somewhere. In fact, if I can get him to walk me into church tomorrow, he might be convinced to stay for the service."

I frown. "Dad's taking you to church?"

"He offered. I accepted."

"And…Mom?"

"Surprisingly, she's the one who suggested it."

Surprising is an understatement, especially as we're talking two things that rub Mom wrong—Grandma *and* church.

"Suspicious, hmm?"

I shake my head. "No, let's stick with surprising and accept it as an olive branch."

"You think?" Her pitch rises with…hope?

"I do."

"Well"—she clears her throat—"that would be a nice change."

As if my mother has never tried to get along with her. "Yes, one I'm sure Dad will appreciate too. So what's this about you signing me up for bowling?"

"I forgot about that. Since I knew I'd be home by then, I thought you would be lonely and in need of company. And that nice fellow Jack signed up. You are going, aren't you?"

"It looks that way."

"Good. Now what is it I wanted to tell you? Oh! William may fly out to see me."

"Really?"

"Yes, he's quite taken with me. And though I can't say I return the intensity of his feelings, I do miss him."

"That's great." I think.

"How's your article on Steeple Side coming?" She makes no attempt to couch the question in genuine interest. Disapproval is more her style.

"The paper has given me a deadline. I have two weeks to get them the story."

"Getting impatient then."

"They *are* paying me."

"As is Steeple Side." She tut-tuts, slathering on another layer of guilt, though I have yet to cash a single Steeple Side paycheck. "Ironic, if you ask me."

I glance at the clock in search of an excuse to get off the phone. Five thirty. Too early to turn in for the night.

"Did you see what that book of yours has to say about integrity, Maizy Grace?"

I drop my face to the bedspread. "Nuh-uh."

"Well, you should."

A knock at the front door brings my head up like a shot. Expelling the mouthful of bedspread, I say, "Grandma, someone's at the door."

"Probably that dreadful Halston woman. Don't answer."

"I have to. I'll talk to you soon. Bye."

To my surprise, Woofer has his nose to the door when I enter the living room. Meaning it can't be Tessie, as her visits warrant little more than a crooked ear.

As the knock sounds again, I falter. Who other than Tessie would come knocking on a Saturday? I have my answer a moment later when I peek through the curtains. Jem.

Before I can formulate a reason for her appearance, movement draws my attention to Tessie, who has stepped out her back door. She halts at the sight of Jem and says, "Can I help you?"

Jem turns to her. "I need to talk to Grace. Her car's here, but she's not answering the door."

Oh, yes I am. I throw the door open wide. "What are you doing here, Jem?"

She swivels around. "You're here."

A glance at Tessie subjects me to raised eyebrows. "Want to come in?"

Jem nods and steps past me.

Avoiding Tessie's gaze, I raise a hand to her and close the door.

Awkwardness stretches over the next several moments as Jem and I face each other. Finally I say, "I'm glad to see you."

She shifts her slight weight. "Really?"

"Yes. I was afraid you weren't going to talk to me again."

She makes a face. "I wouldn't do that. I was just upset."

"You're not anymore?"

"No, especially since I figured it out."

Figured out her problem? Meaning she is going to get help? My heart constricts at the possibility that my time at Steeple Side won't be entirely defined by deception. "What exactly did you figure out?"

She points a finger at me, closes an eye, and makes the same clicking sound she made my first day at Steeple Side. Only then she was pointing and clicking at Fiala. "I know your secret."

TWENTY

It has to be a rare (or seriously whacked) person who can be horrified, elated, and relieved all at the same time, but I am. And somehow I make it to the armchair. "How did you find out?"

She lowers to the sofa cushion nearest me. "From Jack."

I sit upright. "Jack knows?"

Her brow furrows. "Why wouldn't he? I mean, it is mutual."

That makes no sense. Unless... "What are you talking about?"

"About you two being attracted to each other, becoming an item. What are *you* talking about?"

That's it? *That's* my so-called secret? Going limp again, I blow a breath up my face.

"Grace? What secret are you talking about?"

I wave a hand. "Nothing."

"But all the blood drained from your face. We're talking the extreme end of white."

"Must be the dark hair. Loads of contrast." Time to change the subject. "Is that what you wanted to talk to me about? The attraction between me and Jack?"

"No, I only brought it up because when Jack took me to coffee yesterday to discuss Steeple Side's commitment to me, it became obvious that you told him about my problem because the two of you have grown close."

"How did it become obvious?"

"The way he defended you and assured me you had only my best interests at heart. Of course, then I asked if he had a thing for you, and he said he did."

While it's not news to me, hearing that Jack admitted it to Jem makes it hurt even more that a relationship with him is impossible.

She claps her hands. "Anyway, I just want to apologize for hanging up on you the other night and to thank you for caring about me."

Which is not an act, though she'll never believe it once my story hits the paper. Remembering the card I purchased for her, I jump up. "I have something for you." I dig my purse out of the coat closet. "Just a little something to let you know I care." I hold out the card.

Slowly, as if opening a highly anticipated present, she pulls the card from the envelope, but the chuckle I expect over the plucked, repentant-looking chicken doesn't happen. Rather, she runs her fingers over it, then looks at me in wonder. "I didn't tell anyone, so you couldn't have known."

"What?"

She turns the card toward me. "This is mine."

I frown over her a long moment before dropping down beside her. "You drew the chicken?"

"Last year I submitted a dozen card concepts to a Christian greeting card company, and they bought eight of them. And you liked this one well enough to buy it."

I laugh. "It grabbed me immediately."

She bounces on the sofa in a way that reminds me of Tigger. "Thanks. What did you think of the wording?"

"Yours too?"

"Yep."

"Well, it was the sorry-looking chicken that caught my eye, but the 'My bad. Your grace. Puh-leeease forgive me' made me open my wallet. It's a great card."

She gives another bounce. "This is so exciting—must be how an author feels when she sees someone reading her book."

I give her a hug that she returns with bony arms. When I pull back, I jut my chin at the card. "Open it."

She turns the cover and reads aloud, "I truly care about you and want you to get well. I'm sorry for any hurt I caused. Your friend, Grace."

A moment later, another hug, at the end of which I ask, "Are you going to get help?"

As she draws back, her face passes from light into shadow. "Despite Jack's assurances, I'm afraid."

I squeeze her forearm. "Of what?"

She lays her other hand atop mine. "That the others at Steeple Side will find out about my secret."

She's not alone in worrying about that, but in my case it's only a matter of when.

"I'm afraid they'll think I'm weak and…disturbed." She gives a sad laugh. "Not that they'll be obvious about it—they're nice people—but they'll be uncomfortable around me."

"I believe most of them will understand. After all, you're not the only one at Steeple Side dealing with a life-changing problem. Take the situation with Linda and her son."

Jem's face lightens, but only briefly. "Yeah, but she's not the one doing drugs."

"You don't think her son's addiction is a reflection on her? Nice people or not, some will judge her by what he got himself into…even blame her."

Jem lowers her gaze to our stacked hands.

As silence stretches, I scoot to the edge of my chair. "I haven't been at Steeple Side long, but I've learned that even though its employees have accepted Christ, they face the same obstacles as everyone else. They make mistakes and mess up, whether it's with drugs or gossip or gambling or porn or whatever you want to dig up. But what sets them apart is that they're tied together by faith. Yes, there will be some who don't get it and back off, but I believe there are more who will support you." I lean closer. "You won't be alone."

"I'm still scared."

I smile encouragingly. "What about God? And prayer?"

"I know. And I'm grateful for both."

"But?"

Her hand trembles on mine. "Have you ever been where I am, hating the place you're at, but afraid to move in case the next place is worse? Even if it's where God wants you?"

One moment I'm nodding, the next I'm playing her words back, then mine. And they're running together and through me like an icy wind. I *am* where she's at. I *do* hate it. And I'm just as afraid of venturing too far out and drowning. Again.

"What is it?"

I startle to find her staring at me. "I…"

"Are you all right?"

Get back to her problem. Deal with yours later. "No." *Don't do it. You'll blow it. Then what will you have to show for it? Big difference between starving oneself and full-frontal deception.* "No, I'm not all right." *There's always indigestion…good old menstrual cramps…*

Jem squeezes my shoulder. "Can I help?"

This is your life. "I don't know." I rub my forehead. "I'm into something up to my eyeballs, and I don't know how to get out. But I want to." I meet her concerned gaze. "Like you." *Fine. Kiss your career and dreams good-bye, and while you're at it, say hello to bankruptcy.*

"What kind of trouble are you in?"

Will she hate me? Nose tingling, eyes threatening to spring a leak, I lift my chin. "I guess you could call it fraud. And the name's Maizy."

The voice of dissent stomps off with a snort of disgust.

Jem looks up from the pages of notes that began with the day I put together my 5-Step Program to Authentic Christian Faith. She knows most of the story, including Seattle, and though she has winced, flinched, gasped, shaken her head, and shrugged her shoulders up to her ears, she has yet to turn tail and run.

She sighs. "So that's how Jack found out about my problem."

"Yeah." I stare at her as she sits cross-legged on the floor with my incriminating notebook in her lap. "It went flying, and he got to it before me."

She whistles, and once more I'm struck by how well she's taking this. "I'll bet that about gave you a heart attack."

"Fortunately I snatched the notebook from him before he could thumb through the other entries."

"How did you explain what he did see?"

I'm beyond the blush of shame. "I lied. Told him I was considering writing an article on anorexia. Since he'd asked me to write about my soup kitchen experience, it seemed like it would fly."

Jem fingers the page. "So how many employees were part of the investigation?"

"About two dozen."

She gives a short laugh that borders on bitter. "So this 'freelance editing' you've been doing is how you know that Steeple Side employees face the same problems as everyone else?"

"Yeah."

She rakes her teeth over her bottom lip. "Grace, er, Maizy, is this why you hung out with me...because of my big mouth?"

A conclusion I knew she would reach. "I really do enjoy spending time with you. However, it's true that once the paper put me on the story, you turned out to be a good source of information. I'm sorry."

"But you..." Her eyebrows nearly meet. "...liked me, didn't you?"

"Yes, and I still like you." I collapse back in the chair. "If you can believe that, and I wouldn't blame you if you didn't."

She closes the notebook. "I have to admit to feeling used, but I believe you."

My heart lurches out of first gear into second.

"So what are you going to do?"

Back down to first gear. "I don't know."

"Then we're in the same boat. Knowing we shouldn't be doing what we're doing but afraid to stop. Afraid of what others will think and how they'll react when they find out who we really are."

"Not quite the same boat. What you're doing hurts you. What I'm doing hurts others—not as easily understood or forgiven."

She scoots nearer. "But you're not going to do it, are you?"

The question hangs between us, though I already know the answer. Have known it for some time now despite telling myself I *could* and *had* to do it. "No. What I'm going to do is lose my job at the paper and very likely my friendship with Tessie."

"Maybe that's not such a bad thing. I mean, I know she's helped you out a lot, but if you lose a friendship over doing the right thing, it may not be worth the heart it's written on."

Friendship…worth the heart it's written on. Wow. There's a lot more to Jem than her clothing, penchant for gossip, and anorexia.

"As for losing your job at the paper, eventually Steeple Side will put you on full time."

My jaw unhinges. "I can't stay at Steeple Side. Even if what I did—"

"Were going to do."

"Even if what I was going to do never got out, it wouldn't feel right."

"Because first you need to be forgiven."

"What?"

"You need to tell your boss, Gra—Maizy." She rolls her eyes. "The day we met, I told you I didn't think the name fit, and now it's hard to think of you as anyone other than Grace."

I wave a hand in front of her. "Did I hear right? You think I should tell Linda what I've been up to?"

"Yes, especially if the paper might send in someone else to get the story."

She's right. And yet… "I don't know. This is such a mess."

"What about God. And prayer?"

Thus the question I asked her earlier comes back to me, rubbing my face in hypocrisy.

"Why don't we pray together, Maizy."

"Oh no. I don't do that praying out loud thing."

"We don't have to do it out loud. We can just sit here and silently pray for each other. I promise it will help."

I struggle but finally nod. "Okay. I'll try."

A half hour later, my eyes are red, my nose is running, and I'm all prayed out. As is Jem, who finished before me and traded in the floor for the sofa. I decide not to awaken her since it's going on nine, and scoop up Woofer.

"It helped," I whisper as I settle him against my chest and trudge toward bed, "but I'm still scared."

Woofer lifts his head, gives a snorty little sigh, and flicks his tongue across my jaw.

TWENTY-ONE

VERY BLONDE TIP #43

FORGIVENESS (the receiving end): Okay, Blondie, it can't get any simpler than this. You want forgiveness? Ask for it. That's right. Own up to whatever earned you another's wrath and be done with it. Too chicken to engage in a face to face? Make a phone call. Write a letter. Ask a mutual acquaintance to serve as a mediator. Just do it. *Capiche?*

Exception: in life-threatening situations (what were you thinking?), God's forgiveness may be sufficient.

What am I doing here? I look sidelong at my "pew buddy," as Jem named herself when she rooted out a couple of seats near the front of the sanctuary and dragged me along. I had no intention of showing my face at Sovereign today, *if* ever again, but Jem assured me over bowls of cereal that this is where we need to be. I don't think so, especially as I'm bound to run into Jack. And there's no way I'm attending Sunday school or going bowling with the other singles.

"Are you listening?" Jem rasps in my ear.

"Uh…"

"Your pastor is talking to us."

I look to the man at the podium. "What do you mean he's talking to us?"

"Not directly. En masse." She nods at the projection screen. "We're saints, Gr—Maizy."

That's what it says, but me—a saint?

"Believe it," says the pastor. "If Jesus is your Savior, you are a saint. " He smiles as he surveys the sanctuary. "Let that sink in. Aspire to be worthy." He points to the balcony. "Saint David, Saint Sandi, Saint Elizabeth." His finger lowers. "Saint Max, Saint Robin, Saint Skyler, Saint Jane."

I flinch as that finger sweeps past me.

"Saint Doug."

The big man at the tip of that finger chuckles.

"Believe it," the pastor says. "That doesn't mean you'll never sin. It means you reach beyond your sins to be like Jesus. When you do sin, you get up, wipe off your seat, and try harder. In short, you forgive and are forgiven."

Maybe in the eyes of God, but what about those wronged? I shudder at the thought of asking Linda for forgiveness. Far easier to slink away with no one the wiser about my deception. I bite my lip at the thought of Jack finding out. Jack, who noticed at the outset that there was something crooked about not only my fish emblem, but me. Jack, who should have stuck with his gut feeling but lowered his defenses.

I've messed up, God. Even though this pastor says I'm a saint, I'm not. You know it. I know it. Isn't that enough? Providing I can nip the Steeple Side story in the bud, why does anyone else have to know about my deception?

Twenty minutes later, I feel I'm no nearer to convincing God to let me off the hook than He is to convincing me to follow the advice of my friendly *DBGC.*

Jem nudges my shoulder. "I'll go if you go."

I startle. "What?"

"For prayer...at the front."

I cringe at the half dozen people who have answered the "altar call"—an invitation for those in need of prayer to come forward. Not me. Not that I don't need prayer. But there's no way I'm going up there.

"Please, Maizy." Jem's face draws nearer mine. "At least come with me so I don't have to do this alone. I really need prayer."

I long to bolt, but her moist, pleading eyes tug at me, and she warbles, "Help me."

Oh, God. "All right."

She grips my wrist and pulls me out of the pew. Wide eyed, I look left and right at the men and women stationed at the front to pray for those who trickle forward. When I look left again, I see a big woman coming for us—short, blond curls, a small mouth that doubles in width when she smiles, and beefy arms. When one of those arms reaches for me, I stumble back. "Uh, Jem needs prayer." I nod at Jem, who looks so tiny in the crook of the woman's arm. "I'm just..."

"Maizy needs prayer too," Jem chirps.

"Well come here, darlin'. Don't be afraid." Her large hand cups my shoulder and pulls me in.

Everyone's watching. Pondering the sinner in their midst. Guessing at what bad thing I did to warrant a walk down the aisle that's only missing the dead-man-walking call to seal my fate.

"And how can I pray for you, Maizy?"

I blink at the woman. Is it my turn? Already? Did she pray for Jem? Couldn't have. I wouldn't have missed that.

Jem smiles past welling tears. Oh no. I was so caught up in my insecurities that I missed the prayer spoken over my friend. *What kind of Christian are you?*

Cultural. And I'm tired of it. I want what's shining out of Jem's face. Something like hope, but more. Something that seems within reach. If only I weren't so afraid to reach for it…

"If I can do it," Jem whispers, "you can."

I glance over my shoulder at the hundreds of faces and stiffen. Maybe another time. After all, these people want to get on with their Sunday, and far be it from me to hold them up.

"No hurry," the big woman says. "We have all the time you need, sweet thing."

Sweet thing. Ha! If she knew who she was dealing with—

"Come on." Jem's hand pumps my shoulder. "Spit it out."

How I wish it were only a bad taste in my mouth that could be expelled.

"Maizy Grace."

I blink at Jem's unprecedented use of my first and middle names, the syllables of which cause her encouraging voice to turn musical.

Amazing grace. That's what's shining out of Jem's face—what I need more than anything—and it's within reach if I'll just speak up.

I moisten my lips. "I…" So many people watching. "I'd like prayer for…"

"Yes, dear?"

"Strength. To do the right thing. To tell the truth. And fix my lies." I glance at Jem. "At least to try."

"Then let us go to the Lord."

With everyone watching. *So* glad they can't hear what's being said.

"Lord, Jem's friend Maizy…"

With a voice like that—one that booms between us—I can't believe I missed out on the prayer for Jem.

"…a child precious in Your eyes, needs the strength You give to those who ask for it. And so we come before You—"

"Excuse me?" I rasp.

Her eyes open. "Yes, dear?"

Jem peers into my face. "What is it?"

"Do we have to do this here? I…can't concentrate."

The woman gives an understanding nod. "Let's go to the prayer room."

We enter a small, dimly lit room. There are no windows, only a backlit stained-glass cross at the altar. And a sense of peace. We gather before the altar and bow our heads.

"Lord, Maizy needs strength to do Your good will. Strength to right the wrongs she has done."

Lots of strength.

"Strength to be truthful even when it hurts."

It's gonna hurt.

"We know You can and will give her this strength if she asks for it."

I do. Please.

"And she does, Lord. As do we."

Why do they care so much, especially this woman whose name I didn't even bother to catch?

"Your Word tells us that a person who hides her sins will not prosper—"

Not according to Tessie.

"—but if she confesses and forsakes them, she shall have mercy."

Again, not according to Tessie, who says there isn't one person at Steeple Side who cares as much about me and my future as she does.

"As a tree is identified by its fruit, we pray that Maizy will be identified by her honesty."

And all for the bargain price of one friendship, a career, and a roof over her head.

"So, Lord, give her the strength and confidence to do what You would have her do."

The woman falls silent, but just as I conclude it's over, Jem says, "Lord, my friend needs Your help as I need Your help. We've been pretending to be people we're not and making idols out of our outward appearances."

Our? Ah, her body, my reporter-in-disguise.

"We're afraid to be who You would have us be and who we long to be. Afraid we won't be enough unless we take control of the situation and do things our way. Afraid of trusting You."

Wow. She's good. I open an eye to be certain it *is* Jem whose sincere, sweetly pleading words could crack the hardest heart. It is. Flighty, gossiping, peanut-butter-cracker-crumbling, kicked-out-of-beauty-school, seemingly immature Jem.

"And so I ask You not only to give me the strength to overcome my eating problem but, more importantly, to give Maizy the strength to do what's right."

More importantly? It's her health we're talking about—maybe her life. It's just my career…

Did I just think that? *Just* my career? I did. Because that's all it is—a big *just.* And yet Jem is saying it's more important than her own problem. Or is she? I play her words back. No, it's not my career she's talking about. It's doing what's right. And to her, that's more important than solving her own problem.

Throat muscles tight, I once more steal a peek at her. Her eyes are closed, head is nodding, lips are moving. And for some reason, I can't hear a word she's saying. Can't hear anything except the beat of my heart as something causes it to expand its territory within my chest.

I drop my chin. Strangely, the moment I lower my lids, I hear again.

"…You love her." Jem draws a breath. "One more thing, Lord. I've asked and asked for a friend, someone who will like me in spite of my quirks and failings and sometimes inappropriate behavior. If Your answer is Maizy, and I hope it is, please let her see me as a friend. Please let her know that I care for her."

What's wrong with me? That was sweet, but it doesn't warrant tears. I flutter my lashes in an attempt to clear the moisture and draw a deep breath to give my heart more room in my bound chest. But they aren't cooperating. So when Jem says, "Amen," and the big woman echoes her, I can only squeeze my eyes tighter.

"Are you all right, Maizy?"

"I don't know. I feel kind of dizzy."

I'm urged down into a chair, and the air before me stirs slightly, then more vigorously. Cracking open my eyelids, I see Jem and the woman hovering, their hands fanning my face.

Jem pauses. "Are you going to be sick?"

"I don't think so. I just feel strange." I pat my chest. "Mostly in here." I touch my head. "A little in here."

The woman smiles as if she understands. But how can she when I don't understand myself?

"And I"—I roll my eyes—"feel like having a good cry. Which makes no sense because I don't like to cry. And why should I when the prayer was so nice?"

"Because it was heartfelt." The woman pats Jem's shoulder. "You have a good friend in this young lady."

My chest swells further. Ignoring the discomfort, I reach forward and lay a hand over Jem's. "Thank you. And"—I swing my gaze to the woman—"I'm sorry, but if you said your name, I didn't catch it."

Smile broadening, she reaches out a hand. "Beverly Diggory. It's a pleasure to make your acquaintance, Maizy Grace."

We shake. "Yours too, and thank you for praying for me."

With a satisfied sigh, she takes a step back. "I'll leave you now, but stay as long as you like."

When the door closes, Jem drops down beside me. "You know, don't you?"

"What I have to do?" At her nod, I groan. "I know. First thing tomorrow. What about you?"

She squirms a little. "I guess I'll be talking to Human Resources."

"Good."

She looks at her watch. "So? Sunday school?"

"Not today." After my walk down the aisle, Jack is the *last* person I want to see.

"How about an early lunch?"

I wonder what she'll eat and how much. "All right."

We both rise, but I catch Jem's arm as she turns toward the door. "Thank you for the prayer."

Her cheeks turn pink. "It was nothing."

"No, Miss Modesty, it was everything. And I appreciate it. More, I appreciate that you're my friend."

She gives me a hug through which I feel her ribs like a row of butter knives balanced on their edges. "We start over again tomorrow," I say as we disengage.

She presses her slight shoulders back. "Tomorrow."

Lord, that strength Jem asked that we both receive? Could You start doling it out to her? She's so thin. Of course, I could use some strength myself, as it's only a matter of time before I'm out of a job. And very likely a home.

I am down and out. In the gutter. Again.

With a groan, I turn to my teammates, who smile tolerantly and wave me away from the lane. Wishing I never had to see that scuffed, green marble, three-holed excuse for a ball again, I narrow my eyes at the blur spit out by the ball return mechanism. Can't blame the machine one bit for its disgust.

I head to the table where the others await their turn and drop into the seat farthest from Jack. And I keep sliding down until my nape is on the edge of the seat back. Why did I allow Jem to convince me to come? Yes, I told Jack I'd be here, but everything is different now. Or will be tomorrow, barring the miracle that Jem says I shouldn't be so quick to discount.

"Ready for a few pointers?" Jack says above the *whoosh* and *thunder* and *crack* of balls that echo through the bowling alley.

It's not the first time he's offered to help since I showed up. And I'd like to refuse again, except that I'll be the death of the team's chances to place better than fourth—out of four teams—if I don't hit at least a few pins. "Okay. Point away."

A collective sigh goes around the table, but when I frown at my teammates, they look away.

Jack stands. "Get your ball."

Observing proper etiquette, which was kindly pointed out earlier when I tried to get a jump on my turn by retrieving my ball from the machine, I wait for a break in my teammates' play and those on either side before complying.

Jack extends a hand as I approach him where he stands fifteen feet back from the table. "I'm no expert," he says as I pass the ball to him, "but I can show you the basics."

"Thanks."

He considers me, then tilts his head to the side. "Is everything all right?"

While I'm pretty sure where this is going, I open my eyes wide. "What do you mean?"

"I saw that Jem came to church with you and the two of you went up for prayer. And you didn't make it to Sunday school."

I shift my weight. "Nothing I can't handle." *Right.*

He nods and turns his attention to the ball. "Ten pounder. Looks about right. Slide your fingers in."

I take a step nearer, which transports me from the fringes of his scent into the midst of it. Not good. And yet good, especially if a miracle—or should I say a *series* of miracles?—happens.

Miracle #1: Once I come clean with Linda, everything will work out. She'll keep the matter between us and allow me to remain at Steeple Side.

What about your name? Your real *name? You can't be Grace indefinitely, and eventually someone will make the connection that this Maizy Stewart is* that *Maizy Stewart.*

Miracle #2: The paper will pull out of the story (though probably not without axing me).

What about the work you've been paid to do? The paychecks you've cashed?

Miracle #3: Tessie will forgive me.

Yeah, right.

Miracle #4: Tessie will continue to lease the apartment to me.

And how do you plan to pay for it? Even if Linda keeps you on, the job is only part time.

"Grace?"

I look up into Jack's face. Nice, in spite of the furrowed brow. Maybe there is a future for us.

Only if you come clean with him as well. But don't count on it. This could end as bad as Ben. Or worse.

Jack touches my arm. "Are you sure you're all right?"

I smile so bright that my facial muscles strain. "Yes. Why?"

"You groaned."

"I did?" I search my memory for the sound but catch no echo of it. "Preoccupied, I guess. So how about those pointers?"

He extends the ball. "Show me your grip."

As a cheer goes up from our teammates—one of them must have made a strike—I take the green thing, cradle it in the crook of my left arm, and insert the first two fingers and thumb of my right hand into the holes.

"A bit of a death grip you have there."

I ponder my arthritic-looking hand. "Don't want to drop this thing on my toes."

"Let's go with the conventional grip. Slide your fingers in a bit more...up to the second joint."

Not something I didn't think of myself, but who knows what's in those deep, dark holes?

"Go ahead."

I sink my fingers up to the second joint. Thankfully they don't touch bottom.

He moves to my side and just in back of me, brushing my elbow and heightening my awareness of him. "Now get into starting position."

"Uh..."

He reaches across me, bringing his chest into contact with my upper arm—ooh boy!—covers my hand with his, and turns the ball so that my hand moves under it. "Keep your wrist firm, not too much bend. Let your other hand continue to support some of the ball's weight."

The only time I've been closer to him was when he kissed me, and though there can't be a kiss between us now, I'm tempted to change all that. Trouble. Or not. Miracles do happen.

"Keep your bowling elbow close to your side." He gently presses my upper arm against my ribs. "Brilliant. Now you're ready to deliver your shot."

I am?

"Though you'll move toward the lane when you start your swing, let's go through the motions here." Once more he reaches across and places his hand atop mine on the ball. "Now grip it only hard enough to—"

"Jack! You're up."

He gives our teammates a nod and disengages. "I'll be back."

Anchoring the ball on my hip, I admire his long strides and sigh over the flexing of his shoulder as he hefts his black bowling ball.

"Thank goodness he's on the auction block again, hmm?" someone says.

I locate the petite brunette to my left. Dinah something-or-other, who's on Avery's team two lanes down and who, according to Jem, is a shameless flirt. "Auction block?"

Pulling her gaze from Jack, she wrinkles her nose. "I'd bid on him, wouldn't you? Yeah, he's a Christian—a definite plus—but he's also good looking, has a melt-in-your-ear accent, and seems fairly well off. It doesn't get much better than that."

I look back around in time to see Jack take out three pins, and I catch the face he makes at me as he retrieves his ball for a second try. Actually it does get better. He's nice and thoughtful and not too serious once you get to know him. And a good kisser.

"Speaking of well off, you must be yourself."

Dinah can't be talking to me, especially in light of my worn jeans, slightly pilled top, and these u-u-u-u-gly rented bowling shoes. However, when I return my regard to her, it's just the two of us. "What?"

"I said you must be well off."

I shift the ball to the other side. "What makes you think that?"

"You haven't cashed any of your Steeple Side paychecks."

It's then I remember that she works in Payroll, and I'm stirred with unease that shifts into purée mode when Jack heads toward us. I have to tell him the truth. But not like this. Not because I'm cornered. "Not well off at all. Just busy."

Oh, believable, Maizy.

I seek and find Jack, who smiles as he advances. "Nice talking to you." I nod at Dinah and step forward. "I'm up next." Well, not next, but after the guy who comes after Jack.

"Cash those checks, won't you?" she calls. "We'd like to get them off the books."

Holding my breath and praying—yes, *praying*—her words are lost amid the din of balls, pins, cheers, groans, and high-fives, I intercept Jack within feet of the table. "Seven pins. That's great."

He gives Dinah a nod past my shoulder but shakes his head at me. "Hardly great, but not bad…for me. So where were we?"

"My swing, but my turn's coming up, so—"

"I'll be quick about it." He draws me toward the spot where he demonstrated how to grip the ball. Fortunately Dinah is headed back to her team.

"Grip it firmly, but not too tight." Once more, he moves in back of my elbow, reaches across, and slides his hand over mine on the ball. Then he lightly sets his other hand at my waist.

My mouth goes dry. Nothing to get excited about. This is simply how a person shows another how to swing one of these holey balls.

"Now move the ball out…" He guides my arm. "…down…"

Nothing.

"…back…"

Nothing at all.

"…and forward…"

Maybe a little something.

"…keeping it in as straight a line as possible."

Maybe a lot.

He eases the ball back to starting position. "How did that feel?"

I look across my shoulder and am a little surprised that his expression isn't the least bit suggestive.

He raises an eyebrow. "Awkward?"

I wouldn't call it that. Of course, if I called it anything, I would hardly be referring to the bowling ball. I have no idea how that felt. "I wouldn't say that."

As he frowns, my attention is drawn to his mouth, and I'm struck with remembrance of our kiss.

His mouth turns further down. "I believe I'm receiving a signal here, Grace. Are you sure it's one you want to send? Because I distinctly remember you telling this bloke—"

Bloke. That is *so* adorably British!

"—that you aren't at a good place in your life for a relationship."

Just yesterday. And here I am thinking this might not be such a bad place after all. Once he knows the truth, of course, and providing he still wants anything to do with me. Will he forgive me for my deception? extend to me the same grace that Steeple Side extended to him years ago when he came clean about Bette?

"If you keep looking at my mouth like that, I'm going to have the answer to my question whether you like it or not."

I jerk my eyes toward Jack's and am lightened by the teasing glint there. "You have your answer," I say more boldly than I feel, then narrow my lids at him. "The answer you were looking for."

His lips twitch. "What do you mean?"

"Tempting me like this, showing me how to swing a bowling ball."

The twitch turns into a chortle. "You found me out. Just as I found you out, Grace Stewart."

No he hasn't. And he won't, because I'm going to tell him.

His laughter falls away. "Did I say something wrong?"

Realizing my smile is down around my chin, I pull it back up. "No, I—"

"Hey, lovebirds," one of our teammates calls. "Grace is up."

As Jack releases my waist, I turn around. Sure enough, I'm up. No telling how long they've been waiting on me. As warmth spreads across my face, a whistle sounds to my left and I follow it to Avery, who's watching us. In fact, everyone's watching us. And smiling—except Dinah, who looks dejected.

Jack comes around to face me, and he appears only slightly discomfited. "Show them what we were really doing. Send that ball down the middle."

Fat chance. Still, I put my chin up and shoulders back as I lug my ball past my teammates.

Second joints. Firm. Not too tight. Ball out, down, back, forward. Er, he said something else. I pull the ball back in. Oh yeah, keep it in as straight a line as possible. Here we go again. This time I release and the ball thuds onto the alley and slowly rolls forward. It doesn't look promising, as it veers toward one gutter, then the other, but—lo and behold!—it centers itself right before it reaches the pins.

The pins go down, leaving only two standing, one of which wobbles before tipping into the other and taking it down.

"Strike!" I squeal. Forget etiquette. I did it! "Strike! Strike! Strike!"

A hand curls around my arm, and I look up into Jack's face. "I did it!"

"Grace…"

Etiquette, schmetiquette. I embrace him. "Did you see that? I knocked them down. Every one." I pull back and laugh with a glee I haven't felt in a long time. And, of course, the laugh ends on a purr. But I don't care. "I got a strike."

"You didn't get a strike."

"What?" I snap my head around. My pins have been swept away and replaced with ten standing perfectly upright. "But I…you saw…"

"You fouled." He smiles apologetically. "You stepped over the line."

And just like that my strike is voided? "A technicality," I mutter. "Well, I don't care what that silly scoreboard says, I'm not letting it take away my joy."

"Good for you." He urges me toward the ball return. "Give it another go."

"All right." However, once more eschewing etiquette, I halt. "Are you doing anything after bowling?"

An eyebrow goes up. "That's a promising question."

"I'd like to go somewhere and talk."

"Dinner?"

"That would be nice. But somewhere quiet. I have something I need to discuss with you."

"That doesn't sound as promising."

No, it doesn't, but it depends on him. And grace. Real grace. Not fake Grace.

A score of seventy-six. My best game. I'd be embarrassed if I didn't have more important things on my mind. Namely, dinner with Jack.

"Are you certain you don't want me to pick you up at your place?" He steers me away from the din and toward the doors.

"This time around"—*Lord, please let there be more*—"let's meet at the Green Hills Grille."

"If that's what you prefer." He moves forward and holds the door for me.

Like a gentleman. An English gentleman with a melt-in-your-ear accent. Dinah's words, not mine, but God willing, I'll soon have more right to them.

Jack takes my arm as he steps alongside me into the late afternoon sunshine. Squinting against the brightness, I pull my sunglasses from my purse. No sooner do they come to rest on my nose than the man striding toward us on somewhat bowed legs comes in to focus.

He registers recognition a moment before I do and raises his bowling bag in acknowledgment. "Hey, Maizy."

TWENTY-TWO

Please, God. Not Porter. Not now.

"Maizy?" Jack murmurs.

I could say it's a case of mistaken identity. Lie Number—

No. Heart knocking as I scramble to avert disaster, I draw to a halt within feet of Porter and another man also toting a bowling bag.

Porter grins. "Don't tell me you're a closet bowler?"

"Just giving it a try." What do I do? "Well, it was nice seeing you." I start to skirt him. How am I going to explain this to Jack? And it will have to be explained, probably before our dinner date.

"Hey, aren't you the guy I saw with Maizy at the Mule Day event?"

I freeze. Porter saw me with Jack? But I was practically lying down in my seat.

"You know, at the liars contest." Porter shifts his attention to Jack's hand on my arm. "Is that where the two of you met?"

I hazard a look at Jack.

He briefly meets my gaze before offering a hand to Porter. "Jack Prentiss."

"Porter Mitchell." He gives Jack's hand a jerk-shake, then introduces his friend.

"Nice to meet you," Jack says.

"And this is Maizy Stewart," Porter tells his friend. "We work at the paper together."

Jack's hand on me stiffens. "The paper?" In the blink of an eye, the reserve I haven't heard in his voice for some time kicks in.

"Yes, the *Middle Tennessee Review*. I'm a staff photographer." Porter chuckles. "Nothing as interesting as what Maizy does, but I enjoy it."

Jack's razor-sharp stare slices into me, and it's all I can do to hold it.

He releases my arm and looks back at Porter. "Unfortunately, as close as *Maizy* and I have become, she's been a bit secretive about her work at the paper, so I wouldn't know anything about it."

Porter gives a comical grimace. "Sorry, Maizy. Hope I didn't blow your cover." *Chuckle, chuckle.*

He thinks he's being funny, but he has no idea that Jack is—*was*—part of the Steeple Side investigation, and that I *am* undercover.

Porter steps forward. "We'd better get inside or they'll start without us. Nice meeting you, Jack."

Jack inclines his head, and a few moments later it's just the two of us.

"Jack—"

"I'll walk you to your car."

I follow him, using the length of the parking lot to search for words to explain what he surely thinks of me and what I've been doing at Steeple Side. But when we reach my car, all that comes out is, "I was going to tell you over dinner."

He lowers his palms to the hood of my car, leans into them, then slowly turns his face to me. "Oh. Right."

I don't think any man has ever looked at me like that—disillusionment wrapped in disappointment wrapped in disgust.

Lord, won't You step in for me like You did for Mary with Joseph? Send an angel to inform Jack that I'm telling the truth?

I touch Jack's arm but pull my hand back when he stiffens. "When I said I had something to talk to you about tonight, it was this. My job at the paper." Deep breath. "And what I'm doing at Steeple Side."

His nostrils flare. "Confession time? How convenient."

I'm not surprised that he's set against believing me, but I am hurt. Even though I have no right to be.

"Tell me, is Teresa Halston involved in this…" He looks overhead, then slams his gaze back to me. "…investigation? Because that's what it is, isn't it, Grace?" He laughs harshly. "Pardon me—*Maizy.*"

"Grace is my middle name." *Oh, that will clear up everything!*

"As I said…convenient. So? Teresa Halston?"

I drag a hand down the side of my face. "Yes, but—"

"The taped bumper sticker and crooked fish." He nods. "The liars contest. I told you you'd be good at that. The notebook and notes on Jem's anorexia. I wonder what else I would have seen if you hadn't snatched the book away. Notes on Linda and her son's drug rehab, the young man struggling with porn, Bette and me?"

Two out of three. "Look, you may not believe me, but—"

"I *don't* believe you, Gr—" He pushes off the hood of my car. "I'd be daft to. And I've been daft enough as it is."

"Please listen." I grab his sleeve as he steps past. "When I started at Steeple Side, it wasn't in an investigative capacity. I just needed a job. When this opportunity arose, I didn't want to do it, but it was the only way to get my career back after I messed it up."

"I don't care about how you messed up your career, *Maizy*. All I care about is how you intended to rebuild it on the heartaches of people who befriended you. Fellow Christians, or so you had us believe."

Releasing his sleeve, I ball my hands at my sides. "I am a Christian. One who makes mistakes just like Linda's son did. And you with Bette."

"Turning it all to your advantage now." He shakes his head. "You're too clever for me. Good-bye, Maizy Grace Stewart." He strides past but at the rear of my car looks over his shoulder. "I'd like to say that under different circumstances it would have been nice to know you. But no."

Tears rush my eyes at the remembrance that he had said the same thing to Tessie all those years ago—only gently—when he put her story to rest. He said it would have been nice to meet her under different circumstances. And left it at that.

Jack resumes his stride.

"You're wrong about me," I say, but it comes out so choked that I doubt he heard.

I watch him walk to his car, then slip inside my own and drop my chin to my chest to indulge in an old-fashioned cry. It doesn't help, and when I finally let up enough to insert my key in the ignition, I wonder if I'll ever laugh again.

Of course, you will! Don't be so dramatic.

Okay, but I'm pretty sure purring is out. And maybe that's not all bad.

This is bad.

Tessie doesn't say anything, just grips the edge of the counter and stares out her kitchen window. As the words I loosed in a rush sink deeper, her arms begin to tremble. But that's not all. There's her sharply drawn reflection in the darkened window. Her big blue eyes are narrowed to slits, nostrils flared, and jaw set forward. All evidence that her frigid anger does, indeed, have more than one setting—as Jack discovered the day they met. In fact, she might boil over.

Oh, to be anywhere but here, but I owed it to her to tell her first.

She draws a breath that I hear across the ten feet between her and the kitchen table, where I sit with my hands clasped between my knees.

Please, God, I'm doing what's right even if she doesn't agree. Give me a break, won't You?

She slowly turns. "I can't begin to tell you how disappointed I am in you."

Darts again, but unlike Grandma's, which zeroed in on my conscience, Tessie's are aimed at my self-esteem.

She leans back against the counter and lifts her chin to peer down her nose at me. "I thought you could rise above Seattle's foolish mistakes and sentiments, that the hunger to redeem yourself would prevail."

So did I, but once again I got too close to those I was investigating. However, I'm doing what's right, and no matter what it costs me, I'm done with the Steeple Side story. Done squatting on toilet seats, scribbling notes about others' personal lives and pain. Done using friendships to my advantage and others' downfall. "I can't do it."

Her mouth bunches. "After all I did to help you?"

"I'm grateful, and I owe you." I moisten my lips. "But not like this. I cannot go against my conscience."

"Conscience?" She jerks to her full five foot eleven and smacks the counter. "You mean that silly Bible."

I stand. "I suppose the two go hand in hand. Regardless, if you would just step back from whatever you harbor against a faith you once called your own, I think you would understand why I can't do what the paper has asked me to do. "

Color rushes her cheeks. "Don't you mean what it *paid* you to do?"

I keep my shoulders back. "Yes, what it paid me to do." I sigh. "I'll have to figure out how much that is, lifestyle editing aside, and repay the salary I drew. Hopefully Ray will allow me to make monthly installments."

Tessie swings away, glares out the window again, then whacks the faucet so hard that the handheld sprayer snakes out of the head and smacks the side of the stainless steel sink. "You're quitting, aren't you?"

"I am."

"You'll be ruined. The best you'll be able to hope for is that some backwater excuse for a newspaper will let you write classified ads."

So hard to be strong when faced with reality, but I believe this is what God wants me to do. Meaning, surely He has other plans for me. *Oh, please do. And not classified ads. Maybe more lifestyle writing, which I'm pretty good at. Which isn't all that bad. In fact, most times I enjoy it.*

Tessie turns back around. "Is that what you want?"

"It's a chance I have to take. If it proves the end of my career as a journalist, I'm young enough to find another career."

She rolls her eyes. "Well, aren't we the little martyr destined for sainthood."

I am a saint. I long to tell her so, but she wouldn't understand. I step toward the back door. "I should probably go."

"First answer me this. What happened?" She turns her palms up. "You were among my best students. You could dig up anything, put together a compelling story, and rejoice in the difference you made."

She's right. Among other things, I exposed the mishandling of scholarship monies, discrimination in grading practices, and the use of steroids in athletics. "Yes, but that was for the campus paper, and I was dealing more with issues than a specific person behind them. I wasn't trying to ruin someone's life, innocent or otherwise."

Tessie snorts. "Some people's lives deserve to be ruined, as your ex-boyfriend proved to his gain—not *yours*—when you waffled on the state senator who compassionately addressed the concerns of the underprivileged. And all the while she not only had her own little Watergate underway but was stuffing her Gucci bag with political contributions."

Emotion stings my eyes. Yes, the story that Ben stole held water, but when I stood on the rim of it, I didn't think it would—rather, didn't *want* it to. Despite the evidence, I simply couldn't risk ruining the life of a woman I had come to care for.

I startle when Tessie is suddenly at my side. "Maizy..." She grips my shoulder. "You can't allow people to get away with lying and hypocrisy. If you turn your back, you're condoning what they do, and that makes you just as guilty."

I stare into her intense face and catch a glimmer of pleading in her eyes, but I am not going to do what she asks. "If I knew without a doubt that someone had committed a terrible act and I did nothing,

I would be in the wrong and my conscience would let me know, but that isn't the case with Steeple Side. There isn't a story there. At least, not the one you're looking for."

She releases my shoulder. "There's always a story."

I shake my head. "A good friend and mentor once told me that writers have to put stories behind them when they reach a dead end. This is a dead end. I only pray you'll respect that and let it go."

"Pray! This whole religion thing has you messed up."

"No, it's cleaned up my mess." I reach toward the doorknob. "Obviously I won't be able to afford the apartment, so if you'll give me a couple of weeks to find something else, I'd appreciate it."

Her only response—besides staring holes in me—is a shrug.

Wonderful. She'll probably have the eviction papers served tomorrow. "Good night."

I open the door, but as I pass through, her bitter voice strikes. "Is it Jack Prentiss? Did he get to you?"

Air eludes me for a moment, but when I turn back, it's in full supply. "What do you mean?"

"Have you fallen for him?" Her mouth curves into a not-so-pretty smile. "Not that I'd blame you. He's attractive in a foreign way, especially when he opens his mouth and out come those deep, round vowels. Did you get taken in?"

I try to hold her gaze, but my eyes refuse to cooperate.

"Surprise, surprise. And I'll bet that you do indeed have something on our local Brit you aren't letting on about."

A moth slips past me into the brightly lit kitchen. I know I should close the door before others join its ranks, but I just stand there.

"Was it really scandalous?"

I look up. "There's no story."

"Not from you."

"What does that mean?"

She crosses her arms over her chest. "Everything you've given me, as lame as much of it is, has been paid for by the paper. I could write the story myself. Open up the can of worms on the hypocrisy running rampant through Steeple Side—drugs, gambling, porn, divorce, blasphemy, eating disorders."

I grip the door's edge. "You would do that? Be Linda Tripp to my Monica Lewinski?"

She stills, the only evidence of life found in her flaring eyes; however, an instant later she laughs.

I don't want to dislike her, but in that moment I do.

Fortunately it doesn't take long for her to regain her composure. "Bad comparison, Maizy. You knew what you were doing when you passed on the information and where it would end up. In print."

"You're right, but that doesn't mean it's fit to print." I take a step toward her. "There isn't a story."

"There will be when I'm done with it."

That's no empty threat, and it makes me mad. I close the distance between us. "What happened to your insistence that a journalist's writing be based on the known and observable?"

Is it my imagination or did her gaze waver?

"That he or she not allow personal biases to seep into and twist a story? That she not lose sight of the goal, which is to change things for the better?"

Her lips tighten.

"Why are you compromising your high standards? Because of what happened to your own faith?"

Her eyes flash. "You know nothing about that."

"I know that you did believe and that something made you turn your back on your beliefs."

Tessie's jaw slackens only to snap back. "Do you really want to know what happened?"

"I do."

She glares at me. "All right. It begins with my father—an upstanding member of the community who worked for a Christian publishing company."

I catch my breath. "Steeple Side?"

"No," her voice wrings out disgust, "though the two companies do paddle around in the same hypocrisy pond."

I can guess where this is going. "Your father was laid off?"

She rolls her eyes. "No, but that's the least of what they should have done to him."

"I don't understand."

"My father—that fine, upstanding Christian man—verbally beat my mother and Bible-thumped all in the same breath. Day in, day out."

"I'm...sorry."

"Yeah." Bitterness sharpens her expression. "Still, I was a good little Christian and even at times felt something not dictated by my father when I sat in my Sunday school class." She touches her chest. "When I got older and my father started turning on me as well—demeaning me, finding fault in my efforts—I was comforted by the knowledge that I had another Father who loved me and my mother and would never hurt us."

Silence creeps in, and on her face I glimpse a range of emotions that I wouldn't have believed her capable of feeling. "When I graduated from high school with a full college scholarship, my mother filed for divorce." A derisive laugh pops from her lips. "Turns out she was biding her time until I was out on my own. She'd suffered all of those years for my sake."

At my frown, Tessie continues. "You see, she wasn't educated beyond a GED, so she depended on my father's income. And my father's job depended on him modeling those Christian values, which did not include divorce. He pleaded with her to reconsider. Know why?"

I shake my head.

"For the sake of his job. Not her. Not me. His job."

"Did they...divorce?"

"Yes." She scowls. "And with his company's blessing."

I startle. "What?"

"Adultery—that's how my *Christian* father was absolved of the 'sin' of his divorce."

"But it wasn't adul—"

"No." Her nostrils flare. "But it satisfied them and allowed them to keep their top salesman on board. As for our church, they rallied around my poor, wronged father."

"Then no one believed your mother?"

A snort. "She didn't defend herself, but had she, who do you think they would have believed? My quiet little mother who kept to herself or my outgoing, upstanding, model *Christian* father?"

328 | Tamara Leigh

"But you can't turn your back on your beliefs just because one person wasn't the Christian he convinced others he was."

The set of her jaw turns stubborn. "Yes, I can. And did. And will continue to do so." And there's that "discussion closed" sigh.

Though I know I'm wasting my time, I step toward her. "I'm sorry about what happened, but it's wrong to take out your anger on Steeple Side. Those who work there are good people facing the same problems everyone faces. They're just trying to handle them in a different way—by leaning on God and helping one another."

Her only response is a raised eyebrow that says I have worn out my welcome.

I turn away but at the door look back at her. "Please let the story go, Tessie."

At her further lack of response, I walk outside and pull the door closed.

Woofer is up on his peg legs when I enter my apartment, tail ticktocking and tongue lolling. I scoop him up. "So to what do I owe this nice reception?" Might he finally accept that we're back to normal? I almost laugh at the thought, as "normal" isn't going to last. Soon we'll be moving.

I press the Play button on my blinking answering machine.

"Hi, it's Jem. I just wanted you to know that I called my boss at home. She was understanding, and she's going with me to Human Resources in the morning. So depending on what happens, I may not see you at lunch." She draws a deep breath. *"I'm going to do this, Maizy. What about you?"*

"I did," I breathe as the automated voice announces the time and date of the message. "I already did."

TWENTY-THREE

No one looks at me funny. No glares, no sidelong glances, not a single raised eyebrow. From all appearances, it's just another day at Steeple Side, which can only mean that Jack hasn't exposed me. Yet. I tried to talk myself out of coming in today, burrowing beneath the covers and hugging on Woofer until he yipped and fought his way to the surface, but I can't leave without talking to Linda. Though Jack may not want to know, I owe her the full story. Even if she doesn't believe me.

As I near my desk, Fiala appears—the true test of whether or not Jack ratted me out. I warrant little more than a meeting of eyes before she slips past.

"Oh, Grace," she calls.

I turn around. "Yes?"

"After you left Friday, Linda put a copy of the editor's letter for the next issue on your desk. Said she wanted fresh eyes to look at it before it goes to press. I told her I'd do it, but she says you're ready to assume all responsibilities as her assistant."

Now that I'm on my way out. Poor Fiala will soon be training someone else.

"I'd advise you to get right on it so it's done when she returns from her meeting."

Meeting? It's about me. I'm sure of it. They're all sitting around a conference table arguing over who gets to can me.

"But it's your call." Fiala smiles—a first in that it's as close to genuine as I've seen from her. Then she's off again, a bit of a bounce in her usually un-bouncy step. Because she's no longer responsible for me? Or perhaps she and her husband are working through their problems? I hope the latter, which would mean answered prayer. And, God knows, I could use a bit of encouragement.

As I cross to my desk, my fellow editorial assistant looks up. Phone pinched between cheek and shoulder, she smiles before returning to her pencil and yellow pad.

I drop into my chair and light on the manila folder on my desk. Though I know I'm wasting time that would be better spent clearing out my desk, I retrieve a red pen and begin to read the editor's letter.

Dear Reader,

It's hard to be real and no less hard when you're a Christian. In fact, from where I sit now, it seems even harder. As a Christian, there are expectations that you'll be the perfect wife, mother, friend, and co-worker. Expectations that your family will be in tune with one another and held together by the love of Jesus. Expectations that, in times of trouble, your faith will provide all the answers and bring you and your loved ones swimmingly through the trials of life. But that would be too easy, and life down here is never that easy. This is not heaven.

Among Christians, a person's journey through hardship and tragedy is often expressed as "going through a wilderness." While my life has not been without its trials, until recently I had never used the term *wilderness* to qualify them. It seemed dramatic and cliché—until we nearly lost our teenage son to drugs.

The morning after he was admitted to a treatment facility, I startled awake at the realization that I had met my wilderness. There I lay, awash in guilt, despair, grief, and anger, a sick feeling in my heart that nothing would ever be right again. Somehow I had failed my son. I must not have prayed enough for him, must have been unavailable when he needed me to counter peer pressure. I certainly had not picked up on the signs.

The wilderness closed in, the canopy above refusing the smallest ray of light, the path before me impassable, and the shadows on every side promising worse things to come. I thought I would die, but then I reached for God with an urgency I'd never felt before. That's when light pierced the canopy, when the path opened up enough to allow me to take a step forward, when the shadows began to recede.

Though I have yet to emerge from this wilderness and may not for some time, I am getting through it, not only with God's help but that of family, friends, and co-workers who do not judge but pray for our family.

Whether you are a parent or not, regardless of the age of your children, I encourage you to read this issue's feature article, "Drugs and Our Children." You need to know.

I lower the red pen. There's nothing to ink up. It's perfect, especially in light of the hypocrisy Tessie believes is rampant at Steeple Side. Aching at the knowledge that this is the last task I'll perform for Linda, I retrieve a sticky note, jot down, "I wouldn't change a thing," and apply it to the outside of the folder. Then from my purse I pull the folded paper I printed off at two this morning.

"Overwhelming Grace." I titled the short piece Jack had asked me to write about the soup kitchen. A bit of wordplay, but meaningful, as not only was there overwhelming grace in that place but this Grace was overwhelmed by it. I slip it in the folder with the editor's letter, step into Linda's office, and place it on her desk. As I turn to leave, through the windows that look out across the department I see Linda heading toward her office, Jack at her side.

I'm about to be busted, and it will look worse that I'm alone in Linda's office—no doubt rifling through her desk in search of more dirt. Slapped with a vision of being escorted off the premises in cuffs, I nearly scuttle behind a chair before either of them notices me. Instead, I send up a prayer devoid of any promises of "if You'll do this, I'll do that" and brace myself.

Linda halts in the doorway, eyes widening at the sight of me before her desk.

I hold her gaze, unable to bring myself to look at Jack.

"I didn't expect you to come in today," she says.

"I felt you ought to hear from me what I've been doing at Steeple Side." Not secondhand from a man who passed judgment on me based on the little he heard and the lot he surmised.

As if realizing the doorway is not the place to hold such a discussion, she says to Jack, "We'll talk later."

"No, I'd like Jack to stay." The smidgen of hope inside me shivers at the chill in his eyes.

Linda looks at him. "Jack?"

"I'll stay."

As he steps inside and closes the door, Linda continues to her desk and pulls out her chair.

I see her hesitate at the sight of the folder with its sticky note. "The letter is wonderful. Very honest."

Which is more than can be said of you, Maizy Stewart.

"Thank you." She gestures to the chairs before her desk. "Have a seat, Gr—" Her mouth curves with what seems part sorrow, part bitterness. "But it's Maizy, isn't it? Maizy Stewart."

Guilt scampers through me on clawed feet. "Yes." Giving my skirt an upward tug to ease the material against my backside, I sink down into the chair.

Linda nods at the other chair. "Jack?"

I hold my breath at his hesitation, certain he finds the prospect of being so near me distasteful. But he sits and even angles toward me—the better to protect his back?

Linda regards me with a lined brow, then leans back. "I'm familiar with your writing, having followed your articles in the Lifestyle section for several months. You're quite good...witty and entertaining."

Under different circumstances, I would beam. "Thank you."

"So tell me why that piece on Columbia's Mule Day is the last that *MTR*'s readers have seen from you."

I lift my chin. "When I applied here—"

"Before we begin," Jack interrupts, "we ought to clarify whether what is said is on the record or off."

The severity of his inflected voice makes me catch my breath. "Off. I don't work for the paper anymore."

I'm not surprised by the skeptical lift of his eyebrows.

"I e-mailed my resignation last night." Along with a plea for time to repay the part of my salary that covered my investigative work. "And intended to do so before we ran into Porter outside the bowling alley."

"Really?" His disbelief has a bite.

I give my attention to Linda, whose face reflects the strain I've added to her already strained life. "I didn't take this job to investigate Steeple Side. I took it to pay my bills."

"On your application and résumé," Linda says, "you claimed you had no previous work experience in the field of journalism."

"I did."

"A lie."

"Yes."

"The first of many, I assume?"

"There were eight in all… That is, big ones." *You don't have to be so honest.* Or maybe I do…

Bewilderment softens Linda's face. "You tracked your lies?"

I doubt I've ever been as aware of a man's presence as I am in this moment with Jack's tension thickening between us. "Despite appearances, I'm not good at lying. I wrote them down so I wouldn't forget." I open my eyes wide. "I did fix two of them, though, so it's really just six lies."

Jack makes a sound of disgust, and Linda clears her throat. "If you originally took the job to pay your bills, why did you feel it necessary to lie about your lack of journalistic experience?"

"A friend—" *Was* she? As angry and disappointed as Tessie is, I want to believe she cares for me, even if I did become a means of retaliation. "A friend warned me that if it were known I worked in mainstream media, the chances of being hired at Steeple Side were nil."

Linda inclines her head. "Your friend may be right. So how did you go from working here to pay the bills to working here undercover?"

"And why did the Seattle paper sack you?" Jack asks, evidence that he's been digging into my past.

Acting as if Linda posed the question, I keep looking at her. "That's where it begins…with the Seattle paper and my promotion from general assignment reporting to investigative reporting."

Over the next quarter hour, I ignore Jack as I tell Linda about my first failure to deliver an investigative story, being scooped by my boyfriend, the firing, the breakup with Ben, and the move to Nashville prompted by Tessie's promise of a job at the *Middle Tennessee Review* that didn't work into full time as expected. When I lightly touch on my plan to increase the chances of snagging the job at Steeple Side—not a word about *The Dumb Blonde's Guide to Christianity*—Jack shifts in his chair. Thankfully he doesn't say a word about our bumper sticker encounter.

"Then you're not a Christian?" Linda asks.

"No! I mean, yes. I'm just"—my hands flutter—"not Christian enough."

Her forehead furrows. "Go on."

I attempt to moisten my lips, but my mouth is so dry that the tip of my tongue drags across my bottom lip. "I need some water."

I start to stand, but Linda waves me down. "Jack, would you grab a bottle from my fridge?"

He rises and returns with two. He passes one to Linda, the other to me. As I accept it, I hazard a look into his face in hopes of a softening there. None.

After a long drink, I tell about Tessie's reaction to my having met Jack, which led to Tessie's tale of the story she believes he pulled out from under her with divisiveness.

"I remember Steeple Side's big layoff," Linda says. "The company was going through a rough time, and it was the only way to preserve the rest of our jobs. However, your friend is wrong in believing that the disgruntled ones were bribed to keep them from airing Steeple Side's dirty laundry." She looks to Jack.

He pushes up from his reclined position. "The employees who had been let go were asked to come in and talk with us. No threats were made, no offer of money for their silence. It was a time of reconciliation between Christians. That's all."

I want to say I believe him, but his eyes show no invitation of reconciliation between *us*. I tell Linda about my move from part-time to full-time status at the paper and the strings that were attached. "I'm sorry. I should have refused, but I thought it was what I wanted—to be an investigative reporter again and to write life-changing stories. It seemed to be my only chance to redeem myself after the mess I made in Seattle, so I took it."

Jack makes a dissenting sound. "You admit that you took the private failings and struggles of people who had befriended you for your personal gain."

I peer at the man who revealed his own private failure that day at the café…who kissed me in the park two days ago. "I told myself that if hypocrisy were rampant at Steeple Side, our readers had the right to know who was telling them how to live, but it was just as much about climbing out of the hole I got myself into."

"Then you regret not pursuing the story on the state senator?"

Linda's question is uncomfortably direct, but I refuse to soft-pedal the answer. "I have regretted it. After all, in trying to preserve a reputation she didn't deserve, mine was destroyed."

Linda looks away and nods as if to herself. When she looks back at me, her brow seems somewhat smoother. "Why did you resign from the *Middle Tennessee Review*?"

"For the same reason I was fired in Seattle: failure to deliver a story."

"Why didn't you deliver this time?"

"Because..." To bring God into this, though He does belong, would only fuel Jack's disbelief. "The only story here is one the paper isn't interested in—people caring about one another and forgiveness."

Linda leans forward. "There won't be a story then?"

I look down. "I don't know."

"What do you mean you don't know?"

I turn to Jack. "Tessie—er, Teresa—was overseeing the investigation. She has my notes." Though I want to clarify that those notes aren't complete and don't include his revelation about Bette, I can't do it in front of Linda.

"So they could still go forward with it," she prompts.

"Yes."

"Will they?"

I recall Tessie's face, her disgust, her anger. "It's possible."

Linda rubs her temple. "What kind of things are we talking about?"

"Everything—gambling, porn, divorce, drugs."

She holds up a hand. "That's enough."

From outside her office, I hear the phone ring, and as I'm not at my desk to field it for her, she picks up. "Linda Stillwater." She listens, glances at Jack, then me. "Thank you." She lowers the handset. "I'm told you haven't cashed any of your Steeple Side paychecks. Why?"

My heart *zings* at the realization that here is proof I didn't go into this investigation without reservation. "It didn't seem right."

"From the start?"

"Yes."

"Noble," Jack drawls, "but is it? After all, it would hardly reflect well on your integrity if you accepted payment from those you were in the process of betraying. And what about all those bills you needed to pay?"

Would I have cashed the checks if I hadn't been able to meet the minimum payments? I don't know. "Once I was put on full time at the paper, I was able to pay most of my bills without the Steeple Side checks."

Linda sighs. "I suppose there's nothing to do but wait and see what Teresa Halston does with your notes."

What will she do? And has she already done it? "I could ask her."

"Might be hard to get through to her now that you've resigned."

"Actually she's my landlady. I live in the apartment over her garage."

Linda's lids rise to reveal more of her eyes than I've ever seen. "That could prove uncomfortable."

"Obviously I'll be looking for another place to live."

She considers me, then pushes back from her desk and stands.

"Unless there's anything else you need to tell us, we should adjourn this meeting."

Feeling like a coiled spring, I jump up. "Thank you for listening." I see that Jack has also risen. "It shouldn't take more than ten minutes for me to clean out my desk."

"Not today, Maizy."

Nearly missing the placement of my forward-moving foot, I turn with Jack and ask, "What?"

"Go home. I don't know how we're going to handle this situation with your story hanging over our heads, but you haven't been let go. At least not yet."

A glance at Jack reveals his jaw is clenched.

"I'll call you at home this afternoon or early evening," Linda continues. "You'll be there?"

Where else would I be? Unless, of course, Tessie kicks me out. "Yes."

She comes around the desk, takes my arm, and leads me to the door, where she leans in. "One thing you need to know is that none of us, not one, is 'Christian enough.' We're always reaching for what's out of reach. We just want to get as close to it as we can." And with that kindness, she pats my shoulder, opens the door, and nods for me to go through.

According to the message on my machine, Jem has been admitted to a program for eating disorders. Another answered prayer, as it happened so suddenly that we didn't get the chance to talk. Thus my troubles remain mine, allowing her to focus on her own while she undergoes treatment.

I push up from my slump amid the sofa cushions and open my hand to consider the necklace I'd scooped up hours earlier when I stationed myself beside the phone to await Linda's call. I start to curl my fingers back over it, but the imprint in my palm makes me peer closer. I've been branded, though only temporarily, as the impression of the cross will soon fade. Regardless, I find myself searching for the symbolism of that cross figured into my flesh. Sacrifice? Just like—

I roll my eyes. "Yeah, right. Not at *all* like Him, you self-pitying faker." I pour the necklace onto the table beside the phone, only to jump when it rings. Is this it? I want it to be, and yet I don't.

The phone rings twice more before I lift the handset. "Hello?"

"Maizy, it's Linda."

Gulp. "Hi."

Silence, then a rustling like that of termination papers. "I read your soup kitchen piece. It's good. Honest and insightful."

"Thank you."

"I have to tell you that I met with resistance when I suggested that we keep you on at Steeple Side."

I know where this is going. A prayer not answered the way I wanted it. "I understand."

"However, once I showed the committee—"

Committee? *Oh, Lord.*

"—the piece you'd written, several of the members thought you deserved a second chance."

Meaning grace for Grace? All because of what I wrote? With a sudden urge to read it through—to see what they saw—I look at my laptop on the kitchen table.

"So the job is still yours if you want it."

Gasp. Grace. I am being shown grace. Grace I wasn't shown at the *Seattle Sound.* What about Tessie's grace? Joy pounded by guilt over what she did for me and what I was unable to do in return, I bite my lip only to shake my head. No, I did what was right, even if she doesn't see it that way.

"The only thing is, the job is likely to remain part time."

I can always find another job to supplement my income. Say… writing classified ads? "That's great." Well, not exactly. "I don't imagine Jack is too happy with the decision."

"The two of you were seeing each other, I believe?"

Good thing I'm sitting down. "Is that what he told you?"

"Simple deduction, which means it's going to be sticky if you stay at Steeple Side."

In other words, Jack doesn't believe you deserve grace, even though he was treated to a full serving years ago. The resentful little voice wheedles its way into me. While he wasn't fired for his indiscretion, the offer of the position he sought was withdrawn, and it wasn't until months later that he secured it. Grace, but a little at a time perhaps. And I suppose that's a good thing.

Still, just thinking about the quelling looks and cold shoulder I'm bound to receive from Jack is almost enough to make me pass on Steeple Side. But I am not going to scurry out of the light like a cockroach seeking the cover of dark. Far worse things lurk there.

I press my shoulders back. "I'd like to stay."

"I'm pleased to hear it. Now there are a couple of things we need to address. The first is your name. If you want to go by Maizy Grace, that's fine, but your co-workers need to know that you're Maizy

Stewart. Meaning it will get around that you wrote for the *Middle Tennessee Review*."

"How much will I have to explain?"

"I don't believe you need to go into your move from lifestyle reporting to investigative reporting, at least not at this time. Should the paper go forward with the story, that may change. We'll deal with it then."

Lord, I know this is the chicken's way out, but won't You please have a little talk with Tessie? And maybe Ray?

"The other thing is that the decision to allow you to stay at Steeple Side was not an easy one, and our belief in you isn't without risk. So I'm asking you to guard the trust we're placing in you."

I can't help but draw a parallel between her request and the one Tessie made when she vouched for my ability to deliver the Steeple Side story. I failed her. Will I—?

Not this time. "I won't let you down."

"I'll see you in the morning then."

Lightheaded with a mix of dread and relief, I say, "Thank you, Linda."

Five minutes later, I settle before my laptop with Woofer on my lap and open the OverwhelmingGrace.SS document:

Overwhelming Grace
by
Maizy Grace Stewart

My grandmother signed me up to volunteer at the soup kitchen this past May—without my consent. To be fair, she also placed her name on the list. To be unfair, when the day arrived and my "mysteriously" flat tire proved insufficient to absolve me of the commitment, Grandma deserted me. Where did that leave me? At the side door of the old church hoping no one would hear my respectfully subdued knock.

Evidently, church folk have keen ears.

In the basement I was given an apron and a hair net before I took my place in front of a steaming tray of carrots. The smell…well, one would have to be desperate to ask for a scoop of my offering. But when the homeless and hungry came through the line, they did ask. Most were grateful for the color I added to their plates, and some even looked at those canned carrots with the same enthusiasm with which I regard a slice of apple pie. Amazing. But not really, I soon discovered. They were hungry, and all that seemed to matter was that the vegetables were edible and would nourish them until their next meal. Whenever that might be.

Though the hundreds of homeless people who came through the line weren't all pleasant—and what right did I have to expect them to be?—most were appreciative. Now that I look back on the experience, I realize they weren't all that different from me. Regardless of the circumstances that landed them on the streets with little more than clothes that were once less threadbare and soiled, they needed help. They needed hope. They needed grace.

I need help. I need hope. I need grace. Actually, I need overwhelming grace. Though I am hardly in need of food, clothes, or a warm and safe place to sleep, I need the acceptance, forgiveness, and love of others. I need to be real and trust God with the same certainty as one of the homeless women I met.

Despite one woman's terrible circumstances, she blessed me for the carrots I slid onto her plate. Not knowing what else to say, I blessed her back. She smiled and said that God blesses her by giving her a new day each morning, keeping her safe, and placing me there to feed her when she can't stomach more garbage scraps. *Me* feed her? No, *she* fed me. As a fellow volunteer noted, such an experience puts things in their proper perspective.

What did I take away from the experience? As a Christian who more fittingly bears the prefix "cultural," I consulted a book that has proven useful in recent months. In *The Dumb Blonde's Guide to Christianity,* under a chapter titled "Punching the Time Clock God's Way," I found reference to Ephesians 4:28: "Use your hands for good hard work, and then give generously to others in need."

I will, starting today.

I turn my palm up to search out the impression made earlier by the cross. It's gone. Not the slightest trace left. Well, not on the outside…

I lean over to meet Woofer's gaze. "We're starting over again. A new chapter. Are you up to it?"

He gives a little rumble.

"I'll take that as a yes."

A quarter hour later, I answer a knock at the door, and there stands Tessie with a cardboard box. She eyes me over the splayed flaps. "Ray had your desk cleaned out. I offered to bring you the contents."

I have no reason to wince, as this was to be expected, but knowing it doesn't make it any easier. "Thank you." I reach for the box.

"I've got it." She strides forward and sets it on the sofa table. "So?" She turns to me as I close the door against bugs in search of light. "Did you spill the beans to your boss at Steeple Side?"

"I did."

She crosses her arms over her chest. "Fired you on the spot, I'll bet."

"No."

Her tough stance falters. "No?"

"Linda is giving me another chance."

She looks momentarily away, then shakes her head as if to clear her confusion. "What about Jack?"

"He was there when I told Linda everything."

"And he agreed to give you a second chance?"

"Not exactly, but the decision wasn't his."

She frowns. "You said you told Linda everything? How much of everything?"

"Everything that should have gotten me fired. And she knows the paper may still publish the story." I step toward her. "Will they? Has Ray asked you to write it?"

"He has."

"Will you?" *Please, God.*

"It's a strong consideration."

I bolster my sinking insides by latching onto the word *consideration*. Maybe she won't write the article. Of course, another of Ray's writers might. "Was Ray angry?"

She gives a short laugh. "You got that right."

"He took it out on you?"

She hitches an eyebrow.

"I'm sorry."

"Yeah, well, I can handle him." She heaves a "discussion closed" sigh, then looks around. "Are you still planning on moving?"

I nearly groan at the thought of packing my belongings. Fortunately the furnishings are Tessie's, so I won't have to move them. "Yes. Until I can find another part-time job, it's going to be tighter than ever."

"Wise decision." She glances at her watch. "My column's due tomorrow, so I'd better get on it."

I return to the door and open it. "Thank you for bringing my stuff."

She crosses the threshold.

"Tessie?"

She turns to face me.

"I really am grateful for all that you did for me. And I'm sorry for disappointing you. I just…couldn't do it."

After a long moment, she says, "It's not as if you didn't give me adequate warning. Good night."

I watch her walk all the way to her back door. When it closes behind her, I close my own door and cross to the box. It contains the usual personal items found in or on one's desk: coffee cup, comb, dental floss, spare sweater, pack of chewing gum, lipstick, framed picture, knickknacks, and name plaque. I hold up the latter and eye the letters that spell out "Maizy Stewart."

"This ought to set everyone at Steeple Side right," I murmur, then roll my eyes at the thought of the questions to come.

I certainly have my punishment cut out for me.

TWENTY-FOUR

Still nothing on Steeple Side. Nothing snide, speculative, or remotely scandalous. As I've done nearly every day for the past seven months, I send up a silent prayer of thanks, then close the *Middle Tennessee Review* and reach for a stack of unopened mail.

"Let me guess…" My roommate's pert voice makes the rounds of the kitchen. "No article." Jem stands in the doorway wearing a plump old bathrobe marked by a wayward splash of bleach. Tucked beneath her arm is her baby, formerly known as *my* baby. It's a good thing I'm over Woofer.

I nod. "Good guess."

Jem pads forward, lowers Woofer to the floor, and drops into a chair. "That'll be your New Year's resolution, won't it? To stop worrying about a nonexistent article?"

Dare I believe it would have happened by now if it was going to happen at all?

"Well?"

I look to Woofer as he rolls over near her feet and offers up his belly. "Yeah, but you know how resolutions are—hard to keep."

She lifts her foot and scratches Woofer's belly with painted toes. "I know, but if I can do it, you can."

Jem has done it and looks better for all of her struggle to over-come anorexia. Though still tiny, she's fuller and has a glow about her. She credits me for much of her success, but she's just being kind. After all, I needed an affordable place to live, and her offer of a room in her apartment helped me more than it helped her. Too, there's Fly-boy—the same guy who knocked me down months ago in his flight from Todd. Jem has been dating him for a couple of months, and he might just be a "keeper."

Jem stands up, causing Woofer to startle. "Stop taking the paper, Maizy." She scoops up the scattered sections and tosses them in the garbage can. "You're in the clear."

"I know, but every time I start to relax, I have this urge to look over my shoulder."

She resumes her seat, and once more everything is right in Woofer's world. "Look, you are where you're meant to be, and you're doing a fantastic job." She gives a little laugh. "Once Fiala is pro-moted—likely at the beginning of the New Year—the junior staff writer position is yours."

It's what I'm hoping for and what Linda alluded to last week when I turned in another editorial piece. She said my writing was excep-tional and, as I started for the door, added that it was time she did something about my overqualification. I turned my head, but Linda merely winked before returning to her computer screen.

I smile at Jem. "It looks that way."

"It is. And if that's not enough, everyone likes you."

I arch an eyebrow.

"Well, maybe not everyone, but you're accepted."

I can't argue that. Not that it was easy. Within hours of placing my name plaque on my desk, everyone knew I had been a staff writer for the Lifestyle section of the *Middle Tennessee Review*. I quickly became the talk and speculation of Steeple Side.

Q: Why didn't you tell us you were Maizy Stewart?

A: I didn't think I'd be hired if it were known that I also worked at the paper.

Q: Are you still working at the paper?

A: No, I quit.

Q: Why?

A: I didn't like the direction my career was heading.

Q: And you like the direction it's heading *now* as a part-time editorial *assistant*?

A: I like working for Linda. Hopefully the job will work into full time and I'll be writing articles again.

I didn't lie. I just didn't elaborate. Not surprisingly, that first month was rough as many of my co-workers viewed me with suspicion, Fiala being foremost among them. But it's tapered off, and even Fiala has let down her guard. However, if that story ever appears—

Jem's right. I have to believe it won't. Have to believe that Tessie, despite her aloofness those last weeks I resided over her garage, tossed out the copies of my notes. Have to believe, because she isn't going to confirm it. Despite my attempts to maintain contact, she hasn't returned my calls or acknowledged my e-mails or notes. It's made me question if our friendship ever existed, but I always conclude it did. Which means there's hope for healing. When she's ready.

"You're thinking about Jack, aren't you?"

Though Jack figured nowhere in my thoughts, heat invades my cheeks. "No, not Jack." Not that I don't think about him, especially lately as he doesn't seem as intent on avoiding me. Still, it can only be because he's learned to tolerate me. From time to time we even exchange a word or two—entirely work related but better than the tense silence between us those first few months.

"I saw him looking at you today while we were having lunch." Jem smiles as I open my eyes wide. "Meant to mention it, but you were so fixed on my anorexia and your piece on eating disorders." She's referring to the article Linda gave me permission to write, which will be my fourth for the women's magazine.

I wish I didn't tingle at the possibility that Jack voluntarily looked my way. "Stop encouraging me. I'm sure he was only making certain I wasn't eavesdropping on anyone."

"No, I've seen *that* look. This was not it. Then when he saw that I was watching him watching you, he started pretending that whatever Todd was droning on about was interesting."

I shake my head. "You're wrong. Jack doesn't want anything to do with me."

"Then why is he still not dating?"

She has a point—*no, she doesn't. No point. No pain.* "Maybe he is dating. And even if he isn't, that doesn't mean I figure into his life in any way other than as a thorn in his side."

Jem opens her mouth to argue, but a glance at the clock makes her jump up and Woofer scramble to his peg legs. "It's after six. If you don't want to be really late, we'd better get moving."

Steeple Side's Christmas party. Though I've looked forward to it,

I suddenly feel uneasy. Because Jack was watching me—or so Jem says? Maybe I should stay put.

"Come on." Jem heads out of the kitchen, Woofer on her heels. "I'll zip you up if you zip me." Over her shoulder she wrinkles her nose. "I'll even do your hair."

Right. I've made peace with her Elvira-inspired attempt on my hair, but that doesn't mean I'm going to let her loose on me again, even if it is with only a brush and bobby pins. Having returned to a semblance of natural color—as in over-the-counter (I'm still poor), semipermanent hair color that returned me to the realm of basic brown—I'm not taking any chances.

As I start to follow Jem, my cell phone rings. "Just a minute." I reach into my purse on the counter. "Hello?"

"Maizy, it's Tessie."

"Tessie…" I blink. "Uh, how are you?"

"Good." Her voice may not be chill, but it has the ring of business. "Ray asked me to give you a call."

Is this about the salary I drew for the investigation? Though I accepted Grandma's offer of a loan in order to repay the paper and completely sever any ties, perhaps I miscalculated. *Deep breath.* "Oh?"

"A full-time position in the Lifestyle department has opened up, and he wants to give you first shot."

I can only stare at the air at the end of my nose. "Me? Ray wants *me* back?"

"You may not have the stomach for investigative reporting, but you're good with the lifestyle stuff." That last word spoken with derision. "I'm not supposed to tell you this, but since you stopped contributing articles, the paper has received numerous inquiries. Apparently you developed something of a following. Are you interested?"

My ego perks up, but the one multisentence scripture I've memorized due to its relevance and ability to comfort swats it aside: *"Make a careful exploration of who you are and the work you have been given, and then sink yourself into that. Don't be impressed with yourself. Don't compare yourself with others. Each of you must take responsibility for doing the creative best you can with your own life."* Galatians something-or-other in *The Message*.

"It's full time, Maizy, which means a generous increase in salary."

Bolstered by a longing for security, my ego snaps back to attention. Full time, meaning far more than what I make at Steeple Side and freelancing, meaning I could make good on Grandma's loan, meaning I could exceed the minimum payment on my bills, meaning I'd be writing—and not just the occasional editorial piece.

"Of course, if Steeple Side has already put you on full time…"

"Not yet, though it may happen after the New Year."

She harrumphs. "You can't bank on possibilities. And why should you when a sure thing is knocking?"

Temptation. And in that moment, I wish I had memorized scripture to help me fight it off. Feeling watched, I glance at the kitchen table, where my unopened mail sits. Mostly bills.

Leave Steeple Side. Leave the friends I've made. Leave those who gave me a second chance. Leave Ja—no, leaving Jack would not be a bad thing.

"So?" Tessie prompts.

Yes. So? Financial security working for the paper? Or financial uncertainty in a job that allows God to do His work in you—that means you have to trust in Him, not yourself? As far as I believe my faith has come, the decision isn't easy.

"Are you still there, Maizy?"

Struggling against the current that urges me back to a semblance of self-reliance, I draw a breath. "It's been hard, Tessie, but I like it at Steeple Side, and the people care about me. I'm going to stay put."

Silence ensues, and just as I'm about to ask if she's still on the line, she says, "I thought that would be your answer. So you're happy there?"

I'm warmed by what I dare to believe is interest. "I am."

"What about your faith?"

A thrill goes through me. "Growing. I'm attending Jem's church, and though it's small compared to Sovereign and there isn't much of a singles' program, I like it." I give a short laugh. "This will sound cheesy, but I'm starting to see why some people view other church members as family."

Rather than scorn, my words elicit a long drawn, "Hmm."

So I push the envelope. "What about your faith?"

Scorn is delivered in the form of laughter. "What faith?"

For fear of losing any ground I might have gained, I decide to keep it light. "Guess I'm not cut out for evangelism."

"Not where I'm concerned. Well, I have a deadline to make, so I'll let you go."

Just one more thing. "What about the Steeple Side story? Is it— I mean…"

She keeps me hanging, then says, "I should have let you know, but I've never been quick to forgive. Ask my exes."

"So?"

"There isn't going to be a story, Maizy."

Oh, thank You, God! "Why?"

"Because a writer needs to know when she's at a dead end. And Steeple Side is a dead end."

Hardly, but who am I to argue? "Thank you."

"For what?"

She knows for what, but no need to press it. "For calling. And will you thank Ray for me for the offer?"

"Sure."

"I'd love to have lunch with you sometime."

A long pause. "We'll see. Good-bye, Maizy."

"Bye." I consider the phone a moment before I flip it closed and glance overhead. "You really do have incredible timing, You know." Of course He does.

We're a half hour late when we pull into Steeple Side's parking lot. Approaching the doors, Jem and I gasp over the glittering lobby visible through the enormous glass panes. Though it's been in the process of transformation for two weeks as Christmas trees, lights, banners, freshly cut garlands, and a life-size crèche have moved in, it's come together beautifully. And that's further apparent when we step through the doors. Past the milling employees outfitted in gowns, tuxes, sports jackets, dresses, pantsuits, and even jeans, white-clothed tables stretch left and right. Set with a variety of appetizers, they're flanked by chattering men and women whose voices are rendered indistinct by the Christmas music that pulses from a band on a dais at the foot of the towering cross.

After we check our coats, Jem grips my arm. "Food or dancing first?"

Easy for her to ask, as *she* has someone to dance with. In fact, I wouldn't be surprised if Flyboy steals her away entirely. I nod at the nearest table. "I'm hungry."

"Okay." She bounces ahead.

Once more struck by how fairylike she appears with her hair caught up in the high ponytail we fashioned into ringlets that cascade down around her face, a pink chiffon dress, and sparkly heels, I smile. No red or green for Jem. Too predictable, she had pronounced as she zipped up my new evening gown that follows my curves down to my ankles—all in a predictable shade of Christmas tree green. Adjusting my lace and sequined shoulders, I follow her.

Amid chattering, laughter, and an occasional squeal of delight, Jem and I fill our plates with appetizers marked as crab-stuffed mushrooms, sausage puffs, and prosciutto-wrapped asparagus. Then there are the tamer items: shrimp with cocktail sauce and cold cuts. All good.

"So you didn't come with Jack?"

I'm broadsided by the question asked by a woman whose voice I don't recognize; however, it's not directed at me, I discover as I look her way. It's directed at Dinah, the flirt from Payroll and Avery's Sunday school class. She and the other woman are loading their plates on the opposite side of the table.

"No." Dinah's mouth puckers. "He brought someone else."

Bette? The ribs in the vicinity of my heart take a pounding.

With a snicker, Dinah nods at a table to her right.

Smarting from pain I do not want to feel, I follow her gesture. But Jack isn't at the table. I recognize the one man there as someone I've seen around Steeple Side, but the three women with whom he shares the table are unfamiliar—two young, one quite old. Not Bette then.

"Which one is she?" Dinah's companion asks.

Dinah gives a strangely self-satisfied smile, only to drop it when she notices me. "Oh hi, Gr— er, Maizy." She corrects herself, as some still do, with a measure of suspicion.

"Hi."

Her companion frowns at me, then turns with Dinah and walks away.

I glance at the table again. Though both women are attractive, I hope it isn't the redhead, as she's a knockout. However, an instant later, the brunette leans near the man and lays an intimate hand on his.

Okay, so Jack has himself a redhead. Telling myself I don't care, I trail Jem to the beverage table. Shortly, we turn away with punch cups in hand.

"This way." Jem alters course to snag the table being vacated by the same man and two women that Dinah pointed out to her friend. That leaves only the old woman.

"Mind if we join you?" Jem asks.

"Puh-lease do," the woman says, her southern accent tacking on an extra syllable. "I'm Buh-renda. And you are?"

"Jem." She lowers her plate and drops into a chair. "This is my friend Maizy."

"Nice to meet you, Jem, Maizy."

It may take more muscles to frown, but the smile I aim at her nearly drains me. Attempting to distract my emotions, I peer into the bubbly red punch with its floating bits of oranges. My first Christmas party without alcohol. Not that I'm much of a drinker. It just seems odd that there should be this much merriment in the air without the assistance of wine or beer or something stronger.

I scan the revelers in search of signs that their spirits have been boosted by *spirits,* but they just look happy, regardless of whether they're simply engaged in conversation or moving on the dance floor. So maybe that "something stronger" is just the fact that they're among family, friends, and fellow believers, celebrating the birth of Christ.

I finger the cross necklace that I talked myself in and out of before clasping it around my neck as Jem and I went out the door. I've avoided wearing it for fear of appearing to do so merely to advertise my Christianity as I did the first time I put it on. I finally decided that I *wanted* to wear it—for me.

"Puh-retty necklace, dear," the old woman says.

I look across the table. "Thank you."

Brenda smiles—a nice, creased smile. "Did you two come alone?"

The question surprises me, but Jem takes it in stride. "Yes, but my boyfriend is supposed to meet me. He works here too."

"And you, Maizy? No boyfriend?"

I'd be offended if she weren't so old. Seventy-five or so? I open my mouth, but out of it—sort of—comes Jem's voice.

"No boyfriend." She sighs. "Poor thing."

I gasp. "Jem!"

Peering at the old woman, she frowns. "A really sad case of unrequited love."

Love? I never paired that word with Jack. And I don't love him. Yes, I'm attracted, but attraction does not love make, especially when reciprocation is nipped in the bud by deceit. I wince, achingly aware that while I get to live with the consequences of my deceit, Jack gets a stunning redhead. Probably deeply Christian. And so successful she easily pays her bills. Doesn't even carry a balance on her credit cards—

"See that?" Jem points at my brow. "The way her forehead wrinkles and she bites her lip? That means she's thinking about him."

"Jem!"

"It's true." She gives an impish grin and sucks sauce from her fingertips. "Just can't get her mind off him."

I open my mouth to deny it, but a side effect of having to log one's lies to keep them straight is an acute awareness of the stealthy approach of one headed toward the lips.

With a sympathetic pout, Brenda pats my hand. "Buh-roke your heart, did he? The dirty dog."

I nearly laugh at her affront. Instead I shake my head. "He's not a dog, dirty or otherwise. It was my fault."

"Oh." Her wrinkles deepen but then smooth. Green eyes sparkle with such vitality that she suddenly seems decades younger. "Did you apologize?"

"She did." Jem picks the crab stuffing from a mushroom and pops it in her mouth. Despite my annoyance with her, I'm pleased that she's making a dent in her food—unlike me, and all because I'm having a personal conversation with a total stranger.

"He didn't forgive you?" Once more Brenda sounds offended, and I could almost believe she's my grandmother. But Grandma Grace is far away and will be farther yet when she and William (I hear wedding bells) embark on a Christmas cruise next week.

"Thinking about him again, are you?" Brenda shakes her head sadly.

Who *is* this woman?

She pats my hand again. "If you have given him the opportunity to forgive and he hasn't taken it, he isn't deserving. So it's time for you to move on. Speaking of moving on"—she peers over her shoulder—"my guh-randson…"

The old "Have I got a grandson for you!" matchmaking scheme. Not good.

"He's around somewhere…" Brenda turns her slightly tottering head. "I'm afraid he's in much the same boat as your fuh-riend." Her expression turns sympathetic. "Unrequited love. Well, maybe not love, but he liked this young woman. And now he has to work with her."

"Well, Maizy knows all about—"

"Jem! Don't you think Flyboy's looking for you?"

She wrinkles her nose and addresses Brenda. "That would be my boyfriend. But don't mind Maizy. She's just jealous."

Teasing—one of two disadvantages to having a good friend. As for the other, that would be said friend thinking she knows what's best for me. "See you, Jem."

"Okay, okay." As she rises with her plate, she whispers in my ear. "Let me know how it goes with the grandson."

I bristle, but since there's concern in her eyes, I sigh. "Yeah, time to move on."

She twirls away and merges with the throng.

"And then there were two." Brenda sighs and once more looks around. "Where is that boy of mine?"

Boy. Probably younger than me. Though tempted to ask her grandson's name, fear of encouraging her matchmaking makes me hold my tongue.

"Oh well. Tell me about this young man who buh-roke your heart."

Back to that, are we? I should probably disengage, but where would that leave me? Alone. Besides, Brenda appears harmless, and it's not as if I'll see her again.

I adjust the skirt of my gown, spear a sausage puff, and regard the woman across the flaky morsel. "It hurt, but as for my heart...while there may be a few cracks, I'll get over him." I pop the puff in my mouth and savor the spicy sausage and pastry.

"How long were you together?"

Swallowing prematurely to keep laughter from spewing my mouthful across the table, I nearly choke.

Brenda jumps her chair closer and thwacks me on the back. "Heimlich?"

The thought of this creaky little woman performing the maneuver gives rise to more laughter, but I resist and clear my airway without further mishap.

"I didn't mean to upset you." Brenda peers into my face.

"You didn't. That was laughter I choked on."

"Laughter?"

"Yes. When you asked how long we were together, I was struck by how silly it is to be so caught up in a man I really wasn't dating. After all, we'd only seen each other a few times outside of work."

Her spotty lashes flutter. "He works here?"

"Yes. He's not in my department, but we interact from time to time."

She's thoughtful a long moment, then says, "And, of course, every time you see him, it duh-redges up old feelings."

"Old?" I pause in the midst of dipping a shrimp in cocktail sauce. "Eventually, I imagine they will be old. Of course, I don't know why I'm telling you any of this."

She taps her chest. "Psychologist."

I frown. "You were a psychologist?"

She laughs. "*Will* be when I complete the program, hopefully next spring."

Maybe she just looks really old...

"I know. What's an old thing like me doing pursuing a degree?" She chuckles. "Just living and learning and making good use of the years the Lord has given me."

Now that's something to aspire to. I smile. "That's a wonderful attitude."

"You should try it; then maybe you wouldn't get caught up with the wrong kind of man."

Implying that Jack is the wrong kind of man? Hardly. "Or maybe the right kind of man wouldn't get caught up with the wrong kind of me."

She shakes her head. "Though it's true there are always two sides to every conflict, it's likely you're shouldering more of the buh-lame than you should."

"No." I push my plate away. "The lies were mine." I look across the lobby and consider Fiala, who is pressed affectionately against her husband's side as the two converse with Linda. I no longer listen in on stall conversations, but several months back I innocently overheard Fiala tell Linda that her husband is getting help for his gambling. I only pray—and I do mean *pray*—it's working.

"Those lies could have hurt a lot of innocent people here," I murmur, only to realize I've spoken aloud when Brenda makes a little sound.

Her smile seems forced, especially in light of the deepening wrinkle between her eyebrows. "Including...the one your fuh-riend said you haven't gotten over?"

Embarrassed at having verbalized my musings, I grimace. "It could have, though indirectly." As much as I don't want to talk about Jack, I feel compelled to. And what harm would it do? In fact, it might help. This woman is a pending expert in psychology. "More than anyone, he made me rethink the deception under which I was laboring."

"How's that?"

Think: free therapy. Value: in excess of one hundred dollars. "While he annoyed me at first, the more I was around him, the more I liked him. He seemed to genuinely care about me and encouraged me to pursue my faith beyond the shallow grasp I had on it." I sigh. "And so I started to care about him."

Looking deeply thoughtful, she nods.

"Thus I realized I couldn't use him to achieve my end, and that's when everything fell apart."

"And you regret it falling apart, whatever this deception was?"

"Oh no! I'm glad to be out from under it. I lost a lot, but it was worth it."

"That's a good attitude. So what are you going to do about this young man?"

"What is there to do about him? I blew it and…" Whew! What's with the tingly nose? "And that's all there is to it."

She tilts her head to the side. "You say he didn't buh-reak your heart."

My eyes sting. Must be approaching that time of month. Smiling brighter than my silly feelings warrant, I clap a hand to my chest. "Intact. For the most part." I didn't mean to add that last bit, but the woman is trained to pull teeth.

Oh yeah? In your case, the only tooth pulling she did was to those on the way out. You wanted to talk about Jack, and who better to discuss it with than a kindly old stranger?

So why not? "Of course, I could alleviate much of my dilemma if I simply left Steeple Side, and I have been offered my old job back with a considerable increase in salary."

"Maizy." Seeming strangely alarmed, she touches my hand. "I ought to tell you something."

And that's when I see him. Just past her shoulder, standing with a group of men, Jack scans the buffet area. Why does he have to look so good? Must be the black slacks and tuxedo shirt. "That's him."

Brenda sits straighter. "Who?"

"Jack. *Him.*"

"Oh dear." Her hand gives mine an urgent pat. "Maizy, I—"

"Eye contact." Which is best avoided, as it dredges up feelings I do not want to feel. Still, it's Jack who turns away first. As I release my breath, he says something to one of the men and breaks from the group.

"Oh no, I think he's heading our way." Why? "He is." As much as I long to check my hair to ensure that my wisping french roll hasn't wisped itself out of a job, I resist. "ETA three seconds."

With what appears to be distress, Brenda glances over her shoulder.

I jump to my feet a moment before Jack halts between us. "Jack, this is—"

"Grandmother," he says in that clipped British accent. And as disbelief bounds through me, he places a hand on Brenda's shoulder, leans down, and kisses her cheek.

TWENTY-FIVE

Oh no. *This* is Jack's date. Not the redhead. This elderly woman with whom I entrusted my thoughts and feelings about her grandson. Guessing this is how bowling pins feel when whacked by three-holed, two-ton balls, I grip the chair back and seek Brenda's gaze. She smiles apologetically, and now I understand what she tried to tell me before Jack appeared. Timing can be so cruel.

"Sorry to keep you waiting." Jack straightens. "But I see you found someone to visit with. I trust you introduced yourselves?" The unspoken question: do you know who you've been chatting with?

Brenda does. But what I want to know is at what point she realized that I'm the one Jack told her about all those months ago—the one with whom she told him to play nice.

She nods. "First names only, I'm afraid."

"Then allow me." The face he turns to me is genial enough—providing I steer clear of the eyes. And I do. "This is Maizy Stewart, Grandmother—Maizy *Grace* Stewart."

She pats his hand where it rests on her shoulder. "I did figure that out, only a short while ago."

I look back at Jack and catch the frown on his brow that matches the one on his mouth.

"Maizy, this is my grandmother, Brenda Wood."

I detach my fingers from the chair back. "That I figured out a much shorter while ago." I force a smile. "It was nice meeting you, Brenda." Wishing that were the extent of our encounter, I sidestep her and her grandson.

"Maizy?" Her tone is urgent.

Can I pretend I didn't hear? It is, after all, a party. Exceedingly noisy. And I do need to find a quiet place to pull myself together. In fact, maybe I ought to go home.

No. No matter what Brenda tells her grandson, I am not running away. After all, this is my party as well, even if it is the last place I want to be. Too many people, too many voices, too much laughter, and as for the music…

I falter, only to grind back into gear. Until Jem is ready to head home, I'm going to forget about pseudo-psychologist Brenda, Jack Prentiss, and the humiliating position I placed myself in. And I'm going to do it by dancing.

I slip between groups of partygoers and, after much weaving and dodging, find the outskirts of the dance floor. I hesitate at the sight of Todd with his hands in his pockets and eyes searching the crowd, but he'll do.

Soon a surprised Todd turns me onto the dance floor and begins to move rather spastically to the lyrics of "Jingle Bell Rock."

I follow his lead as best I can, but I'm hampered by thoughts of Jack. So what if he concludes that I'm still affected by him? That would be his interpretation of hearsay—even if said hearsay is from one sly grandmother who just had an unguarded conversation with the source.

"Are you enjoying the party?" Todd leans toward me.

I cannot tell a lie, but neither can I say I'd rather be elsewhere. "It's different from what I'm accustomed to."

"I'll bet." He wiggles his eyebrows. "You look pretty tonight."

Until that moment, I hadn't realized how much I wanted to hear that from a man. Todd is not the one I would have chosen, but my first choice is out of the question. "Thank you."

We make small talk through two more upbeat selections that maintain a respectable foot and a half between us. However, when the band starts in on "White Christmas," I hesitate. Might a slow dance send Todd the wrong message?

The ranks of couples on the dance floor thinning, Todd opens his arms wide. "I'm game if you are."

"Uh…" I glance past him and catch sight of a certain grandmother tugging her grandson onto the dance floor. As much as I long to head opposite, I say, "I'm game."

Todd clasps my left hand in his right, settles his other hand at my waist, and turns me to the beat of the music. For the first minute, I avoid looking beyond the tip of my nose. When I do venture past it, I practically fall into Jack's eyes as he and his grandmother dance ten feet away.

Wrenching my gaze away, I stumble against Todd.

"Hey, I like you too, Maizy, but don't forget where we are." He grins.

"Sorry." The next time I look over his shoulder, I meet Brenda's eyes as she peers around Jack. Though I'm sure she means to be discreet, what follows is so exaggerated that there's no way anyone who is paying attention could miss it. A finger jab in my direction, as in "you," a head jerk in her grandson's direction, as in "him," and crossed fingers doing a jig, as in "dance."

I shake my head, as in "no way."

She mouths, "Please."

I mouth, "no," and catch the determination in her eyes before Jack turns her around. To avoid another encounter with those eyes, I give Todd a smile. "You're a good dancer."

"Really?"

He sounds so hopeful. "You lead well." Which is true. Had I stumbled into a lesser partner, we might have gone down.

He turns me, which brings me nearer Brenda and her grandson. Before I can look away, she repeats the pointing, head jerking, and finger dancing.

I shake my head. Unfortunately Jack chooses that moment to look around, as does Todd.

The latter groans. "I'm about to lose my dance partner."

He thinks Jack wants to dance with me? Though it's certainly what Brenda is after, Jack is not about to cooperate.

"Too much to hope that you two had really called it quits."

As if we ever called it "starts." "You're mistaken, Todd. There's nothing between Jack and me."

He chuckles. "That's right up there with complimenting me on my dancing. No, you're in denial, same as Jack."

I stare at him, only vaguely aware that "White Christmas" is transitioning into another slow song. "You're wrong, I—"

A finger taps my shoulder, and at the end of it is Brenda, who has maneuvered her dance partner alongside us. "I hate to put you out, Maizy, but I'd love to dance with dear Todd. Do you mind if we swap?"

To my surprise, Jack looks more apologetic than put out.

"It's settled then." Brenda releases her grandson. "Thank you, Maizy."

I'm confused. Regardless, a moment later I'm in Jack's arms, and all of me thrills at the feel of his palm against mine, his other hand at my waist, and that citrus-y scent I haven't been near enough to catch in ages.

"Play nice," Brenda says as Jack turns me aside.

Jack gruffly murmurs, "Sorry about that."

"What just happened?"

"My grandmother got her way."

"I know, but why?"

He tenses. "First, answer a question for me, Maizy."

I almost sigh over my accent-inflected name. "What?"

"Are you going back to work for the paper?"

How did he—? Oh. Right. Not only did I open up to his grandmother about my feelings for Jack, but I told her about the job offer. Though I have no reason to feel guilty, the errant emotion scratches at my door, causing heat to rise in my cheeks and Jack's mouth to tighten.

"You are going back," he says with finality.

Realizing we've come to a standstill, I look around. The only one on the dance floor who seems to have noticed is Brenda.

"No, I'm not."

His lids tense. "You're staying at Steeple Side?"

Hope shivers through me. Brenda did say that her grandson was suffering from unrequited love—or a precursor to it. Now that I know who that grandson is, it follows that I'm the recipient. If the precursor is real. "Do you want me to stay?"

His mouth tightens, and he urges me back to the beat of the music. However, because of my awareness of him, it's all I can do not to step on my own toes. "Are you staying?"

I open my eyes wide. "I answered your question; now you have to answer mine."

His hand splays against my back in what seems a helpless gesture. "Point taken." He draws a breath. "Yes, I'd like you to stay…providing it's what you want."

Are we really having this conversation? "I like Steeple Side, yet I have to say that the paper's offer of a full-time job was tempting."

"They asked you to return to investigative reporting?"

I laugh, pulling Jack's attention to my mouth. "No. Lifestyle reporting. After what I did to the Steeple Side story, they know I'm not cut out for taking a can opener to people's lives and splashing the contents on the front page." I give another laugh, the slightly bitter edge of which surprises me. "A failing of mine."

Jack's gaze sinks into mine. "Failing?"

"Not really, but it has complicated my life."

Brenda and Todd appear. "Did you tell her how much you liked her soup kitchen piece, Jack?"

He sighs. "I'm getting there, Grandmother."

"Hmm, this could take longer than expected." She turns back to Todd, whose face is a picture of puzzlement. "Give them some space, dear."

As they sway away, Jack smiles almost sheepishly. "I did like your piece. Though it fit the Grace I thought I knew, after what we learned of your investigation, it didn't seem a true reflection of you or your faith. So when Linda used it to convince the others you could be trusted, I didn't believe it." He glances away momentarily. "I was angry, and I felt betrayed."

"Because of what you told me about you and Bette."

"Yes."

"You may not believe me, but you and Bette never made it into my notes. In fact, after you told me about your past with her, my real struggle against the investigation began. I didn't want to do it. I just didn't know how to get out of it."

His eyes search mine. "I do believe you."

He does?

"Do you know why I told you about me and Bette?"

I'm afraid to answer, as I may be wrong.

"Because I thought if you knew me better, you might open up and allow me to know you better—that there was a future for us."

I would have answered right. Now the question is, is it too late?

Jack and I startle as Brenda sidles alongside, a weary-looking Todd in tow. "Has he apologized yet?" The old woman's bright eyes swing to Jack.

"Grandmother, I was getting there."

"Well, don't mind us." She gives Todd a nod and they scoot away.

"So"—Jack tilts his head—"would you prefer the abbreviated version of what my grandmother said to me after I ran you off from the table, or a blow-by-blow?"

Precariously near joy, I smile. "I think the abbreviated version will do just fine."

To my toe-tingling dismay, he draws a deep breath, causing his chest to expand against mine. "I am a prideful, foolish git who, despite having received forgiveness time and again, has yet to extend the same to a woman who is just as deserving...perhaps more."

I blink. "Your grandmother called you a git?" Roughly equivalent to "jerk," I believe. "And prideful? And foolish?"

His short laugh moves the wispy hair around my face. "Actually, she left it to me to fill in the blanks."

I giggle, barely managing to keep the purr in check. "But I thought this was the abbreviated version."

His face momentarily sours. "Believe me, it is."

Though happiness seems within reach, I don't close my fingers around it just yet. "Why are we dancing, Jack?"

"Because I like the feel of you in my arms." He draws me nearer. "However, what led to our dancing is the apology I owe you, which I've wanted to make for months now."

I lean back to better see his face. "Months?"

"That's where the prideful part of 'git' comes in—knowing I was wrong about you yet justifying my behavior by reminding myself of your deception. I watched you the first couple of months, believing I could prove that Linda's trust was misplaced. But later I was impressed not only by your ability but your determination and commitment. And frustrated when I was unable to stop thinking about you."

I lightly probe happiness.

Jack brings his face closer. "I am sorry, Maizy."

My throat tightens.

"And now I have to ask what happened at the park. When you kissed me back, was it part of the investigation?"

I gasp. "No, not at all."

He searches my face. "What did it mean to you?"

I nearly close my eyes in remembrance. "More than a kiss has ever meant. What about you?"

"It felt like the beginning of something real."

"Well?" a voice sounds from the left.

I give Brenda a watery smile. "He apologized."

She beams. "Excellent." Back to Todd. "We did good."

With an uncertain nod, Todd turns her away as the slow song ends. "Come with me?"

I return my attention to Jack. "Where?"

"Outside."

"Why?"

"What happens next is just between you and me."

And what might that be? Another kiss? "All right."

He leads me from the dance floor and through the throng. As we near the lobby doors, I stumble on Jem's gaze as she and Flyboy stand near a buffet table set with desserts. Eyebrows raised, she looks from me to Jack and back, then shrugs and gives a thumbs-up.

A minute later, huddled in my coat, I precede Jack out into the crisp air of early winter. Will it snow? Though the weatherwoman said not to count on it, as December snow rarely sticks in Nashville, I'm holding out for a white Christmas. Looking to the thick clouds overhead, I shiver as the chill nips at my cheeks.

"This will do." Jack halts before a bench halfway down the sidewalk.

I lower to it and angle my body toward him as he joins me.

"I see you're wearing the cross again."

"This time for me."

He inclines his head, and the light pouring through the lobby's windows weaves in and out of his dark blond hair. "Forgive me, Maizy?" He reaches up and touches the cross at the base of my throat.

I catch my breath at his brief contact with my skin. "Yes. Do you forgive me?"

"Months ago." His rough exhale mists the air between us. "I should have told you sooner. Pride is a terrible thing."

Though I long to jump for the happiness that seems within reach, I have to ask. "What if I hadn't spoken with your grandmother tonight? What if she hadn't pushed you to dance with me?"

Despite the shadows, there's no mistaking his regret. "I'd like to believe I would have gotten my act together and thrown myself on your mercy. Unfortunately, it's possible I would have missed out on you."

Missed out on me… I don't know how he manages to imbue those few words with romance (maybe it's his accent?), but were I wearing a tight corset, I would swoon. "It sounds like we might be indebted to your grandmother."

"Spectacularly, and believe me, she'll collect on it." Jack chuckles. "But it's a debt I'll gladly pay." He lowers his gaze to my mouth; then his head follows and I feel his breath against my lips.

Faking Grace | 377

He's going to kiss me. After all these months, he's going to kiss me. I close my eyes.

"Maizy?"

Did I miss something—namely, a kiss? I open my eyes. "Jack?"

"What does *The Dumb Blonde's Guide to Christianity* say about kissing?"

For a moment I can only stare at him, but then I glimpse the light in his eyes. "What does it say? In a word...don't."

"Don't kiss? It really says that?"

"At least not at the beginning of a relationship."

"Are we at the beginning?"

I make a face. "Sort of. And I do put a lot of stock in that book's advice." I remember Very Blonde Tip #101:

THE LOWDOWN ON DATING

1. Exclusivity: one man at a time—got it? (And it does go both ways.)
2. Spend time getting to know one another (read: months).
3. Keep tabs on *all* of your body parts at *all* times!
4. A kiss is *not* just a kiss, so don't go there until you've gotten to know the kisser.
5. Once you know the kisser, kisses should be brief. (No extended kissing!)

"Of course…" I smile. "As long as we keep it brief."

Jack peers at me, then murmurs, "Pleasure." A moment later he wipes the smile off my face, but in a very nice way. And when a snowflake lands on my nose, I laugh into the kiss. A laugh that ends on a purr.

Oh well. Love me, love my purr.

1. Grace accepted Christ at a church summer camp when she was a teenager, but ten years later her life shows little evidence of her claim to be a Christian. How should a person's life reflect her acceptance of Christ as her Savior?

2. Grace utilizes "Jesus junk" to enhance the perception of her faith in order to secure a job. She also employees "Christian speak." Have you ever "faked" your faith? Do you use Christian speak? If so, is it a conscious effort, and how do you think nonbelievers feel when it's used in their presence?

3. Just as preachers' kids are often held to higher standards of behavior, so are those who work for Christian companies. What are your feelings about this?

4. As Grace's deception escalates, she finds herself telling lies to stay afloat, which leads to the necessity of tracking her lies. When have you thought it necessary to lie? What were the consequences of your lies?

5. When Grace is overwhelmed by the language of the King James Bible, Jack recommends that she try a different version. How important is the translation to your understanding of the Bible? Which translation do you prefer and why?

6. Many women struggle with eating disorders. It takes prayer, compassion, and understanding for Jem to finally get the help

she needs. Is an eating disorder part of your past? How did you overcome it? Is it part of your present? If so, what will it take for you to get help?

7. Though Grace was initially put off by Jem's attempt to befriend her, Jem proves to be a genuine, if unlikely, friend. Have you ever been surprised by friendship? If so, describe your experience.

8. Grace is amazed to find out that, as a Christian, she is considered a saint. Does that surprise you? Why?

9. When Grace is dragged forward to answer an "altar call" at church, she is mortified. Have you ever gone in front of a congregation for prayer? If not, have you felt the need but held back? Why?

10. Have you ever been shown the depth of grace that Jack and Grace were shown? If so, what did it look like? If not, what would you like it to look like? What steps can you take to be shown grace? Who needs *you* to show them grace?

Girls you can relate to

Kate Meadows is a successful San Francisco artist looking for a nice, solid Christian man. So when not one, but two handsome bachelors enter her orbit in rapid succession, her head is spinning just a bit. The question now is, what kind of work will Kate do on herself...and who exactly is she trying to please?

Harriet Bisset used to be a rebel. And she has the tattoo to prove it. Join Harri on the spiritual journey of a preacher's kid turned rebel turned legalistic Christian who discovers the joy of trusting in God's security—and the fun to be had along the way.

Laugh, cry and identify with
Kate and Harriet

...available from your favorite bookstore or online retailer!